# THE SAVAGE
# HIGHLANDER

# THE SAVAGE HIGHLANDER

## HEATHER McCOLLUM

Entangled Publishing, LLC
2614 South Timberline Road
Suite 105, PMB 159
Fort Collins, CO 80525
rights@entangledpublishing.com

Amara is an imprint of Entangled Publishing, LLC.

Edited by Alethea Spiridon
Cover design by EDH Graphics
Cover photography from Deposit Photos and 123.rf

Manufactured in the United States of America

First Edition November 2018

*To those whose worlds have been shattered. May we all find the strength to pick up the shards, dust them off, and make them into something even more beautiful.*


*And a word to my first boss, who thought it was sexy to trap a sixteen-year-old girl in the restaurant basement to steal a kiss—you are very fortunate that I did not yet have my hair spike.*

# Scots-Gaelic used in *The Savage Highlander*

*Sgian dubh*—Black handled knife

*Dia mhath*–Good God

*Eigh*—Ice, the name of Aiden's white horse. Pronounced like age.

*Caora*–Reed, the name of Scarlet's horse. Pronounced like coo-ra.

*Sassenach*—Englishwoman

*Falbh!*—Go!

*Mattucashlass*—Short dagger

*Ionnsaigh!*—Attack!

*Mo chreach*—My rage

*Tha thu cho teth*—You are so hot ("hot" was used as an adjective that meant full of sexual desire from the 1500s)

*Tha thu m'anam*—You are mine

*To Charles, King of England, Scotland, and Ireland*

*I, Nathaniel Worthington, son of the late Benjamin Worthington and 5th Viscount of Hollings Estate in Lincolnshire, write to inform you that the traitors, Captain Cross and Lord Philip Sotheby, have been vanquished, and that I, with the Chief of the Campbells of Breadalbane and Finlarig Castle, am traveling to bring you the heads of the would-be assassins. We will travel by coach to reach Whitehall a score of weeks from the time you receive this missive.*

*The castle, which was taken from the Campbells under false accusations of treason, has been returned to the Campbells and my sister, Lady Evelyn Worthington Campbell, new wife to Chief Grey Campbell. The castle has been made into the Highland Roses School under the tutelage of my two sisters. While away, Aiden Campbell, Chief Campbell's second-in-command, will continue to guard the area against possible traitors, keeping the Campbell clan and surrounding Scottish peoples loyal to your rule.*

*May this missive find you in excellent health and vigor.*

*Your servant, Nathaniel Worthington, Viscount*
*18 November 1684*

# Chapter One

*November 1684*
FINLARIG CASTLE, KILLIN, SCOTLAND

Scarlet Worthington lifted a crimson-colored piece of broken china from the pile in the basket. The thin red edge was chipped and jagged, reminding her of broken teeth. "I suppose I will just throw the pieces away," she said to her sister, Evelyn.

Evelyn tsked, staring down into the basket of collected remnants. "They were beautiful tea bowls and fine pottery and plates before Lieutenant Burdock destroyed them when setting the castle on fire. I can't stand to throw them away."

It had been months since Scarlet and Evelyn had journeyed to Scotland to start Evelyn's Highland Roses School for ladies. After the initial battle for ownership, Evelyn and Grey Campbell, the chief of the Campbells of Breadalbane, had wed, uniting the chiefdom with the school.

Scarlet held the piece up to the light that filtered through the glassed windows along the upper walls of the great hall.

The entire great hall and part of the second floor had been scorched. Although all the tapestries had burned, leaving discolored walls, Evelyn, Grey, and the Highland Roses School students and instructors had replaced the furniture and scrubbed the soot away.

Scarlet picked up another piece of red china. Turning it in several directions, she tried to hold it against the first shard, but they didn't fit. "Once shattered, the pieces are useless." Was it the same with people? She exhaled, tamping down the self-pity. She despised the gnawing ache of it. "I will be rid of them while you are gone."

Evelyn touched her arm, ducking her gaze to catch Scarlet's. "Broken things can be put back together."

Scarlet gave her a weak smile and shook her head. "Some things can't be fixed." She turned out of her sister's grasp to toss the pieces back into the basket. They clanked against the other remains of china and pottery, their colors mixed into a pile of brokenness.

"Scar," Evelyn said, obviously not willing to drop the subject. "Everyone is shattered in some way." Scarlet glanced toward her. "But," Evelyn said, "if we pick the pieces up and dust them off, we can make them into something even more beautiful." Evelyn nodded with encouragement. "You're the artist, Scar. I'm sure you can create something lovely if you try."

Were they still talking about the fractured tea bowls and plates? Of course not.

The door of the keep opened, letting in a shot of winter air. "The coach is ready," Molly, their maid from England, said, hustling in to grab a wool blanket. "You'd best take this to keep warm," she said. "The pixies in the hills are liable to trick you into rolling about in the snow, freezing you into an icicle." Molly nodded, her eyes wide.

"There is no snow," Evelyn said, knowing better than to

argue with the slender woman's strange ideas.

"It will come," she said with resolute confidence. "Mark my words."

"It is nearly December," Scarlet said. "And those pixies are tricky." She smiled at Evelyn, who took her arm.

Evelyn leaned close to Scarlet. "I will be plenty warm." She lifted the edge of her skirt to show the trousers that one of their students, Kirstin, had made for her last spring. "Between these and Grey, cold will not be a concern."

Scarlet smiled, letting loose a small chuckle. "If you can keep them on you with that vigorous husband nearby."

Evelyn joined in the quiet laughter. They walked through the dark entryway, stepping out under heavy clouds. "Are you certain you are fine with me leaving for London with Grey and Nathaniel? If King Charles hadn't sent word that he was coming to see the heads of the traitors, I wouldn't think of traveling back to England."

She glanced at the carriage where two bound lumps sat anchored to the roof. "As it is, the thought of riding with two severed, decaying heads tied to the carriage makes me shiver. I would much rather remain here, but I don't trust Grey to not get himself killed or arrested while trying to clear his parents' names with the king."

Scarlet looked at the stone facade of the massive castle, hiding the unease in her middle behind a practiced smile. "I will be perfectly fine and busy. I will keep up the lessons with Alana's help—and welcome the onslaught of female students who will surely come knocking at the gate any day now."

Evelyn quirked her smile into a wry grin. "We have two students now, besides Alana, Kirstin, and Isabel. And I'm this close"—she held up her gloved fingers, pinched close together—"to getting Cat to come for formal lessons." Cat was Isabel's older sister, who lived alone in the forest, an angry, completely freckled redhead who was the only experienced healer around Loch Tay.

Scarlet nodded. "I will welcome any that come before you return. Especially if they have money to pay."

"We will teach them without funds."

"Certainly, but to buy supplies for the students, eventually we will need coin," Scarlet said, patting Evelyn's arm. "But I will welcome and teach all the uneducated ladies in the land while you are away."

Their brother, Nathaniel Worthington, walked up, catching the last of their conversation. "If any sheep wander by, welcome them, too." He had plans to graze sheep on the fertile land around Finlarig, since the wool trade was becoming a highly profitable business.

"Yes, brother," Scarlet said, smiling as he bent to kiss her cheek, his dark hair matching her own. "I'll round up any stray sheep walking about." He smiled widely, gave a nod, and walked back to the coach where Evelyn's husband stood.

"That would mean you will step beyond the walls of the castle?" Evelyn asked, her voice low as she searched Scarlet's eyes.

It was true that Scarlet hadn't left the grounds except for an occasional festival in the meadow where she was surrounded by people. Instead of riding daily, as she had growing up in England, Scarlet had busied herself in the garden by the kitchen. "I might," Scarlet said without adding that it was unlikely. "Though I prefer to stretch my legs inside."

"Pish," Evelyn said, sliding her arm through hers. "You used to ride every day, roaming the lands around Hollings Estate."

Scarlet slid her gaze to the thick stone walls that gave her a tangible sign that she was safe. "I'm not accustomed to the wilds here."

Evelyn sighed but didn't ask her usual questions. *What*

*happened the night of the St. Valentine's Ball? Did I hear you crying during the night? Was it another nightmare? Why do you watch the gate like you're afraid someone sinister will show up?*

Scarlet pulled her sister close, appreciating Evelyn's silence. They walked toward the carriage that had carried them to Finlarig last spring. Just approaching it made Scarlet's stomach tighten, remembering their hasty escape from England. "I don't like you going back down there," she said to Evelyn, her words low. "Especially to court. There are dangers everywhere, Evie."

Evelyn squeezed back. "I think Grey is as determined to keep me safe as I am to keep him alive. And Nathaniel will be there. Charles is bound to be pleased that we've foiled the assassination plans *and* brought him a gift of two heads." She snorted, but then her gaze grew serious as she lowered her voice. "If I see Harry Covington—"

"Say nothing of me," Scarlet cut in, the man's name kicking her pulse high.

"He will ask where you are, though he likely knows by now."

Scarlet clasped her hands before her. "He means nothing to me, Evie. If he asks, say I am happy and well, with no plans to return."

Evelyn nodded, and Scarlet exhaled, shaking off the taint of Harry's name. "You must be back by Christmas Day," Scarlet said, watching a flock of chickens pecking the ground. It seemed the coop was overflowing with hens. "We will have a grand celebration."

"The Scots don't celebrate Christmas, Scar," Evelyn said.

Scarlet frowned, pinching her lips. "Well, I do."

"The country is very Protestant, and most view Christmas as a Catholic celebration or a pagan one. We can exchange gifts like they do on the eve of the new year, on Hogmanay."

Scarlet frowned. "Hmph."

"We don't want to offend anyone," Evelyn said.

Scarlet's gaze slid to the open portcullis as a white horse trotted into the bailey, a tall Highlander sitting proudly on its back. "Some offending can be good for people," she said, watching the most offensive Highlander that she'd met since they'd arrived in Scotland. "Jostle them out of their ill humor."

"Scarlet," Evelyn said in warning, but Scarlet was too busy observing Aiden Campbell dismount, his long, powerful legs taking his weight easily as he jumped down. He stroked a strong hand along the horse's neck and tossed the reins to a stable boy who had just led Grey's dappled horse out.

Aiden held his usual frown and stared straight ahead as he strode toward them, making his handsome face look as if it were chiseled from the granite boulders that poked up through the grasses across this wild country. His hair, the rich color of wheat in the sun, was sheared short, growing out from being burned away in the castle fire seven months ago. Evelyn said the man would always carry the burn scars across his back and shoulders, but Scarlet hadn't seen them.

Aiden walked with power evident in each stride. He wore an undyed shirt, tied at the neck, and a blue and green plaid kilt with black leather boots. A scabbard held his long sword, strapped to his side. It moved with him as if it were part of his body. Even though he'd nearly died in the fire, it was obvious that he'd recovered his strength.

Scarlet's heart thumped a little faster, a simple awareness of a rugged, powerful man. She'd felt this awareness before as a naive fool, months ago in the gilt ballroom at the court at Whitehall Palace in London. Fear followed the memory up her throat, making Scarlet cough into her gloved fist.

Evelyn frowned at her, but Scarlet waved off her unspoken concern. "Some dust," she said, and pulled the mask of wry happiness across her features. One could hide almost anything behind flippant comments and a coquettish smile. Scarlet forced a small laugh and cleared her throat. "A price one pays for roaming the yard with chickens." Her gaze wandered back to the large Scotsman.

Aiden stopped before his chief's horse and pulled a small apple from his pocket. Rubbing the horse's muzzle, he let the animal lip the treat from his palm, ran a hand down the stallion's neck, and turned to Grey and Nathaniel. Scarlet couldn't pull her gaze away when she saw the relaxed grin on Aiden's lips.

She leaned close to whisper into Evelyn's ear. "I'm fairly certain I've never seen surly Aiden Campbell smile."

Evelyn hid a chuckle in her gloved hand. "He's smiled at his sister, Rebecca, and of course, Grey. But you are correct. He's made it quite clear he despises the English, which unfortunately includes us. Luckily, Rebecca doesn't seem to be as stubborn in her view of us."

The wind whipped about the bailey, whistling as it shot through the arrow slits high up along the roof walkway of the four-story castle. Scarlet shivered, pulling her shawl tighter around her arms. The freezing temperatures were a good distraction from the foolish warmth the man elicited in her on the few occasions she'd spotted him.

"Good Lord, it is cold," Evelyn said. "Scar, you should open my Hogmanay gift now to keep you warm. It's in the trunk at the end of Grey's bed in our room, under my smocks. It's bound by a ribbon."

"I will if needed." Scarlet gave her sister one more hug.

Evelyn pulled back. "And when I return, we will figure out a way to celebrate all the holidays without offending the good people of Killin."

Scarlet let out a small laugh. "Very well, but unless I keep to my bedchamber, I'm sure to offend people before you return. Another reason I should stay within the walls of Finlarig." They walked toward the carriage. Scarlet breathed through her parted lips even though Nathaniel had said the severed heads of Philip Sotheby and Captain Cross were frozen solid and free of the stench of death.

The three men stood close together, the white fog from their breaths making clouds as they spoke. "Ye will live here at Finlarig then? Rule in my stead?" Grey asked Aiden.

Scarlet's gaze snapped to Grey and then to the frowning Highlander. Aiden? Living at Finlarig? With her? Her heart thumped hard, but she smiled past it. After all, Aiden hadn't shown any interest in her.

"Aye. I'll defend the seat of our clan," Aiden answered, looking at Grey. "From all the bloody English."

Nathaniel frowned, his lips tight. "Now that Captain Cross is dead, and Ensign Morris has been made the lieutenant at the English encampment north of Finlarig, you shouldn't have to worry about the English invading Finlarig," Nathaniel said in his clipped British accent.

Scarlet watched Aiden's jaw harden as if he clenched his teeth. He held Nathaniel's gaze with sharp conviction. "I will always be on guard against English invading Finlarig," he said, his gaze slipping briefly to Scarlet before going to Grey.

*God's teeth.* The man still despised them for taking Finlarig Castle, even if Nathaniel gave it back to Grey when he and Evelyn wed. Of course, Aiden had been recovering through the whole battle between them and the traitorous English commander who'd planned to use Finlarig as a place to assassinate King Charles. But surely Grey had explained it to his friend.

Despite being English, the Worthington family had done nothing to jeopardize or thieve away the Campbell stronghold. Evelyn would continue the Highland Roses School for ladies at Finlarig, but the castle was still the seat of the Campbells of Breadalbane parish and the village of Killin.

"I will keep the castle ready for war," Aiden said to Grey.

"Lord," Scarlet said, glancing at Evelyn. "It will be all parties and frivolity with Aiden Campbell in charge of defense."

Evelyn let a small chuckle slip before curling her lips inward to suppress more. Grey pulled Evelyn into his side. "Let us go then," Grey said. "The quicker we give Charles his traitors and explain my parents' innocence, the quicker we return." Grey leaned in to kiss Evelyn on the mouth, the heat between them evident despite the months of wedded play.

"I will ride your horse, Campbell," Nathaniel said with one raised brow. "I have no desire to be enclosed with the two of you in the carriage."

"Nat," Evelyn said.

Grey produced a wicked grin, making Evelyn swat at his arm before he guided her to the carriage. He whispered something in her ear that made her smile up at him, the look on her face full of unabashed love. Scarlet had never been a jealous creature, but watching her sister and brother-in-law tugged at the annoying pocket of self-pity Scarlet tried not to notice within herself.

She would miss her sister, but it would be nice not to have to announce herself about the castle to avoid walking into the kitchen or pantry or library to find them loving each other with passionate abandon. Even the noises the two made could inflame one's body, which was something Scarlet had sworn never to let happen to her again. Maybe she should revisit the idea of joining a cloister. No men, no passion, and no leaving the grounds. It certainly had its merits.

The carriage rolled out under the raised teeth of the gate. Nathaniel gave her one last tip of his head. Next to her, Aiden raised his arm to Hamish in the gate tower. The portcullis began to lower, the chains rattling as they released the iron bars to bite into the dirt below.

Aiden stood next to her like an unmovable mountain. Had she ever been this close to the ornery Highlander? He'd been healing for months, but even when he was visiting Grey at the castle, he'd leave when she'd enter the room. "You are ordering the gates shut?" she asked.

"Aye." His brief answer was punctuated with a pivot on his heel to walk toward the keep. He nodded to the boy, who walked his horse toward the stables.

She grabbed her skirt to follow quickly. "During the daytime?"

"Aye," he said, continuing on.

"I have students coming." She hurried, cutting through a cluster of chickens and making them squawk and dance about with their wings extended. Where had all these chickens come from, anyway?

"Aye," he answered a third time.

"God's teeth, Aiden Campbell. If you persist in giving one-word answers, make them informative words."

He spoke without looking back, his strides long and sure. "'Tis a precaution. Neighboring clans and the English north of us will have heard that the chief was leaving this morn."

Scarlet tried to keep up with the blasted man. "Stop running away from me."

Aiden halted on the second step to the keep, turning on his heel. His usual frown looked even more fierce. "I do not run away. From anything."

Scarlet climbed the steps, going two above him so she could look down into his face. She met his frown with her own. "How will my students come to class if the gate is shut? Will Hamish open it for them?"

"Hamish will direct them to the door in the wall," he said without shifting his gaze from her. The muted sun that filtered through the dense clouds shone on his face. His eyes were blue, a beautiful jewel-like blue, though they were usually squinted in coarse annoyance.

She blinked, forcing her gaze to run across the thick granite wall that had just been fortified around the castle and bailey. "There's a door in the wall? Don't you think that the inhabitants of the castle should know about a door in the wall?"

"Likely, ye were busy taking tea when Grey talked about it." He climbed past her.

She followed. "Aiden—"

"'Tis to the right of the gate tower, disguised as a crack in the wall. It's only the size of a bent-over man. Your students will have no trouble getting to their lessons on tea and *contredanse* steps."

*Hmph.* Frustrating man. "If you care to stop in for lessons, you will see that the ladies of the Highland Roses School learn much more than dancing and serving tea." She walked briskly through the dark entryway into the great hall, trailing him to the large hearth where he squatted low to add several more logs to the fire. "They are schooled in art, music, embroidery, reading, writing, mathematical figures, and most importantly, how to skewer a man's brain when one is intent on evil things."

"When *one* is intent on evil things?" He glanced over his shoulder, scratching one finger behind his ear. "The student or the man?"

She cocked her head to the side. "It depends whether the man is an irritating, condescending, ornery fellow. The student might find herself daydreaming about using her hair spike on him just to cease his offensive ways."

Aiden's face remained grim, but something in his eyes hinted at merriment. "Do ye often daydream about me, Lady Scarlet?" he asked.

The edge of her lips turned up into something of a true

smile. Perhaps there was humor buried within the Highlander. "If I answered that truthfully, you might be too frightened to help Kerrick with our defensive lessons in Grey's place."

His mouth twisted, his brows lowering as he turned back to prod the logs with an iron poker.

"Grey said that you would take his place," Scarlet said. "'Tis too difficult for Kerrick alone to teach us."

With his head bent, his broad back to her, she could see the red lines of his scars peek above his collar, like fingers reaching to his scalp. Lord, how the man must have suffered with the burns. She stepped closer to view his side. "Are you still in pain? Perhaps that is why you are surly all the time?"

His back straightened, his head snapping up to look at her. "Nay," he said.

"So, you are just churlish by nature? Or do you lie about the pain? Or perhaps, unbeknownst to me, I've caused you great insult?"

"Aye," he said and stood, turning so that he faced her.

"Which one? And don't you dare say aye or nay."

The side of his mouth edged upward. "Ye've taken away my two favorite words." He crossed his arms over his chest, his legs braced apart as he stared directly into her eyes. "My sister would say that I'm churlish by nature. I am mostly recovered from pain. And you have done nothing to insult me except to be born in England and, I suppose, to daydream about skewering my brain."

She flapped her eyelashes and patted her chest as if the biggest relief had released her heart from an iron grip. "Thank the good Lord. I was beginning to think you couldn't string together more than a couple of words."

He grunted and looked past her toward the entryway where two students from the village stood. Fiona wore braids looped to hang near her ears and nodded, making them swing forward. Martha waved, her large green eyes growing even wider at seeing Aiden.

"See, they made it through the wall unscathed," he said.

"Hello," Scarlet called. "Please go on up to the library and begin to write out your letters. I will find you shortly. Alana and Izzy may already be there." The two girls walked shoulder to shoulder to the steps that wound up to the library on the second floor. One of them whispered while the other giggled.

Scarlet took up the basket of china shards, setting it in a corner. After Evelyn had used her hair spike to save herself and then Grey from Philip Sotheby, Scarlet had decided that the daily defense class was an even higher priority than reading and ciphering. Perhaps if she'd known how to wield a *sgian dubh* at Whitehall Palace, she wouldn't still avoid dark corners and wake shaking from nightmares.

She turned back toward Aiden and dusted her hands together. "Once you get settled, come up—"

"Where shall I bed down at night?" Aiden asked, his gaze slicing to the steps the girls had taken and then back to Scarlet.

"Bed down?" Scarlet asked, a smile curling her lips. "Like a horse?"

His scowl returned. "Grey asked me to sleep in the castle," he said. "What bed shall I use?"

Scarlet indicated the steps. "The third and fourth floors have rooms with beds. You could always take the largest, since you're…" She moved her hand to encompass his frame. "You're so mountainous. It is Evelyn and Grey's, last room on the right on the fourth floor. However, their exploits have likely soaked the walls with passion." Could she possibly win a true smile from him? It was the most interesting challenge she'd had in months.

She waited a beat, but his grim expression continued. Scarlet shrugged. "But it is big and roomy."

"I will find another bed," he said, his voice gruff.

Scarlet chuckled. "You are welcome to any of the other unoccupied rooms. Molly, Izzy, and Alana with her pack of wild pups sleep on the third floor, and I'm all the way to the left on the fourth." She turned to the steps to join the girls at their lessons.

*Bang.* The front door smacked against the stone wall, and Kerrick, Grey's second-in-command after Aiden, jogged inside, his boyish smile gone. He scanned the room until he saw Aiden. "Menzies are at the gate."

Aiden slid his sword free.

"Friend or foe?" Scarlet asked, running after him to the entryway. Grey had just left, and already swords were drawn.

Aiden stopped at the top of the steps, and she caught his upper arm, immediately feeling the muscles through the linen. His bicep was solid, like a thick oak, bulging easily as he raised his arm.

"Friend or foe?" she repeated.

He looked down at her with a pinched brow. "Both."

# Chapter Two

Aiden heard the crunch of her quick steps behind him as he crossed the bailey. "Go inside, Scarlet," he called over his shoulder, striding to the ladder leading up inside the gate tower.

"You represent the castle and the Campbells," she yelled back. "I represent the Highland Roses School and my brother's interests."

*Bloody hell.* The *Sassenach* did not take orders well. The last thing he needed was for the young, cocky Menzies chief to see her. There'd be no getting rid of the man after he got a look at Scarlet's glorious mane of auburn hair, creamy skin, and soft womanly curves.

Aiden leaped up the ladder and headed to look over the wall of the gate tower.

"And still no Grey Campbell," Finlay Menzies called up. The chief of the Menzies was only a score in years and hadn't yet filled out his muscle. Known for his cleverness and wit, he never seemed short of female attention. He'd brought six men with him, one of which held a white lamb before him on his horse.

"Grey has gone to take the traitors' heads south to King Charles at Whitehall. I am in charge while he is away. Name your business."

Behind Aiden, a muffled curse and the ruffle of petticoats heralded Scarlet up the ladder. He should have locked her inside the castle. If anything dangerous befell her while he was in charge, there'd be hell to pay from her sister, who was a force not unlike a hurricane when angered.

"Grey came to Castle Menzies months ago and asked…" Finlay's words trailed off as his gaze slid to Aiden's side. "Well, hello?" he said, the question obvious in his voice. "And did Grey leave this lovely lass in charge of Finlarig as well?"

"I am Lady Worthington, sister-in-law to Grey Campbell and the matron in charge of the Highland Roses School for ladies here at Finlarig."

The way Finlay smiled at her, like a cat with a cornered mouse, made Aiden want to shove her behind him. Aiden clutched the hilt of his sword.

Finlay chuckled and shook his head. "I'd heard that Finlarig was changed into a school for lasses." He looked pointedly at the iron-toothed portcullis. "Is the massive gate to keep the English out, or keep the lovely lasses, like Lady Worthington, in?"

"State your business," Aiden yelled down, annoyance edging his words.

Finlay crossed his arms over his chest. "I also heard that the Englishman who took Finlarig is looking for sheep to start his own flock." He indicated the lamb on the other horse. "I have fifteen sheep that I can't feed this winter. Either we will have mutton stew until spring, or I can sell them to the Englishman."

"I represent my brother's interests," Scarlet said.

Finlay clapped his hands together once. "Aye, good, then!

Let us in, and ye can inspect this sweet lamb. It represents the flock."

Finlay only had a handful of men, and they didn't have muskets, only swords. Aiden turned from the wall. "Hamish, raise the portcullis when I reach the ground."

Hamish moved to the coiled mechanism. Scarlet rushed to the ladder as Aiden climbed down. He looked up to see layers of skirts above him. *Mo chreach.* Her shapely legs showed above the edge of her boots, rising up into the darkness that shrouded the lass's heat. He snapped his gaze level and shifted to avoid being kicked by her flailing boot as it sought the next rung.

"Bloody useless skirts," Scarlet murmured above him. She slapped her hands down on them to shove the puffed layers through the square-cut hole.

He reached to grab her heel. "Ye're going to fall. Probably knock me flat and break your bonny neck." He held on tightly as she continued to tap in the air. "I will put it on the rung." Aiden dodged the opposite foot, grabbing it to set it on the next rung. Down they went. Aiden kept his gaze straight ahead on the seam up the back of her leather boots. The breeze blew down through the hole past her, washing him with a flowery smell.

"*Dia mhath,*" he whispered and jumped the rest of the way down. She was close enough to the ground now that if she fell, she wouldn't hurt more than one of her trim ankles.

Aiden heard the crank of the gate and turned to meet the Menzies, Kerrick coming up next to him. They drew their swords. Finlay Menzies flattened low over his horse's neck to ride under the gate as it rose. He touched the point of one iron bar as it continued up. "Aye," he called. "Thick enough to keep the lovely lasses inside." He laughed at his own humor. Several of his men grinned, but they all remained quiet as they followed him inside.

Finlay dismounted and signaled for the man with the lamb to do the same. "We have more than enough sheep for wool," he said, walking forward. "And we lost some of our hay crop to fire when one of the farmers was using a torch to drive away a pack of wolves."

The man's gaze slid to Scarlet as he continued. "I stopped by Balloch Castle yesterday, but your cousin, Donald Campbell, wasn't interested," Finlay said. "He reminded me that Grey was looking."

The man with the lamb set it down. It immediately began to hop about playfully, bleating. "As ye can see," Finlay said, looking to Scarlet. "The lamb is flawless."

Scarlet bent down as the lamb butted against her skirts. "Of the fifteen, how many are lambs and ewes? And is a ram included?"

"Five ewes, nine lambs, and one potent ram," Finlay said. "'Tis a flock that is sure to grow. A great business opportunity."

"And they are all as healthy as this lamb?" she asked.

"Aye, but ye must come to Castle Menzies to see them."

"I will come," Aiden said.

Finlay shrugged. "Do what ye like, Campbell, but if I'm taking the lady's coin, she needs to inspect the flock. I won't have the English harass me if they think I tricked one of their lords into giving coin for inferior stock."

"What of this one?" Scarlet asked, scratching its curly white rump before it leaped away to try to butt a chicken with its head. She smiled at its antics, not even bothering to hide the leaning of her heart. Foolish woman.

"'Tis a gift to ye, milady, if ye agree to come see the rest on the morrow," Finlay said, a grin of triumph already on his face.

"We will let ye know by messenger if we can come," Aiden said.

Finlay pursed his lips and shook his head. "Then I'll be taking my dinner home with me."

"Dinner?" Scarlet's head snapped up.

Finlay laughed. "Just a name, but if ye worry, promise that I will see ye at Castle Menzies on the morrow, and the little lamb will remain with ye."

*Blasted cod.* The man's tongue slipped out to wet his bottom lip as he watched Scarlet kneel before the prancing sheep. Aiden scowled, but apart from the appreciation, he saw no hint of trickery, though the man's father had been a lying scoundrel. They would stop at Donald Campbell's small castle on the way around the loch to the Menzies' stronghold to verify that Finlay had stopped there first. If Finlay lied about that, then Aiden would count everything the man said as false.

"Snowball will stay with us," Scarlet said, straightening tall.

Finlay smiled widely. "Dinner has a new name." The Menzies behind him chuckled. Finlay's gaze slanted to Aiden. "Then I have your word, Campbell? Ye will bring the lady around tomorrow to see her flock?"

Aiden stared hard at the grinning chief. "Aye, on the morrow, but just to see the flock."

"Lo, but we will have a meal together," Finlay said, and ignored Aiden's shaking head. He looked back to Scarlet. "My sister will have returned from her time at Inverness. I would have her meet ye as she is in need of proper schooling."

"She is welcome at the Highland Roses School," Scarlet said. She turned at the sound of the door to the keep opening.

*Bloody hell.* Aiden cursed at the erupting chaos as Alana's pack of puppies and the mother, a huge wolfhound, hurtled down the steps into the crowded bailey. Scarlet gasped, running for the lamb. Two groups of chickens scattered about the yard, squawking, wings flapping, as the dogs chased them.

The mother wolfhound barked at the Menzies, her deep voice drowning out Alana's reprimands.

One large puppy, Robert, the only male, was trying to reach the lamb, yet Scarlet tried to hold him back. Unafraid, the lamb knocked its head into the dog, who bent his head low, ready to play. "No, Robert," Scarlet yelled. The puppies were so large now that they were difficult to handle. Alana needed to work harder at training them.

Aiden strode to Scarlet and hefted the male dog into his arms. Scarlet ran after the lamb, who'd hopped toward the still flustered chickens. Finlay bent over in a fit of humor, hands on his knees. His men roared behind him. He straightened, shaking his head, and sauntered over to mount his horse.

He looked down at Aiden, who still held the wiggling Robert. "Ye have your hands full, Campbell," Finlay yelled over the barking, squawking, and bleating. His laughter calmed, and he gave a more serious smile. He called out to be heard. "Just make sure to keep your promise on the morrow."

"I keep my promises, Menzies," Aiden said, shifting the dog to avoid its lapping tongue.

Finlay lifted his gaze to Scarlet, who cradled the lamb in her arms. "Good day to ye, milady." He bowed his head, smile in place.

Damn, the woman had no idea what a bonny vision she was, her red cape flung back to reveal her curves in the dark dress, the white lamb sitting sweetly in her arms. Her hair lay in waves over one shoulder, and her lush lips curved in a smile that seemed to beckon. *Blast!* Was Finlay Menzies feeling beckoned?

Aiden walked forward, lowering the dog to the ground. "Farewell, Menzies," he called and slapped his hands together. *Crack!* The horses shifted, and Finlay was forced to look away from Scarlet. Aiden purposely put himself in the way of his view, moving his arms as if the action would shoo the mounted men out of the bailey. "We have work to do."

"All right, Campbell," Finlay said, turning his horse. "I'll leave ye to your lessons at the school for lasses." Laughing again, the men rode out through the gate. Aiden raised his arm to Hamish, who was waiting for his signal to lower the portcullis.

Aiden turned away when the points reached the packed dirt. "Alana," he said. "Ye have to work more on training these beasts."

"Aye," she said, shaking her head. "I've not had the time, with learning and teaching at the school." She whistled, and the calmer mother followed her back up the steps. The puppies, nipping and tumbling with Robert in the lead, eventually climbed the steps after her.

Scarlet set the lamb down, and it quickly pissed and left a pile of pellets. "Good girl," Scarlet said and patted her skirts. "Come along, Snowball." The lamb actually hopped toward her, following her to the steps into the keep. "Look how clever you are," she said.

"Ye can't keep it in the castle," Aiden said, striding over to head up the steps. "It will shite everywhere."

"Just until I get Kerrick to help me build a cozy pen for her, or until her mother and siblings arrive." Scarlet continued to lure the lamb up the steps. "I'll clean after her."

Aiden snorted, pushing into the dark entryway.

"I keep my promises, too," she called behind him.

"Doubtful," he murmured. What English woman ever kept her promises?

• • •

Once cold seeped into the bones, it was hard to get rid of it. Scarlet shivered in her bed, pulling her blanket tighter. Making a spy hole in her inadequate covering, she could see that the coals in the hearth were nearly black. Surely it was the cold that had woken her and not the strange dream of dancing with Aiden Campbell, his strong arms around her, whirling her around the ballroom at Whitehall Palace. At least she hadn't woken choking or sobbing like she usually did when finding herself in that nightmarish setting.

With the curtain drawn back from her one window, silver moonlight showed Snowball curled up in Scarlet's second blanket before the hearth, slumbering peacefully. Perhaps she should lift the lamb to sleep next to her. God's teeth, her mother would toss in her grave if she knew her daughter ever considered bringing a barn animal into her bed.

Scarlet pushed up off the mattress, and before she could talk herself into suffering further, she jammed her stockinged feet into her slippers and rose. She would have to find more blankets. The lamb didn't move as Scarlet slipped out her door and into the inky-dark corridor.

*You should open my Hogmanay gift now to keep you warm.* Evelyn's words came back to Scarlet, and she hurried forward. Aiden said he would find a different bed, but when Scarlet reached Evelyn and Grey's bedchamber door, she pressed the iron latch softly. The door opened without hesitation. Surely Aiden would have locked it or put the bar across if he were slumbering inside. Scarlet peeked in but couldn't see anything with the curtains drawn across the two paned windows. But the hearth was completely dark. No fire. Not even embers.

Scarlet released her breath and walked inside the vacant room. She cursed softly as she bumped her knee against the chest at the end of the bed. She needed some light, so she continued past it toward the window, feeling with her hands out before her as she shuffled her slippers along the thick rug lying across the wood floor. Coming off the end of the rug, she teetered forward, her fingers grabbing for a wall, bookcase, or hopefully the curtain. Her fingers brushed something, and she pressed her palms against it, her breath catching in her clenched chest.

Instead of cold stone or wood, her palms pressed against… warm skin. She couldn't speak without breath, but her fingers curled inward as if the contact burned her. A sprinkling of hair, solid muscle, hot skin.

"Oh, God," Scarlet said, her stomach flipping.

The mountain before her moved, and the curtain whooshed as it was thrown aside. Moonlight blinded Scarlet, and she blinked.

"Nay," Aiden Campbell said. "Not God, although a Highlander is close."

Scarlet's mouth hung open as she saw that Aiden stood with his legs braced apart and his arms crossed before his massive chest, which she'd just stroked. He was completely naked.

He studied her. Was she blushing? Surely the silver of the moonlight would hide it.

"I…I…" Scarlet's mind felt numb, and her heart pounded as if letting her know it was ready if she needed to sprint away. "I came to get warm," she said.

His frown softened, and his eyebrows rose slowly. "Ye came for me to warm ye?"

Scarlet blinked, her breath ragged. She closed her eyes and spun around. "I thought you were sleeping elsewhere." Her breath came rapidly as she surveyed the rumpled blankets and furs across the large bed.

Without his glorious, brawny, very naked body before her, Scarlet's numb shock faded, replaced by irritation when she spotted the open door. "Who sleeps without locking the door? You lower the gate during the day but won't bar your room at night?" She threw an arm out, angling it toward the dark hearth. "And you don't bank a fire?"

Silently, she saw him step past her. Moonlight sliced across his toned buttocks, making her choke. She coughed, swallowing. Her gaze lifted up his broad back where lines of scars ran, but before she could study them, he grabbed a fur from the bed, lowering it before his narrow hips as he turned to face her.

"The other beds are too small," he said. "I didn't require a fire."

Scarlet shivered, realizing that she'd dropped her blanket by the door. She stood in her sleeping smock and the robe she donned before getting into bed. "Well, normal people do. It's freezing, and mine has burned low."

"So…ye came here for warmth?" he asked, leaving off his early question about her searching for him. As if she would seek Aiden Campbell out to warm her.

*The dream warmed you, didn't it?*

Her traitorous thought made her frown.

Scarlet flapped her cold fingers toward the end of the bed. "Evelyn told me to open a gift if I was cold. That it would help me stay warm. I was retrieving it." She strode to the chest, tripping slightly on the thick rug as her loose slipper caught on it, falling off. Leaving it, she lifted the lid and felt under the cool cotton smocks, which Evie had piled to one side. Underneath was a soft, folded something, tied with a ribbon. She worked it out without completely scrambling the smocks.

"See," she said, holding it up, and turned toward the hearth where Aiden had moved. "Good God," she said. The offending man had dropped the fur in order to strike a flint to light a candle. She slammed her eyes shut. "Stop doing that."

"Doing what?" he asked, and she heard the slide of glass being set in place over the flame in the lamp.

"Being naked."

"I sleep naked," he said. "I am covered."

Scarlet opened her eyes to see that Aiden had tied a

length of plaid around his waist like a loose kilt. He tucked the side in, but it didn't look very secure.

"What is the gift?" he asked.

The package was made of soft black wool, the softest she'd ever felt. She untied the ribbon, tucking it into her cinched sleeve, and shook out the woven fabric. Two legs dropped down.

"Trousers?" Aiden asked.

Scarlet smiled. "Yesssss," she drew out, running a hand over the soft trousers, like the ones Evelyn was wearing under her skirts for travel. Without waiting another moment, Scarlet lifted the edge of her smock and robe to shove her slipper-less foot into one leg. She kicked off the other slipper and did the same, shimmying the trousers up under her smock. The worked wool caressed her skin in luxury.

"Thank you, Evie," she whispered, already feeling warmer. Or was the tingle of heat coming from Aiden's stare? She stooped to grab her blanket, throwing it over her shoulders and shoving her one foot back into the slipper. "I will leave you to your chilly slumber," she said, glancing about for her errant slipper. Damnation, she'd abandoned it after her small wobble at the rug's edge. Of course, it was right next to Sir Large and Frowny.

A quick retrieval and she'd be away to grab an extra blanket from one of the other rooms. Though with her heart beating like a bird's rapid wings, she'd likely be awake for hours. And the more Aiden stared at her, the more agitated she felt. It was as if he had a thin blade that scraped off more and more of her composure the longer they stood together. Alone. In the dark night. Nearly naked.

She stuck a hand out to point. "My slipper." Taking a quick step, Scarlet caught her toe in the drape of the blanket. Wrapped so completely in it, she couldn't catch herself. She squeaked as she fell forward. Squeezing her eyes shut was the only self-defense she could take before she surely smashed her face into the floor.

Instead of pain and cold floorboards, she felt solid arms pull her against the same hot skin she'd encountered in the dark. Aiden dragged her upright, and Scarlet realized that her nose was pressed into his chest. She inhaled. Lord, he smelled good. Like wild outdoors and clean man.

"I…apologize," she said. "I'm not usually such a bungle." She tipped her head back. The moonlight cast half of Aiden's face in silver while the other half was composed of shadows. His perpetual frown was relaxed, as if he'd forgotten to don it. The slight golden hue from the lamp showed a merriment in his eyes, making him look almost happy. Is this how Aiden looked while holding a lover in the night? Relaxed and merry, his chest warm and inviting? He kept a hold, as if he were afraid that she'd fall if he let go.

Scarlet stared back, mesmerized by the change in his features. He was…beautiful and powerful. Her mind tumbled with an urge to step closer, sensation shooting through her. *Oh Lord.*

She should step back, turn away, retreat as quickly as she could. Yell "no" and run like she'd learned in her self-defense lessons. Didn't she know, firsthand, that men were dangerous in the shadows, away from eyes, without rules of propriety keeping them honorable? Why then did she want to lean into Aiden Campbell?

Scarlet's breath grew shallow, and she felt the press of him against her chest. Had he leaned forward, or had she?

Down the hall, a faint bleat sounded, as if a far-off lamb was lost. Scarlet pulled back. "Snowball," she whispered, turning to the door. "I…" She didn't manage to say anything. Not an apology, not a thank-you. What were the proper words for nearly falling prey to a passion she'd sworn never to allow again?

Scarlet was out in the dark corridor before she realized that she was walking unevenly, her slipper left behind. "Snowball," she called, her voice soft. "I am here." She stuck a hand out of her blanket to skim the wall next to her. Behind her, the golden haze of light funneled down the hall, reaching her and illuminating farther ahead.

Her heart jumped as the scene from her nightmares came to life. A candle glow that grew brighter until brutal fingers…

But this was Aiden Campbell, a man who showed no interest in her, not some flattering suitor in King Charles's bedecked court.

But could Aiden have felt the tether that had held her there in his arms for a moment? Was he coming after her to…? What? Throw his surly frown away and ask to kiss her? Could he want to…love her?

*You were fashioned by God to be desired, Scarlet. Every man will want to bed you.*

The deep voice in her nightmares surfaced like a bloated fish on a stagnant pond. Scarlet scooped up Snowball without pausing, moving quickly but not running. No footsteps sounded behind her, but the faint light brightened. He was gaining on her.

Snowball squirmed in her arms, and she realized that she was clutching the lamb. "There now," she whispered. "I'm sorry." Reaching her room, she strode into the darkness to place the lamb back in the blanket nest that she'd made earlier. Light illuminated the room. "I have found her. You can return to your bed." Her words came breathlessly, as if she'd run the whole length of the hall.

Aiden stood, still without his shirt, beside her bed. In her smaller room, he looked even larger, his shadow dark and looming across the ceiling. He didn't say a word but strode toward her. Scarlet held her breath, her palms pressed tightly against one another. As he moved past her to squat before the hearth, Scarlet let her exhale out in a silent huff.

Aiden patted the lamb's head and reached around it to set down his lamp on the stone before the open fireplace. Scarlet's legs felt weak from being so tense, and she stepped back, perching on the edge of her bed.

Aiden broke the cinders apart with the iron poker and set dry kindling and peat on the iron grate. "I didn't know ye could go this long without saying anything," he said, the back of his head toward her.

He was teasing? The quiet humor helped Scarlet inhale fully, but her fingers still curled into the edge of her mattress. She should respond with some flippant remark, a witty comment, but her fear in the hall had washed her wit away.

"Ye should have a fire if ye're cold," Aiden said when she didn't reply. He grabbed something wedged under his arm and tossed it toward her. It clunked on the floor near her feet. "And ye forgot your slipper."

Scarlet watched a small flame catch on the dry twigs, and Aiden bent to blow under it. As light grew in the room, she again saw the angry scars from the castle fire across his broad back. "Thank you," she said, finally finding her voice. She watched the muscles in his back and shoulders stretch and tighten as he lifted two logs from beside the hearth, placing them into the grate.

"Ye should have bricks to heat for your bed." He looked over his shoulder at her, and the openness on his face had disappeared in the tight set of his eyes. "That is what cold ladies do, isn't it? Wrap hot bricks for their beds?"

The return of his frown calmed Scarlet's nerves. He wouldn't come closer, discovering that her heart pounded. "I suppose, yes," she said and cleared her throat as the tightness there lessened. "I will have to find some in the morning since I seem to have left my heating bricks in my other robe."

The flames licked along the logs, and Aiden stood,

bending once more to arrange the blanket around the lamb. He glanced briefly at Scarlet before heading toward the open door, his steps quick, almost as if he were fleeing. "Get some sleep," he said on passing. "It will be a long day tomorrow going to the Menzies."

He shut the door behind him. Scarlet strained to hear his footsteps, but all she heard was the crackle and sizzle of the flames. She wrapped the blanket over her, burrowing once more into her own nest, feeling warmer. Scarlet breathed deeply for long minutes, yet sleep remained a specter, hovering close but unable to lull her.

She stared at the bright glow of the flames. Did Aiden have nightmares about flames flaying his back open? Even hardened Highland warriors must fear torture. Yet he seemed to have no problem building fires, blowing life into the sparks. Perhaps he couldn't fear fire, since it was something he dealt with every day.

Scarlet exhaled long. She encountered men every day: charming Kerrick, serious Grey, faithful Hamish, and half a dozen other Campbell warriors. But none of them haunted her nightmares, and none of them made her heart flutter like Aiden's nearness had. Blast. Scarlet forced herself to shut her eyes, but the red glow from the fire played behind her lids until she rolled over onto her other side. Never again would she allow her heart to rule her mind.

# Chapter Three

Aiden let his horse, *Eigh*, lip up a small apple as he watched Scarlet walk across the bailey toward the horses. After he'd left her in the dead of night, he'd tossed in Grey's gigantic bed, the feel of her warmth and the smell of her skin making him ache. Damnably beautiful woman.

"She's a young mare and will need a strong hand," Kerrick said, holding the bay's bridle as Scarlet peeled off one of her white gloves to let the horse smell her hand.

"What is her name?" Scarlet asked.

"Caora," Kerrick said. "It means reed in Gaelic, because she was such a slender little filly when she was born."

"Aren't you beautiful, Cooo-ra," she said, drawing out the *ooo* sound in the name. She almost purred like a cat. Damnation. Even with her bloody English accent, the woman's voice lured him. It was like God or the fates were tempting him, testing his convictions.

Aiden turned away, swinging up into the saddle of his horse. Let Kerrick hold her small foot and hoist her up.

"Don't worry about the lamb," Alana called. "She's

getting along fine with Robert now." The lamb pranced around the steps to the keep with the large wolfhound puppy. "Poor pup paced the room all last night. I think he wanted to go sniff her out."

Aiden knew the feeling. He inhaled against the weight of his own sleepless night and ran a hand along his face, stretching his back and shoulders. "We should be back by tonight," he called to Alana. "Hamish will keep the gate closed after us. Any students will come through the door in the wall."

Scarlet adjusted herself in the saddle. It wasn't a sidesaddle, so her legs were spread about the mare, inching her skirts up so that he could see the black wool of her trousers peeking above her boots. Good. The woman would be warm enough. Even so, he'd packed an extra wool blanket on the back of Eigh.

"Do you think it will snow?" Scarlet called toward him, even though there were six other mounted Campbells closer to her in the bailey.

"Most certainly, since we are forced to travel to save a lamb from becoming a stew," he said, his words dark, yet Kerrick laughed.

"How long is the ride?" she asked, ignoring his irritation.

"With a *Sassenach*, two to three hours," Aiden said.

Scarlet leaned forward to stroke her horse's brown neck, calming it with soft words. She clicked, rising up in the seat, and guided the young mare toward him. "How long for a Scottish lass, ye churlish man?" she asked, slanting her accent to imitate a brogue. Kerrick laughed again, and Aiden had the urge to punch him. Luckily, Aiden always had a rein on his urges, except the ones that kept him awake most of the night. *Mo chreach.*

"I was practically raised on horseback," Scarlet continued. "There's no reason to hold back the pace for me."

"We can get there under two hours at a brisk clip, though a bit longer since we are stopping at Balloch Castle on the way," Kerrick said, nudging his horse alongside Scarlet.

The man's gaze traveled along the lines of Scarlet's legs. "Ye have a strong seat," Kerrick said with a nod. "Though, I've never seen ye ride before." Kerrick's gaze slid along Scarlet more than the horse. It lingered on the waves of reddish-brown hair that flowed out of the side of her red hood to lie along her breast.

Scarlet flipped her gloved hand. She wore a smile that looked completely fabricated. "I don't get the chance to ride with such a group of strong warriors."

Kerrick nodded. "Aye, we are usually busy training or building, but I'd be happy to take ye riding."

Aiden's hands clenched around his reins. He touched his heels to Eigh's sides and raised his fist to the sky, moving it forward, a silent command for everyone to follow. Aiden led the way out under the portcullis, nodding to Hamish as the man waved from the gate tower. He pressed Eigh into an easy trot down the curved path leading to the main road through the village of Killin. They would take the road north for a mile and then veer east to ride along Loch Tay, passing his own cottage.

The clip of horses followed behind him where his men and one distractingly bonny *Sassenach* rode. Scarlet said that she could keep up with him, so he didn't bother to slow Eigh when the horse picked up speed at the edge of town. Kerrick knew the way and would guide her there. They could talk and laugh together without Aiden having to listen. He grunted and leaned farther over Eigh's long neck as they settled into a canter.

Snowflakes began to fall, pocking his face as he rolled along with the gait of his horse. Eigh ran in the middle of the thin path that wound beside the loch. Aiden sucked in large drafts of cold air, calming the heat inside him. His blood pumped in his ears, blocking out the sounds of the other horses. Unfortunately, it wasn't loud enough to block out the purr he'd heard in Scarlet's voice as she crooned to her horse back in the bailey. How would it feel to have the woman purr his name?

A meadow stretched out before him, and he had the urge to let Eigh have his head. But would he look like he was running away from them, tearing off across the snow-speckled moor? Before Aiden could decide, the sound of galloping hooves broke through, coming up behind him. He twisted in his seat just as Scarlet flew past, the bay filly in a full gallop.

Panic clutched at his middle. Had Caora gone wild? Scarlet leaned low over the mare's neck, its tail streaming out behind it, much like Scarlet's mane of brown waves that had pulled free of her hood.

"*Falbh*," he yelled with a press of his heels, and Eigh sprang forward in chase. His larger horse caught up halfway across the moor. "Scarlet," he yelled, and she turned her head while still in her low position.

Aiden's breath caught for a beat at the joyful smile that reached every part of her bonny features. Pure and exuberant, her face radiated such happiness that it made all the happiness that he'd felt in his entire life incomparable to this one moment. Her high cheeks were flushed pink, her lips parted, her eyes sparking with life and freedom.

Sitting slightly up, she slowed Caora into a canter. "I've missed this," she called.

"Slow down," he said as they neared the far edge of the meadow. "The woods ahead are thick." He matched Eigh's gait to the slowing mare until they finally trotted and walked in a circle just before the wood line.

"That was purely wonderful," Scarlet called, her breath

puffing out before her. Aiden couldn't agree more. Behind them, Aiden watched Kerrick and the other men race across the meadow.

"Ye ride," Aiden said.

She laughed, a real laugh, not one twisted with wryness or cleverness. Just an open, authentic laugh. "Yes, but not since I've come here. My legs are bound to be sore on the morrow." Her smile said that she wouldn't care one bit.

"Why haven't ye ridden here? The Highlands are made for riding across as long as ye stay away from the boggy areas."

Her smile lowered a notch, some of the earlier spark extinguishing from her eyes. "'Tis truth that I haven't thought it safe to venture from Finlarig alone."

"Someone could surely take ye," he said, watching the snowflakes land on the dark fall of her hair.

"I don't want to bother anyone." She shook her head, looking off toward the trees, but then leaned to stroke Caora's neck. Aiden was completely certain that there would be a line of men waiting to escort her if she asked.

"Bloody hell," Kerrick called, his usual grin dimmed with a lowering of his brows. He pulled up on his horse's reins to wheel the large gray around in a circle as the other men reached them. "I conclude that ye can ride, and that little filly should be entered into races."

Breaking the gaze that had held Aiden captive, Scarlet turned with a laugh, which had reverted to her usual witty flutter. "Caora is a natural," she said, patting the horse. Caora tossed her head as if agreeing. She pulled the mare around to point toward the woods. "Let us continue before snow covers us."

. . .

Scarlet guided Caora through the woods behind Aiden's

charger, watching the man shift occasionally in his seat. Good God, what an example of Highland ruggedness. He rode as if he'd been born in the saddle, something Scarlet appreciated in a man. He was light with the reins, using his knees to guide his horse and scratching between its ears periodically. There was a tight bond between them.

"Winterberries are favorites of the local birds," Kerrick said, pointing to some red berries, frosted in small clumps. "We can pick some branches on the way back if ye'd like some to decorate the keep."

"That would be lovely," Scarlet said, though she hardly saw the red berries with her gaze following the steely line of Aiden's back. She huffed quietly at her foolhardiness. The man hated all that was English, and her ability to seat a horse wasn't likely to change that. Although it had been wonderful to show him that her talents didn't stop at pouring heated tea into dainty bowls. Not that she wanted to attract the man, but it would be a victory to win the friendship of one who despised the English.

They emerged from the woods to skirt Loch Tay, and Scarlet spied a medium-size cabin up a low hill on the left. As they neared, Aiden veered off toward it. He raised an arm overhead.

"Excuse me, Scarlet," Kerrick said. "Time for me to lead the way."

"To where is Aiden off?" she asked.

"'Tis his home," Kerrick answered. "He will catch up to us before we reach Balloch Castle."

The cabin looked solidly built, a two-story rectangle with a slanted roofline. The door was painted blue, and logs were piled under a wide eave that ran the length of the front. Several paned windows sat in the log walls. A barn, of similar construction, stood some ways off in the back.

Aiden dismounted, jumping from his white horse at his

front door. She watched him pull a lever high up, and the door swung inward. Then, unless Scarlet was willing to twist completely in her saddle or turn her horse toward him, she had to look away. She followed Kerrick with the other five Campbells bringing up the rear of their party. When the path widened, she pulled up level with the tall, affable Campbell.

She cleared her throat, and Kerrick turned his head her way, smiling brightly. "I thought Aiden lived with his sister, Rebecca, on the edge of Killin Village," she said.

Kerrick's smile slipped a bit but came back as he looked forward. "Nay, that is only Rebecca's house now that their da died a few years back. Aiden built his cabin...oh, about ten years ago now. He only stayed at Rebecca's while she cared for his burns."

Scarlet rode along, letting her body sway with Caora's smooth gait. "What did his father die from?"

"Jack Campbell?" Kerrick looked up as if trying to remember. "Fever I believe, an infection of sorts. It killed a couple of the elderly folks in town that winter." He shook his head.

"What about Aiden and Rebecca's mother?" she asked, watching Kerrick's profile.

He shrugged. "Dead, I think. I came to Killin with my grandmother back when I was a lad. Aiden must have been about thirteen then. I don't remember his mother being around."

Had he been close to his mother? Maybe the absence of a female in the household had hardened Aiden's heart. "I would think it difficult to grow up without female attention."

Kerrick laughed, his eyebrows rising. "Oh, Aiden hasn't been neglected by the lasses. They seem drawn to him like flies to dung, have been since I met him way back then." He looked at her. "And he doesn't send them away wanting." Kerrick held her gaze, until she frowned and looked toward the loch.

So, Aiden was a rogue? Did he save his brooding attitude and frowns just for her, then? *Hmph*. It was good, then, that she felt no attachment to him. Surely, the heat she'd felt last night in Grey's room was due to the darkness and the warmth he gave off. She had no reason to fear falling into lust with the man, losing her reason and jeopardizing her newfound safety.

She glanced at the dark-haired Highlander riding beside her. Kerrick was handsome, in a boyish way. Someone with whom she could tease and laugh without fear of losing herself to his influence. All the ladies said he was also very gentlemanly and reliable like a good brother. Unlike Aiden, Kerrick was safe. "So, Kerrick Campbell, tell me about yourself," she said with a grin.

• • •

Balloch Castle was older than Finlarig, and Donald Campbell did not keep it up as well as Grey kept up Finlarig. Parts of the wall around it had fallen in, and the thatching on the outbuildings needed repair. Aiden would talk with Grey about sending some of the young warriors to work on it when he returned. After all, Donald was a Campbell cousin.

Aiden had caught up with their party before they had ventured too far ahead. He'd just wanted to check in and gather some fresh shirts and take his father's daggers, which were now hidden upon his body. They rode away from Balloch castle, along the loch that would take them to Castle Menzies. They had only visited long enough for Aiden to verify Finlay Menzies's claim that he'd approached Donald first with his offer.

Scarlet hadn't said a word to him but had spent her time talking with Donald's two younger daughters, persuading them to attend the school. Watching their suspicious frowns,

Aiden could tell that her English accent had put them immediately on guard. They seemed to judge her poorly by her voice alone. He frowned. But hadn't he done the same?

He shook off the slight tug of guilt with a physical shake of his shoulders. Scarlet rode behind him again, next to Kerrick. He could hear the bloody besotted man regaling her with stories of Campbell prowess.

"Grey and I rode out to meet the riders on the field beyond the village while the warriors were roused in town," Kerrick said.

"We were there right behind ye," Lawrence called over.

"Aye," William said. "'Tis not like ye and Grey were meeting the whole raiding party on your own."

"You were all incredibly brave," Scarlet said.

Aiden kept his snort quiet and his gaze before him. In the distance, he could see Castle Menzies, soaring up on the swell of a bare hill. Situated with a low mountain at its back and a wide moor before it, it didn't have a wall for protection. Either the Menzies weren't threatened by the English, or they were too cocky to worry about protecting themselves.

Scarlet rode up level with Aiden. "They have no wall?"

"Nay."

"Why is that?"

He shrugged. "Something ye can ask Finlay Menzies."

They rode up to the front of the Z-shaped fortress, much like Finlarig except without a wall to define the bailey. Several outbuildings sat about it and held horses, the kitchens, and pens for other animals. A small village lay beyond the castle, where snow drifted onto thatched cottages.

"Hello," Finlay called as he stepped out the front doors, followed by several of his men, whom Aiden recognized as some of the clan's seasoned warriors, including Edgar Menzies, an advisor to the late chief.

"We've come to view the flock," Aiden said, tipping his

head to Edgar.

"Welcome, Lady Worthington," Finlay said, walking up to her horse. He looked up at her. "I have learned a secret about ye," he said, and Scarlet's eyes widened slightly.

He smiled up at her like a besotted fool. "Your Christian name is Scarlet, like the reddest rose."

She gave him a gentle smile. "I am a Highland Rose now. 'Tis the name of our school."

"Ah, of course," he called, laughing abruptly, making Scarlet's mare shy back.

Scarlet stroked the horse's neck, calming her. "Would someone be able to water and shelter our horses, so they will be ready to return after our inspection?"

"Certainly," Finlay called. "Though, I'm holding ye here for a meal before ye leave. My sister has returned, and I would like her to meet ye. She is such a senseless lass, loud and in need of discipline."

Finlay grabbed Scarlet around the waist to lift her down. "Sir," she said, her tone admonishing, but he'd already slid her from the horse, the reins still in her hands.

Aiden swung his leg over to dismount and strode to her side, followed by Kerrick. "Menzies," Aiden started, but before he could say anything further, the young man lifted both hands from Scarlet and stepped back in surrender.

Finlay grinned broadly. "Och, I was but helping the lady down."

Scarlet regarded him coolly. "I am very capable of dismounting on my own."

Aiden's hand lingered near the hilt of his sword, and he met the wide-eyed stare of Finlay. Had the man read the unspoken threat? The side of Finlay's mouth curved upward as he rubbed his chin. He turned, speaking over his shoulder. "Let us inside, out of this snow."

"I would see the flock," Scarlet said, apparently not

comfortable with the greeting, either.

"After a warm drink."

As if the winter weather agreed, a gust swirled thick flakes around them. Aiden passed a look to Kerrick and the other Campbells. They would all be on guard.

Aiden moved before Scarlet, while Kerrick took up the position at her back. If she thought it unwarranted, she didn't object. Stepping inside, Aiden was struck by the richness of the great hall. Thick tapestries graced the walls and floors, insulating the room against much of the winter cold. A cheery fire crackled in the giant hearth at the end, and a long wooden table with chairs filled the middle of the room. A lit iron candelabrum hung on a chain to illuminate a basket of rolls and plates of meat and root vegetables. A serving man filled tankards along the table, and two more hefted a steaming iron pot.

"A bite, and then we will see the flock," Finlay said. Grinning like a benevolent prince, the cocky chief held a chair out for Scarlet. Aiden had the impulse to sit in it himself but held back.

Scarlet moved forward with the grace of a woman used to walking across a ballroom. She gave Finlay a brief nod and sat in the seat he held, letting him push it under her. Her back remained stiff and straight. "There," Finlay said and motioned for the men to take seats around his table with him at the top. He leaned toward one of the servers. "See if Cici is presentable enough to come down." The man hurried away.

Finlay's own men also sat, several of them nodding to the Campbell warriors. They were neighbors, after all, and even though there had been feuds and raids in the past, they had grown up meeting and competing at festivals through the years. Aiden was fairly certain that one of the Campbell lasses had wed a Menzies.

Scarlet untied her red cloak and let it slip from her head

and shoulders. A lady's maid came forward to shake the melting snow from it. Aiden scanned the well-appointed keep, noting corridors and the exit.

Finlay lifted his tankard. "A blessing on this exchange." He took a long haul off of his ale. As the Campbells had been taught to do, Aiden, as the acting chief, took a drink first. The others would wait for the count of ten before the next in line, Kerrick, would drink. No fast-acting poison could wipe out the whole party of men, leaving Scarlet without defense.

Finlay didn't seem to notice as he jabbered away to Scarlet about the castle and Menzies' vast lands. "Our village has a chapel, smithy, apothecary, and a tavern."

"But not a school?" Scarlet asked as she spread butter on a roll.

"Nay," Finlay said. "Which is why I wish to send my sister to Finlarig."

Scarlet took a small bite, chewing. From the corner of his gaze, Aiden watched her slender throat swallow, making his mouth go dry. He took a long drink from his tankard.

"Tell me, Chief Menzies, why you do not have a wall around Castle Menzies?" she said.

"Don't need one," he answered with a smile. "Our warriors are known for their fierceness, so we are never bothered."

"That sounds like a challenge, Menzies," Aiden said without looking up from his plate.

Finlay chuckled. "We are always up for a challenge, Campbell."

Scarlet tipped her head, regarding Finlay. "Strange how you do not worry about the English."

Finlay took a drink and smiled. "Like I said, we are renowned."

The conversation started up slowly along the rest of the table. The food was well seasoned and hearty, but Aiden noticed that Scarlet ate little, preferring the stew that was served from the iron pot. He turned back to his plate. All English women must eat sparingly.

A bubbling of high-pitched laughter brought Aiden's head up, and his gaze joined the others to turn toward the arched throughway to the back of the castle. A rustling of skirts preceded a lass with reddish hair and wide eyes over a full smile. Plump and joyful, she practically ran into the hall. "Halò!" she called in greeting. The Campbell men pushed back their chairs and stood.

Finlay snorted and kept his seat, though several of his men stood. "And here she comes, the banshee of Castle Menzies." Finlay threw a hand out toward her. "Cicilia Menzies, meet Lady Scarlet Worthington."

"Hello," she said, her smile dipping slightly. Her gaze took in the Campbells around the table. It stopped on Aiden, her one brow rising as if she were appreciating his appearance.

Scarlet rose, but Cicilia motioned for her to return to her seat. "I wouldn't dream of interrupting your meal, Lady Worthington," she said, taking a seat across from her, where one of the Menzies men had vacated.

Scarlet smiled pleasantly. "Please, call me Scarlet."

"And ye can call me Cici," the happy woman said and grabbed a plate, adding meat and a roll to it. Her gaze moved back to Aiden. "Now, I know who some of ye are, Aiden Campbell," she said, and he bowed his head toward her. He remembered her from a harvest several years ago. She seemed just as boisterous as she had been then, though her father had still been alive and had tempered her exuberance with his bellows and frowns. "Did ye all come to welcome me home?"

Scarlet cleared her throat. "We were actually invited to Castle Menzies by your brother to inspect a small flock of sheep, which I plan to purchase for my brother."

Cici turned her smile on Scarlet. She lowered her voice to a hush that still reached everyone in the hall. "That's right. Your brother stole Finlarig from Grey Campbell, but then Grey fell in love…" She clasped her hands before her heart. "And won an English lady's heart and his castle back. So romantic."

Scarlet smiled. "I suppose it was."

Cici leaned forward. "Are they really soooo in love?"

"They certainly seem to be," Scarlet said and took a sip from her cup. "So Cici, your brother mentioned that you might be interested in attending our new Highland Roses School for ladies, at Finlarig Castle."

Cici's eyes widened, and she glanced at Finlay, who'd taken another long drink of his ale. "Getting rid of me so soon?" she asked but didn't sound disgruntled.

"Certainly," Finlay responded with a broad smile. He coughed into his fist and rested his hand on Scarlet's on the table. "Lady Worthington is teaching lasses to read and cipher. Even though ye've been taught letters and your name, your simple mind hasn't caught on to reading."

Aiden frowned as he watched Scarlet slide her hand out from under Finlay's. She looked to Cici. "I'm sure you have a very clever mind. We would love to have you as a student. Our curriculum includes etiquette, art, and practical endeavors, including how to defend oneself."

"Defend oneself?" Finlay asked, his face splitting with laughter. "And how would a lass defend herself?"

Kerrick sat across from Aiden, his usual grin gone. "Lady Scarlet could probably kill ye in ten seconds, Menzies."

Both Finlay and Cici raised their eyebrows to their hairlines at the same time, making Aiden almost laugh. Despite the differences in their statures, they had the same humorous expressions, likely inherited from their mother, since their father had been a grim old cur.

Everyone stared at Scarlet. She didn't recoil at the attention but tipped her chin a bit higher. "I wouldn't put my skills to the test," she said with a confident smile, "else find yourself skewered."

Silence followed for several heartbeats before Cici leaped up. "I will pack now." Everyone around the table laughed.

"Good God," Finlay said. "Loud and lethal. How will I marry ye off, then, Cici?"

"It will take a strong, confident, and kind man to win my heart, brother," she answered, taking up her plate to walk toward the back. She flapped her hand at Scarlet. "Just let Fin know the school fees. We may have suffered a bad harvest for hay, but our Da saved gold like a miser. Best to spend it before Finlay spreads it around."

Finlay leaned low across the table toward Scarlet. "I think ye'll be going back with a flock of sheep and a high-spirited virago." He pushed himself back up, reminding Aiden of a man with too much whisky dulling his mind. Maybe his tankard held something stronger than ale.

Aiden rose. "We've supped. Time to see the sheep, Menzies."

"All right, Campbell," Finlay said, his humor muted, but he returned a smile to Scarlet, standing. "Lady Scarlet, to your flock."

Aiden watched Finlay help her into her red cloak that the maid returned. She murmured her thanks, and before Finlay could offer her his thin arm, Aiden took up her hand. Slightly startled, she looked down where he held it. He laid it on his own arm, turning to lead her toward the door. Her fingers curled into his sleeve, and he glanced her way. The hint of a smile touched her lips, and she gave him a slight nod. Aye, she wanted nothing to do with the buffoon.

"Well, then," Finlay mumbled, hustling around the front to grab his scabbard by the door. The sword clattered in its holder as he wrapped the belt around his middle. "This way," he said, pushing through the doors.

Aiden followed, keeping Scarlet close where he could keep her safe. She was his responsibility while Grey was gone. As temporary chief and a warrior of Clan Campbell. Not because she smelled of flowers and her eyes sparkled with unguarded joy when she flew like the wind on her horse. They stepped out through the doors of the keep, and Scarlet gasped, stepping closer into him.

*Bloody hell.*

The world had disappeared.

# Chapter Four

White and gray. That was all Scarlet could see. Wind whipped ice about them as she clung to Aiden's strong arm. Finlay, two steps down, was nearly obscured by the tempest. It was if snow had engulfed the world.

"This way," Finlay called, arm raised as he trotted down.

"I've got ye." Aiden's warm breath slid along her cheek as he spoke close to her ear. She felt him tug her hood up, covering her head. Down they stepped into the white wash. She linked her arm tighter with Aiden's, her shoulder right up against him.

Kerrick cursed in Gaelic. He appeared through the snow on her other side. Flanked by the two large Highlanders, she felt less of the wind's bite, but it still pushed through her woolen cape, making her feel like she was drowning in the storm. "How in hell are we leaving in this?" Kerrick asked over her head.

"We will wait for it to abate," Aiden answered. The wind shrieked, trying to steal his words away, a warning that he, too, could be snatched up in such a storm.

Ahead, the dark shape of a structure began to emerge.

"Inside," she called above the wind, feeling the prickles of snow hitting her face. Fingers numb under the thin leather of her gloves, Scarlet pressed forward, tripping on an unseen rock. She gave a small, unheard gasp as her feet left the ground, and she realized that Aiden had lifted her against him, his arms around her waist as they thrust ahead and pushed inside a small barn.

They breathed hard against one another, and she looked up into his face. His eyebrows, hair, and short beard were iced over with snow, making him look like a frosty barbarian. She reached up to dust his brows with her hand. He blinked as the crystals fell down to his cheeks to melt. He backed up and shook his head like a wet dog. Scarlet dragged her cloak from her head.

"Wild weather today," Finlay said as he turned toward them. "Looks like ye'll have to stay the night." He clapped his hands in one loud crack, making the sheep startle in the corner. "And if ye find fault with my flock, a couple of these will make us a fine lamb stew."

Whether he'd issued the threat as a business strategy or not, Scarlet knew that she'd never surrender the little bleating lambs to a stew. Within moments she agreed to purchase the flock and the ram, who was kept separate.

"See that they are brought over after the storm abates," Aiden said. "And there will be coin."

"Yes," Scarlet said. "I will pay twenty pounds for the full flock, including the ram."

Finlay raised his arms in the air. "This calls for a celebration!"

• • •

Scarlet sipped at the dark wine that the Menzies had served with venison pie and fresh bread. For dessert, sugared apples were placed in bowls with frothed cow's milk, and a barrel of whisky had been tapped. Musicians wielded their instruments in the corner as if it were a festival, and a dozen villagers had braved the storm to eat and dance. Wood smoke mixed with the smells from the food and dancing people.

Aiden stood with Kerrick on the other side of the room, where Cici laughed and spoke with large gestures. Scarlet sipped the dry wine and leaned back against the edge of the table, watching Aiden. Even at a party, the man was ready for battle, his legs braced and his hand resting on the hilt of his sword. He interjected a word or two, but Kerrick seemed to be the one to carry the conversation. Aiden turned his body and scanned the room. Scarlet kept her eyes on him, and when their gazes met, Aiden said something to Cici and strode toward Scarlet.

Scarlet took another sip of wine, her toe tapping to the rhythm of the drum. Aiden dodged a line of dancers and lowered his weight into the chair next to her.

"Seems Chief Menzies needs little reason for a celebration," he said, his mouth close to her ear.

A tickle of awareness shot along her skin. "No wonder he needs the gold," she said, watching Finlay laughing with some of his warriors. They all had been drinking whisky freely, along with several flirtatious young ladies from the village. At first, Scarlet thought to talk to the women about the school, but they seemed to become drunk quickly.

She frowned, a tightness in her chest. "I wish we weren't stuck here," she said. The wind and snow had become bars around this merry cell. Unease hardened her spine.

"Aye," Aiden answered. "The storm is slowing, but it is late. Better to head back in the morning." He didn't sound any happier than she about their circumstances.

The music continued, and Scarlet watched Cici tug Kerrick out to dance with the others. His gaze kept drifting toward Aiden and her, which was probably why he tramped on poor Cici's foot nearly every time they passed one another.

"You don't dance?" Scarlet asked Aiden, already knowing the answer.

"Not for a long time," Aiden said, his muscular arms obvious through his shirt as he crossed them over his chest.

Scarlet's eyebrows rose. "Pardon? Do you mean to say that at one time you did dance? This brutal, ornery Highland warrior?"

He cut a glance her way. "I was taught. As a lad, when I had little say in the matter."

Scarlet tipped her head to the side. "Which dances?"

He nodded to the line across the floor, ladies on one side with men on the other, passing through the middle and turning. "You know how to dance a minuet?" she asked, her voice full of surprise.

Aiden pointed one finger down and spun it slowly. "Along with some turns where I would lift the woman."

"You know La Volta?" Scarlet turned her body toward him. "Who are you, Aiden Campbell?"

The ghost of a smile played across his full lips, making his features darkly handsome. He'd taken some time before the meal to wash and trim his short beard, shaving the rest smooth. He grunted a laugh but didn't answer.

As the song ended and another began, Kerrick turned around, his gaze going directly toward Scarlet. "Oh dear," Scarlet murmured without moving her lips. "I fear my feet will be trampled very soon."

Aiden's smile faded, though he raised an eyebrow as if in jest. "Not if you're standing before him. Finlay's sister suffered because he kept looking over here."

Scarlet sighed. "Blast, here he comes." She took another sip of wine, hiding her lips in the cup. "Help," she said.

Aiden cursed in Gaelic next to her, inhaled deeply, and

pushed up out of his seat. "Come along then." He held out his arm. Scarlet just stared at it for a moment. "Quickly, before he reaches us."

She leaped up, taking his arm. "I would love to take one turn of the dance before retiring," she said. "Thank you, Aiden. Oh, hello, Kerrick. Aiden is taking me through the steps before I head to bed."

"Aiden?" Kerrick asked, incredulous as Scarlet had been. "The steps are tricky."

Aiden said nothing, just marched out toward the line with Scarlet on his arm. She couldn't keep her smile inside and nearly laughed at the look from the other guests, wide-eyed surprise and suspicion from the ladies' suitors.

Scarlet was familiar with stares on the ballroom floor, as she'd been paraded around the English court, her father wishing her to make a profitable marriage match. Her stomach fluttered with a slice of panic at the memory of her risky, flirtatious behavior, and the consequences that haunted her still. Her steps faltered, making Aiden glance her way, a question in his eyes.

She gave a quick smile and opened her eyes wide. "I must still be in shock," she said, rotating her free hand toward him and then the dancers. He gave a small chuckle and left her at the end of the line of females. Cici waved to them both from four partners higher in line.

The musicians began another minuet, and she guessed that Aiden would work a few La Volta turns into it as some had done during the previous dance. Schooled from the age of five, Scarlet knew dance steps forward, backward, and sideways. She doubted Castle Menzies could throw anything at her that she couldn't swiftly grasp. At Hollings Estate, her mother would receive published pamphlets on the updated dances yearly and tutor her daughters and son on the current tweaks to the traditional steps before they left for court.

Instead of gilt walls, bright mirrors, richly costumed courtier peacocks, and a thousand flickering candles in golden chandeliers, Scarlet took the graceful steps to the music surrounded by stone walls and simple country people. She smiled broadly. Even if the Menzies whispered about the dirt on her riding habit or that she'd left her hair down and unadorned, they were not the viperish whispers of the royal elite.

Scarlet passed Aiden, twisting her head to keep their gazes tethered. After another pass, she began to relax and followed Aiden as he added a small step in the middle of their pass to add a level of complexity. She nodded and kept his gaze, their bodies moving together to slide past each other at the last moment. It was like a caress, and prickles of awareness spread across Scarlet's skin. The music continued, and the laughter around them faded as Aiden pulled her complete attention, his dark, serious eyes looking deeply into her. Normally, she would look away, laugh, or make light of some pretended misstep that she didn't take, but Aiden's gaze reached inside her.

He stepped close, his hands reaching for her middle. La Volta. With his large, strong grasp, he lifted her, spinning her past him in an elegant turn, and Scarlet stepped right back into the minuet with a grace that had been pressed into her. Again, they approached, and again, he reached, his warm hands holding her waist, lifting her as if she weighed nothing. And through it all, they ignored the onlookers, the world around them. Only the music, the rush of her blood, and the feel of Aiden's gaze and hands mattered. It was like being caught up in a dream—not a nightmarish memory but something new and exhilarating. She trusted his steps and hold, his strong gaze securing them together so they moved as one.

With one last La Volta turn, the music ended, and Aiden let his hands slide down her waist so that she could back up. For a heartbeat, Scarlet stood there in the center of the floor. People clapping set her in motion, and she joined the applause. But when she looked around, she realized that instead of applauding the musicians, everyone seemed to be looking at Aiden and her. She gave a brief curtsey to Aiden, and he took her arm, escorting her toward the arched alcove that led to the bedroom she'd been given above.

"Nay," Finlay called out, following them. He tripped, looking down as if the floor had sprung up on purpose to foil his grace. "Wait, Scarlet. I would have a dance with ye."

They turned to watch the young man right his shirt and run a hand through his longish hair. With a flourish, which only showcased how much whisky he'd consumed, he bowed. "Lady Scarlet, may I have the honor of—"

"Forgive me, Chief Menzies," Scarlet cut in. "I find that I am exhausted from the travel today and will be retiring for the night."

Finlay's red face screwed up into a playful scowl, and he huffed. "Blast. Ye are the loveliest lass on the floor this eve." His glance went to Aiden. "Lucky bastard. Stole her right out from under me."

Scarlet felt the muscles in Aiden's arm tighten, and she drew herself upright. "Sir," she snapped. "Your insinuation against your guests are rude, and I am not, nor ever will be under you. I must think your base lack of manners stems from consuming whisky and your lack of years. Your mother would certainly be ashamed."

She turned toward the stairs, Aiden beside her. Finlay said nothing, and they climbed the winding staircase. "What a baboon," she said, watching the steps before her in the dim light of glass-enclosed candles mounted to the stone. "I was worried that you would run him through."

"Your tongue was just as deadly and didn't leave blood stains," he said, his dry answer making her chuckle. After several turns, they reached the third floor where a vacant room had been made ready for Scarlet. Aiden entered first. "Cold but empty," he said, going to the hearth, where he pulled wool and flint from his satchel to light a fire.

"Thank you," she said when the flames began to catch, lighting the small room. She wrapped her arms around herself. It would be a long night.

Aiden straightened. "Bar the door when I leave. I will return at dawn for our trip back to Finlarig."

She nodded, glancing at the door where a heavy oak slat leaned against the wall.

"Or," he said. "It would be best if I sleep outside your door."

"No," Scarlet said, shaking her head. "Find a bed. A sleep-hungry Aiden Campbell is a surly fellow, indeed," she said. With him outside her door, it would be too easy for her to give in to the unsettling heat that seemed to coil inside her when he was near.

He walked out. "I won't leave until I hear the bar drop," he said.

She hefted the wood and let it slide down heavily. "Good night," she called through the door. He didn't respond, though she hadn't expected it. Scarlet turned to the small room with the cozy fire and wrapped her arms around herself. With Aiden gone, it felt like a dungeon cell.

She snorted. What dungeon cell had a warm fire and blankets?

She shivered and took up her cloak, tucking it around her. She'd sleep dressed to leave in the morning. Fingering through her hair, she lowered onto her side on the lumpy bed, her cheek against the flat pillow. Watching the flames dance in the hearth, the strains of the minuet played in her mind, lulling her to sleep.

*Tap. Tap. Tap.* "Lady Worthington?" Scarlet blinked, her gaze opening to the glowing embers in the hearth. *Tap. Tap. Tap.* "Are ye in there, Scarlet?" It was Finlay. Scarlet took a full inhale and pushed up in bed.

"It's the middle of the night," she called, her mind still wrapped in a dream of dancing La Volta with Aiden. "What is it?"

"There's a lass ye must see," he said. "She's burning."

An image of Aiden's scars filled Scarlet's mind, and she threw back the covers, planting her feet into her boots. "Burning? She's on fire?"

"Aye," Finlay said. "Ye must come see."

Scarlet strained to push up the heavy bar. Blinking, she opened the door. *Bar the door.* Aiden's words came back to her, and she hesitated, stepping back.

Finlay reached in and grabbed her wrist. "Quickly, do ye hear her screaming below?"

Scarlet heard the faint call of someone, a woman. Good God, what had happened? Evie had treated Aiden's back with snails, or rather their slime, but where would she find snails under all the snow?

Finlay hurried her through the dark corridor and down the winding steps. Scarlet smelled smoke, but it didn't seem thicker than the usual hearth fires. A woman yelled out as if she was in agony, making Scarlet's boots clip faster. The whole time, Finlay kept looking back at her to see if she followed. As they reached the bottom, he tugged her into the shadows by the archway.

"What are you—?" she asked, realizing he'd wrapped around her from behind.

His whisky-thick breath was hot in her ear. "Watch, Scarlet lass," he said. "Watch her burn." He reached one arm past her to point at the table in the great hall where a woman kneeled on all fours, her skirts raised as a man thrust into her. Her breasts hung out of her bodice before her as she moaned, rocking, the pitch of her voice rising to the point where she was nearly screaming.

Scarlet's knees felt weak as fear crushed through her. Despite the thickness of her skirt and cloak, she could feel the press of Finlay's erect member against her backside. His arm held her tightly around the ribs, trapping her. "Let go," she said. The man on the table looked over his shoulder and smiled, knowing they watched.

"Just enjoy. Jack doesn't mind us watching," Finlay whispered, his lips brushing her ear, sending a wave of nausea down through Scarlet. "Doesn't it make ye ache?"

Flashes of her nightmares caught at Scarlet's breath, nearly suffocating her. Trapped, forced to watch the passion of another couple while held, a mere moment from being raped. Any heat that might possibly flame up within her at viewing a scene of mutual passion froze to ice in her veins. For she knew what could come next.

Weakness made her legs buckle, but Finlay held her hard against him, bending his height over her. He breathed heavily against her cheek, pressing into her as if he were the one rutting.

The man pulled out of the woman. "Don't stop," she said, pouting.

"Never, lass," he answered, laying her back on the table and raising her legs high to rest over his shoulders, the skirts ruffled about her middle as he entered her again. She crooned, and he began to pump harder.

The man smiled at Scarlet where Finlay held her within the archway. But instead of the Scotsman, Scarlet envisioned the long, dark wig of King Charles, the press of Harry Covington against her back. "Watch," Harry whispered, his hand coming up to touch her breast. Shock, fear, and shame washed through her body, making her chin grow numb and stars spark in her periphery.

But this wasn't Harry, it was Finlay Menzies, his hand roaming under her cloak. *Get away*. The calm words of

Grey Campbell, as he taught them self-defense back at the Highland Roses School, cut through Scarlet's paralysis. *Get away with surprise, then attack.*

Scarlet inhaled and exhaled slowly, resting her hands on the arm anchoring her to Finlay's chest. She raised her booted foot, tipping her toes up so that the heel would come down first. Finlay was entranced with the show before him, even loosening his hold as his free hand found his rigid member, where he began to stroke.

With one more inhale, Scarlet threw herself into action, stomping her heel down on the bastard's bare toes. He hollered in pain. "Fok!" His arm dropped from her, and she spun to face him, her one hand grabbing his shoulder as the other raised her skirts, liberating her knee to jam upward. Her target was obvious, and she threw all her weight, fear, and growing fury into the thrust, hitting his cod. Finlay doubled in half immediately, falling to the stone floor.

Scarlet wasted no further time on him, whirling away to run through the great hall, past the couple. The woman screeched in Gaelic, grabbing her clothes. Apparently, *she* hadn't been aware of the viewing. Scarlet dodged empty tankards and hopped over one unconscious Menzies warrior on her way out the front door. *Escape. Get away.* Just like when she'd woken Evie up at Whitehall that horrible night. But this time, Scarlet was on her own.

Again, she'd been foolish enough to believe a man and had walked into his perverse escapade. Shame heated her face even in the cold night air. Shame at her stupidity. Shame that she would believe anything a man would say.

The moon had come out from the clouds, its light glistening against the fresh snow. Scarlet didn't stop running until she reached the stables, where she spotted the white coat of Aiden's horse. Where was Aiden sleeping? Her gaze snapped left and right along the moonlit bailey where she could see several outbuildings, including the one that housed her sheep. She didn't dare search for him, not when she might run into other rutting couples or drunken men.

With the stable door open, the moonlight allowed her enough light to find Caora. Unlatching the stall, Scarlet threw her arms around the horse's neck, hugging her, taking in her strength to stop her legs from shaking. "We are going home," Scarlet whispered, and the horse's ears flicked, her wide, intelligent eyes seeming to accept the risky plan. Evelyn and then Aiden had asked her why she didn't ride. Well, now she would, as fast as she could to Finlarig to bar herself away from the world.

The storm had blown itself away, leaving a clear, moon-washed night. Galloping, Caora would fly her back to Finlarig in under two hours. They would ride southeast until finding Loch Tay, which they'd follow until coming to the familiar road to Killin.

Not wanting to spend the time saddling Caora, Scarlet slipped a bridle over her head and a padded blanket onto her bare back. She climbed the slats that made up the stall and pushed herself onto the horse's back. "That's it," she whispered. "Good girl." She breathed heavily, the whole time keeping her ears alert for anyone giving chase. But the night was silent, even the wind dying down.

Clicking her tongue, Scarlet pressed Caora into a walk out of the barn. Blast, the moon was so bright. But no one ran out of the keep or the thatched buildings. Scarlet kept Caora walking until they reached halfway across the snow-blanketed meadow. Four or five inches had fallen, creating a soft, bright surface.

With one last adjustment to the direction, Scarlet let up on Caora's reins. "Fly," she whispered, and the horse shot forward.

# Chapter Five

Aiden woke, his fingers wrapping around the *sgian dubh* he kept under the pillow. Where was he? Castle Menzies. From his spot on the small bed in the thatched outbuilding that served as quarters for soldiers when needed, Aiden could hear several of his men snoring. Was that what had woken him?

In the distance he heard horse hooves. A Menzies headed home after waking up in his own vomit on the great hall floor? When Aiden had left Finlay and his guests, the wild drinking and dancing had settled down, with several men passing out along the table. Finlay's sister, Cici, had gone above to bed shortly after Scarlet. With the celebration ebbing, Aiden and Kerrick had headed out with the other Campbell men to sleep in one of the empty buildings.

Aiden tossed onto his other side and paused to listen, but only snoring prevailed. Still, something pulled at his instincts. *Scarlet*. Aiden sat up in the bed, still dressed down to his boots. He clipped across the floor to the door and out into the bailey. Brow furrowed, he mounted the steps to the keep two at a time.

Striding through the entryway, he came up short as he saw Finlay sitting at the table, puking into a wooden tankard. One of his men stood close, an undone woman beside him, clutching her bodice closed over her chest. Aiden strode past him on his way to check on Scarlet. "Can't hold your whisky, Menzies," he said and shook his head. "Time to grow into your chiefdom."

The other Menzies cursed. "'Twas that lady, kicked him in the ballocks so hard he's sick."

Aiden froze, his boot on the first step leading up, and turned. "Lady?"

Finlay couldn't talk doubled over, his hand to his chest as if his heart might break through his ribs and skin.

"Aye, the lady. Kicked him hard enough to almost kill him."

"Ye should have been kicked, too, ye bastard," the woman said. "Not telling me we was being watched like that. I'm going home."

Aiden's hard stare moved between Finlay and his man. "The Lady Scarlet?" he said slowly.

"Aye," the man answered, and before he could say another word, Aiden leaped up the stairs, using his hands on either side of the narrow, curling stairway to propel him faster. He came out on the third floor, running down to her room.

"Scarlet," he called. His heart dropped as her door pushed open under his knock, and he raced inside. Empty. He grabbed up her satchel, the only thing that showed he had the correct room. Nothing else of her was left.

Back down the stairs, he ran into the great hall and straight up to Finlay. He grabbed the man under his arms, hoisting him upright. Pale and pained, the man panted.

"What did ye do to Scarlet?"

"Nothing," Finlay said, his eyes floating about in his

head. The man was drunk, his head lolling about on his skinny neck. Aiden had the urge to shake him until his head snapped off.

"Where is she?" he yelled into the arse's pale face.

"She ran out of here," the other man said, shrugging into his shirt and pointing toward the entryway.

*Mo chreach!* What had gone on in here that sent Scarlet fleeing into the cold night? He shook Finlay, throwing him back onto the bench where he pitched to the side, falling face first onto the floor. "If anything happens to Scarlet because of ye…" Aiden crouched down to turn the man over so Finlay could see his face. Finlay's nose bled from hitting the ground. "If anything has happened to her, I will be back to gut ye."

Aiden turned to the other man. "Make sure this drunk fool remembers what I just said."

The Menzies' lips thinned into a hard line, but he nodded. Aiden ran out of the keep and scanned the snow in the open bailey. Scarlet's small boot prints were easy to spot in the moonlight. He strode along them. "Bloody hell," he cursed as they led him to the stable. He pushed into the building. "Damnation." The bay filly was gone, her stall door gaping open.

• • •

Speed was no concern for Scarlet, even bareback, and the young horse seemed to understand Scarlet's need to fly. Once the meadow, which extended past Balloch Castle, disappeared under Caora's flying hooves, they slowed to enter another set of dark woods. After this, they would come out near Loch Tay, and she'd follow it past Aiden's cabin.

Moonlight slashed down through the winter-bare trees, making eerie, finger-like shadows across the ground. Thin bramble stuck up through the snow on all sides. Luckily,

Caora had excellent reflexes and dodged the saplings and trees with precision while Scarlet held on, lying low over the horse's neck.

Lord, what was she doing riding a horse in the winter forest at night? She'd escaped her demons once by flying away from London, and now she flew from Castle Menzies. But this time she didn't have James with his musket and Evie telling her that all would be well. The center of her chest tightened, and she bit back a sob. Would she always feel like she must flee? Awake or asleep, it didn't seem to matter. She was always escaping from her memories or from new horrors.

Scarlet clung to the horse's neck, needing the feeling that she wasn't alone. Her nose and her gloveless hands felt the bite of the wind. Thank the heavens she'd worn her boots and cloak downstairs when Finlay had called her, thinking she might need to run for an apothecary.

"So stupid," she hissed. How could she have fallen again for trickery? She'd thought herself clever. Evie had always said so, and she could make a table of courtiers titter with her wit. But to fall for another man's lies, after Aiden had told her to keep the door barred… Shame washed along her skin, prickling her face until her vision swam with tears. She held a bare hand to her mouth, realizing it still shook from cold and fear and anger at herself.

In the distance, Scarlet heard the howl of a wolf. She pushed upright on Caora's back. "Dearest God," she whispered into the wind that blew like an icy rebuke against her face. The young mare's ears twitched as she tipped her nose to the breeze that cut through the bare trees. She whinnied softly, a nervous note in her pitch.

They broke out from the trees and rode toward Loch Tay. The moon's white orb reflected on the calm, frozen surface, where several shapes stood farther above them along the water's jagged edge. Prickles of fear cut along Scarlet's skin.

Wolves. A small pack, lapping water from the thinned ice. Scarlet's thoughts raced as fast as the wind that swept past her toward the beasts. Her fingers clenched around the reins. Would running make them chase? She had no weapons at all, not even a hair spike to act like a dagger.

The largest wolf raised its pointed snout to the sky as if inhaling the wind that carried the fragrance of her fear. "Oh God," Scarlet whispered as the beast began to trot toward her, its head low. The others followed on its heels.

"Run," Scarlet said, kicking into Caora's sides. The horse needed no encouragement, having sensed the danger from the first scent. Caora's hooves seemed to leap through the air, barely touching down as she ran, the muscles of her legs surging in time with Scarlet's wild heartbeat. Would she die tonight? Would her continued foolishness doom the beautiful bay filly who raced so hard to carry them away?

Scarlet lay over the horse's straining neck to hold on for dear life. Without a saddle, her feet dangled, trying to find purchase with her heels and thighs. Her numb fingers coiled into Caora's mane. Glancing over her shoulder, Scarlet saw the shapes loping after them, the moonlight shining down to stretch their slanted shadows over the snow. Could Caora keep up this mad dash until they reached Finlarig?

The wind flew past Scarlet's cheeks, filling her hood to blow it off her head. Hair streaming out behind her, Scarlet concentrated on holding on to the horse's back. Raising her gaze, she saw another section of forest before them. The wolves would surely catch them amongst the trees where Caora couldn't run at top speed. The hungry beasts would tear into the poor young horse, even if Scarlet could manage to climb a tree.

Scarlet blinked back tears, and her gaze slid to the right, where a dark structure stood out from the snow. Aiden's cabin. Hope cracked open the panic in her chest. She moved her fingers, willing feeling back into them as she tightened the reins, angling Caora toward the dwelling. Was it locked? Aiden had pulled a chain high on the door to open it. She glanced behind at the pack, closing in. Hungry and fast, the pack was certain death.

Scarlet bent low over Caora's neck, straining in the darkness to see the mechanism of the door. She didn't dare slow the horse until they were nearly to the cabin. Almost there. "Go Caora," she yelled, rising, her thighs straining. Several yards out from the cabin, Scarlet yanked to the left with the reins, turning the horse as she skidded into the side of the cabin. "Hold on," she called and dropped the reins in her desperate pawing at the top of the wooden door. She didn't waste time turning to see the wolves bearing down on them. She knew they were there, salivating, their teeth gnashing.

"Now, now, now," she muttered as she yanked on the chain she felt in the shadow of the doorframe, and a popping sound came from inside. At her shove, the door swung inward. "Inside," she screamed, yanking Caora's mane to get her to turn and digging her heels into the horse's heaving flanks.

Scarlet half fell, half jumped off the horse's back, coming down hard on her ankle. The pinch of pain forgotten, she threw her weight against the door to slam it shut. She opened her eyes wide in the darkness of the room, frantic to find a bar to drop across it.

*Bang! Thud!* The door pitched inward. "Caora!" she yelled, bracing against the door, and the horse moved closer. With strength born of desperation, Scarlet pulled the horse's leg until the mare moved up against the door, her weight holding it closed as the wolves pushed against it, their nails scratching the wood. "Aiden," she yelled in frustration. "Where the bloody hell is the bar?"

• • •

Her horse's tracks were clear in the snow, the moon shining down to light them. What the bloody hell had happened that would send Scarlet fleeing in the dead of night? And in the snow, with no escort or weapons? Even a discontented Englishwoman wouldn't wake and leave in the middle of the night all by herself. Nay, something terrible must have sent her running.

"Finlay Menzies is a dead man," Aiden muttered, rubbing his chin through his short beard. He and Eigh rode next to Caora's tracks. From their direction, it was obvious that Scarlet was retracing the way they'd traveled yesterday. Why hadn't she woken him? Why had she even left her room? Finlay must have tricked her into unbarring her door. "Bloody damned dead man," he said as he tapped Eigh into a canter.

He wove through the trees and came out the opposite end to race across the field that she'd flown over, the horse's tracks stretching long with speed. As he entered the next set of trees, he heard a wolf's howl. "Damn," he whispered and felt a hollow pain in his gut. The beast was close and likely not alone.

"*Falbh.*" He urged Eigh forward to zigzag through the trees. The two of them worked as one, dodging back and forth for long minutes. Aiden leaned low over his horse's neck, visions of Scarlet bitten and torn into by wolves urging him forward. Why the hell hadn't he just slept outside her door? He'd have stopped Finlay from whatever trickery pulled her from her room, and she'd be safe and sleeping in warmth.

Aiden and Eigh broke through the last of the trees, and he glanced down at the tracks illuminated again by the bright moon. "*Mo chreach.*" Scarlet's horse had leaped from walking to a full-out sprint. He spied the jumble of wolf prints farther on. "Go!" he yelled, leaning low to fly. The tracks veered away from the loch, up toward the dark shape of his cabin on the rise. He barreled toward it, his stallion's full weight surging beneath him. Shadows blocked a good view, but the door was closed, and no wolves were in sight.

He pulled up short of the door. "Scarlet!" he yelled. "Scarlet! Are ye in there?"

A muffled noise came from inside. "Come, Caora," Scarlet said, and a moment later the door flew inward. "Get in here!" Scarlet's hand flapped, beckoning him inside. "With the horse."

Eigh whinnied, a high-pitched screech showing his panic. Aiden ducked low, steering his horse under the eaves and into the cabin. Scarlet slammed the door, grunting as she threw the heavy oak bar over it. Kicking his leg over, Aiden dismounted, his boots thudding on the wooden floor of his suddenly cramped home.

"Shhh," Scarlet said, her finger before her lips, and Aiden could hear something running around the exterior of his cabin. *Scratch!* Scarlet jumped back from the door and wobbled on one foot. Blast. She was hurt.

"They've been scratching the door," she whispered and looked at him. Her eyes were round in the dim light filtering inside, round and full of terror. Her hair stuck out in wild disarray, and a smudge of dirt lay across her cheek.

*Scratch!* Scarlet's hands leaped up in front of her chest where she clasped them together, her gaze snapping back to the door.

Without thinking, Aiden stepped forward to pull her against him. She shook, her body stiff, but she didn't push away. His stomach clenched. "Bloody hell," he whispered over her head. "What ye've been through tonight."

He held her, willing his strength into her. He'd seen Scarlet Worthington defiant, stubborn, wry, and floating with joy when riding across the meadow. He'd never seen her filled with fear, and each of her tremors twisted inside him. "They can't get in here, and ye've already proven that ye're cleverer than they."

Placing his hands on her shoulders, he bent so that his gaze would be level with hers and waited until she slid it from the door. "Scarlet, ye are safe now."

She blinked and gave a quick bob of her head. He rubbed his hands down her arms, then held up one finger with a half grin. "Shhh," he said and turned to the door, creeping up on it, waiting.

*Scratch, scratch.*

With the flat of his hands, Aiden slammed into the door, bellowing in a fierce roar. He slapped the door, then pounded with his fists, yelling, letting his anger fly up out of his mouth until his breath gave out. When he turned, Scarlet had gone to the window, pushing back the curtain. "They are running away," she said and turned to look at him, her mouth open. "You scared away a pack of hungry wolves?"

"I startled them," he answered, shrugging, but his gaze connected with hers. "They weren't expecting it, like Finlay Menzies wasn't expecting ye to kick his frigger so hard that he's been puking ever since."

She blinked. "You found him puking?"

He nodded, his gut untwisting enough to let him inhale fully. "Couldn't even talk, doubled over."

"Well, he was drunk, too." She turned back to the window, looking out at the snow.

"They should stay away for a bit," he said. "But they will wander back to their den by morning."

He turned to his horse, running a hand down Eigh's flank, and sighed as the horse pissed on the floor.

"I'm sorry," Scarlet said, gesturing toward the horses. "There was no time to find her shelter."

He shook his head. "It will scrub up." He patted Eigh's white coat before grabbing a bucket. He lifted the bar on the door and filled the bucket with snow to melt. They would all need something to drink, and he doubted Scarlet would want whisky after tonight. Although, perhaps that was what she needed. He set the bucket over the iron grate in the hearth and found his flint for a fire.

As he struck and blew on the sparks, questions churned inside him, relighting his anger. But the lass was still raw. He didn't know much about women, but he did know animals. Wild eyes and a stiff spine required a gentle approach. He waited until she moved from the window and took a seat in one of the two chairs set before the table that he'd built from a hundred-year-old oak that had fallen in a storm.

He kept his gaze on the catching flame. "'Tis late or early, depending on how ye view it. And cold. Finlay must have been the devil himself to drive ye from Castle Menzies." He added a square of dried peat to the kindling and leaned down to blow on it. Scarlet sat silently.

Remaining crouched, Aiden swiveled toward her, peering past the tail of her horse. "What happened, Scarlet?" he whispered.

She looked away, her lips tight.

Aiden inhaled fully and let his long sigh fill the room. "Ye don't have to say. I will return tomorrow to kill Finlay Menzies. We will take the sheep to Finlarig."

"What?" Scarlet said, her gaze snapping back to him. "You...you can't just go in and slaughter a man."

He shrugged. "I will ask the bastard what he did. If he won't tell me, then I will assume the worst offense and kill him. If he does tell me, I'm certain it will require me to kill him."

Scarlet stood, so Aiden did, too. They stared at one another over the back of her bay, the filly's tail twitching. Scarlet's beautiful lips pinched, her brows scrunching together. "I was foolish," she said, her eyes slipping to the table. "He tricked me out of my room." She shook her head.

Aiden looked at the once proud woman, who had walked with confidence across Finlarig's great hall. Her face tilted down, shoulders rounded as if a weight lay across them. To steal the woman's strength like that, Finlay should be flayed open. "Did he touch ye?" Aiden whispered, his fists clenching so hard, his nails cut into his skin. "Hurt ye?" When she didn't answer, he cursed. "I will cut off his ballocks before I kill him."

"He didn't rape me," she said. "Though…I thought he might. So, I…used some of what Grey and Kerrick taught us in classes. Without their lessons…" She let the rest of her thought trail off with a shake of her head.

His fury pounded with the pulse of his blood, but he kept his voice calm. "But he did touch ye, didn't he?"

Scarlet sat in the chair, her gaze dropping to the table where she splayed out her fingers. "He said a woman was burning, and I must come help, so I unbarred the door. The woman was below…naked and…being pleasured by another man. Finlay trapped me with his arms and made me watch. He was aroused and made motions that made me fear that he would rape me, so I kicked him." She said the words quickly, numbly, without emotion.

She swallowed but still wouldn't look at him. "I…I fled without thinking through my plan." The delicate line of her jaw worked. "I wasn't counting on wolves."

Aiden breathed slowly, but his anger still tightened his fists. Finlay would pay, but saying so would only worry Scarlet. He exhaled long and shook his head. "Och, Scarlet, I am sorry I wasn't there."

"'Twas my foolishness," she murmured. "I always thought I was a clever girl growing up, quick with a witty comment to make people laugh." Her face tipped up, her eyes following the lines of his exposed rafters. She gave a dark chuckle as she stared upward. "But turns out I cannot even decipher the simple trick of a fiend." As if noticing that her hands shook, Scarlet balled them into fists and pulled them to lay in her lap.

He hated to see her frightened and even more so to see her blaming herself for the base actions of a dimwitted bastard. Aiden walked around the backside of her horse and threw himself into the chair opposite her. "Yet ye took care of the problem, didn't ye?" He gave her a nod. "With a kick so hard, the bastard may never father children. Ye are a warrior, Scarlet Worthington."

She leveled her gaze at him. "I was panic stricken the whole time."

He shrugged. "I've known many a frightened warrior. It does not matter how ye feel inside, just what action ye take. In fact, ye are even braver when ye act while filled with fear." He nodded slowly to back up his words.

Her lips twitched slightly, but it wasn't a smile. She narrowed her brow. "How do warriors go out to battle all the time, knowing they could face torture and possible death?"

Aiden rested his fists on the table between them. "We prepare, become strong and skilled with weapons and hand-to-hand combat. We learn to anticipate attack and train on how to respond to each situation. When an attack comes, we focus on our defense. It blocks out the fear and saves our lives."

Scarlet shook her head. "To have the strength of a man… 'Tis unfair that women are weaker in muscle."

"Yet it is women who are strong enough to birth life," he said. "Brave enough to act, even when it means torture and possible death."

Scarlet snorted. "Women don't usually have a say in if they get pregnant."

"And warriors don't usually have a say in if they are attacked."

They stared at one another for a long moment. "Teach

me then," Scarlet said. "How to defend myself, to prepare for an attack."

"The only thing that Finlay Menzies and I might actually agree upon is that Grey and Kerrick have apparently done a fine job at teaching ye to defend yourself."

"Not enough," Scarlet said, glancing down. She lifted her hands and held them over the table, letting him see them shake. "I escaped because the man was drunk, slow, and surprised. Yet my fear almost killed me in the end." She glanced up at her horse. "Me and an innocent beast, because fear drove me into the night without thought." She clasped her hands on the table. "I need more lessons, lessons so I can release this heavy mantle of fear." Her gaze dropped. "I have carried it too long, and I am weary," she whispered.

Carried it long? Firelight played off Scarlet's loose curls, adding a golden shine to the dark tresses that lay over her shoulders. "Ye've been frightened before? Another attack?" She didn't say anything, and he replayed conversations he'd had with Grey about the Worthington sisters coming alone to Finlarig. Scarlet came to help her sister start a school and her brother start a sheep farm. Or was there more to her journey north into the wilds of Scotland?

"Did ye flee England because of a man, Scarlet? One who frightened ye like Finlay Menzies?"

Fire crackled in the stone hearth behind him as he waited. The horses shifted, their breath and bodies helping to heat the room. The lack of denial answered for her. "Damn," Aiden said, his voice as low as the wind blowing around the eaves. "Was he a suitor? Someone in your circle?" It didn't matter, but he wanted to know, know the demon who sent her fleeing her home in England. "Someone of high rank?"

Scarlet's eyes were dark in the night shadows as she lifted them to meet his gaze. "The highest."

# Chapter Six

Scarlet pulled her frozen nose under the blanket. Feet and nose. If they were cold, the whole body was cold, as if those appendages were a direct conduit to the marrow of one's bones. Pulling her feet higher under her smock, Scarlet smashed her face into the pillow, listening to the howl of wind beyond the walls. Good God, was it still winter? Was the hearth fire out? She blinked against the gray light in the large bedroom and held her breath. Where was she?

She inhaled, eyes searching the corners of the room, and the haze over the night's disaster cleared. "Hell," she whispered, inhaling the frigid air in Aiden's bedroom.

After her revelation last night, she'd refused to elaborate, asking to sleep. He'd given her his bed while he remained below with the horses for the few hours before dawn. The light filtering into the room looked different from the glow of a winter dawn. She sat up, her hand wrapping around one of the beautifully carved posters at the corner of the bed. Vines, wild grasses, and thistle twined up each of the sturdy arms with a matching scene of a moor carved into the headboard.

Scarlet slid her legs over the edge and looked down at herself. "It certainly makes it easier to dress when one sleeps in her clothes and cloak all the time," she murmured. Lord, she wanted a soak in hot water. She and Evelyn had found a soaking tub at Finlarig, which she would be using as soon as she could.

She hurried across the hewn floorboards to the window, wiping the glass with her hand, but snow lay a coating of white crystals across the pane, blocking the view. Wind shrieked beyond the blind. Another storm? Scarlet washed as best she could, listening to the lulls and whistles of the wind. Nothing else stirred. If she didn't know where she was, she'd think herself completely alone. She paused, half bent over to retrieve her boots. Could Aiden have left to return to Castle Menzies? In the storm? Could the storm have started suddenly after he left? Would he fight his way through the storm and kill Finlay? Would he be arrested? Would she be responsible for Clan Campbell going to war with their neighbor?

"Aiden?" she called, throwing open the door to hurry down the short hall, past the second unused bedroom, to the stairs. She bent over the wooden railing. "Damn," she whispered. The horses were gone. Not even the smell of their manure remained, and the floors looked scrubbed clean. Her boots rapped as she ran down and threw open the front door, her stomach twisting at the sight of deep scratch marks in the thick oak. She shivered as snowflakes shot past her into the room and pushed the door shut.

She rested her back and shivered, despite her cloak and woolen trousers. "Bloody storm," she said, taking strength in what seemed to be a favorite curse of the Highlanders. "Where did you go?"

Above her, the latch rope slid, pulling the toggle. Her head snapped up just as the door pressed inward against her back. She leaped forward, spinning around, hand to her pounding heart as a fur-covered giant blew inside with more swirling snow.

"Bloody hell," she yelled.

"I see ye've learned to swear like a seasoned warrior," the man said, pulling the hood from his head to reveal Aiden, his brows frosty. He shook out of the hood, scattering ice. "Today, we can start teaching ye to fight like one."

"Aren't we going back to Finlarig today?" she asked, her gaze going to the window where the curtain gaped.

"I didn't get nearly frostbitten in a gentle breeze, lass." Aiden continued to pull off wrapping around his legs that he'd tied on with long straps of leather, leaving him in his kilt, linen shirt, and boots. He glanced at the window. "This should blow over by tomorrow, and we'll go." As if to show her how deadly it was outdoors, he swung the door open.

Scarlet retreated toward the fire in the hearth as Aiden dragged in a basket and several frozen parcels. He slammed the door shut on the storm and carried his items over. "An advantage of being stranded in one's own home is that it is typically full of provisions, if a man is wise." He set the parcels down with a clunk on the hearth. "Frozen, skinned hare and plucked partridges, a rasher of bacon, and my hens were busy." Scarlet looked inside the basket to see three apples, two carrots, and ten eggs. "I keep milled flour, yeast, and a crock of lard near the hearth."

"Where are the horses?" she asked, pulling an apple to polish it in a fold of her skirt. The gnaw of hunger reminded her that she'd barely eaten the evening before.

"I have a barn in the back. They are cozy and fed, and my house is again free of their shite."

"The wolves?" she asked and bit into the apple. The sweet juice tasted like the most delicious dessert.

"Nowhere to be found in this storm, and the barn is solid,

or they'd have taken my chickens by now."

She chewed, swallowing. "We should gather some snow for water. Is there ale or wine?"

"Both and whisky," he said.

She smiled over the apple. "It could snow for a fortnight, and we'd still have enough for a feast. You must be a very wise man."

He grunted. "Prepared."

"If you have a pan, I can poach some eggs for us to breakfast. And if the rasher isn't frozen solid, it will go well with the eggs," Scarlet said, taking a bucket to the door to scoop some clean snow, away from the dark lumps where Aiden likely mucked out his cabin. Shivering, she turned with the heavy bucket to find Aiden standing there.

He took the bucket from her hands, carrying it to the hearth, where he'd placed the frozen meat to thaw. "I didn't figure ye for knowing how to cook," he said, pulling out a bowl and cast-iron pan. "Most English ladies stay away from kitchens."

"I didn't know that you were an expert on English ladies," Scarlet said, pulling the eggs from the basket to line up on a small work table. He didn't answer. "I've been helping Molly in the kitchens at Finlarig. We don't have a cook, and it is too much for her with the rest of her duties." With a good night's sleep and a warm fire, Scarlet was feeling more like her old self. Although, given the chance, she'd like to stay right here, locked away from the world in this cozy cabin, which was nothing like her old self.

They worked next to each other in silence, Scarlet cooking the eggs in the hot, melted snow and Aiden working with the sizzling bacon. Even though the space was small, they didn't run into each other. Scarlet knew exactly where and what Aiden was doing even without watching him. It was as if all her senses were alive without the clutter of words.

Scarlet scooped the eggs out of the water and placed them on two wooden plates that Aiden had laid out. They cooled as he finished the bacon, and they sat down across from one another at the table. Aiden paused, looking down at his food. Was he saying a prayer?

Scarlet folded her hands on the table. "Thank you, Lord," she whispered, her words clear over the soft howl of the wind. "For this food provided, for this snug, perfect cabin, for the warmth of a fire…and for the wisdom you've bestowed upon Aiden Campbell. Amen." She didn't look at him but took up her fork.

Aiden added his own silent "Amen" and kept his gaze down at his eggs and bacon. She thought him wise. Although he'd said as much since his house was fully stocked. It didn't mean she thought well of him, or even if she did, it mattered not. For she was a lady, an English lady, and didn't belong in the wild and dangerous Highlands.

"You mentioned training today," Scarlet said and took a sip of the ale he'd brought out of a back room he used just for storage. "Grey and Kerrick have been working with us, but the lessons have been short and sometimes far between as they've been so busy restoring Finlarig and fortifying the wall around the castle."

Did a true English lady learn to fight like a Highland warrior? Maybe Scarlet wasn't as English as he'd thought. "Ye could always benefit with more training," he said, his voice gruff.

"Agreed," Scarlet said with a deep nod. "Most ladies have no knowledge of defense. Which is why we've made it an official part of the Highland Roses School curriculum. Even though we don't brandish it about as a large part of learning, I think it is the most important skill we are trying to teach, right after reading." She tipped her head from side to side. "Well, it's likely an equal priority to reading. They can both be used to defend oneself." Her words slowed as if she realized that she was rambling.

"Wolves or villains?" he asked, scraping the last of his eggs onto his fork.

"Excuse me?"

"Wolves or villains bent on rape? Which do ye wish me to teach ye to defend yourself from?"

"Oh," she said, her brows furrowing.

He drank some ale and wiped his mouth on a napkin. "As a lady, who may not live her whole life in the wilds, I think learning to throw off a man would be of greater need," he said.

She nodded. "Though I'd like to learn to shoot an arrow like my sister or throw a dagger to hit its mark."

"We can get to that, but we will start with how to deal with arse-worms like Finlay." Just the rutting bastard's name made Aiden's hands contract into fists.

"Arse-worm?" Scarlet said, the word sounding comical in her aristocratic English accent. "Another curse I should learn." She smiled as if proud of herself. "I do curse Finlay Menzies with worms up his arse."

"Ye will shock the English aristocracy with your foul language," he said, rising to take his empty plate to the wash bucket.

A small bit of laughter came from Scarlet, a soft melody under her breath. It sounded pleasant like a thawing spring creek. "I don't plan to ever speak before English aristocracy again, so you can teach me all the foul words you know."

He didn't look at her but concentrated on the rag in his hand as he wiped his plate clean. "So ye think ye will remain in the Highlands? Not return to England?" His hand paused, waiting for her answer.

"I will never return," she answered, and he heard her rise, the chair scraping slightly on the wood planks. Her boots clipped as she came behind him. "Evelyn, either."

"Your sister is on her way there now," he countered.

"With her husband who will make certain she returns."

"What if she decides that the conveniences of her homeland and rich life in England are too tempting?" Aiden's shoulders ached at the tension across his back.

"You don't know my sister very well," Scarlet said, humor in her voice. "She's wanted this school forever. She'd no more abandon Finlarig and Scotland than she'd cut off her arm."

He took her plate without looking at her. "Ye have no attachment to the school, Finlarig, or Scotland. And once ye feel secure in how to defend yourself, there won't be any reason for ye not to return to the life ye had before. A pampered woman will always return to her nest of comfort." Someone had certainly frightened her down in England, though she'd refused to give him a name or rank when questioned the night before. But it was certainly someone she viewed as being in the highest station in her circle.

Silence stretched as he finished washing the plate, and he glanced toward Scarlet. She frowned, her eyes devoid of the merriment that usually lurked there. "Shall we begin my lesson?" she asked. "I have a need to kick someone."

Drying his hands, Aiden moved the table and chairs to the side. "Show me how Finlay held ye," he said.

Scarlet stared at him for a moment, inhaling, before stepping to place her back toward him. She took his hand and moved closer, wrapping his one arm around her waist so that her breasts rested on it. She was a perfect size, not so slender that she seemed like she would break, and she was soft, with generous curves. "His other hand was free and… roaming," she said softly.

Aiden's stomach clenched. Finlay had gathered all of Scarlet's softness against him without her permission, holding her so intimately. "And ye did what to get away?" he asked, his words full of anger, making her tip her face up to see his. He cleared his throat. "I'd like to see the effective moves ye made that nearly killed the man despite ye not even having a weapon, save your knee."

She gazed forward again, grabbing the arm that was holding her. "Grey showed us how to surprise an attacker." She shoved his arm outward as the heel of her boot came down hard on his toes, though his own boots protected them.

He relaxed enough to let her spin out of his grasp, and she came forward, grabbing his shoulder with one hand while the other yanked back her skirts to expose her knee. She rammed it high. He was ready for it, sliding instinctually to the side in case she made contact.

"Then he fell forward, and I ran out," she finished, stepping back to cross her arms over her chest.

Aiden stared at her as she breathed hard, her chest rising. His jaw ached, and he cupped it, rubbing it through the bristle of his short beard. "His free hand. Where exactly did it touch ye?"

She stared at him, her lips pinched tight. "That has nothing to do with teaching me."

She was right, but he wanted to know how much pain to deliver the next time he met up with the cocky bastard who tricked women from their rooms and attacked them. Before he could think of a reason he should know the details of Finlay's words and groping, Scarlet stepped back up to him, staring him in the eyes. "I was lucky that he was drunk, barefoot, and distracted. I want to be able to react when the bastard is sober, heavily armed, and focused on getting what he wants from me. If that means I must become a warrior, then make me a warrior. I'm tired of feeling afraid."

His gaze moved from one of her large brown eyes to the other, past the green flecks that encircled her pupils. "Who has made ye feel afraid, Scarlet Worthington?"

She glanced away, and he watched her swallow. "Men," she said. "Men have frightened me."

"Do I frighten ye?" he asked. "We are here alone, trapped by wind, snow, and wolves."

She looked back at him, studying him, judging his intentions, his question. "Not in the same way," she said, her voice low so that the shriek of the wind nearly hid it.

"In what way then?" He didn't move, even fought against blinking as he willed her to speak. Scarlet Worthington had mysteries within her, mysteries he wanted to know. "How do I frighten ye?"

She inhaled, a smile spreading across her mouth that did not reach her eyes. "I'm afraid…" Her chin raised regally. "That you will beat me in a horserace. I'm afraid you will go back and start a war with Finlay Menzies." Her eyes opened wide, and she shook her head. "I'm afraid you will jeopardize my brother's new flock of sheep." She tipped her head to the side. "I'm afraid that you haven't a wash tub for me to bathe in." She flipped her hands about. "I am just full of fears." She set her hands on her hips, giving him a wry smile. "So, let us stop talking and start teaching me to be a warrior."

Aiden pushed his tongue into his cheek and rubbed his chin. No, nothing was easy about Scarlet Worthington. Perhaps that was why she plagued his thoughts. Easy would be easily set aside, forgotten.

He inhaled, sliding up each of his sleeves and crossing his arms over his chest. "It will be a day of battle, and then fortunate for ye…" He met her gaze with a steely one of his own. "I have a soaking tub."

• • •

"Bloody foking hell," Scarlet whispered, gritting her teeth as Aiden latched on to her already bruised wrist. He loosened instantly, which made her glare up at him. "Don't do that."

"Do what?" he asked, his frown fierce as he stood opposite her, playing the attacker.

"Let up on my wrist because you know it hurt," she said. "A bastard like Finlay won't let up."

"He might out of shock at the words that have been overflowing your lips," he said, his fingers tightening again.

"Swearing makes things hurt less, makes me stronger." Scarlet glanced up at him. "Is that why warriors swear all the time? So they can take bruises and slashes without crumpling in pain?"

"Your questions are not going to distract me. Now break my hold."

The last four attempts, she hadn't been able to break through the shackle he held around her wrist, though honestly, she hadn't given it her whole effort. The man had taken a snow bath, whatever that was, and he smelled and looked deliciously clean, in a perpetually fierce kind of way. The soreness on her wrist, along with a foolish draw toward Aiden, may have prevented her escape.

When Scarlet thought back on the dandies at court, their perfectly tailored costumes, plumed hats, and perfumed wigs, she wanted to laugh at their ridiculous posturing. Trying to prove that they were men when their foppish ways just made them look like boys. She hadn't realized it until coming to the Highlands. Aiden Campbell definitely qualified as a real man.

Scarlet glanced down at his large hand and breathed in through her nose, closing her eyes to imagine a different hand shackling her in place. As soon as the face coalesced in her mind, her heart kicked up. Her eyes flew open.

"No," she yelled, hard enough that she may have spit.

"No," she yelled again, stepping into Aiden, the heel of her free hand snapping upward toward his nose. As she hit, she snapped her other hand down, her wrist sliding through the place where Aiden's finger and thumb met.

He grunted, and she spun away, breathing hard.

"Bloody foking hell," Aiden said, repeating her curse as he held his nose. He looked at his fingers where evidence of blood showed, and then his gaze slid to her. A grin relaxed his frown. "Ye're right. The cursing helps."

Scarlet stared at him for a heartbeat and then laughed. "I think I will add swearing to the school curriculum as part of self-defense."

Walking to the hearth, she took a piece of cloth to give to him for his nose. "Sorry about that," she said.

He grinned. "Nay, ye did exactly what ye should do."

Scarlet let out a huff, her smile huge. "You didn't go easy on me?"

"Not in the least," he said, shaking his head. "See, ye have it in ye, Scarlet. Once ye let go of worrying about what someone will think of ye. Yell in their face. Spit in their face. Curse, piss, whatever it takes to get away. Nothing is sinful, forbidden, or wrong when fighting for your life."

Scarlet nodded but felt her face redden. "Did I spit on you?"

His grin turned to a smile big enough to show his teeth. "Aye. Exactly how ye should."

"I'm s—"

"No sorry," he said, crossing to grab up two flasks of watered-down ale. He handed one to her but wouldn't let it go, making her look into his once again serious eyes. "Ye do everything and anything to get away from a foking bastard. Understand?"

She nodded. "Yes."

He grunted something that sounded like an affirmative

and let her take the flask. The cool, wet ale tasted heavenly. They'd been working on various techniques for the last hour while the storm whistled and battered against the cabin.

"When we return to Finlarig, you will teach my students?" Scarlet asked, putting the cork back on her flask. "The yelling, spitting, everything? I think Grey and Kerrick have been too easy on us."

Aiden tipped his flask up to drink. His shirt lay untied at the neck, and she watched him swallow. His hair had dried in a short, tousled look that framed his ruggedly handsome features. He capped the flask and stretched his arms back as if to work his massive shoulders. Scarlet's mouth went dry, and she took another drink.

He nodded. "Aye, I will teach. If the lasses want to have a real chance of saving themselves in an attack, they need a better teacher."

Scarlet grinned. "One who curses and spits."

"As much as she can." Aiden kept his natural frown, but merriment shone in his eyes.

• • •

Scarlet groaned softly as the heated water enveloped her. The muscles in her legs ached as she bent her knees to fit in the deep, short tub that Aiden had filled for her by the hearth fire. With Aiden's promise to stay with the horses for at least an hour, Scarlet had yanked the curtains closed on all the windows, stripped out of her grubby smock, and stepped into the water. Apparently, either she trusted him, or the allure of cleanliness was overpowering her modesty.

Heat prickled her skin as she took up the thin bar of soap that she'd thrown into her satchel. Luckily, Aiden had taken it from Castle Menzies before riding after her. She inhaled the fragrant jasmine as she scrubbed it along her skin. On

Hollings Estate, her mother had gone against popular ideas about water disrupting the humors in the body. No dirty children for Margaret Worthington. She might weep and hide away in hysterics, but she'd smell like a flower doing so.

Scarlet slid down in the tub to wet her hair, the hot water feeling heavenly against her scalp. Blowing out bubbles, she rose to work the soap through her tresses and rinsed. She massaged her arms. "God's teeth," she whispered and stretched the aches in her muscles.

Darkness settled beyond the curtains, and the wind had finally blown itself out before she'd stepped into the tub. She sighed and sunk so that her ears were covered by the water. Her hands floated by her bent knees, palm side down on the surface. They would leave at dawn, but for now, she would let the warmth cradle her.

*Bang!* The door hit the wall, and Scarlet gasped, sloshing up. Aiden stood there, his gaze finding her, and she realized he could see her naked breasts above the water line. "Aiden," she yelled, hands flying to her chest.

"Men are coming. Dress yourself while I keep them outdoors." He charged back out into the night.

Men? Which men? Campbells, Menzies, English? Some horde of raping barbarians? Scarlet propelled herself up out of the water, a small wave washing over the side. The chill in the room, recently enhanced by the open door, made chill bumps rise over her skin. She dashed for her drying sheet, wrapping herself tight as she grabbed her dirty clothes.

Deep voices yelled outside. "She is here," Aiden's voice came through the door. "Safe, thanks to her own quick response to that foking arse."

*Rap, rap.* Good Lord, it was too late to run upstairs. All she could do was hold her dirty clothes before her as the door opened.

Kerrick pushed past Aiden, his eyes growing wide as

Scarlet dripped, her cold toes curling against the bricks of the hearth. "Lady Scarlet?"

Aiden followed, and then two others before Aiden could order them back. "Out," Aiden said, turning to shove Lawrence and William. "Kerrick," he called.

"Ye're undressed," Kerrick said, the words seeming to fall out of his open mouth.

Scarlet's heart pounded hard, but she tipped her chin higher. "A custom we English employ when bathing. Now if you would be decent gentlemen and let me finish dressing…" She let her words trail off as she met Kerrick's gaze with a razor-sharp, unblinking stare.

Kerrick tripped over his own feet as he backed toward the door, where Aiden grabbed him by the shoulder to practically throw him out. Aiden's gaze slid to Scarlet, his face neutral. "I placed one of my sister's clean smocks on the bed upstairs," he said. Giving a nod, he shut the door behind them. Scarlet puffed out an exhale and ran up the freezing steps.

Dressed, her legs warming under the wool trousers and skirts, Scarlet descended to find the room crammed with all the Campbells who had accompanied them to Castle Menzies.

Kerrick had his back to the stairs as he spoke to Aiden. "I will return with Scarlet to Finlarig while ye lead the others back to Castle Menzies."

"No," Scarlet said, the force of the word snapping every angry face her way. "No one is going back to Castle Menzies right now."

"Retribution is required," Kerrick said, his usual smile replaced by a dark look that could only be described as lethal. "For the attack on ye."

She knew Aiden would explain her reasons for leaving Castle Menzies in the middle of the night, but Scarlet still felt her face flame over her foolish flight. Had he told them how easily tricked she'd been? Scarlet swallowed past her tight throat. "Not when everyone is still so angry." She shook her head. "Retribution can come once tempers have calmed."

Kerrick raised his fist to thump across his heart. "My temper will never calm over this attack."

Scarlet gave him a slight smile. "Thank you, Kerrick, but I still insist that we all return to Finlarig. Despite Finlay's sinister soul, I still wish to acquire his flock and entice his sister to attend the school. Even more so, since I now understand to what immoral standards Cicilia Menzies is subjected, living under her brother's roof." Had the poor woman seen couplings in the great hall?

Kerrick looked back to Aiden, whose face had remained as fierce as usual. "Finlay will be giving his sheep to the school without requiring payment," Kerrick suggested.

Aiden's gaze cut back to Scarlet, though he answered Kerrick. "A small price to pay for keeping his balls attached."

Scarlet let out a huff but gave one nod. "I will write to Cici immediately to ask her to come to the Highland Roses School. Now, since we are all thoroughly awake and great in number in case the wolves are about, shall we return tonight to Finlarig and Killin? I'm sure you would all like to sleep in your own beds."

"I will ready the horses," Aiden said.

Scarlet threw on her red cape that sat across one of the chairs. "I will bridle Caora." She strode past them all to follow Aiden outdoors. The cold, clear air made her curl inward, shoving her bare hands into the folds of wool around her. But it was the damp hair that quickly pulled in the icy winter chill. She'd dried it as best she could upstairs with the damp drying sheet.

"Go back inside," Aiden said over his shoulder. "Yer hair is wet."

She grabbed it, coiling it into an icy snake to tuck between her gown and the cloak. "It will still be wet as we ride back." She hurried her stride, following his footprints, which were visible in the bright moonlight that peeked from behind fast-moving clouds.

Scarlet pushed into the barn. Warm and scented with hay, it was a sanctuary from the frigid night. She shook off the cold, striding to Caora while Aiden watched her. "Ye will freeze on the ride back."

"I will be well," she said, though her voice sounded less confident than when she'd spoken inside the house. "'Tis not more than a length through the trees and then the meadow where the Beltane Festival was held near Killin. I will survive it."

Aiden grunted in response. Scarlet turned from him to spread the saddle blanket along Caora and fit the bridle over her head. She rubbed the horse's neck, her warmth helping to thaw her numb fingers. Perhaps she would just hug the horse the whole ride back.

Aiden mounted his tall white horse and watched as Scarlet guided Caora toward the barn doors. She glanced around for a bucket to step upon.

"Here," Aiden said, nudging his giant closer so that Scarlet stood between the sides of the two horses. He reached down, lifting under her arm, his grasp snug around her ribs. Scarlet jumped upward, and Aiden lifted, but instead of setting her on Caora's back, he swung her up, her legs parting to sit astride his own horse before him.

"Aiden?"

"I won't have ye grow ill," he answered, and threw a wool blanket from the back of his mount around them. His lips came near her ear. "If ye're sick in bed, there will be no one to stop me from slaughtering Finlay Menzies before or after my temper settles."

Scarlet swiveled in her seat to tip her face up to him. The moonlight barely lit the stables, making shadows cut along the planes of his face. "I doubt your temper ever settles," she said.

He looked down at her, their gazes locking. "And…I never, ever forget."

# Chapter Seven

Aiden rolled out of Grey's bed and frowned at the bright light streaming through the windows. Getting little sleep the night before, and then returning to Finlarig close to midnight, he'd slept well past dawn. Washing and dressing quickly, he headed out of the room. Walking past the first set of steps, he paused outside Scarlet's bedchamber door. Silence. Was she still asleep? He heard no coughing to signal an illness.

Despite Scarlet's wet hair, Aiden hadn't felt her shiver under the blanket on the ride back through the night. He'd kept her completely covered, pressed against him, their body heat making him almost sweat. He inhaled, still smelling her flower scent clinging to him. *Damn.*

He exhaled through his teeth and took the stairs down to the great hall. The room was empty. Grabbing a cold bun from a tray left on the table, he strode out into the sharp chill of the morning air. Several young warriors worked on a stone enclosure for the flock of sheep that Finlay would be gifting to Scarlet.

Aiden climbed the ladder to the gatehouse where Hamish

stood guard with several of the younger warriors. "Heard that Finlay Menzies is a dead man," Hamish said, wiping an arm across his mouth as he glanced at Aiden and then studied him, squinting his eyes.

Aiden snorted. "The bastard doesn't know how lucky he is that Scarlet wants to bring his sister here to the school. Else he'd already be dead."

"Do ye know ye have bruises under your eyes?" Hamish asked.

"I hit my nose," Aiden said. Or rather, Scarlet had hit his nose. Aye, the woman could become fierce with some training. She was agile, graceful, clever, and surprisingly hardy for a *Sassenach*.

Hamish looked out over the trees toward the empty meadow beyond. "Kerrick said he was organizing a raid on the sheep, in case Finlay doesn't realize how lucky he is to still have his head."

"Kerrick's about?" Aiden scanned the bailey but didn't see him. "Where is he?"

"He's been up at the keep," Hamish said, jerking his thumb over his shoulder. "Some of the lasses from Killin came for their lessons. Said he needed to teach the self-defense class."

Aiden's brows lowered. Kerrick might be wrapping Scarlet up in a hold right now. "I'll be in the class if ye need me," Aiden said.

Hamish laughed. "I don't think ye need any lessons."

Aiden ignored him, sliding down the ladder without bothering with the rungs and strode back into the keep. He leaped up the steps of the main stairwell to the second floor. The library door was open, but the room was empty. The door next was closed, and he pushed inside without knocking.

Half a dozen lasses stood in two facing rows. Kerrick stood near the windows, but what caught his gaze was Scarlet.

What the bloody hell was she wearing? Devoid of skirts, she stood talking to Kerrick in…the black woolen trousers.

"Excellent," Scarlet called. "Our other teacher is here." She beckoned him over.

Aiden strode over, feeling the stares of all the lasses following him. "Where are your skirts?" he asked.

Scarlet looked down at her long, shapely legs encased in the tight wool, as if she hadn't realized her skirts were missing. She raised her gaze to his and planted hands on her hips. "Easier to learn defensive training without the burden of skirts."

Aiden looked to Kerrick, who slowly shook his head. "Lady Scarlet has hired Kirstin and Alana to make a pair for each of the students," Kerrick said.

"Yes," Scarlet said cheerfully. "So we can kick with force and see our target."

Aiden crossed his arms over his chest. It wasn't that he minded seeing Scarlet wearing trousers, or any of the ladies, but he didn't like the idea of dishonorable men staring at Scarlet's legs, the outline leading right up to show the round curves of her arse. "But when the time comes to defend yourself," he said, "ye will be wearing skirts. 'Tis best to train in what ye will have on."

"That depends," Scarlet said with a wry grin. She dropped her hands, bending at the waist to touch her toes. "Perhaps we will start wearing trousers all the time, to be better able to protect ourselves." She straightened and smiled at him. "We might even be able to help protect Finlarig."

"A woman's militia," Alana called out.

Young Isabel, or Izzy, as she was called, made motions with her hands. She hadn't spoken since her mother died a year past, but her sister, Cat, seemed to understand her. "Like the Amazons," Cat said, translating, and the girl nodded vigorously.

The fun challenge on Scarlet's face caught at Aiden's frown. He moved his jaw left to right and rubbed his short beard.

"I'm trying to explain that the idea is foolish," Kerrick said.

Och, was the man so dense? Telling a mule that it was foolish and must move would never make it take a step. And if having their legs free to kick and move taught the lasses to fend off bastards like Finlay, then he wouldn't discourage them. Aiden shrugged. "I won't ask anyone who wants to defend themselves or the clan to stand down."

Aiden was rewarded with a huge smile from Scarlet. Let Kerrick catch her frowns and sour looks.

"Bloody wonderful," Scarlet said, making Kerrick cough and several of the young lasses giggle.

"Lady Scarlet, I don't think Evelyn would approve of all your swearing," Kerrick said, continuing to make himself less likable to Scarlet with each utterance. The more he spoke, the less Aiden needed to worry about Scarlet being seduced by him. Not that it mattered. The woman could love whomever she wanted. He had nothing to say about it.

"In the heat of combat, I have found that swearing gives one strength and courage," Scarlet said.

"Heat of combat?" Kerrick asked, a smile growing on his face.

Aiden walked to the end of the line of ladies, keeping his grin inside. If Kerrick wasn't careful, he'd end up with bruises under his eyes, too.

"Don't you swear during combat?" Scarlet asked Kerrick.

"Well…aye, I suppose I do."

"Then we will also learn to swear. Though, you are correct in that we should never use vulgar words outside of this room or battle."

Scarlet left Kerrick to walk down the short row of facing

women. "Now to return to learning how to break someone's hold." She slid up her sleeve to show a bruise around her slender wrist.

Aiden frowned, but Scarlet held it up like a scar of honor. "We mustn't be afraid to train as if a villain is truly using all his strength. Else if the time comes, we won't know how it feels to break away from an iron grip." She lowered her arm. "Bruises will heal, sore muscles will mend." She stopped to level a resolute stare on Alana, then Kirstin, her gaze sliding down the line of women. "But if you aren't successful in thwarting an attacker, the experience, if you survive, will haunt you the rest of your life."

• • •

*The moon sliced across the dark room as if a polished mirror reflected it. It fell like silver liquid over the man, his black wig a contrast to his pale skin. Scarlet hid in the shadows, panic paralyzing her. She barely drew breath for fear of being noticed.*

*The man's member was erect, and he stroked along it with a bejeweled hand. How could she possibly flee without him seeing her?*

*"Come out, my lady fair," he called, his gaze scanning the gilt interior of the room.*

*Scarlet's breath caught in her throat as she watched another man enter the room, tall, his light-colored hair flattened with sweat as if he'd just removed his wig. Where the king's gaze slid over her hiding place, the other man's gaze stilled on the drapes as if he sensed her hiding there. With strong, silent strides, he walked across. "Where is my pigeon?"*

*Scarlet's fingers curled into the length of the curtain, grasping as if she were aloft, dangling, and the fabric held her life. Reaching forward, the man whipped back the curtain, and Scarlet screamed.*

Scarlet jerked awake, staring out from the quilts that she clutched in tight fists. A lamb slept curled in a heap of blankets by a nearly cold hearth. *Snowball*. Heart pounding, Scarlet breathed from an open mouth. Dawn sunlight lit the window panes across from her.

*I'm in Scotland. At Finlarig. I am safe.* The words helped her breath calm, but she still shook as the dream played through her mind.

"Damnation. Bloody hell," she said, her voice clear in the room, making the little sheep raise her head for a moment before nuzzling back down. "*Mo chreach.*" She pushed the blanket back from her chin, propping herself up. "I am fierce," she whispered, taking strength from the words. "I am powerful, and I resist every man who threatens me. I am free and fierce."

Speaking and hearing the words strengthened her. They battled back the terror that had gripped her in the nightmare. If only she could say them in the dream, but she always felt caught in numbness there, stagnant and helpless, tied by the chains of sleep.

Scarlet slid from the warm blankets, her toes finding her slippers. She stirred the fire, patted the drowsy lamb, broke the ice on the water pitcher to wash, and dressed in a blue wool gown. Her trousers were stiff from drying after she'd washed them, and she'd left them off since they were still damp.

"Come along, Snowball," she called, and the lamb stretched out of her nest to follow Scarlet into the hallway. Scarlet glanced down toward the other end of the corridor. Was Aiden still abed? Sleeping naked under the furs?

The lamb batted at her skirts. "Yes, you need to go outdoors." She hurried down to the second floor, pausing when she heard a thump as if a heavy book had dropped onto the wooden floor. She walked with the lamb down to the library, but when she poked her head inside, the room was empty. She stepped inside and saw the art book sitting on the floor near the fireplace. "Ghosts?" she whispered, picking it up as she glanced in the empty corners. "Maybe Molly is right about fairies roaming the lands," she said to Snowball, who hopped around the table.

Cold whisked under Scarlet's skirts as she walked into the great hall, reminding herself to commission a few more pairs of the warm trousers to survive the Highland winters. The lamb, seeing the pack of dogs near the hearth, ran ahead to join her new friends. Robert, the male dog, leaped up to jump around with her, his shaggy ears flopping about his head. The whole pack ran down the back hallway toward the kitchen gardens when Alana called, Snowball with them.

"Good morn, milady," Molly said as she brought forth a wooden trencher with several tarts upon it.

"Thank you, Molly," Scarlet said, going to the side table to pour some brewed tea into a tea bowl. "Have yourself some, too," she said, pouring another.

Molly's gaze followed the lamb as it trotted off. "Will you be keeping the lamb in the keep like a pet then?"

"No," Scarlet said. "She will move out when her mother arrives and the shelter is built."

Molly nodded. "Best that, less mess in the castle."

They sat together at the table, Scarlet letting the heat from the tea warm her, soothing away the last tendrils of her dream. She sighed. "Do you ever have nightmares, Molly?"

"Oh my, yes," Molly said, her eyes widening. "Rats nibbling on me and ghosts shrieking in my ears as I lie on me own grave." She shook her head. "And sometimes I'm inside the grave, scratching to try to get out."

Scarlet's inhale caught. "How horrid," she said.

Molly tipped her head back and forth. "Aye, but sometimes the rats are with me inside the coffin, so I'm not completely alone." She took a drink from her cup.

Scarlet opened her mouth but had no words. She took a sip of her tea and set it down. "I think we will all be better equipped to rid ourselves of nightmares when we learn to wield daggers and throw kicks and gouge eyes," she said.

"Possibly," Molly said, her face scrunched in contemplation. "Though I doubt I could gouge out a rat's eyes. Me fingers are too fat."

Scarlet shook her head, her lips parting over a slight grin. She cleared her throat. "I think I'd like to make up some glue to use on those china shards," Scarlet said, rising to collect the basket from the corner. "I might have an idea of what to do with them."

"I'll get right to it," Molly said. "Me ma passed down a recipe to me as she was always having to glue her pottery back together."

Scarlet studied the wall next to her that was still darkened by scorch marks from the fire. "She dropped them often?"

"Nay, she threw them often." Molly whisked away down the hall toward the kitchens. Scarlet stared after her, her brows pinched.

The front doors opened, and Kerrick strode in. "Menzies are here," he said, a frown in place. Scarlet nearly pitched forward, feeling like she'd been hit in the chest. "Finlay?"

"Nay, his men are bringing the sheep and his sister."

Scarlet stood, finding her red cloak near the entryway to follow him. "Cici?"

"Aye." She followed him out into the clear morning light. "Aiden's been busy this dawn," Kerrick said.

Good God. What had Aiden been doing? She rushed across the snow-covered bailey where a flock of white sheep were running under the raising portcullis, making the chickens scatter about. A set of peahens trotted in circles in the bailey corner. She didn't even have time to question why there were peahens in the bailey as Cici trotted her horse inside.

"Lady Worthington," she called, her face pale.

Scarlet rushed toward her as one of the three Menzies men lifted Cici down. Scarlet recognized him as one of the older warriors who had left Finlay's feast early in the night. She exhaled as she realized that none of them were the man involved in the scene she'd witnessed.

Cici ran to her, squeezing Scarlet's hands in her gloved ones. "I thought we were all going to die," she said, her words rushed and loud. "Such yelling and cursing."

Scarlet looked to where Aiden dismounted his white horse. He strode to the Menzies, who unloaded Cici's satchels. They spoke, though Scarlet couldn't hear them over Cici's continuing diatribe.

"Finlay sent me and my maids flying above to gather what I could. He only gave me minutes to pack. Surely, I've left crucial things behind. What am I to do?" she wailed.

"We will find you anything you are lacking," Scarlet said, her gaze still on Aiden as he spoke with the older Menzies warrior. The man nodded and reached forward for Aiden to grasp his forearm as if they'd reached an agreement.

"Threw me out," Cici said. "My own brother threw me out and barred the door. Said the Campbells wanted me and the sheep." Her hand pressed against her full bosom. "I feared for my innocence." Her gaze slid over to Aiden. "But then I saw it was your man."

"Aiden Campbell is not my man," Scarlet whispered.

Cici's eyes opened wide. "Oh, I figured from the way ye danced."

Scarlet turned to watch the Menzies ride back out while several Campbells rounded up the sheep. Kerrick yelled orders to the Campbells while Aiden sent one man to run down the road toward Killin. "Aiden went to Castle Menzies this morning?" Scarlet murmured.

"He arrived just after dawn," Cici said. "Edgar, my father's old guard, yanked Finlay from his bed."

"What did Aiden do?" she asked, watching him stride toward them. He wore furs strapped over his legs under his kilt and a wool cloak that parted to show his bleached white tunic. His great sword hung in a scabbard strapped to his side. He looked like a warrior of legends, powerful and lethal, his mouth set in firm lines of anger. And this was hours later. How must he have looked to Finlay this dawn? Scarlet hoped that the arse-worm had pissed himself.

Aiden stopped before them. "Chief Menzies sends his apologies," Aiden said to Scarlet. "He sends the sheep at no cost to ye. He will pay the school for his sister's boarding and education."

Scarlet's mouth pinched into a tight circle as she glanced first at the bleating sheep and then Cici before moving back to Aiden's hard stare. "What did you say to him?"

Alana—her dogs running from around the side of the keep to chase after the sheep—Izzy, Molly, and even Cat had come out of the keep, drawing close. Aiden's gaze flickered to them and Cici. "I would not bore ye with the details, but he sends his best wishes for a long life and great success for your school."

Scarlet looked at the small crowd of women. "Molly, you and Alana please take Lady Cici inside to warm herself and break her fast. We will find her a room."

"Yes, milady," Molly said, stepping forward, Alana with her. "I have the next room ready for a student," Molly said.

Alana looped her arm through Cici's and pulled her around. "Ye are in a safe, warm spot here at Finlarig," Alana said. "I mean to say, the Highland Roses School."

The others followed them inside. Wind whipped about the bailey as Kerrick yelled at the unhelpful puppies, one of them barking at the peahens. "I've sent for others to get the roof thatching up on the corral by tonight," Aiden said.

"What did you say to Finlay?" Scarlet asked, stepping closer to him, as it was hard to hear over the barking, bleating, and yelling.

Aiden breathed in deeply, releasing a puff of white with his exhale. He met her gaze. "'Tis not important." He leaned forward, his eyes pinning her with a stare. Lips pulled back, he spoke mostly through his teeth. "What is important is that he will never touch ye again."

A chill ran down through Scarlet at the hint of death in Aiden's features. She swallowed hard. "And the sheep and Cici?"

"A suggestion that Finlay Menzies took immediately upon my offer," Aiden said.

"Your offer?"

"Aye, to not lose his ballocks this morning. His father's old council, Edgar Menzies, rather agreed with my bargain after I told him what his young laird had been about. Seems it was Edgar's daughter who had come home in the wee hours of the morning the night of your attack." He crossed his arms over his broad chest. "He'll be taking a greater role in the leadership of the Menzies clan."

"You had no way of knowing that when you left during the dark to reach them," Scarlet said, imagining the scene that likely unfolded at dawn. Anger flared up inside her, and she narrowed her eyes. "Alone, with only your fury and sword to protect you if he and his clan wanted a fight."

Aiden's face relaxed, one of his eyebrows rising. "Lady Scarlet?"

"What?" The single word came like a hard clap, but it didn't even make him blink.

"I had no idea," he said, "that ye would worry over me."

She snorted, crossing her own arms. "I doubt that would have made you choose a different course of action."

"Ye are quite intelligent," he said, dropping his arms to stride past her for the keep.

She hurried behind him, tugging at her skirts so she could keep up. "You could have started a war, and I will not be the start of a war."

Aiden turned on his heel, and she pulled up short so as not to run into him on the steps. He bent slightly to meet her stare. "Finlay Menzies started a war the moment he misled ye through your bedchamber door, Scarlet. Nothing that comes of this is on ye." He stood straight, turning back to finish climbing. "As it is, the little coward was only too happy to give you his sheep and his sister, not that it makes up for his actions."

"And we are not at war with the Menzies?" she asked as they strode through the entryway into the great hall.

"The Menzies? No," Aiden said, and nodded to Molly as she handed him a full tankard. He looked at Scarlet over the rim. "But Finlay Menzies knows that he won't survive long if he dares to even glance your way."

Scarlet stared at Aiden. She was torn between gratefulness for his rage on her behalf and irritation because Aiden had risked so much when she'd been foolish to begin with.

Cici chewed on a tart near the flame-filled hearth. "Oh, my brother will never go near Lady Worthington again," she said, her gaze meeting Scarlet's, a smile on her face. "Took him the rest of the night and the next day before he could walk upright after ye felled him."

"What did he do?" Cat asked, her eyes pinching as if she was formulating her own plans for revenge.

Scarlet exhaled, hoping her cheeks wouldn't turn red. "'Tis a story I'd rather not retell, but he was crass, and I thought I would be raped, so I used what I'd been taught in our self-defense class to knee him in the ballocks."

"Hard enough to make him fall?" Alana asked, her eyes wide.

"Hard enough to make him puke the rest of the night," Aiden said, taking one of the tarts himself. "'Tis something ye all should learn."

"I was fortunate to catch him by surprise, and he was drunk," Scarlet said. She smoothed her hair to one side. "We will not always be fortunate, and we must prepare to defend ourselves if needed." Scarlet looked to Cici. "I'm glad you've joined us. I've worried that you were left there."

Cici huffed loudly. "Finlay's always been a lecherous beast, but he's turned horrendous since Papa died, having his parties and drinking. I had to hide half the time I was home. 'Twas why I'd traveled to Inverness to visit with a cousin. I suppose it was good that he threw me out, though I was quite shocked." She smiled sweetly at Aiden, dimples appearing in both of her full cheeks. "Aiden Campbell rescued me. He is my hero."

The woman obviously felt some sweetness toward Aiden. Scarlet looked at him, suppressing the slight tightening of her stomach. Aiden's brows were low over eyes that were a little too wide to show anger. It was more like panic, or the closest she'd ever see to panic in the fierce man's eyes. The overly dramatic woman must not be his taste.

Scarlet glanced at the entryway, where her two students, Fiona and Martha, were pulling off their capes. "We must adjourn to the library for our book lessons." She turned her gaze to Aiden. "But before midday, Hero Aiden…" Aiden's gaze snapped to her, his panicked look dissolving into severe irritation. "And Sir Kerrick will teach us all how to fell a villain with a kick to the ballocks."

She didn't bother to hide her smile. "You and Kerrick

may want to see if the blacksmith has any chain mail that you can wrap around yourselves." Her gaze dipped slightly to the front of his kilt. "I wouldn't want to make you vomit all day."

Cici stood out of her chair. "Kneeing ballocks? Lo. What type of school is The Highland Roses School, exactly?"

# Chapter Eight

Her arse was the most perfect thing he'd ever seen. Aiden stood next to Kerrick in the school's self-defense gymnasium, their arms crossed, legs braced. Aiden heard Kerrick inhale through his teeth as they watched Scarlet show Cici how the woolen trousers she wore allowed her to kick, knee, and touch her toes without the burden of skirts. It was the touching of her toes that stopped Aiden's breath and made Kerrick cough into his fist.

"A gentleman would avert his eyes," Aiden murmured to Kerrick.

"I don't see ye looking away," Kerrick said, frowning at him.

"I've never been known as a gentleman," Aiden said, stepping out from the wall.

"And they keep your legs warm if you wear them under your skirts," Scarlet said. "But the wool is so warm, you can go without the skirts."

"Lady Scarlet," Kerrick said, coming up next to Aiden. "I don't think your sister would approve of everyone wearing…"

He threw his hand out toward her trousers. "'Tis indecent."

Scarlet's hands came down on her hips as she turned toward Kerrick, her frown fierce. "I've noticed that you call me *Lady* Scarlet whenever you think I'm doing something wrong."

Kerrick's brows lowered, and he glanced at Aiden, but Aiden just shrugged. "Ye do."

"And," Scarlet continued, "you seemed to have no problem with Evelyn wearing hers while training. What has suddenly made you so straitlaced? Was Evelyn's backside more acceptable than mine?" She threw her arm out to the other lasses. "Or theirs?"

Nine sets of eyes turned on Kerrick, frowns all around. "I…" he began and stopped, his face red. Kerrick swallowed. "Your backside is quite acceptable, Scarlet," he said. "Carry on."

She gave him a tight smile and turned back to the ladies. "Kirstin and Alana have volunteered to sew pairs for each of us." Izzy raised her hand high in the air. "Yes, and Izzy volunteered, too," Scarlet said with a genuine smile.

"I think black wool will look more…acceptable," Kirstin said, using Kerrick's word.

"*Mo chreach*," Kerrick swore under his breath.

Kirstin glanced at him and then back at Scarlet. "Less likely to see anything through a light coloring of wool."

*Bloody hell.* Did Scarlet own any light-colored trousers? Aiden certainly didn't want anyone seeing through a pair of trousers she wore.

"Black is best for hiding in the woods at night," Cat said, nodding her approval.

"And we will all have the same," Kirstin continued.

"We could embroider a rose on the waistband," Alana said. "Make them pretty."

Scarlet nodded. "Excellent idea. We can each embroider

our own as a lesson." She glanced at Kerrick. "Even Lady Evelyn would approve of that. But if any of you feel uncomfortable wearing the trousers, even if it is just inside for training, you can continue to wear your proper skirts. Though, do consider wearing them underneath to stay warm this winter."

"I might need several pairs," Cat said, apparently planning to wear them more often than in the school. She'd been coming to the self-defense classes regularly now. Perhaps she was sleeping in Izzy's room and had brought her animals.

Cici laughed lightly, shaking her head. "I will try them, but all this," she moved her hands around her full hips, "might be just too much woman for even our proper instructors to handle."

Scarlet smiled, her gaze flashing to Aiden. He kept his face neutral, and she turned back to her students. "Very well. We will work on the trousers to help our three seamstresses get started, and later this week, we will embroider them. But today Aiden and Kerrick will be teaching another lesson in throwing our attackers off balance with the goal of thrusting our knees into their ballocks."

Aiden paired up the students with Kerrick opposite Cici, her wide eyes gazing up at him as he wrapped his arms around from behind. Aiden walked along the row. "Just simulate the punches and kicks on each other, unless you're paired with one of us. At some point I want ye all to have a chance to feel what it's like to actually punch or kick someone. Without that, ye will hesitate in a real situation."

Cici flashed Kerrick a smile, her dimples tilted up toward him. "I would not want to hurt ye."

"We are both wearing chain mail under our kilts," Aiden said and walked close to Kirstin and Scarlet. "Scarlet, show us what ye did to get away from Finlay."

She nodded once, then pretended to stomp her heel onto Kirstin's toes. "Watch, everyone," Aiden said. "She places her hands on his arm, ready to push away as soon as she delivers the stomp, turns, and shoots her knee up. She braces herself for the knee up by grasping the man's shoulders." He nodded at Scarlet as she performed her move and looked down the line. "Now the rest of you try it."

"'Tis difficult to knee up under heavy skirts," Cici said.

Cat snorted slightly. "A reason I wear very light skirts that I can tie. Easier to climb up into trees if needed."

"I pulled my skirt up and to the side with one hand while I grasped his shoulder with the other," Scarlet said.

"Make certain to use your thigh muscle to thrust upward," Aiden said, pointing to Scarlet's raised leg. Och, but she had magnificent legs. Long and powerful, and the trousers stretched snuggly along them. He cleared his throat and looked away, frowning at Kerrick, who seemed fascinated with her legs as well. "Our thighs are strong and often forgotten in battle. A good warrior remembers to use her strengths."

"Her?" Fiona asked. "Are we to become those Amazon warriors, then?" She giggled. "I thought Cat was teasing."

"Aye," Martha chimed in. "Why must we become warriors?" She looked at Aiden as if he were the one to dictate the class curriculum. He gestured to Scarlet.

Scarlet gave a nod. "Good question, Martha." She stood with her legs braced, arms crossed over the small white shirt she wore. She already looked like a warrior, a bonny one with a long dark braid lying over her shoulder. "Because every single man we encounter could attack us, and we, as women of the Highland Roses School, will not allow him to win."

"Every man?" Kerrick asked, brows drawn. "Not sure I agree with that."

Scarlet looked down her nose at him. "You're not a

woman."

Kerrick looked to Aiden for help. Aiden let one eyebrow rise. "She said 'could attack,' and she's correct." Aiden's jaw tightened with anger as he thought of Scarlet having to defend herself, not only against Finlay, but apparently against a much bigger foe. "There are plenty of bastards in the world who would attack a weaker person. Women are at a terrible disadvantage, and if she has no one to protect her, she needs to learn to protect herself."

Scarlet stared at him, the edges of her lips curving slightly up, yet she kept the rest of her face firm. Slowly she turned back to Martha. "As a student here, you will learn the basics, but only you can decide if you want to be fully equipped to save yourself if it is needed."

Cat stepped forward. "Izzy and I will learn everything we can. We have no one left to protect us."

Alana nodded, determination touching her features. "I want to be a warrior, too. I won't allow anyone to throw me back into a burning castle," she said, referring to the horror she'd faced months ago before the school started.

"Well, I certainly don't have a man with strength and integrity left to watch out for me," Cici said, her hands landing on her hips. She nodded to Aiden. "So be sure to don your chain mail, as I'll be kicking for real."

"Aye," Kirstin called, her fists clenched. "I won't be made to feel helpless and afraid."

Martha nodded, as did Fiona. "We will be the Highland Rose Warriors," she said.

"Highland Rose Warriors," Scarlet said with seriousness, as if she was trying out the name. She smiled, but her eyes were hard as she looked at Aiden. "Villains best watch out for our thorns."

• • •

"Pointed and sharp," Scarlet said, nodding to the long, twisted steel hair stick that Craig examined. The ill-tempered old warrior with a shock of unkempt white hair was the blacksmith for Killin. "It should be sculpted in a twist to be at least six inches long, preferably eight, with a knife-like point on the end. The pommel should be smooth so someone wielding it won't harm themselves. Perhaps with something that looks like a rose."

Craig stared at her for several heartbeats, but she didn't blink. "Ye are wanting a dagger then, not a hairpin," Craig said, holding the twisted stick up in the air to squint at it.

"Call it what you will," Scarlet said. "But each lady at the Highland Roses School will use one to secure her coiled hair. I, therefore, will call it a hair stick or hair spike."

Craig chuckled. "A handy hiding place for a dagger." He eyed her the same way he'd studied the hair stick. "I heard ye were training a pack of lasses up there at the castle."

She smiled. The man reminded her of the ornery beekeeper back at Hollings Estate in Lincolnshire who, despite his temper, always saved some of the honeycomb for her and Evelyn. "Yes, a pack of lethal roses," she said. "Especially if we are armed with your hair sticks."

"And twisted, ye say?" he asked, signaling to his apprentice, a younger man named Eagan who shoed all their horses.

"Yes," Scarlet said. "So, once it stabs in, it can't just be yanked back out."

Both men looked at her, their eyes wide, though Craig recovered quicker. He swore softly and rubbed his bristly chin. "Aye, right vicious. Aiden wasn't spouting nonsense."

"Aiden?" she asked, watching Eagan take the hair stick to examine. Aiden was talking about her?

"Aye, said ye were fierce, a warrior in a *Sassenach's* body," Craig said and shook his head, one fuzzy eyebrow rising higher than the other. "The man doesn't throw out compliments very often."

"I take it then that being a fierce warrior in a female body is a compliment," she said. Back in England, any reference to being manly would have been a severe slight, but not in this rugged, wild country.

"In an *English* woman's body," Craig said with emphasis. "Aye, 'twas a boast about ye. Never heard him speak of a *Sassenach* without spitting afterward."

Scarlet watched Kirstin and Cat step out of Kirstin's thatched cottage, Izzy trailing behind them. They carried woven black wool and walked up the path toward Finlarig. She must hurry, but Craig's comment caught at her. She turned back to him. "Aiden doesn't like English because of his burned back."

"Aye," Craig said, scratching his head. "True, but his hate started way before that bastard Captain Cross set fire to the castle." The man pinched his lips tight together as she waited for him to continue. Several breaths later, it was apparent that he had no intention of doing so. "How many of the sticks do ye need?" he asked.

Scarlet kept her frustrated huff soft. "A dozen to start with," she said, placing shillings in his palm. "But each new student will require one."

"Trousers and daggers," Craig said with a shake of his head. "Never thought the English prims would build up an army of lasses. Ye'd be better off letting a strong man and God take care of ye, lass." Judgment twisted with a twinge of mockery in the man's tone.

Tipping her head to one side, Scarlet regarded him with disdain. This man had likely never felt trapped by someone larger than he, stronger than he, someone who wanted to violate his body. She stood tall, staring him in the eyes without blinking. "And I thought God would have already struck down all the bloody, raping bastards with pox, boils, and the clap, but since God only judges them after they are dead, we *lasses* are helping God by sending the bastards to Him."

Scarlet took great delight in watching Craig's beard drop as his mouth opened. Perhaps he'd never heard those particular words come from a woman's mouth before. "I expect the first dozen hair spikes before the end of the week," she said. "Good day."

Scarlet walked away, anger fueling her steps, but she made sure to keep a slow, even gait so as not to appear running away. Something she'd done too much in the past. "Not anymore," she whispered through her teeth.

Her gaze scanned the road ahead of her. Would she be able to defend herself right now if faced with an ambush? Not likely. Women were practically shackled in their own clothing, making them even weaker with the weight of petticoats and the bindings of their skirts and stays. Like trussed up turkeys.

Scarlet snorted softly. Maybe she'd wear her training trousers all the time. Aiden's face coalesced in her mind. Would he be fine with her wearing trousers? He hadn't said much against them the other day, like Kerrick had. Not that it mattered what Aiden Campbell thought of her. "Damn," she said low, because even if Scarlet wasn't truthful all the time with others, she was always truthful with herself. And she knew very well that she did care what Aiden thought of her. When the hell had that happened?

Up ahead, Scarlet saw Rebecca, Aiden's sister. She lived on the outskirts of town at the other end. She'd been coming to the castle for reading lessons, but since Evelyn left, she hadn't. "Hello," Scarlet called and raised her hand.

They met on the road near Kirstin's cottage. Rebecca smiled, glancing down, and sidestepped to go around Scarlet. "Wait, Rebecca," Scarlet said. "Won't you come up to the school for some classes? We miss having you."

"I…I couldn't," she said.

"Why?"

"I…well, I haven't anything to pay ye with."

"The others are paying by helping us get the school up and running. All of them except our newest student, Cecilia Menzies. And I know you've been helping Kirstin sew our trousers. If you attend, you can continue to learn to read the clothing patterns in the library, and more importantly, you'll learn how to protect yourself."

Rebecca pinched her lips tight. "I don't think I'd like to attend, thank ye."

"Why don't you want to attend? You have friends there. Has someone told you that you shouldn't? You don't have to wear the training trousers."

"Nay, it's not that," she said quickly and huffed. "My brother"—she lowered her voice—"doesn't think I should come up to the castle." Her hand went to her mouth as if she'd said too much.

"Aiden?" Scarlet asked. "Why not?"

"See now," Rebecca said, her words muffled from behind her hand as she frowned. "I can't keep words inside. They just spill about." She shook her head. "I must go," she said, practically running up the lane that led through town.

Scarlet stood in the middle of the road, watching her flee. "What the bloody hell?" she whispered, her anger growing like a rising yeast roll. Why didn't Aiden want his sister to attend? He knew they were trying to educate the whole town. Did he not want her learning, preferring to keep his sister ignorant? Doubtful. He seemed to approve of the book learning going on in the library, never wanting to interrupt when it was time for classes in the gymnasium next door.

Scarlet resumed her walk toward the castle. Could it be that he didn't want his sister learning to defend herself?

Maybe he had a problem with the trousers but hadn't said anything. Well, whatever it was, she was going to find out.

• • •

The sheep corral was snug with the daub between the lathe and a sturdy thatched roof. "There now, Snowball," Aiden said to the lamb as it nuzzled against a wide ewe who must be its mother. "Now ye can shite wherever ye want." And Scarlet wouldn't have a reason to run out of his room to save her wandering lamb. He snorted at the foolish thought. The woman hadn't come back down to his end of the fourth-floor since that first night.

He washed in the ice-edged bucket of clean cistern water and walked back into the castle. He'd been away for a night and day, meeting with Donald Campbell at Balloch Castle, to see if he'd heard about any goings-on at Castle Menzies. Kerrick had heard from a man passing through Killin that there'd been crowds up at the castle. Donald had sent a man who'd returned to say that Edgar Menzies was rallying against the young chief, saying he wasn't fit to lead.

It was Sunday, so no classes would be held up at the castle. Except for the chickens, a set of peahens, and what seemed to be a furry, scurrying pine marten, the bailey was empty. A day of rest and biblical reflection were the mandates from the church even if Killin didn't have a chapel, something that Grey said his new wife was planning to change.

What would Scarlet be up to today? The great hall was quiet, but the remains of a fire showed that someone had stirred it before noon. The haunting sound of someone singing came up from the back corridor that led out to the gardens and kitchens.

"And the wind blows low over the bloody moor.

As the raven's beak plucks at frosted eyes.

I'll never again see me Johnny love,

But will hear his voice when err the breeze cries."

Molly with one of her melancholy songs. Aiden climbed the steps, hesitating on the second floor when he heard a *bang*. Walking along, he heard it again and stopped before the closed gymnasium to nudge the door open a crack.

Scarlet bent over, the black trousers hugging her arse, to pick up a dagger from the floorboards. Back-stepping nearly to the door, she held the knife cocked, took a step forward, and threw. The steel blade made it across the room to a straw-filled tick he'd erected at one end but hit the floor right before it.

"Ye need to step more into the thrust," Aiden said, pushing the door open. Scarlet whirled toward him, and he had the briefest relief that she wasn't still holding the dagger, else he'd likely be dodging it. He crossed his arms, walking into the room. "Keep practicing the timing to get the blade to rotate fast enough to hit the mark with enough forward motion to stick."

She was splendid with her fierce frown, rosy cheeks, and hair braided to hang over one shoulder. She wore a man's shirt, tied at the neck, the ends tucked into trousers that showed her long legs. With each breath, her breasts rose under the tunic where he could barely make out some banding, probably to hold her full breasts firmly without stays. He remembered those beautiful breasts resting on the surface of her bath water.

"You've been gone," she said.

He cleared his throat and took a few steps closer, noticing the pink of her lips. What would Scarlet Worthington taste like? Tea and tarts? "Only for a night," he said. "To meet with Donald Campbell at Balloch. I see ye are continuing your training, even on Sunday."

She walked to retrieve her dagger. "I had a need to work

off some ire." She bent down, and Aiden's breath stuttered at the perfectly round display.

"Ire?" he repeated.

She turned on her heel and tilted her head. "You don't want your sister to attend the Highland Roses school."

*Blast.* "Did Rebecca say that?" he asked. He inhaled, bracing his legs.

"Yes, that you didn't want her up at the castle." Her hands rested on the perfect slope of her hips, which he could follow easily while she wore her trousers. The thin, soft wool slid right along her skin, showing all her woman's curves.

"Why wouldn't you want your own sister to come to school here? She doesn't have to wear the trousers, but if she wants to, she can decide on her own."

"She can wear whatever she wants," he said, frowning over his immediate reaction to her attire.

As if feeling the slant of his thoughts, she crossed her arms over her chest. Her hip jutted out, showing her annoyance. "Do you not want her to look in the art book then? I keep putting it away, but someone keeps pulling it out in the library, leaving it open."

"An art book? What art book?" he asked, his gaze following her tightly plaited braid. She reminded him of the female warriors of legends. Though, he doubted Boudica or Joan of Arc could have been nearly so beautiful.

"Why then would you not want Rebecca to come up here?"

Aiden met her steady gaze. The tug, to be honest, was more insistent than he'd ever felt. He rubbed a hand through his short hair, glancing away. "Rebecca can't keep her thoughts and... well, anything to herself. She spouts words, anything that comes into her head." Which was why he didn't trust his sister to keep their family information buried in the past where it belonged. But Scarlet wouldn't understand the feelings he barely allowed himself to recognize—anger, shame, betrayal.

She looked doubtful. "And this is why you don't want her at the school? Because she will talk us to death?"

He grinned past the heaviness of the past. "She could. But really, I'd told her that before," he said, not altogether lying.

"Before what?" she asked, walking toward him.

"Before ye impressed me with being so bloodthirsty," he said, indicating her stance. "Ye aren't the typical *Sassenach*."

The corners of her mouth tipped upward, and she looked beside herself at the mirror they used in training. "No?" she asked. "What is the typical *Sassenach* then?"

Flashes from the past filled him with details, but he shook his head. "Just more easily affected by cold and the wildness of the Highlands. Peevish and easily irritated."

She laughed. "Since when have you known me not to be cold?"

A memory of her in a tub of hot water at his cabin, her glorious display on the surface, pushed away his distasteful thoughts about frigid, complaining Englishwomen.

"And," she continued, "I am almost always irritated."

Her easy admission made the corner of his mouth go up. "I know better than to argue with a lass holding a *mattucashlass* in her hand."

She gazed at him for a moment as if replaying their words. Had he answered the questions about Rebecca enough to suit her? He'd have a serious talk with his sister before she came up to the school for daily classes. Rebecca was clever and quick, but she had no control of her tongue.

Scarlet came closer, their gazes locking. The woman had the longest lashes framing her hazel brown eyes. So clear and confident, as if she wished for him to see her for the strong woman she was becoming. He held his breath as she neared, but then she turned, presenting her back. She raised the dagger in her throwing hand. "I step and throw," she said, simulating the movement without releasing the *mattucashlass*. She looked over her shoulder at him. "Some further instruction will help me be less irritating."

Aiden came forward and closed his hand around her wrist. He leaned in toward her head, his lips near her ear. "Your mark is about sixteen feet away right now, but if a man was running at ye, ye should wait until he's closer to throw, so the blade won't fail to penetrate." He pressed her with his body from behind, making her take several advancing steps.

Aiden's whole body felt alive as his blood surged within him. Without her skirts, she'd no doubt feel him grow against her, but there was no help for it. Everything about Scarlet wrapped around him, her womanly clean scent, tinged with flowers; her warmth and softness; her silky hair, which he brushed his cheek against.

He cleared his throat. "Hold the dagger loosely, so it will slip from your fingers, and raise it over your shoulder." He lifted her arm, her sleeve sliding up to expose the underside of her wrist. Its paleness was soft as he rested his thumb there. He felt the thrum of her pulse. His lips hovered so close to the velvety skin of her neck. Och, how he craved a taste, trailing kisses down it. Feeling her pulse fly.

He swallowed and inhaled her fragrance. "Ye whip it forward with the shift of your weight to the other foot, but keep your wrist straight." He moved her arm through the motion slowly, stepping with her. It took his rock-hard discipline to step back. "Ye try."

Without turning, she took a step back and paused. He watched the slight rise and fall of her shoulders as she breathed. Lifting her arm, she took aim, stepped, and released. The blade flew through the air, bouncing off the target.

"Good," he said.

"It dropped on the floor," she answered and strode forward to retrieve it.

"But your form was right, and ye have strength."

She turned to walk back, and he noticed a flush up her neck. Embarrassment or desire? She didn't meet his gaze but turned her back to him again.

"With this dagger, the blade is heavier than the handle, so make sure the blade is facing the mark when ye release. It doesn't need to spin in the air." He stood there, staring at her straight back, his gaze following the soft coil of her hair down over her shoulder. She didn't move, as if listening intently to his words. "Every blade throws differently. Ye should pick a blade that has a good balance of weight and practice with it. Make it your own."

She lifted her arm, aimed, and stepped forward to release. *Whump.* The point of the blade hit the hay-filled tick, cutting through and quivering where it stuck. She spun on her heel, a broad smile stretching her lips and lighting her eyes.

He smiled and nodded. "Ye follow direction well. Nice throw."

She hurried to the tick and yanked the dagger out, holding it across her finger pads to weigh it. "I like this one." She glanced up at him, happiness in her bonny face replacing the nearly constant unease she wore like a neutral expression.

"Then it is meant to be yours, Scarlet."

"Perhaps I should also acquire a sword," she said. "And become a true Highland warrior." She sauntered toward him, a definite tilt of feminine cockiness in the sway of her hips.

He shook his head but kept his appreciative expression. "Nay."

Her brows lowered. "Why not? I could find one that doesn't weigh as much as yours."

He stood before her. "Apart from not wanting to see ye

in the middle of a blood-soaked field being circled by ravens," he said, "a lass's battles will most likely be more up close. To protect yourself from those who think they can overpower ye with muscle, ye should wield daggers that can be hidden upon your body. A sword is long and meant to slice a man in two. Ye just need to protect yourself."

She looked up into his face, her frown softening. "What if I want to slice a man in two?"

The side of his mouth quirked upward. "Craig said ye were bloodthirsty."

She scoffed and walked away toward a wall that had two practice swords. She hefted one, feeling its weight. The lass didn't really want to slice a man in two, did she?

"If women had the strength of men, we would be treated very differently," she said and slid the blade slowly through the air, testing her arm muscles. He could see the strain in her shoulders as the heavy blade pulled her arms downward. Some of the tightness that she normally wore in her face returned.

"Were ye born bloodthirsty?" Aiden asked, his tone light, but he watched her closely.

She laughed. "Only when my sister stole one of my ribbons or my brother pushed me out of his way."

"But ye've changed," he said.

Scarlet sliced the air again with the blade before lowering it to look at him. "The world changes a person." She set it back against the wall and walked toward him, turning as if she planned to throw her dagger again. "I would think that someone as serious-minded as you would know that. Or were you born bad tempered?" She glanced over her shoulder at him.

He met her stare for several heartbeats. "Who made ye want to slice a man in two, Scarlet?"

She didn't say anything, but her smile faded, leaving a

haunted look in her eyes. He took a step closer. "Who hurt ye before Finlay?" He searched her face, the cheeks that looked soft that may have once showed bruises, her curved bottom lashes that may have held teardrops. "Who betrayed ye, Scarlet?"

# Chapter Nine

*Me! I betrayed me by being so foolish, by believing the flattery and false promises of a deceiver.* The words beat inside her, and with each exhale they threatened to tumble from her lips. Her stomach twisted with the need to bleed out the words, words she'd never spoken, even to her sister.

She looked deeply into Aiden's blue eyes, serious and sharp, as if he were asking for names so he could hunt them down to slaughter. She opened her mouth, but the words wrapped around her tongue.

She wet her lips. "Do you have nightmares?" she asked.

His brows drew closer, and he blinked as if trying to figure out what type of answer she was giving him. "Everyone does, though some more than others."

"Perhaps of the fire," she said. "Slicing along your back, flaying you open."

His jaw tensed. "Aye."

"Yet you must deal with fire every day without flinching."

"Because I control the fire," he said.

"Exactly," she answered. "I must learn to control." Men,

but also herself, so she would never be fooled again by passion. "I must be around men every day, yet I am not in control of them. If one of them strikes again, I must take control of the situation to protect myself. Training in the ways of war teaches control and is helping me replace fear with courage."

Aiden watched her, weighing her words. "So your nightmares will cease?"

"Yes," she answered and swallowed at the sudden tightness in her throat. "The ones that badger me while I sleep." She looked down at the dagger, balancing it on her fingers as she stepped into position. "As well as the ones that stalk me while I'm awake."

*Whump.* The blade quivered with force exactly where she'd aimed it to hit in the middle of the upright tick.

Before she could move, Aiden stepped past her to retrieve the blade. He flipped it in the air, catching the blade between his pinched fingers to hand it back to her, handle first. "Ye can't trust any man?" he asked. "Like ye said in class. Any man can attack at any time?"

She took the blade, exhaling long. "Not all men. I trust some. Like Nathaniel and James, our driver and friend from Hollings."

"But the Scots here?" he asked, prodding. He kept his distance, but his words felt close. "Like me?" He waited, watching her. Trying to decipher her stillness, any telling twitches or change in expression.

Aiden Campbell, the most offensive Highlander in Killin. That's what she'd called him before. Before the night at Castle Menzies. Before the night in his cabin where he let her sleep and then bathe. Before his help in training her students and supporting her ideas about the trousers. Did she still despise him?

Scarlet's frown relaxed. "I think…I think you are a trustworthy man." She inhaled, happy to be off the topic of who she wanted to slice in two. She nodded, feeling quite certain that she was safe with Aiden. "You wouldn't touch me even if you wanted to."

Aiden watched her, his one brow rising only slightly. He was close to her, close enough to pull her into him. What would it feel like to have a man so wild and powerful wrap his arms around her, hold her with true affection? Not judging her as a valuable pawn to use.

Scarlet's heartbeat picked up, thudding behind her breast. It wasn't the rhythm of panic but something else entirely. "Do you want to touch me?" she asked, her voice soft, almost a whisper.

She watched the strong lines of his face. So handsome, even with two days' growth of beard along his jaw, his short hair ruffled by wind and dampness. Finally, his lips turned up slightly. "If I say aye, ye may split me in two for being a rogue. If I say nay, ye may split me in two for being…a liar."

Scarlet swallowed, her pulse flying faster as they stared at one another. Only the occasional whistle of the wind outside broke the silence surrounding them. She slowly raised her arm out straight to the side, the dagger tip pointed down. Fanning open her fingers, one at a time, the blade slipped down to hit the floor, clattering. The noise jarred a blink out of her. "I am… unarmed."

He took a step closer but stopped, as if waiting for her to surrender the small distance to bring them together. The pull was mountainous, a yearning like none other she'd felt. Almost fearful, Scarlet met Aiden in the middle of the room. His hands came up slowly, as if she were a shy horse. They cupped her cheeks, thumbs grazing her skin. She closed her eyes at the sensation, her lips parting.

"Look at me," Aiden whispered, and she blinked open. "See who I am," he said, his eyes kind and clear. "A man ye can trust not to take anything from ye that ye don't want to give, Scarlet." He leaned in, his lips meeting hers. They were soft and warm.

As if the touch had the power to break a mighty dam, Scarlet pressed into Aiden, lifting her arms to capture his shoulders. His arms wrapped around her to slide down her back, pulling her into the curve of his hard body. He slanted across her mouth, and she tipped her face to deepen the kiss.

Her heart fluttered like she'd felt before, but instead of teetering on unease, she just wanted more. More of this powerful, wild, honest man. He played no games with her. She felt it in his heavy breathing. Laying her hand on his chest, she felt the deep thud of his heart and knew it to be real. Her fingers pulled at his shirt, untucking it from his kilt so she could slide them up the taut muscles of his stomach to his chest. A fine sprinkling of hair graced the perfect form of strength and restrained power.

Aiden slid a hand up to cup the back of her head, a low growl coming from his throat. His mouth moved along her jaw to her ear. "Och, lass, I cannot stop devouring ye."

"Don't stop," she said, her damp lips missing the taste of him. She guided him back to her mouth with one hand, while her other fingers grasped his waist to reel him tighter into her. She could feel his thick rod upright between them and remembered the massiveness of it from the night she'd seen him naked. But it didn't bring panic, only a heaviness in her abdomen.

His hands trailed down over her backside, and in the thin wool of the trousers, she could feel every stroke. She moaned into his mouth and sucked in a quick inhale as he lifted under her thighs. Her legs wrapped around his waist, fitting her intimately against his hardness, where he began to rock her.

"Oh God, yes," she murmured against him as they found a rhythm. Heat flooded her body, coursing like strong whisky with every thump of her racing heart. She ached. She wanted.

She needed. "Aiden—"

*Crash!* "Demon!" a woman shrieked.

Scarlet sucked in a silent gasp. Before she could finish a blink, Aiden turned them, lowering her to press her behind his back. Scarlet's fingers curled into Aiden's untucked shirt as she leaned around him, her breath coming from her kiss-dampened lips.

"You're sucking the soul right out of her," Molly yelled from the doorway, a tea tray on the floor at her feet.

Scarlet stepped to Aiden's side. "All is well, Molly," she called. Glancing down, she was relieved to see that her breasts weren't hanging out. A few moments later and they very well could have been. She followed Molly's wide eyes down the front of Aiden, where the man's kilt pitched forward with his arousal.

"Good God," Molly said, hand to her mouth. "All is certainly not well."

Scarlet dodged in front of Aiden. She heard him snort softly. Molly's hands went to her thin hips as she squinted her eyes to glare at Aiden. "What exactly were ye doing to Lady Scarlet, then?"

He cleared his throat. "I—"

"I was sucking his soul out," Scarlet said, interrupting. "Poor man." She shook her head then bent to pick up her dagger, which laid on the floor near her feet. The movement made her backside brush against Aiden, and a rush of longing reignited. But with a maid in the room, wide-eyed with shock, there was no help for it.

She turned to look at him and fought to keep her composure. His hair stood on end where she'd raked it with her fingers. His tunic was out from his kilt and untied at the neck. He looked...ravished. She couldn't help a small grin. "You should learn to carry a *mattucashlass* to fend off the lasses, else they each steal a bit of your soul. Greedy ones might not leave anything behind."

Stepping away from him was like stretching a bowstring between them. At any moment she might snap right back into his arms. Molly's worried gaze was the only thing pulling her away. Tucking her blade into the scabbard she'd belted around her waist, she met Molly at the door. "Let's gather this up and see about that glue you made. Maybe we can make some repairs."

"So sorry, milady," Molly said, tears in her voice. "I really thought—"

"We will make another pot of tea, and you can tell me where you've seen someone's soul sucked from them." With one quick glance at the tall, broad Highlander standing speechless, she lifted the tray filled with broken pottery and left with Molly.

• • •

"It's bloody winter," Hamish yelled down from the roof of the keep. "Ye'll freeze your ballocks off."

Aiden ignored the man and threw more snow over himself where he stood outside the back wall of the castle. He'd stripped down to only his boots, bent on freezing the heat out of his blood. But as he washed his body with snow, his thoughts still churned with raging heat when he thought of Scarlet.

Scarlet, her strong legs wrapped around his waist. Scarlet, running her fingers up the skin of his chest. Scarlet, clawing at his hair, rocking the V of her body against his hardness. His blasted cod was still standing tall. He stroked snow over it, but all he could think about was how warm it would be against Scarlet's skin, in her hands, in her rocking body.

"*Mo chreach*," he cursed. The woman was a witch. Sucking the soul right out of him? *Bloody hell!* Maybe she was. But if pressing her to him, loving her with all the passion he'd felt igniting between them, would render him soulless, then he'd gladly give it to her. Even if she wore the devil's horns.

He paused, his eyes catching the last of the winter sun's rays as it slipped down below the tree line. Would he gladly give his soul to a *Sassenach* who spoke with the devil's *tongue*? Just like his fool of a father?

"Fok," he said, wiping the snow from his limbs. But Scarlet wasn't a typical Englishwoman. She was fierce and brave, hardy and not afraid to live in the Highlands. She didn't simper around and complain of the dirt and cold, blaming those around her for her discomfort. She worked hard and now fought to recover her courage.

Anger prickled inside his skin. Those bastards, Finlay and someone down in England, stole away the bright light he'd seen radiate from Scarlet when she was riding her horse, when she'd sunk her *mattucashlass* into the hay-filled tick, when she relaxed in the safety of the keep with one of her cups of cream tea.

Over these weeks, he'd come to realize that her smiles were mostly masks. He could pick out her injured spirit by looking in her eyes. Just now, when he'd kissed her, he'd only seen the fire of her desire in her eyes. No fear, and no remorse when Molly had found them. Och, what would have happened if the maid had decided to bake instead of bringing tea?

Aiden grabbed his shirt, throwing it over his head, and wrapped his kilt loosely around himself. A snowball flew past his head, and he glanced up to find Hamish grinning down at him from above. He glared back and trudged along the wall to enter the hidden door where Kerrick stood watch inside.

"A snow bath?" Kerrick asked, his brows high.

Aiden didn't feel the need to answer the obvious and continued toward the keep.

Kerrick followed him. "What did ye find out at Balloch about Finlay Menzies?"

The great hall stood empty, though people would likely gather soon for the late day meal. Would Scarlet wear her trousers? He hoped Kerrick would go home before that. Aiden strode to the dying fire and fed it some dry peat squares.

"Seems Finlay will be ousted as chief, though I don't know yet who will take the reins," Aiden said and leaned forward to blow.

*You deal with fire every day without flinching.*

*Because I control it.*

The heat from the growing flames prickled against the skin of his face as Kerrick spoke behind him. Aye, fire was needed, welcome for the warmth it gave. Desired even, when it wasn't deadly. Was he fire in Scarlet's mind? Desired but possibly deadly if she lost control? The thoughts percolated through him.

"So, Cici must be asked," Kerrick said, his pause bringing Aiden around.

"Asked?" Aiden said.

"Aye, if she wishes to stay here," Kerrick said. "Without Finlay being able to pay her tuition, she'll have to work to pay her way. A lass raised as a chief's daughter may not wish to work."

Aiden frowned. "Where would she go then, if Finlay's been thrown out of their home? The new chief isn't likely to take her in."

Kerrick nodded. "Ladies raised watching others do work for them don't respond well—"

"Aye," Aiden said, interrupting. "I'm well aware that some high-born ladies do not like to dirty their hands, Kerrick. But there are others who do not mind, like Scarlet and Evelyn."

Kerrick stared at him, nodding slowly as his eyes narrowed. "Ye have something good to say about the *Sassenach* sisters? I think your snow bath froze your brain." He smiled.

Aiden crossed his arms over his chest. "Do ye think they will decide to leave Scotland? Go back to England and their estate in Lincolnshire, or to court in London?"

"Evelyn married Grey, so—"

"That means nothing," Aiden said with a slice of his hand.

"Well…" Kerrick drew out as if annoyed at being cut off again. "She seems to want nothing to do with her former home and is passionate about her school and Grey. So, I don't think the chief has anything to worry over."

"What of Scarlet?" Aiden asked. "Do ye think she will grow bored of the country, irritated by the cold and wind until she despises everything here?"

Kerrick made a foolish face and shrugged. "Who can predict the ways of an unattached lass? She does seem more likely to tire of life here than her sister, and she is always cold."

*Except when her legs are wrapped around my waist.*

"Gentle-born ladies don't like to be cold," Kerrick said.

Aiden turned to face the fire when the heat penetrated his shirt, stinging the still-sensitive skin on his back. Bloody hell, he was playing a dangerous game. He'd lived the devastation of such weakness. Maybe he should thank the maid, Molly, for stopping him from making a mistake. For Aiden was certain, one real taste of Scarlet Worthington, and he'd risk his soul to play her game.

# Chapter Ten

Scarlet's legs twitched under the blankets of her bed, and she slid them up as she turned on her side to stare at the dying fire in her small hearth. Between the fiery ache in her belly, pooling between her legs, and the feel of Aiden's mouth branded on her lips, she couldn't calm her churning thoughts enough to sleep.

She huffed and flopped over onto her stomach, no longer worried about disturbing her lamb, since Snowball was snuggled with its mother in the new corral. Her gaze fastened on the shadowed door. Was Aiden having as much difficulty falling asleep?

She huffed. During the evening meal, the man had hardly looked at her, instead talking mostly with Cici about her horrid brother. He'd done a fine job making the pretty woman feel welcome at the school, even though she would likely have to work within to pay her fees. Although, as Scarlet had pointed out, all the students worked in the school, even if they did pay fees.

*Hard work is good for the soul.* The only time Aiden had

made eye contact with her was when she'd declared that to the room. She'd remained after dinner, embroidering a rose on her black trousers with the ladies who resided at the school: Alana, Izzy, Cici, and, apparently, now Cat, who had been very reluctant before. The extra chickens tripping people in the bailey must be hers, along with the peahens.

Aiden had left the keep, saying that he might stay with his sister overnight. Hopefully he'd ask Rebecca to come to the school. Or had he just used his sister as an escape from the castle?

Scarlet had been raised by her manipulative mother to read the subtle glances, grins, and glares of a man. It was this knowledge that told Scarlet that Aiden had nothing really important to say to his sister. Whether he ended up sleeping there or with some loose girl in the village, she couldn't say.

After poking her finger a dozen times with the embroidery needle, she'd retired to her bedchamber, where she now stared at the stout walls surrounding her. Had she misread the passion in Aiden's earlier kiss, his touch, the groan that had come from deep within him? Had he ignored her at supper so Molly wouldn't say anything? Or did he avoid Kerrick's jealousy?

"Gah," she said, pushing up in the bed. Asking herself the same unanswerable questions over and over would lead her nowhere except to an exhausted day tomorrow when she had a full set of classes to teach. If the man were here, she'd just knock on his door and ask her questions. But he wasn't.

Scarlet slipped out of bed and donned her warm robe and slippers. With a glance toward Aiden's empty bedroom, she stepped down the drafty stairwell, skimming her hand along the rough stone wall to help guide her around and around past the sconces that had burned low. She hesitated on the second floor, thinking she saw candle glow coming from the library. She blinked, and the light was gone. Maybe she'd imagined it.

At the bottom of the stairs, she hastened to the fire and added some peat, thumping it with the iron poker. She turned around to survey the shadowed, silent room. The walls were still bare, since the tapestries had burned in the fire that the English captain had ordered set before she and Evelyn had arrived. Then Finlarig would be free to trap King Charles in an assassination. Even though they hadn't been successful in ridding the castle of what Captain Cross had called Scottish vermin, the castle had been scorched, the beautiful tapestries destroyed.

Scarlet's gaze traveled along the largest of the stained walls, the plaster daub mottled with black and brown streaks. The basket of shattered fragments sat next to the glue she'd helped Molly prepare earlier to fix the cups Molly had dropped when finding Aiden sucking out Scarlet's soul.

She strode across to the basket. Maybe that's why she couldn't sleep. Aiden had sucked away part of her soul with his kiss. It certainly had sucked away her practical, non-heated thoughts.

The shards clinked together as she tilted the basket toward the lamp she'd lit on the table nearby. Reds, blues, greens, whites, nearly all colors of the painter's palette collided together. Lady Campbell, Grey's mother, must have had a rainbow of china. It was a tragedy that they'd been crushed under English boots.

*If we pick the pieces up and dust them off, we can make them into something even more beautiful.* Evelyn's words smothered some of the questions swirling in her head.

She picked up a red piece that was curved into what looked like a flower petal. As she studied the wall, a form took shape in her mind. She poured the shards slowly onto the table and picked out a rounded swirl piece. Perhaps it had been a decoration on a platter or bowl. And now it was rubbish unless Scarlet used it separate from its original purpose.

She stood, lifting the horsehair brush out of the pot of glue, and made a thick dot on the wall and pressed the swirl there. The glue was sticky and held the piece in place. She added the petal next to it, then dug through the pile on the table, extracting petal-type shapes. She also separated out green and brown pieces for the stem and leaves.

Working in silence, she focused on the shapes, colors, and the vision she had for the mosaic. Sharp, small, flat, swirled, darker red, light red, rounded…

One by one, she glued over the constant questions about Aiden's kiss with the individual shards. She added a series of slivers downward to make a stem, vines veering from it. The sharpest brown pieces made perfect thorns.

"A rose." Aiden's voice shot through her, making her spin.

"You're back," she said, looking toward the window. Was it already dawn? But the windows were filled with the inky blackness of night.

"I've been spoiled by Grey's massive bed," he said. "Couldn't sleep on Rebecca's floor."

So, he had gone to his sister's cottage. She turned back to the wall, placing the little brown shard into the glue she'd just dabbed.

His footsteps came closer. "I didn't know ye were also an artist."

She continued to study the wall, hiding the rapid thud of her heart. "I wouldn't call me an artist," she said softly.

He walked up next to her, leaning in to stare at the arranged pieces in the glow of the lamp. "Aye, an artist to see what these broken pieces can become." Gently he touched one of the brown shards sticking out from the main stem. "Complete with thorns."

"Those who wish to draw close to the beauty of a rose, risk the sting of its thorns," she said with a smile, although the words came out as a warning.

Even without touching or seeing him next to her, she felt his presence, his strength, pulling her in like he'd done in the practice room. It lit a rush of sensitivity along her skin, making her feel flushed. "It's worth asking," she said softly. "Is the rose worth the sting of its thorns?"

God help her, she had more thorns than most. If he knew the mess that tangled within her almost incessantly, he'd surely keep his distance.

She heard his inhale in the silence of the night, and his voice came rough. "I think…'tis the thorns that make the rose sweeter won."

She gave one chuckle, sliding her gaze to him. "You are a poet?"

"Don't tell Kerrick," he said, still looking at the beginnings of her mosaic, hands clutched behind his back. But she could see the corner of his mouth tipping upward in a half grin. She didn't say anything but placed another thin green shard into the leaf. "Why are ye working on this now?" he asked.

She pressed the piece firmly, watching the glue fill in the cracks between. "Evelyn says that if we pick up the pieces, dust them off, we can make the most shattered mess into something beautiful. I was thinking about it and decided to start since the glue was fresh." She picked up another piece. "And I couldn't sleep."

He stepped closer as if studying her design. "Why couldn't ye sleep?"

Scarlet paused, her eyes following the lines of her design. She could throw wit at him, make him grin. She could tell him that she couldn't stop thinking of their kiss, which was the truth and might lead to another. But standing there in the dark, still feeling the loneliness of him leaving without talking to her, she felt more like throwing her dagger than giving in to the passion that had plagued her all night.

She turned to lean against a clean part of the wall and crossed her arms over her chest. "Why did you ignore me at supper and then retreat to your sister's cottage for the night?" she asked, meeting his gaze without blinking. "Are you afraid of me sucking away your soul?"

Her straightforward question made his gaze sharpen. He took a step to the side to look at the pile of pottery and china shards. Heart pounding, she waited as he pushed his finger through the pile that she hadn't sorted. "It's possible," he said. "For all I know of ye, ye're a witch out to ensnare me to do your bidding." He picked up a green piece and moved to the mosaic to grab up a second paintbrush sitting in the glue. "I know nothing about ye really." He glanced over his shoulder and then back to the rose. With a dab of glue, he placed the green piece as part of the vine she'd begun.

"I was born in June, over a score and four years ago," she said, moving to pick up a yellow piece that could start another rose. "I've been taught all the socially expected feminine arts such as embroidery, the harpsichord, French, and dance. I also paint and sketch with some degree of precision." She lifted another glob of glue, setting it higher where she envisioned a climbing yellow rose, and set her round piece. "I had a beautiful bay horse, named Margarette, when I was a girl. She was my best friend, besides my sister, and I cried for a month when she died two years ago."

Scarlet walked around Aiden, who had picked up another green piece, holding it before him as if trying to follow her vision for the mosaic. "And," she continued, picking up a few yellow petal-like pieces, "I was christened as an infant in the Church of England, I've never attended a coven before, nor prayed to Lucifer, so your soul is safe."

"No devil's horns," Aiden said, glancing sideways at her. "But plenty of thorns."

"Is that then what frightened you away?" she asked, turning toward him. "My many thorns? I am not a sweet, tame peony, and never will be now that you've taught me to arm myself."

Aiden squashed his brush on the wall with more force than needed, and she watched the glue drip. "I do not retreat, and I am not frightened by your thorns, Scarlet," he said. He used the pottery piece to wipe up the glue and stuck it into place on the wall before stepping back to look at her.

Shadows hid his blue eyes so that she couldn't read them, but she stared at them anyway. "Then why did you leave?"

He let out an exhale. "I was born in February almost a score and ten years ago. I was taught by my father, Jack, and Grey's father to wield all types of weapons from the *mattucashlass* to a mace to a claymore to a bow. I prefer the claymore. I drink whisky at festivals but prefer ale daily. My favorite sweet is baked pudding. I had a small dog named Pearl when I was a lad. And I have plenty of thorns, though I'm no rose. I'm more of blackberry bramble."

She blinked, taking in all his little facts. He wasn't going to tell her why he left earlier. Perhaps he had no answer. She wet her lips. "What type of dog was Pearl?" she asked.

"A spaniel," he answered, without looking away.

"A spaniel? Up here in the Highlands?"

"Aye," he said, turning back to the pile of shards. "She was cold and shook most of the time. She hated it here and died."

Scarlet's tight face released with sympathy that she only allowed because he looked away. "I am sorry," she said. "Pets are our friends."

He picked up another piece. "She wasn't my pet." Before she could say anything else, he held up a blue shard. "And ye trust me to put pieces into your picture?"

Exhaustion from the day and the heavy thumping of her heart seemed to catch up to her. She sat down in one of the chairs close by. "I can chisel your mistakes out in the morning if they are atrocious."

Aiden dabbed and placed his piece way out in the middle of nowhere on the wall. She chuckled, and he turned toward her, dropping the brush into the glue pot. "I expect that will be gone by noon," he said.

Scarlet ran her fingers up through her hair, which she left free for sleeping. She shook her head a bit, meeting Aiden's gaze. "What are we doing here?" she whispered.

He crossed his arms and leaned against the bare wall near his planted blue piece. His jaw moved back and forth as they stared at one another. "Let's see," he said. "I surprised ye. Ye started questioning me when I asked why ye couldn't sleep. I accused ye of being a witch because I know nothing of ye except that ye have a fire of passion like I've never felt before. Ye told me about your schooling and horse, Margarette, and that you've never known Lucifer. I told ye that I don't retreat and that we had a spaniel named Pearl when I was a lad. And I'm happy to help ye with your mosaic if ye can fix my mistakes."

"Back up," she said, moving her finger in little arches through the air as if jumping backward on a written page.

"To your horse?" he asked, his stare intense.

"No." She shook her head. "To the passion like you've never felt before. I'd like to…hear more about that."

A slow grin tipped up the corners of his mouth. Lord, he was handsome, in a rugged, full of warrior's grace kind of way. Scarlet was glad she was sitting, as the sudden rush that accompanied his grin made her legs weak.

Aiden exhaled and grasped the back of his head with one hand, which made his bicep strain against his sleeve. "I couldn't stop thinking about ye, the kiss earlier. 'Tis why I came back, not because Rebecca's floor is hard. I can bloody sleep on a pile of rocks if need be."

*Truth*. She heard it, knew it. Aiden Campbell had spoken plain truth to her without innuendos, orneriness, or cleverness.

A shiver rushed through Scarlet. "I couldn't sleep because I kept thinking about kissing you again," she said. "And I worried that I'd done something wrong to send you away."

He stepped closer to her chair. "Ye did do something wrong," he said and squatted down so they were on eye level, his hands braced on the arms of her chair. "Ye made me break my own law against kissing a *Sassenach* without regretting it," he whispered.

Her brows pinching inward. "I'm not your enemy, Aiden." Her gaze slid from eye to eye, studying him. She shook her head slightly. "I have no evil plans against you. I am just a woman…" She swallowed, her tongue wetting her bottom lip. "A woman who again wants to feel what I felt in the room above."

"What was that?" he asked, his face leaning closer.

"A wildfire that consumed me without scorching my skin," she answered, her whisper just above a breath.

"Scarlet, lass, ye are a poet, too," he whispered, and then his lips met hers.

The warnings that Aiden had bombarded himself with as he'd walked back through the night to Finlarig turned to ash under the heat that sprung up as he pulled Scarlet into him. Lifting her to stand, his arms encircled her warm, soft frame, and her face tipped to the side as she returned his kiss.

The darkness and silence in the hall covered them, making it seem like they were the only two people alive.

Nothing else mattered as Aiden's heart strummed a wickedly fast beat. Not Scarlet's English, aristocratic tongue, not her family home back in Lincolnshire, not her fragile form that could become ill in the harsh Highland winter. None of it could withstand the onslaught of her sweet woman's scent and the lushness of her curves and hair as she pressed into him.

Sliding his thumbs along her soft cheeks, he tasted her deeply. She responded, touching the tip of her tongue to his lips. A groan, born of the ache he'd been unable to rid himself of all day, wound its way up his throat. "Bloody hell, lass," he murmured, stroking down her back. Her fingers dug into his shoulders, but he barely noticed the bite of his burns over the raging heat within.

"Bloody hell, Aiden," she murmured back, pressing her body against him, feeding his coiled need. Her hands slid up under his shirt to stroke his chest. She wore only a smock and a robe that lay open, the thin linen barely hiding her from his view. Och, he wanted to see her without it. But not here, not in the great hall, where anyone could see. Not like she'd witnessed at Castle Menzies.

Breaking the kiss gently, Aiden laid his forehead against Scarlet's, both of them breathing in quick gusts. "Lass," he said. "I will not make ye feel tricked into lying with me. I am not like those bastards."

Her fingers, still inside his shirt, wrapped around to his back, and he held his breath. Feather-soft, her fingertips slid across his bare scars, the ridges of thick skin. She didn't pull away, but placed her cool palms against them. "Are you tricking me, Aiden? Telling me we are going to marry and raise our children together just to get me to buckle in and raise my skirts?"

"Nay, I've said noth—"

She silenced him by pulling her hand out to lay a finger over his lips. "Are you promising me riches and luxuries?"

"I have none," he said against her finger. "Only my cabin and a large bed."

A small chuckle came from her, and she pulled back her finger. But then her smile faded as she inhaled through her perfectly shaped nose. "Will you tell me that you love me beyond the heavens and then order me to sleep with another man?"

Aiden stared at her, trying to read behind the words. "I will never wish for ye to give yourself to another, unless that is what ye desire to do all on your own." He shook his head slightly without breaking eye contact.

She nodded once. "Are you keeping secrets from me?"

Och, his stomach tightened. "Everyone has secrets, Scarlet." The lass had several of her own. "But none of mine have to do with ye." His past was better left behind.

A slow smile returned to her lips, lips he longed to taste again. "You have no idea how attractive the truth is to me." She stepped into him. "Tell me more."

# Chapter Eleven

Scarlet pressed her body to Aiden's, her softness up against his gloriously hard everything. The aching that had pooled within her sprang anew as his arms lifted around her. "Ye want more," he whispered at her ear and then slid the tip of his nose along her exposed neck, inhaling. "Ye smell like my favorite flower."

"What flower is that?" she asked, tiny bumps of sensation rising across her skin.

He kissed her neck. "Scarlet flower," he said and bent, his strong arm lifting under her legs. His lips met hers as he carried her across the room, leaving the fire in the hearth and the lamp to burn out under the glass. He tucked her head under his chin as he climbed the steps.

"Let me down," she whispered. "You'll be too exhausted by the time we reach the fourth floor."

She felt his nearly silent chuckle through his chest. "Too exhausted for what? I'm going to bed."

"Exactly," she answered, her heart flipping about in her chest. Aiden let her slide down his body but held her hand as they climbed the chiseled rock steps together. His largeness seemed even greater in the dark, tight tower, leading her toward what her mother would call disgrace, though she wasn't fearful at all.

Protecting one's body was vastly different from protecting one's heart. *This has nothing to do with my heart.* She wanted Aiden and the heat he kindled in her. She wanted to take charge of her virginity and give it to whom she chose. She wanted to be an independent woman without a prized maiden's status to woo a royal lover. None of that had to do with wanting to capture a Highland warrior's heart.

They reached the fourth floor, her heart beating fast with the climb. It was completely dark with only the faint glow of the last sconce on the stairs. He seemed to wait, giving her time to retreat. He didn't know that her mind and body were, for once, in agreement.

"My turn," she whispered, although there was no one else sleeping on their floor.

"To lead me?" he asked, his voice gruff even though he teased.

"To tell a truth."

He held her hands but didn't pull her one way or another. The large bed that was his, for the time being, was way down the hall to the right. Her much smaller bed was to the left.

She cleared her voice softly. "I saw you washing in the snow earlier." Thankfully, the darkness hid any blush that might be infusing her cheeks. She lifted one hand to her face and felt the heat there. "Is that something you do all the time?"

He stepped closer into her until she could feel him brush the front of her through the wool of his kilt. "Nay," he answered. "Only when a thorny rose has left me aching and so hard I couldn't be seen by my men."

"Oh," she said, smiling. "Did it help? I might have need

of a snow bath myself."

"Ye'll have no need to douse your fire, Scarlet," he said. The air between them seemed to change, the lightness of their banter growing heavier, and her heart quickened. "Let it burn between us," he said, a beat before his lips brushed across hers, warm and full of promise.

He held her there in the dark, his hands resting on her shoulders. They kissed, tasting, giving, and taking, and the heat built higher inside Scarlet. "Truth," she murmured against his mouth and parted, tipping up to find his face in the shadows. "I want you, Aiden Campbell. Tonight."

He grasped her hips, pulling her against him, but she held a hand to his chest. "But I would not keep this secret from you," she said, moving slightly back and forth against the hardness she felt through his kilt. She stepped back. "I'm a virgin."

His breathing seemed as ragged as her own, and the ache at standing away from him nearly buckled her knees. "I don't intend to marry, so you needn't worry that I expect that," she said. "But I need you to know…if I give to you my maidenhood, you…might make an enemy. A powerful enemy."

He reached forward, his hand stroking her cheek. "Are ye promised to someone else, lass? Is that what made ye run from England? Like your sister?"

*Promised?* She almost laughed a dark, wry chuckle. She'd certainly been promised to someone, though not in marriage. "I am not betrothed," she said. "There is no suitor contracted or waiting to marry me."

He stared at her in the dark for long moments. "Ye don't need to tell me tonight." Had he picked up the pain in her voice? "But one day, Scarlet, consider telling me about your nightmares."

She swallowed hard, nodding as he held the side of her

head gently. "But the enemy—"

He brushed a kiss against her lips, stilling them. "I'm a Scot, a Highlander. We are born with enemies," he said. "Another one makes no difference to me."

*No difference to me.* She wanted it to be true.

She stepped closer, pressing herself against him. "Know this for truth, that I give myself to you," she said. "With no reason except that I want you, Aiden." She needed to hear the words as much as he. Her fingers curled into his shirt. "I want you," she whispered, rising onto her toes. "Do you want me?"

"Och," he said, his hands cupping her face. "I want ye more than my own breath, Scarlet."

"Say my name again," she whispered, kissing him.

"Scarlet, lass," he said, his thick brogue wrapping around her name. "I want ye, Scarlet." He lifted under her legs, but instead of turning toward his room, he went left toward hers. He backed in through the door and set her on her small bed, going to the embers in her hearth.

She shivered as the cool air replaced Aiden's body heat, and she watched him tend the fire until flames danced to life. He rose, turning back to her, and she could see the evidence of his need. He helped her up from the bed.

"You prefer a small room?"

"I prefer a room that isn't soaked with Grey's passion," he said, using her warning from his first day. She chuckled softly as he dragged her mattress from the roped bedstead to lay before the crackling flames.

"A nest," she said, walking before the flames. She let her robe slide from her shoulders, the fire spreading heat along her back as she stared at the glorious man before her. His gaze raked across her, and she knew that the fire must be lighting her from behind, making her form visible through the thin fabric. She watched his broad shoulders move with his inhales, and he untied his shirt at the neck. Lord, she wanted to lay her mouth along his pulse.

Aiden raised his shirt, peeling the garment off over his head, and Scarlet's breath caught. Golden firelight played along the outlined muscles of his chest and shoulders, his biceps full and tight with relaxed power. Everything about him was beautifully hard and strong.

Scarlet's insides clenched as heat poured through her, and she swallowed, raising her hands to her breasts. She lifted under them, brushing her thumbs over her taut nipples through the fabric.

Aiden groaned, stepping forward. "Scarlet," he said again, wetting his lip as if tasting her already.

"I love to hear my name on your tongue," she whispered, his accent so very different from the voice in her nightmares.

A wicked smile curved his lips. "I have a talented tongue, Scarlet." His words shot through her, bringing a sensitive flush across her skin.

Her fingers picked at the knot at the top of her smock, rotating her shoulders one at a time to lower the sleeves so the garment slid down. Heavy breasts fell out, peaked and full. She held them up and reveled in his deep groan. If he didn't touch them soon—

Aiden took two steps forward. His mouth descended to capture hers, stealing her breath and the faintest worry of consequences from her mind. The only thought she had was need, a deep, aching need to be closer to him. Careful not to scrape his back, she wrapped her arms around him and tilted her head to deepen their kiss. Her breasts pressed against the muscles of his chest, the fine hairs on it teasing her peaks.

With a tug against her, Scarlet heard the thud of Aiden's kilt hitting the floor. The heavy, hot length of him pressed against her belly, and she rotated her hips, standing on tiptoe to press him against her ache. She moaned. Aiden cupped her backside, lifting to fit her against him, rocking them together as they tasted and explored each other's kiss.

Wild heat coursed through Scarlet. Aiden's hand reached in front to palm her breast, squeezing her nipple gently. He released her mouth to trail kisses down her neck, and she threw back her head, panting as he encircled her peak, teasing it with his teeth. "Bloody hell, Aiden," she rasped, raising one of her legs to wrap around his hips.

"Ye like to climb," he ground out against her flesh and lifted her so that she could wrap both her legs around his middle, the V of her spread wide to cradle him. Raw need swept her along as his mouth devoured her breasts with slow, deep suction. Nerves coiled tight within her, Scarlet ground against him, rubbing, Aiden helping her to increase her rhythm. The pleasure tightened until a dam of passion broke within her.

She moaned out her pleasure. "Aiden," she cried, feeling the ache crash over and out through her body.

"Aye, Scarlet, feel the fire in ye." He raised his head, slowly lowering her along his hard body until her toes touched the blanket at their feet. Her hands wrapped around him, sliding the velvet skin over the hardness of his length. "*Tha thu cho teth*," he groaned, closing his eyes. Scarlet watched, reveling in the pleasure she gave him.

She swallowed, looking down at how thick and heavy he was. What would he taste like? She'd seen a woman take a man in her mouth, and the man had nearly lost his mind with passion. "I want to make you burn with pleasure," she said.

"Ye are, lass," he said, looking down.

"Even more," she said and wet her lips. Before she could explain, she opened her mouth and lowered onto him. He sucked in breath, his body going rigid as if he were in pain. But his groan filled the room. Gaelic words leaked from his lips as she explored, his response making the ache within her begin to build again.

"Scarlet, 'tis too good," he said, his voice rough, and he gently pulled her from him, capturing her face in his palms to kiss her. He looked into her eyes. "My plan was to taste ye." He caught her up, his mouth against hers as he lowered them to the mattress before the fire.

Heat prickled along her skin, warring with the cool air in the room. Her skin was raw with sensation as Aiden worked her smock up over her head, ridding her of it. He sat back on his heels to gaze at her, his words tumbling in his ancient language that she couldn't understand. But there was reverence in it.

He leaned into her, changing his words to English. "Och, Scarlet lass, I've never looked upon anything so beautiful before." The emotion in his tone caught at her heart, making it speed. She wanted to be all for him, anything he wanted.

Lifting onto her elbows, she cupped her breasts and smiled. "And it is all for you," she said, her knees falling slightly apart, opening to him. With another groan, he leaned forward, lowering his mouth between her legs, his hot breath adding to the heat there.

Scarlet's head fell back, a flood of molten sensation taking away any rational thought. There in the embrace of passion, she only sought the fire that was Aiden, her core pulsing with need as he pleasured her, making her buck and clench. "Please," she said, her voice fierce with need. "I want you inside me."

He lifted his face. "Aye," he said, rising over her. She watched him, her lips open with ragged breath. When he braced his arm beside her head, she felt him against her.

"I'm on fire," she whispered as he guided himself, teasing her.

"Aye, ye are, lass," he said, strain in his features. "Ye are sure?"

Panting, she grabbed the sides of his head. "I'm sure that if you don't take me now, I will hunt you down with my *mattucashlass.*"

A small grin lifted his lips. "My fierce rose," he murmured and covered her mouth with his, his fingers teasing the most sensitive spot on her until she writhed beneath him. She moaned into his mouth, kissing him with a wildness, and clung to his shoulders, her nails curling inward.

With a sudden thrust, Aiden pushed into her aching body, sheathing himself. Scarlet gasped against his mouth, feeling the sting she knew meant that there was no going back. Tears pressed against the backs of her eyes, not for the pain, but for…the relief.

She opened her eyes to find Aiden above her watching, not moving. He looked tortured, and she reached up to touch his cheek, smiling. He lifted a finger to capture a tear that had escaped her eye, but she caught the digit into her mouth, sucking the salt from it. "'Tis the sting of thorns that makes the rose sweeter won," she whispered, quoting him. She reached down a hand to slide along his tight arse and pressed upward. "Make me forget it."

He kissed her, gently stroking her arms and breasts, tasting and tickling a path down her neck. The heat still simmered inside her where he waited, giving her body time.

"Aye, Scarlet," he said. His deep voice sent another thrill through her, and she moved against him, feeling a delicious heat. He kissed a line to her ear. "Another truth, lass."

"Yes?" She looked at him.

"My back is fine if ye want to hold on." He grinned. "The sting of thorns won't slow me at all."

Had he noticed how careful she'd been to avoid his burns? She slid her hand around to his back, feeling the thick lines. His mouth moved over hers, and she opened fully. Could he taste himself on her tongue like she could taste a hint of herself on his? The thought made her core contract, clenching with renewed want.

Sliding his hand down with strong fingers, Aiden reached the juncture between them, teasing her. A surge of heat flooded back down through Scarlet, and she rocked against his hand.

"Och, lass, 'tis hard to stay still in ye."

"Then don't," she said, pressing upward.

He looked into her eyes, breathing through slightly parted teeth. "Hold on, Scarlet." Pulling back, he sunk back into the pool of heat they'd created between them. Sensations ignited like wildfire through Scarlet, and she clung to his upper back as he began a steady rhythm that she met, the sting lost in the movement.

Mouth on her neck, he tasted her skin in kisses as she tangled her legs around his, finding leverage to meet his thrusts. "Yes," she called out, opening her legs even farther, giving him total access to her core. "Oh, Aiden. Yes."

His fingers continued to work down between them. Powerful, deep, filling her, branding her. Surely this was what it meant to have one's soul sucked away.

"Aiden," she pleaded.

"Scarlet!" She watched his face harden as he pulled his lips back in a roar. The look so wild, raw, and honest, that her own passion broke, making her cry out as they rode the fast cadence, crashing over like a massive wave onto the shore.

*I'd cling to him forever.* The thought infused her as they moved with the natural heat, slowing as wave after wave of pleasure rolled along her limbs. No wonder women risked their reputations for this. Though she doubted the ladies she knew, those bought with pretty gems and gowns, could feel the inferno that faded slowly within her, leaving behind a languid contentment.

Aiden rolled them together onto their sides and pulled a

blanket over her shoulder. Legs still intertwined, he cradled her against his chest, and she listened to the deep thud of his heart. She felt him kiss the top of her hair and tipped her face up to meet his gaze. "Can we stay here like this forever?" she whispered.

A grin spread across his features, not just on his lips, but all the way into his eyes, golden from the reflection of the fire behind her. "Molly will call a cleric to pull your soul back out of me."

She laughed lightly. "I thought I was pulling the soul out of you."

He kissed her, his smile growing more serious. "Aye, I think ye did."

She held her breath, her heartbeat a gallop. Swallowing, she finally inhaled. *Truth?* Had she pulled out a part of his soul? She couldn't ask it. Their relationship balanced on the passionate thread they'd just woven between them, and she wouldn't risk the weight of that question.

She smiled and turned over, scooting so she could curl her back into his chest. With the warmth of the fire before her and the heat of Aiden behind, his heavy arm draped over her, she'd never felt so safe before. Could she find safety in a man? The thought had been ludicrous before, a childish fantasy shattered.

She found his hand and threaded her fingers between his. He curled them in, clasping hers back. She stared down at the hold between them, solid and golden in the glow of the fire. Truth? Did Aiden truly care for her? Was there more than just passion between them, something that involved the heart? She hadn't the courage to ask.

# Chapter Twelve

Aiden glanced up through a clearing in the woods at the snow that fell from the gray sky. He smiled. Some liked the spring with all the green. Others rhapsodized about the autumn leaves. But Aiden liked winter with its shrieking wind and blinding white, crisp and always looking for a good fight. Just like his father, Jack Campbell, Aiden was hot-blooded and didn't mind the icy sting about which others complained.

His visit with Rebecca just now had been brief, but hopefully she could help him today without giving away all their family secrets. He filled his lungs, the cold air like ale to a thirsty man, and stretched his arms out wide. Hell, he almost whistled.

As he walked out of the woods, he spotted Kerrick staring at Izzy's parents' abandoned house with the sagging thatched roof. He nodded when he saw Aiden. "We should still fix the roof, make it habitable in case Izzy and Cat decide to move back in. Or it can be used for visitors to Killin or the chapel that Grey said Evelyn wants built."

"Agreed," Aiden said, stretching his arms wide again

and continuing down the road toward the smithy.

Kerrick caught up. "Embracing the cold?" he asked, his one eyebrow quirked up over a frown.

Aiden grinned. "Aye." He certainly had embraced fire, leaving Scarlet with a kiss when he roused her to say he had to go. It would take him most of the day to accomplish his mission, and he needed it complete by the time Scarlet retired that night.

Kerrick narrowed his eyes and quirked his lip upward. "I've never seen ye smile for no reason. Has someone brought ye the head of an Englishman or trussed up Finlay Menzies for ye to slice open?"

Aiden scooped up a handful of snow to fashion a ball. *Whack!* He hit Kerrick in the chest. "Nay. Just enjoying the winter."

Kerrick looked down at the snow print on his woolen jacket. "Ye hit me." He looked at Aiden. "With a snowball."

"Ye have a keen sense of observation," Aiden said, continuing on toward the smithy. Craig, as the town blacksmith, would have a sledge Aiden could borrow for the day.

"Keen sense of observation?" Kerrick repeated, dusting his front. He jogged to catch up. "Truly. What's changed your usual, I'm-going-to-spit-on-ye mood?"

Aiden glanced at Kerrick. "I won't be at the self-defense class today. I need to get something from my cabin."

"I thought ye liked seeing all the lasses in their trousers," Kerrick said.

There was only one woman that pulled Aiden's attention, and he'd gotten to explore all her lovely curves last night. Aiden's hand came down on Kerrick's shoulder. "They are all yours today. Perhaps ask Craig here to accompany ye. His blustering could liven up the instruction."

"The lass's trousers will make the old man's heart stop,"

Kerrick said low as Craig came out from behind the billows.

Aiden chuckled, making Kerrick's brows narrow farther in suspicion. "Cat will be there to get it beating again." Better to have the ornery blacksmith viewing Scarlet in her black wool trousers than roguish Lawrence or William.

Craig raised a bent arm in greeting. "Cold morning."

"Perfect for working over hot fires," Aiden said.

"Aye." Craig scratched his full beard. "What can I do for ye today? A new dagger to keep the lasses away?" He laughed and coughed into his fist.

"Can I borrow your sledge for the day?" Aiden asked. "The one to pull behind a single horse?"

Craig nodded. "I keep a couple of different sizes behind the smithy. Take whichever one ye need."

"Much appreciated," Aiden said, also appreciating that the man didn't ask questions about what he needed it for. He glanced at Kerrick, who still frowned. "Also, some daggers might be needed up at the castle."

"Daggers?" Craig snorted. "On top of the twisty skewers?"

"Twisty what?" Aiden asked.

Craig raised his stained hands to his thinning hair as if making a lady's updo. "Scarlet Worthington requested hair spikes made. Long, pointy, and lethal."

Hair spikes? Like the one she wore? Aiden grinned. "'Tis the perfect weapon for a lass. Hidden but deadly."

"Wasn't it a hair stick that Evelyn used to skewer that Englishman?" Kerrick asked.

"Aye," Craig said, pulling one from a pocket he had tied to his kilt. He held it point up.

Kerrick bent closer. "What's that on the other end?"

"Och, the woman wanted a rose on the end." Craig shrugged. "Tried my best, but I'm no artist." He handed it over to Aiden. The whole piece measured about eight inches long, a twisted length of steel, leading to a needle-sharp point. The other end had a coiling of steel wire wound into the vague shape of circling petals.

Aiden rested it on his open palm. He nodded. "'Tis well made. Nicely balanced." He glanced at Kerrick. "We can work this into the class."

Craig crossed his arms over his barrel chest. "Ye making these lasses into warriors?" He grinned, showing a few broken teeth that he'd gotten long ago on the battlefield.

"They are becoming fierce," Aiden said, making the old man laugh. "But I'd like to teach them to throw a dagger, too. If ye have some made, they don't need to be sharp."

"Better that they're dull," Kerrick added, and Craig barked out more laughter while heading toward the back.

Aiden crossed his arms and met Kerrick's questioning look. "Ye and Craig can teach the lasses about finding the dagger's balance today. Show them the form for throwing."

Kerrick nodded. "What are ye getting at your cabin that needs a sledge to haul it?"

Aiden didn't have to tell Kerrick or anyone anything. Only Grey, as his best friend and chief, held his pledge of obedience, and that only when Aiden felt the order made sense.

Aiden walked out from the fires at the smithy to circle behind it. Kerrick followed, waiting for an answer that would never come. A medium sledge, with two arms, stood among several others. The arms would hook to Eigh's working saddle, and Kerrick jumped forward to help him line it up out in the open.

"Thank ye," Aiden said, striding away toward the castle to get his horse. With the day set for the ladies, he'd leave right away.

"Ye aren't going to tell me, are ye?" Kerrick asked, striding next to him.

"Ye have a keen sense of observation," Aiden repeated, and Kerrick cursed low under his breath.

"Rebecca got all the words in the family," Kerrick said, shaking his head. "She talks, and ye won't say a word."

Aiden nodded to Hamish up in the gate tower. The man was stuffing his mouth with a tart. "Best of luck with the lasses today," Aiden said.

Kerrick crossed his arms, stopping as Aiden turned toward the stables. "Best of luck with your secrets," Kerrick called after him, his tone accusatory.

His secrets. *Hmph*. Everyone had secrets. Those who told them were considered gossips or tongue-waggers. Those who kept them were considered suspicious and ornery. Frowned upon either way. It was best never to have any secrets, but they were thrust upon people without consent. Aiden's only defense was to pretend they didn't exist.

• • •

"Holy Mother Mary," Craig swore as he walked into the training room.

Scarlet turned to Kerrick. "Where did Aiden go? I thought he'd be back by now." He'd left her with a kiss early that morning. She'd been too dazed after the night of uninhibited play and hadn't asked any questions.

"He said he had to get something from his cabin and that Craig could bring a bunch of daggers for your ladies to practice with."

"Who stole your skirts?" Craig asked.

In answer, Izzy spun around in a circle, kicking sporadically in uninhibited glee, her arms wide. If any of the students had taken to her training costume, it was Izzy Campbell.

"Thank you for bringing the daggers, Craig," Scarlet

answered. "We train in our trousers so that we are better able to see where we are kicking our attackers."

Craig looked at Kerrick. "We aren't attacking them, are we?"

"If you brought daggers," Scarlet answered, "we will attack the mattress tied against the wall."

The old man frowned, grumbling in Gaelic, and produced something from his pocket. "I also brought a sample of your hair skewers. If ye like it, I'll make more."

Scarlet's stomach tightened with excitement, and she hurried over. "Thank you, Craig." She lifted it from his hands as the other ladies gathered behind her for a look. "This, ladies, is a hair spike or stick. Some of you have seen the one Evelyn wears. I asked Craig to make more for the school out of twisted steel. Each Highland Rose will receive one."

"It looks sharp," Fiona said.

"Yes," Scarlet answered, holding it across her palm like Aiden had taught her about daggers. "And balanced." She noticed Craig's chest puff out, and she smiled. "The rose is quite clever on the end."

"That's a rose?" Cat asked, her tone flat with apathy, but she stuck her hand out. Scarlet laid the spike on her open palm.

"I'm no artist," Craig muttered.

"I think it is fun," Cici said. "A tangle of lines that becomes art representing the complexities of womankind." Everyone looked at Cici, and she smiled. "Ye were talking about that yesterday during our art lessons."

"That I did," Scarlet said and looked back to Craig, his face pinched. "I think it is perfect, Craig. We can use it to tie our hair up and have it available if we are attacked. Yes, please make more."

"We might slit our own heads open or stab our brains while putting it in," Kirstin said.

Martha leaned in to get a better look. "Or shear off our hair."

Craig shook his head. "Only the point is sharp. So, I guess ye need to try not to skewer your own brains, but the edges are dull, so ye can keep your bonny locks."

"We will practice with them in class, like we do with any weapon," Scarlet said. "Once you get comfortable with wielding it, in and out of your hair, it will be safe, and the perfect surprise for a villain."

Scarlet took the hair stick from Cat's palm, holding it point up like a mighty sword, though it was tiny in comparison. "Behold," she said with a broad grin. "And beware, villains. The Highland Roses now have their deadliest thorn."

. . .

Scarlet pushed up the dim steps in the curving stairwell. She hadn't bothered to bring a lamp, and she extinguished each of the sconces as she stepped past the quiet floors. Lessons all day, a longer than expected visit at Rebecca's house where the woman changed the topic to weather whenever Scarlet asked about Aiden, supper, and then working on her mosaic in the great hall, made her crave her bed. She'd left Aiden's blue china piece glued to the wall, smiling to herself as she thought of the surprise Aiden would get when he saw that she'd worked it into another rose.

Aiden must still be out at his cabin along Loch Tay. She hadn't seen him since he'd woken her with a farewell kiss at dawn. Perhaps he would come to see her in the night. She sighed, recalling the way Aiden had held her on the lumpy mattress before the fire. It would certainly be colder this eve alone in her dark room.

With the last candle pinched, Scarlet felt her way up the last few steps. Looking down toward the far-right end where

Aiden had taken Grey and Evelyn's room, all she saw was darkness. No, he hadn't returned. She turned left at the top and blinked, halting in the pitch-black corridor. The soft glow of firelight outlined her door.

Scarlet stepped silently forward to push into her room, her eyes nearly blinded by the bright fire leaping in her grate. She blinked, her hand flying to her chest as she saw the bulk of a huge bed.

"Good God," she whispered, hand moving to her lips. She glanced around to see her pitcher still in the corner, her robe hung on a hook beside the door. It was her room, although now, a huge bed took up most of it. Stepping to the edge, she ran her hand over quilts and a couple of furs that lay across the mattress.

Her fingers felt along one of the four posters on the corner closest to her. Leaning in, she examined the vines and flowers carved into the hard, polished wood. The bed had no canopy, but one would just block the beautiful carvings on the posters, headboard, and footboard. A sweeping landscape had been painstakingly cut into the headboard. She ran a hand over the smoothness of it, the dips and curves. Someone had spent hours working on it. The carving reminded her of Aiden's bed at his cabin, though this was of lighter wood.

She spied a small piece of paper on the pillows. The letters were formed in heavy, confident script, elegant yet filled with masculinity. She picked it up, reading it in the glow of the fire.

*Your old bed was puny.*
*Don't burn your toes.*
*A*

Scarlet stared at the note and looked at the bed. "Burn my toes?" She ran a flattened palm down the top quilt, feeling the warmth creeping up from the blanket as she reached the bottom where her hand hit something hard. A brick? Reaching under, the blankets at the foot of the bed were warm where a wrapped, hot brick had been placed. She smiled, a quiet laugh bubbling out. "Aiden," she whispered. The man was trying to keep her warm.

So, he *had* been back to the castle today. Where was he? She turned toward the door, but it stood empty. She walked out into the dark corridor and caught sight of a glowing lamp way down at the other end. It hadn't been there when she'd climbed up to the fourth floor moments ago.

Her heart gave a few hard pounds, and she drew in a full breath to feed her racing blood. Heat crept along her, making her skin feel sensitive as if anticipating Aiden's touch. Without hiding the sound of her boots, Scarlet walked down the corridor toward his room. Her gaze focused on the single lamp sitting on the floor, its glow splashing up on the stone wall behind it.

"Aiden?" she said, her voice soft yet carrying in the silence.

"Aye."

The deep resonance sent a thrill down through her middle. She still didn't see him, but he was there. Her shoulders relaxed as she smiled in the darkness. He was letting her come to him, like she had done with skittish horses back at Hollings Estate.

Her fingers curled into the doorframe, and she rounded the corner. His room was dark, but she could see him in the glow of the lamp from the hall. The sight of him caught her breath.

*Aiden Campbell.* Quiet strength radiated from his stance, legs braced, his kilt wrapped loosely around his narrow hips where it rode low on his taut abdomen. His chest was bare and beautifully broad, the muscles of his upper arms and shoulders full of relaxed power. She shivered slightly, knowing how warm his skin would be sliding against her own.

Wetting her lips, she stepped before him. "So, my bed was puny."

"Aye."

"Not for one person."

His grin flattened. "I didn't give ye the bed because I expected to be invite—"

"I know," she said, cutting him off. He could have been waiting for her in her room, but he'd remained far away, giving her a choice. "Thank you. It is beautifully carved." She watched him lean against one of the bedposts in Grey's room.

"Where did you find it?" she asked. "I want to examine all the details in the morning."

His frown relaxed into a tentative grin. "My father, Jack Campbell, carved it. I helped a bit, but I was a lad. He had a talent for working wood."

"It was your parents' bed?"

He shook his head. "No one has slept in it. I've had it wrapped up at my cabin for nearly a score of years." He shrugged. "It deserves to be seen and appreciated, and I felt ye could do both. It is yours."

"Rebecca doesn't want it?" Scarlet asked, taking a step closer.

He shook his head. "Nay. I asked her this morning."

Scarlet smiled. "Rebecca got me out of the castle today, so you could sneak the bed up to my room."

His grin returned. "A gift is better when it is a surprise." He studied her. "I half expected her to tell ye about it."

She laughed lightly. "Well, she did talk a lot, but always brought the conversation back to the weather." Scarlet's fingers floated up to the ties at her sides, plucking them so that they loosened. "And the heated brick…?" she asked.

"An Englishwoman gets cold easily, but if her feet are warm, the rest of her will warm."

Scarlet shrugged her shoulders until the bodice slid

down, exposing her smock over her full, sensitive breasts. She stepped directly in front of him and laid her palms flat on his chest. He didn't even flinch from her cold touch. "How do you know so much about Englishwomen?" she asked.

"I don't," he said, reaching up to slide his fingers through the stray curls at her temple. "With ye, I feel like I'm walking blind."

"Well, Aiden Campbell," she whispered, leaning up on her toes to brush a kiss against his warm lips. "I am perfectly content with you feeling your way around me."

He exhaled, a small rumble in his chest. Her hands went up to the back of his neck, pulling his face closer as she pressed her body into him. His mouth took hers in a kiss that poured heat down her, a heady liquor to loosen her spine, making her limbs heavy, her stomach fluttering with anticipation.

She inhaled through her nose. He smelled fresh, like clean water and masculine heat. "You smell so good that I want to taste you again," she whispered close to his ear.

"Och, Scarlet, if ye talk like that, I'm likely to go mad."

"Go mad with me, Aiden," she whispered back, and he wrapped her up in his arms, surrounding her completely to kiss the very soul from her. Her hair tumbled down, and she realized he'd pulled her hair stick from the twist she'd secured. She heard it clatter on the floor.

"You've disarmed me," she whispered, breathing against his lips.

"Ye disarmed me from the moment ye saved yourself and your horse from a pack of wolves." His arms tightened around her, and she closed her eyes, reveling in his strength and the promise of pleasure. The feel of his body heat penetrated her, and the press of his mouth on hers, sliding together in a perfectly wild dance that bespoke absolute passion, made her legs weak. For long moments they touched and kissed, exploring, giving, and taking.

Scarlet opened her eyes. "Come," she whispered.

He smiled, merriment in the relaxed lines of his face. "If ye keep touching me with those sweet, soft hands, lass, ye know I will."

"To my room," she said with a small laugh.

"That, too," he said.

Dousing the lamp, Aiden followed behind her, their fingers intertwined. He made it obvious that she was leading him to her room, not the other way around. When they reached the end, Scarlet paused as she heard a strange noise from below and stared into the darkness leading down the steps. "Did something just bray?" she whispered, but there was no further noise.

"Bray? Like a mule?" he asked. "I can go—"

"No," Scarlet cut him off, tugging him into her room. She released his fingers to go to the bed. The glow from the hearth bathed the room in gold. Scarlet ran her hand up one of the four soaring posters, her fingers finding a rose. "Exquisite," she said.

"Aye," Aiden said, and she turned, but he wasn't looking at the bed. He was looking at her, his bare, thickly muscled arms over his head as he held on to the top of the doorframe. "The most exquisite woman I've ever known."

Scarlet's heart pounded. The emotion in his voice almost spoke of love. He did care for her, maybe even respected her. She beckoned him with her fingers, and he dropped his arms to step inside. Without breaking eye contact, he shut the door, moving forward. Such sleek grace sparked a thrumming of excitement through Scarlet, and she had the feeling of being stalked by a wild animal. Although instead of fear, there was only delicious eagerness.

She loosened the ties completely on the sides of her bodice, letting it slide down to rest on her hips, and went to the ties of her skirt. Aiden caught her hands, stopping her, and slowly raised them over her head until she felt the carved bedpost graze her fingers.

"Hold on," he whispered, opening her hands to grasp around the firm post. He kissed her slowly, his hands slaking down her arms, shoulders, breasts, and stomach to pull the ties of her skirts. They dropped to pool around her boot-clad ankles. He slid the bodice down her legs.

"Don't let go," he said, lifting one foot to remove a boot, setting it down. He discarded the second one, sliding his warm hands up to the top of her stockings, untying the garters. "No trousers today?" He untied first one and then the next. With slow strokes, he caressed and kissed a path on her bare skin as he worked each stocking down and off her leg, leaving her in her untied smock, completely bare underneath.

"I washed them," she said, breathlessly. "They are still damp." Scarlet watched him stand, and he leaned in to kiss her, first on her lips and then down her neck to the open edge of her smock. Nudging the lace lower with his nose, she heard him breathe in deeply as if savoring her scent. He lifted his head to stare into her eyes, capturing her as if she were truly tied and vulnerable to his attentions. Yet fear didn't linger anywhere between them, as if Aiden's mere presence banished the shadows. With one finger, he edged the lace line of her smock down until her heavy breasts came out, their nipples jutting outward, begging for his attention.

Aiden groaned, his lips closing around one where he began to suck. The heat of his mouth coiled down through Scarlet, making her rub her thighs together at the ache building between her legs. He moved to the next breast while palming the first.

Behind them, the fire crackled as if mirroring the fire building inside Scarlet. She pressed her body forward without letting go of the poster but couldn't get close enough to feel him. "Please. Aiden, I want to touch you," she whispered.

He raised his head to look into her eyes. "'Tis a sweet torture, isn't it?" He stroked lightly over her bare arms, his palms heavy as he reached the sides of her breasts, sliding slowly down over her ribs, the indent of her waist, and her hips, his thumbs gliding down the V through the thin linen of the smock.

His fingers captured the material, inching it up. He bent, sliding his open hands up her legs until he reached the ache that pulsed within her. Scarlet moaned as his fingers worked magic along her flesh, throwing her head back against the poster. Somewhere at the back of her consciousness, she heard the sound of his kilt thumping to the floor, and she dropped her gaze to take him in. Bold and brawn, Aiden stood there, working to pleasure her when it was so obvious that he could be taking his own.

Letting her fingers release, Scarlet reached forward to grasp him. A deep, guttural groan came from Aiden as she slid along his member. "Och, lass, this is about ye tonight."

She unwrapped her fingers, stepping back to slowly shake her shoulders, releasing her smock. It floated down to join her skirts and bodice on the floor. His gaze washed along her like a heated caress, making her insides contract even tighter. She reached both hands behind him to grab his tight backside, pulling him into her. The feel of his skin up against her own sensitive skin caught her breath. She swallowed, staring up into his handsome face. "Tonight is about us."

Aiden's arms came up and around, reeling her into him as he bowed his head. She melted into his kiss, the power of it conquering all of her thoughts, her worries, her past.

# Chapter Thirteen

She always smelled of flowers, her creams for which she sent away came with letters from the south. The air seemed especially filled with the scent as the trees danced overhead, and a muted sun shone down without adding any warmth to the summer day. The yipping of a dog shot from the window of a rich carriage that stood behind her.

*"Don't go," Aiden said, grasping her soft hand. "Stay."*

*Sad eyes stared at him, her lips moving, but then she looked away, her gaze going to the coach that waited. "Don't leave me," Aiden said, but she turned her back, walking quickly to board the conveyance. "Nay," he yelled, running after the coach as four horses pulled it down the road. "Nay. Lady Beckett. Don't leave us. Lady Beckett!"*

*Tears flooded Aiden's eyes, but he would say no more. She looked at him from the carriage window, but her hazy visage sharpened until every detail slid into place. It wasn't the woman he'd known. Instead, brown eyes framed by long, dark lashes looked back, her lush lips tight, subduing her natural smile. Scarlet watched him as she rolled away.*

Aiden jerked awake, blinking at the image of Scarlet staring down at him in the pre-dawn light, her brows furrowed. "You were dreaming," she said. "It didn't look pleasant."

Aiden's arm came up to his forehead as he closed his eyes again, taking in measured breaths to calm his pulse. It had been a long time since he'd had the nightmare. He slid his hands behind his head, cradling it. "Sorry. Did I wake ye?"

She lay her head back on her pillow, her face turned to him, her gaze searching with a pinch between her brows. "A bit."

Aiden stretched, trying to shake the heaviness sitting in his chest, and wiped hands down his face. He pushed up in the bed, the carved posts soaring toward the ceiling. "Perhaps we should knock down the wall into the next room, like Grey did, to accommodate your new furniture."

"That would raise some eyebrows," Scarlet said, still staring at him.

He chuckled, even though the nightmare clung to him, and rose, bending to gather up his kilt. "I best get started with the day." He turned back to her. "Ye sleep. I kept ye up much of the night."

"You got as little sleep as I," she said. "But I despise mornings, especially cold ones." She snuggled back into the covers, giving him a slight grin, though her face still looked tight.

He leaned in to kiss her, his lips brushing the softness he'd enjoyed so thoroughly. His fingers slid across her cheek, relishing the velvet cream of her skin. "Catch some more dreams, lass." He straightened, heading toward the door.

"Aiden?"

"Aye?" He turned to see her eyes filled with questions.

"Who is Lady Beckett?"

The name felt like a boulder growing in his gut as he held his breath. He gave a small shake of his head. "No one to concern us. She is dead and gone."

Scarlet stared without blinking. "She may be dead, but she's apparently not gone."

"She is no one," he said. "I'll be back in time for class. Get some more rest."

Aiden pulled the door shut behind him, and he stood for a moment in the dark hall. His blood pounded through him, and his hands fisted as he tried to shake off the feeling of disapproval. From Scarlet? He scratched his scalp through his hair. Perhaps. From the woman turning her back on him in the dream? Absolutely. Pray God, that they weren't one in the same.

. . .

"No," Scarlet yelled, letting some of her tension out in the word. "No," she repeated, her hands going to Aiden's arm. With a kick backward, she shoved his arm away, escaping his hold. Wrapping her hand around the hair stick holding her coiled tresses, she snatched it free. Her heavy hair fell down her back, but the side pins kept it out of her eyes as she brandished the lethal spike before her. With two forward steps, she shoved the weapon toward the dip in Aiden's neck, the one she'd kissed in the early morning.

He kept his ground, and she stopped the point inches from him, a slow smile spreading on her face. "You didn't even flinch," she said, dropping her arms. The students in the room clapped.

He leaned near her ear. "After what I've done to make ye moan over the last week, I'm fairly certain ye don't want me dead."

His whispered words sent a giddiness through Scarlet. Since the gift of the beautiful bed, they'd slept together every night. He hadn't spoken through any further nightmares, although some nights she watched him sleep, wondering what transpired behind his eyelids. *Lady Beckett? Who were you?*

Their passion was hotter than anything she could have dreamt, but Scarlet knew time was required for full trust to develop between them. *One day, Scarlet, consider telling me about your nightmares.* If Aiden could ask it of her, she surely could ask it of him. The time just hadn't been right, as passion consumed them quickly when they met in the night, each time with her having to invite him from his room down the hall. The days had been full with students—eight in total, now, with Rebecca attending and Cat showing up regularly. Nine when Molly stopped in at Scarlet's continual urging.

Scarlet gave Aiden a smile but puckered her lips to stop herself from laughing. Whenever they were together, they attracted questioning looks from the ladies and frowns from Kerrick. Was their attachment so obvious?

She stepped away from him and clapped her hands twice to catch everyone's attention. "I want you all to practice putting your hair up with your hair stick. Try very hard not to poke or cut yourself." She made sure to catch twelve-year-old Izzy's gaze and held it until the girl nodded.

Cat gave a dark chuckle, tossed her hair stick in the air to catch it by the rose knot, and quickly fashioned a bun to shove it through. "Well done, Cat," Scarlet said. The woman had a natural way with weapons.

Rebecca stepped forward, stabbing the air with her stick. "Och, the trousers make it so much easier to move."

Molly shook her head but smiled a toothy grin. "I just don't know if I could get accustomed to wearing trousers." She'd opted to keep on her skirts.

"It's time to change back to skirts and have tea in the library before we start our lessons in summing numbers," Scarlet continued. Kerrick and Aiden gathered up the daggers they had brought for further training. Most of the ladies were starting to have success with throwing, though Fiona and Cici were less coordinated. Perhaps a separate class could be arranged to give them more practice.

"'Twas a good class. Ye are a natural teacher," Aiden said as he neared her on the way out. His compliment warmed her inside. Apart from her beauty, Scarlet hadn't received many compliments.

Had Lady Beckett been beautiful or studious?

*God's teeth*. She needed to put the woman from her mind.

"Thank you," she said. "It helps that the students are eager."

Aiden met her smile. "I will check on the sheep before heading to the smithy to let Craig know that none of ye have lopped off your heads with his skewers. Yet."

She gave him an exaggerated glare.

"'Tis true," Kerrick said. "The old goat is worried about ye all slicing your own throats."

"Tell him that my Roses are doing wonderfully with their training. He will want them on his side in battle," she said, loud enough for the ladies to hear her boast.

Aiden paused near her at the door. Without a glance toward any of the ladies or Kerrick, he leaned into Scarlet's face, brushing a slow kiss over her lips. Eyes wide, Scarlet stood there stunned.

Aiden nodded to the ladies who were no doubt staring open mouthed behind her. "Good day." He walked out, Kerrick's head twisting between her and Aiden before he took off after him.

Scarlet turned around, the feel of Aiden's very public kiss still on her lips, though she didn't dare touch them with a finger. Nine sets of eyes stared at her, mouths set in all sorts of smiles and frowns and shock. Rebecca's eyes and mouth were open the widest.

"He...is going to check on the sheep." She indicated

the empty hallway behind her as if nothing apart from the ordinary had happened. "My lamb, Snowball, seems secure with her mother in the new corral." She paused. No one said anything.

"Nathaniel will be surprised," Scarlet continued and crossed her arms over her chest, flipping one hand out to all of them. "The school has come a long way in a short time. Hopefully Evelyn will like the direction I've taken the self-defense classes."

Was she rambling? "Because, in order for you to truly protect yourself, you must be willing to hurt the attacker." Face flushing, she wove her own hair stick through her bun to secure it and walked across the room toward the changing screen to retrieve her skirts. "I'm determined to equip all the Highland Rose students with weapons, strength, and technique."

"Does that technique include kissing the brawniest Highlander I've ever seen?" Cici called as Scarlet dipped behind the screen.

"Aye? If I'd known that was part of the curriculum, I would have signed up on the first day," Kirstin said, her voice a bit strained.

"No wonder Aiden wanted Da's bed," Rebecca said. "Not just for ye, but for the both of ye."

This whole thing was spiraling out of control. Scarlet stepped out, once again attired in her skirts, which she finished cinching. She raised her hands. "Enough, ladies."

"In the Highlands, sleeping with a man practically makes ye married," Alana said, nodding. She turned to Martha. "I heard about a MacPherson who lay with a Menzies, and her clan made her go with him as if they were married."

Scarlet sighed, lowering her hands to walk out of the gymnasium. Let them go beyond propriety with their questions without her. She gritted her teeth as she strode to the stairwell. "Bloody hell, Aiden," she whispered. What had he been thinking, kissing her before everyone? Hopefully Kerrick was giving him an ocean of trouble.

"Scarlet? Where are ye?" Alana's voice came from behind her as she climbed the stairs toward her bedroom.

"Ye dolts," scolded Cat. "If the woman wants to bed one of our strapping men, it's her business."

"He's my brother," Rebecca countered. Their voices were getting louder as if they followed. Good Lord.

"Since when does being someone's sister give ye the right to know where he lies at night?" Cat asked.

"She's English," Rebecca said, though her voice was softer. "Aiden hates Englishwomen."

Scarlet paused on the steps. Englishwomen? Not English or Englishmen. She said English*women*.

*She is no one.* Scarlet would bet a pound of tea that Lady Beckett was an Englishwoman.

"Perhaps she's bewitched him," Cici said, making Scarlet roll her eyes and continue her upward climb.

"Shame on all of you," Molly said, her voice snapping. "My lady is neither a witch nor a loose woman. If anyone's had their soul sucked out of them, it's Aiden Campbell sucking on Lady Scarlet."

*Good Lord, Molly.* Scarlet shook her head and alighted on the top floor, traipsing toward her very crowded room. She closed her door, stepping to her polished mirror to practice using two hair spikes to hold her heavy tresses. She'd return to the library in a few minutes, once her blush had receded.

*Knock. Knock.* She didn't answer. *Knock. Knock.* She sighed. "What is it?" she called, turning toward the door.

"We want to see the bed," Kirstin called. "Rebecca says she remembers it being bonny."

Truly? They wanted to see the bed. Scarlet stared at the door. If Evelyn was here, she'd shoo them away and remind them that ladies did not barge into their teacher's bedroom or gawk at their bed or question them about what they did when they weren't teaching. But Evelyn wasn't here. "Blast," she whispered. Although, if Evelyn were here, then Grey would also likely be here, and Aiden would still be frowning at her from a distance.

Scarlet whipped open the door and crossed her arms, barring their way. All nine students crowded in the hall, eight of them still wearing their black trousers and white men's shirts. She met their gazes with a steely frown and waited. Her one eyebrow rose slowly as she looked down upon them, even Cici, who was taller than she.

Heartbeats passed as one by one they lowered their gazes until Alana cleared her throat. "We don't mean to pry."

"But you do anyway," Scarlet answered. "Whom I kiss and what I do after school hours is none of your concern."

Rebecca opened her mouth, but Scarlet spoke first. "Even if it involves a member of your family." Rebecca's mouth clamped shut.

"It's gorgeous," Cici said, gazing over Scarlet's head toward the bed. "Did your da carve it?" she asked Rebecca.

"Aye," she said, her frown relaxing.

Scarlet sighed. How could she refuse to let Rebecca show off her father's craftsmanship? She stepped aside with an ushering wave of her arm. The ladies filled the room. They ran their hands over the vines, flowers, and birds carved into the light oak.

Outside the door, the sound of heavy footfalls echoed, and Kerrick appeared in the doorway. Good Lord. Was he coming to view the bed, too?

He stopped, eyes wide as he took in the room, every bit of floor space filled with ladies in black trousers. "Scarlet," he said. It was the edge of panic that snapped Scarlet to attention. She'd never seen a Campbell warrior frightened, not that

Kerrick was filled with fear, but he looked as if someone had told him the moon was about to fall to the earth. The babble of female voices stilled, the whole room seeming to hold its breath.

"What is it, Kerrick?" Scarlet asked.

"Aiden told me to prepare ye," Kerrick said. He flapped his hands at the students. "All of ye." He looked back at her. "Because he's asking for you. Lady Scarlet Worthington, daughter of the late Viscount Worthington of Lincolnshire," Kerrick said. Her formal name sent a shiver up Scarlet's spine.

"Who is asking for me?" she whispered on what little breath she had left.

Kerrick swallowed, looking her directly in the eyes. "Bloody King Charles."

* * *

Aiden stood in the bailey with Lawrence and William as Hamish raised the portcullis. The foking king of England, Scotland, and Ireland was paying an unexpected visit to Finlarig. But what made his warrior instincts roar was the fact that the man was asking for Scarlet. *A man of the highest rank*. One couldn't find a higher rank than king.

A tall man with sand-colored hair had taken the black drapes off the two richly appointed coaches outside the gate. The man asked for entrance, but the lion and unicorn heraldry emblazoned on the conveyances demanded it. It wasn't until Charles himself, dressed in rich ermine splendor, stepped down from the carriage that Aiden ordered the portcullis raised.

As far as he knew, Grey Campbell wouldn't bar the king, and Aiden must act as steward. Any move that could seem treasonous would affect not only his own life, but the lives of his clan. *Mo chreach*. Grey walked this line all the time.

Aiden was damned happy to be an independent man, except when he must represent the Campbells of Breadalbane parish for Grey. Had Grey passed the king on the road?

Both the king and the tall man climbed back into the carriage, and the conveyances rolled under the thick teeth of the raised gate. Two red-costumed soldiers rode on top of each carriage, along with one driver. Two horses led each. They stopped before Aiden near the steps to the keep, and the door swung open again.

The tall man jumped out, his smile pleasant as he scanned the area. His short trousers and hose showed strong legs, and his tailored jacket fit snuggly across a broad back. Unlike the monarch, who stepped down after him, the man didn't wear a wig, though his short hair hinted that he likely did. Unless, of course, it had all been burned off by sadistic bastards and was still growing in.

The king was richly garbed in an elaborate blue and gold waistcoat and coat, trimmed with fur, over white silk breeches that showed the man's thin legs. His long wig was a tumble of dark curls that rested past his shoulders. His thin dark mustache tipped up at the corners as he smiled mildly.

Lawrence gave Aiden a small poke in the ribs with his elbow, which prompted Aiden to bow his head. "You are welcome to Finlarig Castle, home of the Campbells of Breadalbane."

"Yes," Charles said, stepping closer, his dark eyes shifting about as if anticipating an attack, though he didn't relinquish his smile. "'Tis cold and damp and away from everything civil," he said. He sounded happy about the complaints. "'Tis perfect, as you said, Lord Covington."

"Yes, sire," the tall man answered and stepped forward, his gaze focused on Aiden. "I am Lord Covington, Earl of Salisbury." He swept his hand toward the king. "Advisor and personal assistant to our sovereign, Charles, King of England,

Scotland, and Ireland."

Aiden bowed his head briefly to the king and then nodded to Covington. "Greyson Campbell is not in attendance at Finlarig as he is taking the heads of two traitors down to London."

"Ah, yes," Covington said. "Captain Cross and Lord Sotheby. We received Viscount Worthington's missive."

"Yet ye came all the way up here?" Aiden said.

The king chuckled slightly. "The safest place for a monarch is where a treasonous scheme has been disrupted and flushed out."

Covington nodded as if bolstering up the idea. "The perfect place for the king and queen to spend Christmastide amongst good country folk where no one can reach them."

"But Chief Campbell—" Aiden began.

"Will turn around and return once he finds the king is not in residence," Covington said. "When he returns, we will be here to greet him with a cup of wassail."

Lawrence made a choking sound next to Aiden, making him look past the king toward the coach where a richly dressed woman emerged, followed by two other ladies. Aiden bowed his head. The king looked to them. "My queen, Catherine, and her ladies."

The two ladies curtsied, and Aiden bowed his head again. One was the age of the queen and had dark hair. The other woman was bonny and young with blonde hair. Her face seemed familiar, something in the tilt of her eyes.

"Ye...may come inside Finlarig," Aiden said, his words slow. *Ballocks.* He felt completely inept dealing with bloody royalty. As much as he wanted to stuff Scarlet away in a hidden cave, her guidance could only help the stilted situation. He tried to remember what his mother had told him about kings and queens of England, but it had been long ago, and he'd paid more attention to his father's teachings on weaponry. The only thing he knew of the monarchy was that encountering any member of it increased the chance of a man's head leaving his shoulders.

The king turned on the thick golden heel of his shoe to survey the bailey, where chickens scratched about with two peahens, a donkey bit at tufts of grass, and a large peacock strutted toward the stables where the sheep were held. "Where now is our friend, Lady Scarlet Worthington?" His dark eyes turned their intensity on Aiden. "I am told that her sister married the chief of the Campbells, and that Lady Scarlet was in attendance, despite her brother reporting that they journeyed south toward Plymouth." The king frowned slightly but recovered his smile, one of his dark eyebrows rising.

"Lady Scarlet is a teacher here at the Highland Roses School," Aiden said. "She was beginning a class in ciphering numbers in the library, but I have sent word of your arrival."

The wind blew a gust, making some light snow swirl around them. A prompt from God? Aiden cleared his throat. "Ye are welcome to enter Finlarig, where it is warmer."

"I dare hope it is," Charles said, laughing. He held out an arm for his queen to take, and they proceeded them toward the steps. Aiden had no idea if he was supposed to walk in front since the king had never been to the castle or continue to follow behind. No doubt he would insult the king numerous times while he was here. By the time Grey returned, his head might be cleanly cut away and residing in a basket.

Covington walked up next to him, an easy smile in place as he spoke low. "Keep his cup full of good Scottish whisky, and this visit will go quite smoothly."

Behind him, several men emerged from the second coach. Two were soldiers in their red uniforms, but the one who caught Aiden's eye was a large blackamoor, his dark skin a contrast to the white wrappings he had about his head.

One soldier lowered several deer from the roof while another caught them. The Moor squatted down to examine them. Lawrence and Hamish talked with two of the guards, who nodded, and all muskets remained unlit. Aiden followed the royal group inside, their colorful garb reminding him of the peacocks sauntering over to peck with the chickens. He took another glance toward the flock. Since when did Finlarig have peacocks? And a donkey?

Aiden took the steps quickly, catching up to Covington as he entered.

"'Tis dark as a tomb," he heard the king say.

"Just the entryway, my majesty," Aiden called ahead. "Inside the great hall it is quite light."

"Your majesty," Covington whispered.

"What?"

"You say your majesty, not *my* majesty," the man said, a wry smile quirking his lips.

Aiden had thought saying your majesty would sound like he was saying the king wasn't the king of Scotland. *Ballocks.* He'd much rather be on a battlefield than paying court to a jewel-encrusted king and his fancily-costumed cocks.

The king walked the ladies directly to the hearth fire. Where was Kerrick? Hadn't he been able to find and warn Scarlet?

A movement from the arch made him turn. Scarlet stood beside the unfinished mosaic of roses on the burned wall, his blue piece sitting at the center of a half-finished red rose. Scarlet wore a gown that he hadn't seen before, its blue material smoothed with a shine that looked like silk. It billowed around her and was trimmed with lace and sewn beads. Her hair was piled up high on her head, but he could see the coil of steel in the shape of a rose sticking out of the wavy mass. Seeing her armed helped him draw breath.

She wore a sophisticated smile that he knew was false

and held her head high as she practically floated across the floor. Behind her, the ladies came quietly, their dresses back in place and looking shabby compared to the English gowns. The Rose students walked slowly, in pairs, their expressions a mix of fear, torturously fake smiles, and in the case of Cat and Izzy, open hostility.

*Foking hell*. He needed to start pouring whisky for the king and possibly himself.

"Your majesty," Scarlet said, her voice a practiced purr that made Aiden's middle clench. She curtsied low before him, rose, then curtsied to the queen. "Your majesty," she repeated. The queen smiled at her, and the sentiment reached her eyes.

When Scarlet rose, the queen caught Scarlet's hands with her own gloved ones and squeezed. "It is good to see a familiar face here in the wilds of Scotland," she said, her voice thick with her Portuguese accent. It was her foreign ways and accent that had made her unpopular with her people, much like the Scots. And just like the English in Scotland, Aiden reflected. He frowned, focusing his attention on the stiff, silent stances.

Scarlet ignored the man Covington and dipped her head to the king. "What brings you to Finlarig Castle?"

"Christmastide," the king said, his arms flying out wide as if announcing the plans for a grand siege. "Though, it would seem that nothing is yet prepared." He looked around, the queen and her ladies following his lead.

"The Scots do not celebrate Christmas," Aiden said, his deep tone seeming to draw all eyes, which grew wide. "In a very Protestant country, Christmas is viewed as a Catholic holiday. We celebrate the last night of the year, Hogmanay."

The queen pressed a hand against her heart, her face drawn as if she might weep. "However," Scarlet said, her voice high and merry, "since the Highland Roses school is run by two English sisters, we intend to celebrate Christmas from now on."

Had Evelyn informed Grey? Since none of them had been raised acknowledging the holiday, Finlarig Castle would likely be the only part of Breadalbane making merry.

"How fortunate," Queen Catherine said, a soft smile returning. The woman seemed remarkably genuine. Perhaps it was her Portuguese heritage, so different from *most* English. At a time, Aiden would have said *all* English. His gaze slid back to Scarlet. Her whole body seemed stiff, coiled, and restrained, very unlike the warm woman he'd come to know. It made his heart pound as if readying for war.

"Excellent," the king said, clapping his hands. "Harry, see that my men help them in any way. They must find holly and mistletoe to hang. And a yule log to burn. Christmas Eve is only a few days away." The king sounded like a child excited by the thought of candy.

Scarlet looked between him and the queen. "We are very honored to have you for Christmas; however, I fear you will not be comfortable here as we are still making improvements. There is only one large bedchamber, Chief Grey's chamber on the fourth floor."

Charles flapped a beringed hand. "My queen and I will share the chief's room."

Catherine's eyes widened, and the king took her hand. "Of course we will," he said and looked to Scarlet. "My queen may be with child again. 'Tis another reason to leave London, where my enemies will do anything to squash out the life of a legitimate heir to the throne. Once I received the letter from your sister about the traitors, and then your brother about their visit to London, Lord Harry suggested we venture north to the wild and secluded countryside where the traitors have already been thwarted." He threw his one arm out to take in the bare great hall. "Hence our visit."

*Unannounced and unwanted visit.* Aiden's gaze drifted amongst the visitors. The more mature woman, who had accompanied them, had such a low-cut bodice that her breasts nearly fell out. Her gaze remained riveted to the king as if he were a feast. She was most likely one of Charles's many mistresses. His audacity to bring her along with his queen spoke to his immoral character.

When he glanced at the younger woman with light-colored hair, she met his gaze as if she'd been studying him. She was bonny, rather like Rebecca.

"We will make do with the lodgings," Harry Covington said, staring at Scarlet. "And we will make merry together."

Scarlet would not make direct eye contact with the man, whereas Covington nearly devoured her with his gaze. What the bloody hell? Aiden's fists clenched. They knew each other. He was certain. And Scarlet would rather entertain the king's conversation than Harry Covington's.

"We have no cook, either, your majesty," Scarlet said, though her tone showed no sign of trying to dissuade the visit and held a note of cheerful resignation. Aiden was certain the cheerfulness was a learned role she'd been required to play often.

The king looked to his queen. "See, my dearest, it was good to bring Titus with us." His gaze slid to Scarlet. "He is our dark and mysterious Moor, who is also an exceedingly talented cook. He is likely filling your kitchens with the foods we stuffed into the second carriage and the deer we shot this morning as we neared this quaint village."

Scarlet bowed her head. "Royal forethought, your majesty."

The king laughed. "Of course. And our ladies of the queen's bedchamber are quite talented," he said, his gaze roaming over them, especially the lady who displayed her breasts in the lifted, open bodice.

Covington smiled. "How rude I am. Let us introduce our two brave ladies who have accompanied us into the wilds. Lady Scarlet, you know her grace, Louise de Kérouaille, Duchess of Portsmouth," he said, his hand out to indicate the more mature of the two. "And…" he smiled, indicating the younger, bright-eyed woman, "Lady Jacqueline…Beckett of Nottingham."

Everything inside Aiden clenched. *Beckett*? The name tore through him like vicious daggers flowing through his veins. *Beckett from Nottingham.* He stared as the young woman bowed her head in a slow curtsey, rising, her gaze directly on Aiden. It couldn't be… The woman in his nightmares had come back to life before him.

# Chapter Fourteen

Scarlet nodded to the two ladies, even though her stomach ached with knots. The first woman was one of the king's high-ranking mistresses, one that the queen tolerated best. Louise had born Charles a son and lived at Whitehall Palace, her rival being the actress, Nell Gwyn.

Scarlet breathed evenly to dispel the sparks of light that signaled a possible swoon. Did Louise remember last St. Valentine's night or had wine numbed her memories? The flush that rose along Scarlet's neckline might never recede.

Scarlet turned her focus on the second lady, who was beautiful, young, and…watching Aiden. While Aiden stared back. The connection between them was obvious, and Scarlet's stomach turned in on itself with a wave of nausea. *Beckett?* That was the name that Aiden had uttered once in his nightmare. He'd said she was dead, but this woman was exceedingly alive and mysteriously riveting.

Scarlet swallowed down the acidic air coming up her throat as Aiden's possible lie twisted inside her. "Molly, we will prepare rooms on the third floor for those in the king's party, along with the room adjacent to Grey's room for the queen's attendant," Scarlet said, the words coming softly, a part of her mind still functioning even if the rest of her was numb. "I will help you."

She bowed her head to Charles and Catherine. "Please warm yourselves and take refreshment," Scarlet said. She nodded encouragingly to her wide-eyed students, donning her practiced smile. "The wine. Alana, Kirstin, please pour and serve." Hopefully Cat wouldn't try to skewer any of them.

Without waiting for an acceptance, Scarlet willed her legs to move toward the archway with Molly. She wanted to flee from the room, flee from Finlarig. Harry Covington, with his arrogant confidence, had brought the king and someone from Aiden's past. All her carefully tended courage seemed to desert her. She clutched her skirts as she met Molly just inside the archway.

"They will lop off our heads," Molly whispered, ending in a panicked hiss.

Losing her head was certainly not the worst that could happen, but Scarlet wasn't about to feed the woman's odd slant toward the grim. "I won't let them lop off your head, Molly," she said. "Go above and start making beds with the fresh linens. With the cook, the ladies, and Aiden needing a new room, we should freshen four smaller bedrooms along with Grey's large room. The soldiers can sleep in the guardhouse. I will be along in a moment."

"Yes, milady," Molly said and scurried up the stairs.

Scarlet rested her open palm on the rough stone wall and breathed slowly to combat her pounding heart. "Lord. Help me."

"I don't think the Lord readies rooms." Aiden's voice lurched through Scarlet, and she wobbled slightly as she turned. He stood in the archway.

Scarlet leaned against the wall, her fingers pressed

between it and her back. Questions spewed up inside her. Why wasn't the woman dead? Why had he lied? Had he loved her? But all the questions boiled down to one. Scarlet wet her dry lips and met Aiden's gaze in the shadows. "Who is she?"

Scarlet watched Aiden carefully as her heart pounded in her ears. His frown did not change. "Do you love her?" she whispered before he could answer the first question.

Aiden let out a huff from the back of his throat and shook his head. "Love her? I don't even know who she is!"

Scarlet narrowed her eyes. "You've dreamt of her, Aiden. How could you not know her?"

He shook his head. "I've never seen that woman before."

"Lady Beckett?" she said, the name snapping on a whisper.

He scratched his neck, glancing down at the floor as if answers were painted there. "'Twas a different Lady Beckett."

"A different Lady Beckett?" Scarlet repeated. "How many blasted Lady Becketts are there?"

He met her gaze. "Apparently one that your Harry Covington wanted to bring up here."

"*My* Harry Covington?" Scarlet asked, her gaze shifting to the room behind them, where the man of her nightmares laughed lightly with Cici as she handed him a goblet of wine. She'd have to warn the ladies to stay far from him. "He is not *my* Harry Covington."

"His gaze on ye is heavy with ownership," Aiden said softly, the frustration in his voice softening to a lethal tone. "And ye avoided looking at him completely. Is he the high-ranking bastard who sent you running from London? Is he the man of *your* nightmares?"

Scarlet pushed off the wall, grabbing Aiden's sleeve to pull him toward the stairs. "Don't go after Harry Covington. He's currently King Charles's closest confidant. Any slight against him will be viewed as one against the king. With

Charles's fear of traitors, especially Scottish ones, he's liable to act without thought. And what thought he does have will be influenced by Harry Covington."

With a hushed growl, Aiden pulled her with him behind the stairs, the shadows hiding them. He captured her shoulders with his large hands, keeping her between the back wall and his chest. Fear rolled through her. Not of Aiden but of what might happen if he drew his sword, threatening Harry. "What did he do to ye?" His words gritted out, and she knew Harry's life teetered on her next words. Aiden's life balanced there with it.

"Nothing permanent," she said. "I was a virgin when I asked you to take me."

The questions on his face hardened to condemnation. *Blast.* She'd said too much.

"Nothing permanent?" he repeated, his voice deep and hard. "You've fought your fear for months, but it's still there. I could see it in the set of your shoulders." He glanced toward the great hall and back at her. "He may not have raped your body, but he raped your soul."

Scarlet shut her eyes, willing the tears to stay in place. Shame prickled her skin, and she sniffed. She wouldn't let Aiden jeopardize his life over her folly. "I let him touch me, Aiden," she said. "I was foolish. I thought he loved me, would wed me. He led me along with talk of children and a home but never promised me anything. He's broken no vows. I... encouraged his attention. Evelyn even warned me that Harry was a rogue, but I didn't listen." She shook her head. "Foolish and naive, I..." Her words trailed off.

She listened to Aiden pull in a breath. He didn't move away, but she couldn't bring herself to look up at him. Luckily the shadows covered her.

His voice was strained, as if tortured. "He convinced the king to travel two weeks in a carriage to come up here to see ye."

"I have no idea why," she said, meaning it. She was just another one of Harry Covington's conquests. Surely, he'd found others when she fled. At first, she'd feared he would follow her north, but as the months went by, she'd realized more and more what a fool she'd been.

Aiden's hands lifted to her cheeks, and he ducked down to capture her gaze. His eyes were dark in the shadows and impossible to read. "I know why. He realizes he wants ye. Maybe loves ye."

She shook her head, but Scarlet wasn't willing to explain more. She clutched her shame tightly around herself. Hopefully, she'd told him enough to stop him from confronting Harry, but she couldn't give him more details. How she knew Harry Covington couldn't possibly love her.

"I think he does," Aiden said. He paused to brush a kiss over her lips and backed up. "Before a fortnight," he said. "Harry Covington will ask ye to return to England."

She shook her head again. "No, and even so, I will never return."

"Are ye so sure?" he asked, backing up farther, giving her room to escape the corner. "Ye are a lady, born and bred to drink tea and dance the minuet."

Anger ignited in Scarlet, pushing back the shame and worry. "Just because I enjoy tea and dancing doesn't mean I don't love the wildness of Scotland."

He nodded. "But, Scarlet, will the wildness of Scotland be enough for ye?"

She would swear to it right there, but she knew that a quick assurance wouldn't sway him. Nothing as easy as words would impact the opinions of a man who apparently disliked Englishwomen. For some reason, he thought she would leave easily. The small shoot of hope that he would be upset by her leaving gave her strength.

Scarlet pushed past him to climb the stairs. "I need to help Molly freshen the rooms."

"I will find a room to move my things. I didn't bring much," he said.

Scarlet made a low growling noise of annoyance. "Good bloody hell, Aiden." She glanced over her shoulder at him. "Put them in my room." The thought that he'd abandon her so easily cut her hope at the root, shaking her to the core.

Which begged the question, what did she want from Aiden Campbell? More nights of exquisite, naked pleasure? A thousand times yes. A man who could care for her enough to want her for more than carnal pleasure? For her mind and determination? For her bravery and fierce independence? Yes. Yes, she wanted that, too. The realization made her even more vulnerable than when Harry had pressed her up against the wall outside the king's salon the night she'd fled London.

She swallowed, climbing the stairs, her breath loud in her ears as she listened to Aiden's footfalls behind her. The darkness and the narrow stone passage around her made her suck in more air, bringing dizziness. If she swooned, would Aiden break her fall? Humiliation hunted her like hounds after a fox. She inhaled, counted to four, and exhaled just as much.

Making it to the third floor, she swung out to walk along the corridor. "Scarlet," Aiden said, making her pause. She felt him come up behind her, his large frame warm against her back. She wanted nothing other than to curl into him, breathe him in, and feel his strength around her. But right now, with the ghosts of her past just downstairs, specters that could order Aiden's death without question, she couldn't just hide away and let him protect her.

"Yes?" she whispered without turning toward him.

"Are ye certain, about the room? I could—"

"Aiden," she said, turning so that they stood together on

the shallow landing. "Right now, you sharing my bed is about the only thing of which I am certain. Don't abandon me."

"*Mo chreach*," he cursed low, catching her chin with his fingers to stare into her eyes. "I will never abandon ye." He brushed a kiss over her lips and turned to disappear back into the stairs to continue his climb to the fourth floor.

Scarlet released a breath that shook more than she wanted to admit. What was she doing? The king was downstairs, but he'd brought his queen and his mistress. What use would he have for her? She closed her eyes. Unless Harry had reminded Charles of his obsession with her before. *Lord, help me.*

Throwing herself into action, Scarlet whisked through the rooms behind Molly, helping her wrap clean sheets over the ticks that they'd filled that fall with fresh hay. Luckily, with Evelyn's optimistic plans, the rooms were spotless, awaiting future students.

Blast, where was her sister? The king had probably left before Nathaniel had arrived in London. Perhaps they returned to Hollings in Lincolnshire when they realized the king wasn't at Whitehall. Evelyn had planned to be at Finlarig for Christmas. Had a blizzard delayed them?

Evelyn was the strategist, always laying plans to get them out of trouble. When Scarlet had gone to her that awful night almost a year ago, Evelyn had set their escape in motion. "Hell," Scarlet whispered as she set dried peat in one of the grates. She needed her sister.

"Aye," Molly said behind her. "We certainly be in Hell, milady."

Scarlet stood, and even though she was living her version of fire and brimstone with Harry Covington and the king under the same roof with her, she certainly didn't need the others frightened. "You have nothing to fear, Molly," she said, helping the woman spread a heavy quilt over the sheets. "Apart from the flurry of work to do when royalty visits, they are like the titled aristocrats who used to visit Hollings Estate when father was alive."

"I had no love for any of them or their servants," she said, sniffing. "They'd rather sacrifice a friend with a well-placed lie than own up to any fault of their own. Vicious trolls, the lot of them."

"If anyone gives you trouble, let me know immediately," Scarlet said. "Starting with their cook, Titus, who's likely already taken over your kitchen."

Molly's eyes went wide. "He'll upset my stew for this eve," she said, already deciding the man was a fiend. Her gaze jumped to the open door.

"Go on," Scarlet said, shooing her. "I will finish the last two rooms."

"Thank you, milady." Molly gathered her skirts and ran off.

"Try not to skewer anyone," Scarlet called after her when she saw that her hair was held up tight with one of the hair sticks.

"Skewer anyone?" The deep voice sliced through Scarlet, sending her heart racing even faster. She turned to see Harry Covington in the doorway, tall, fair, and as handsome as he'd always been. Without the court wig and pomp, he looked more rugged and kind, but she knew his true nature. The room suddenly felt like a cell.

Without missing another beat, she fluffed one of the pillows for the bed. "We train our ladies to protect themselves by any means possible," she said, her voice flat and firm. She gave the pillow a hard punch. "There are villains everywhere."

He entered the room, and she turned toward him. She would never let him at her back. She frowned, her eyes watching closely for any sign of attack. Let him know that she saw him for what he was.

"I see you are furious with me, Scar," he said, his voice

low. "Am I one of your villains?" She didn't give the obvious answer.

"You never let me explain before you fled Whitehall and then Hollings," he said. "I did follow you there, but your brother said you'd gone to Plymouth."

"Explain what?" She clutched the pillow close to her chest. She could use it to throw at his face if needed, catch him off guard.

He opened his hands, palms up, in an act of pleading. "That I was acting under direct orders from the king. That no matter how I loved you, I was forbidden to take what you offered me."

What she offered him? Shame prickled over her skin as she remembered sneaking out of her room. To seduce the handsome rogue and make him marry her. It had begun like a game until her young heart fell for his ruse.

"I was foolish and believed your talk of a home away from court, about children you wanted with me. You led me to believe you would ask for my hand, that you truly loved me," she said.

"I do love you, Scar."

Anger ignited within her, mixing with her own shame. "Don't lie to me," she said through gritted teeth. "You would give me to another man without so much as frowning over it."

"Not just another man. The king," he said. "'Twas not something I could refute or discourage."

"Your political stance was worth more than me," she said. She threw the pillow on the bed. "Excuse me," she said, traipsing forward to leave the room. He caught her wrist, his grip tight. At a time, the manacle would have sent her into a panic. Now her unease changed to anger.

With a twist and a jerk, she was free. "Do not touch me again," she said, her words low and fierce.

She stomped out into the corridor, her heart pounding so

that she needed to take fast breaths. She refused to run but kept her senses alert.

"I've come for you, Scarlet," he called after her as she walked to the stairs. "Why else would I convince the king to travel way up here for Christmas?"

She ignored him, taking the steps down. Aiden was right. But she would not leave Scotland, not for the king or comfort, and certainly not for Harry Covington.

• • •

"I want eight Campbells sleeping within Finlarig's walls each night, one for each English soldier the king brought. Send someone to Donald at Balloch Castle to tell him of the visit and retrieve any muskets he can spare. Craig can store them so it doesn't look like I'm arming Finlarig." Aiden's gaze scanned the dark bailey. Everyone was settled in for the night, the king and queen having taken Grey's bedchamber after an extravagant dinner that their cook constructed.

"Ye expect trouble then," Kerrick said, following his gaze.

The bloody king of England was there. Even though they said they were hiding away for Christmastide, Aiden was certain that Covington had at least one ulterior motive for visiting. Scarlet.

"There will be trouble," Aiden said. "But if muskets are required, the Campbells will be labeled as traitors to the crown. So, keep them hidden. 'Tis a precaution."

"That short-haired prig, Lord Covington, kept staring at Scarlet," Kerrick said low, his voice rough. "I don't like him."

Aiden hated him. Even if Scarlet didn't believe it, she would see soon enough that the Covington cock would try to convince her to leave Finlarig. And despite her confessing her part, the man had hurt her in some way, and it was only the cost of his retaliation for all the Campbells that kept Aiden from dragging the man out of the castle. "Set a man to follow him about discreetly. I want to know where he goes, who he talks to, and especially if he goes near Scarlet," Aiden said. He looked at his friend. "What did ye find out about Jacqueline Beckett?"

"She seems sweet, had been invited to the court right before the queen asked her to accompany them to Scotland. She's only just turned seventeen years old."

"Her parents?"

"Are dead, she says."

"Her mother? Did she say what happened to her mother?"

"Died soon after she was born. Her grandmother raised her on their estate. Seems Harry Covington contacted her grandmother, asking her to bring her to court."

The timing of Covington's invitation to Jacqueline would be just before they left for Finlarig, after Grey's letter had arrived heralding their upcoming visit.

Aiden grabbed the back of his neck where knots threatened. Bloody hell, Jacqueline Beckett's grandmother must be senile to let her granddaughter go to Scotland with the king and queen and the bastard, Covington. Riding for two weeks with aristocratic vipers... It was a wonder the girl wasn't poisoned.

"Tomorrow, find out the date of her birth," Aiden said.

Kerrick nodded. "Any chance ye'll tell me why ye want to know so much about her, especially after ye kissed Scarlet in front of everyone." His tone bordered between jealousy and anger.

Aiden turned on his heel to walk toward the keep.

"Thought not," Kerrick called after him and turned to his task of relieving Hamish in the gate tower.

Aiden strode through the great hall. It was empty, and the fire was low in the grate. He climbed the steps, slowly, listening for footfalls or movement in the castle. On the third floor, he heard muted snoring coming low from one door, and he continued up to the fourth.

Scarlet had said he could share her room, but he wanted to give her every chance to change her mind. A lot had happened since he'd left her in bed this morning, warm, sleepy, and undone with complete satisfaction.

With the king's arrival, they had been forced to spend the evening and night dining and sitting in uncomfortable extravagance. Candles lit to excess, and the fire banked until Aiden was so warm that he had to step outside several times. There'd been tittering and boisterous laughter, and the king had brought a minstrel who played the fiddle. Thankfully, they all decided that they needed a night of good sleep before dancing.

They'd dressed in silks and wigs for the dinner, making the Scots attendees look rough and poor in comparison. Not that he cared what these English prigs thought of him, but he wouldn't have Rebecca feel inferior to the painted, bejeweled elitists. He'd overheard the students talking about embellishing their best gowns for the Christmas dance that the king had announced they would have in three days' time. Meanwhile, the great hall would start sprouting tufts of holly and mistletoe that the ladies planned to gather tomorrow.

He walked silently along the corridor, extinguishing the candles but for the one outside Grey's room. All seemed silent, and he tread back to Scarlet's door. Was she already asleep? Perhaps he should sleep in the gate tower or in a room on the third floor. He braced his hands on either side of her door and bowed his head. Should he knock, or should he retreat?

Raising his knuckle, he tapped softly. *Tap, tap, tap.*

"Who is it?" Scarlet's voice came immediately, as if she'd been waiting.

"Aiden Campbell."

He heard the heavy board used to lock the door scrape along and thud softly on the floor. The door swung inward, and his breath caught.

Scarlet stood in her smock, the lace-edged neckline low to show her creamy skin. Hair unbound, it lay about her shoulders like a silk mantle. The fire glowed behind her, outlining her in gold. Without a word, she stepped forward into his chest, burying her face there. His arms came up to hold her against him, and he felt her fingers curl into his shirt.

"I thought…" Her voice seemed small, muffled against him. "You might not come."

Aiden's heart tightened, and he inhaled fully, smelling the light floral scent from her hair. He stroked one hand down her unbound curls and pulled her tighter against him. She wanted him there. It was true that he hadn't spoken to her during the dinner but sat taking in every detail he could about the threats within his walls. Could she think he didn't want to hold her?

"I am here if ye want me here," he whispered.

In answer, she tilted her face up, her eyes connecting with his as she pulled him inside the room and shut the door. When she moved to take up the board, he raised it out of her hands, lowering it across the door, locking the world out. He turned and stopped, watching her stand with her back to the fire. The glow illuminated the lush slopes of her body through the thin linen. He'd never seen anything so beautiful in his life.

As if words would break the peaceful spell that engulfed them, they came together in silence, each of them capturing each other's face in their palms. Lips melted against lips, opening and inviting as if a desperation twisted around them. Hands and arms stroked, giving pleasure and taking pleasure, Aiden guiding them to the luxurious bed. Gentle tugging became frantic as Scarlet loosened his kilt, dropping it to the floor, and her smock floated down as he slid it from her shoulders and over her round breasts.

Scarlet clung to him, and Aiden kept her close, loving her with hands and kisses until both of their bodies begged to become one. The fire crackled in the grate as they breathed and sighed and moaned low together, the sounds of skin sliding against skin and sheets finding a rhythm to rival the grandest melody.

The tight coil inside Aiden built higher as he moved within her. Scarlet writhed beneath him, and he looked down to see her hair curled like dark ribbons about the pillows, lips parted, and her beautiful eyes wide open. He kissed her, rocking them faster, as he stroked a hand down to their joining. She moaned, her eyes fluttering, though she kept her gaze connected to his.

"Aiden," she whispered, and he felt her body begin to convulse, pulling him over the edge.

He growled as the pleasure took him, sweeping through him as he pumped into Scarlet. "*Tha thu m'anam*," he said, his words coming like a vow. *You are mine. You are mine, Scarlet Worthington.* The oath echoed through his mind with his surging fire. Even if he didn't speak them in English, he was claiming her with his body.

She opened her eyes to stare again into his as the passion rolled through her. Did she know enough of his language to understand? Or was his inflection enough?

Aiden held her to him, kissing her and stroking her face. She met his gaze as he rolled them to one side. The firelight played across her features, and as her brows lowered into a tiny pinch, he felt his stomach tighten.

"I am yours?" she whispered.

*Bloody hell.*

# Chapter Fifteen

Scarlet knew enough Gaelic after living amongst Highlanders for nearly eight months to understand his words. These were the same words that her sister's lover and then husband had said to her. *You are mine.* It was even an oath spoken in wedding ceremonies.

She pushed up on one elbow, the cool air in the room a balm against the fever they'd just shared. "I am yours? What does that mean?" she asked, making sure to keep her voice neutral. Neutral because she didn't know how she felt about the words. A sense of excitement washed over the initial desire to yell that she didn't belong to anyone.

Aiden's gaze slid to the ceiling as he rolled onto his back, the sheet draped only partly across his toned body. "I would have ye be mine, Scarlet," he said finally. "And no one else's."

"Your what, exactly?" He didn't answer. She lay down on her back, glancing up at the ceiling. Did he want her for a mistress? The thought pinched through her. Wasn't that what she already was?

"'Twas just something one says during pleasure," she

murmured, deciding that perhaps it was better not to hear his answer.

"Och, Scarlet," Aiden said and turned on his side, his large hand cupping behind her head to roll her to face him. She watched the shadows play across his high cheekbones and rugged jaw, his nose sloping down with the smallest of bumps where she may have broken it. His thumb traced her cheek.

He frowned. "Could ye be content here, surviving the frigid winters, eating only what ye cook yourself, living in a cabin instead of a castle or on an estate, riding horses instead of in carriages? Could ye really be content here for your *whole* life?"

"Yes," she said, blinking at the moisture that ached behind her eyes.

He stared hard at her, and she watched him inhale. "If ye didn't have fear driving ye from England, Scarlet? Would ye choose to stay here rather than anywhere else in the world?" he asked and then pressed a finger to her lips. "Just think about it, think all around it, inside and outside of it, until ye are completely sure." He shook his head on the pillow. "I would know your true answer before I ask ye to be mine."

"You just told me I was yours," she reminded him. "You will also ask?"

A grin relaxed his lips. "'Tis very different, that. Telling ye that ye are mine doesn't mean anything if ye don't want to be mine. 'Tis the asking and answering that binds two people."

Marriage? He hadn't said it and hadn't spoken words of love, but it sounded as if he hinted of it. The idea shot like lightning through her blood, straight to her heart where it pounded. Instead of the slow flooding of nausea that used to accompany her thoughts of tying herself to a man, she only felt light as if it were... joy.

Wiggling closer, she nuzzled into his chest and peeked up at him. He leaned down, kissing her gently, arranging the blanket over her bared back. She closed her eyes, letting contentment infuse her limbs as she listened to his heart beat against her ear.

*Tap, tap, tap.*

For a brief moment, Scarlet thought Aiden's heart had rapped louder against his ribs. His body stiffened, and he rolled away. He stood out of the bed, his tight backside leading up into all that wonderful muscle shaping his back and shoulders. He didn't say anything but stared at the door.

*Tap, tap, tap.* "Scar, are you awake?"

Good bloody hell. Harry.

Aiden looked at her, questions in the pinch of his brows. Questions that ignited anger inside her. She shook her head. Did he really think she'd invited the devil to her bedchamber? Maybe she was reading his expression wrong.

Scarlet slid from the warm blankets, catching up her smock to throw it over her head. Not that being in her smock would make this scenario any less scandalous if Harry were to somehow see through the door. Aiden didn't seem to care so much about being completely naked. He grabbed his sword from off his kilt, sliding it from the scabbard slowly. The steel hummed as if it thirsted for English blood.

Scarlet moved around him to the door. "What do you want, Harry?"

"Open the door so we can talk." Her heart kicked inside her ribs as she heard him push against the door. Did he think her foolish enough to sleep without a lock between them?

"I will not. There is nothing else to say," she said.

"You may not have anything else to say, but I do."

"Not tonight," Scarlet said, glancing at Aiden. What would he do if Harry began revealing details of the night she'd fled Whitehall?

"Come now, Scar," Harry said. "Open the door, or I will find the key." He said it playfully, but it was still a threat.

"No key will open this door," she said. "Go back to your bed. I am undone and not going to discuss anything with you alone in the middle of the night, especially in my bedchamber."

He paused for a long moment. "What is Aiden Campbell to you?" he asked.

Scarlet looked at Aiden, but he didn't move. It was as if he were chiseled like the statue of David, although with a much more impressive male member.

Good Lord. If she told Harry that Aiden was her lover, Harry would tell the king, and the two of them might devise a way to rid the world of Aiden, or at least threaten him. If she said he was no one of consequence, the lie could plant a wedge between Aiden and her when they'd just forged something of a bond.

"What?" she asked.

"He watches you. Did you know that?" Harry asked. "At dinner and after, no matter where you were. He stayed away from you, but his gaze followed you when he thought no one was looking. I don't like it, Scar."

She almost laughed. Harry Covington warning her about a possible rogue. "Good night, Lord Covington," she said. "Your foolish tales do not interest me."

"You haven't answered my question," Harry said. "What is he to you? Answer me, and I will leave."

Scarlet flinched when Aiden moved toward the door, his one hand dropping to the bar to lift it. Was he going to throw open the door, exposing them as lovers? She ran over, shaking her head, and pressed his arm down. *No*, she mouthed.

She met Aiden's gaze as she spoke. "Aiden Campbell is an honorable man, bound by duty to protect this castle and our school, which includes me. He is a warrior of amazing strength, skill, and cunning. You would do well to stay far from him and curry his favor instead of his anger, Lord Covington."

Harry didn't say anything for a long pause. "But what is he to *you*, Scar?"

"He has become an ally and friend, someone I trust when the world has taught me to trust very few. I will say no more, so leave my door before you chance to wake the king down the corridor."

"I will let you sleep, my dearest pigeon," Harry said, the endearment grating on Scarlet's composure, but she didn't respond except to bare her teeth at the door. Aiden watched her and lowered his sword until the tip touched the wood floor.

"But," Harry said. "Beware. Every man has secrets, Scar, and a personal agenda. Trust is a dangerous thing."

She glared at the door. How dare the man, who'd broken so much trust with her, warn her of trusting anyone. If the door weren't between them, she'd likely shove her knee into his ballocks, punch him in his aristocratic nose as he writhed in pain, and stomp off.

She flinched slightly as Aiden lowered his hand on her shoulder, turning her away from the door. He rested his ear on the heavy oak for several moments and turned back to her. "He's walked away," he whispered.

Scarlet sunk to the edge of the bed and dropped her face in her hands. Everything was a tangle. She heard Aiden squat down before her.

He took her hands, making her raise her face. The anger had drained from his features, and he studied her. "I hate seeing ye afraid or shamed, Scarlet." His eyes asked the questions his mouth wouldn't form. He wanted to know what had happened to her, what Harry had done, how the king might be involved, what had driven her from the luxury of her former life to the wilds of Scotland.

She closed her eyes, unable to answer. "I… can't," she whispered, swallowing hard against the self-loathing in her throat. Aiden's thumb grazed her cheek, and she opened her eyes to see him move closer, placing a kiss across her lips.

Without another word, he climbed over her in the bed and pulled her down with him. Cradling her in his arms, he held her, just as she was. Even though he wanted an explanation, his silent comfort showed that he didn't require it. At least, not right now.

· · ·

*Twang.* The slam of steel upon steel vibrated up Aiden's arm as his blade met Lawrence's. Warrior's fire rushed through his veins as he sparred in the bailey, and each strike and parry made him feel better. Every word uttered by the bastard, Covington, last night, along with his silence through it all had wound itself into a tight tangle of fury within his gut. And fury could lead to mistakes, so he was burning off some of it with his men. Several of them stood off to the side, resting or nursing bruises he'd delivered when they weren't quick enough to evade his strikes.

Scarlet had explained her need to keep their…whatever their relationship was, a secret. He didn't agree that he needed protection, but if the king decided to despise the Campbells in any way, it could harm the clan, something Aiden couldn't allow to happen. Once again he was glad he wasn't the full-time chief.

Lawrence moved forward, his guttural yell showing the strength he was throwing into his attack, determined to thwart his teacher. But the lad was using a much heavier blade, which had tired his arms, giving Aiden the advantage, whether Lawrence knew it or not. Aiden ducked under the singing blade and spun away before Lawrence could raise his sword again. Aiden raised his knee high and kicked the young warrior away, making him fall on his arse, his claymore clanging as it hit the hard ground.

Kerrick walked over to help Lawrence up. "Aiden's sword was lighter than yours," Kerrick said, grasping the man's hand. "So, unless ye are twice as strong as your opponent, ye are going to be slower, so raising the sword over your head takes too much time and strength to bring it around."

Lawrence cursed and spit in the dirt, but he nodded as he walked to the group to drink some ale. Kerrick walked up to Aiden. "Ye seem more vicious than usual this morn," Kerrick said, offering him a leather flask.

The cool ale washed the dryness from Aiden's throat, and he wiped his mouth. "We have the bloody king of England sleeping under our roof, Kerrick. Why aren't ye more vicious this morn?"

Kerrick gave him a wry grin. "Aye, foking horrid, isn't it?" He looked about the bailey, spotting several of the students walking together with baskets of collected holly to decorate the great hall. "Even making us celebrate their Catholic holiday."

The whole Christmas celebration didn't bother Aiden. In fact, it gave Scarlet's students something to focus on. It was not knowing what King Charles wanted of Scarlet that made Aiden's skin crawl, not to mention the bastard, Covington and whatever he'd done to Scarlet in the past. Could the King really be hiding in the wilds for Christmas?

"Ready for another victim already?" Kerrick asked with a chuckle, and Aiden realized that he'd raised his sword, the muscles in his bicep contracting as his body tensed. He much preferred battle to this blasted intrigue. How did people spend all their lives playing at court politics without losing their minds, running through the gilded ballrooms and slaughtering everyone?

"Ye haven't had a turn yet," Aiden said to Kerrick as he watched the door open at the top of the steps.

Kerrick chuckled. "I know better than to go up against ye when ye're ornery. How about Covington?" He nodded toward the man who walked with the king down the steps, the queen and the two ladies following. No wig this morning, the man wore more rugged clothing. With Kerrick's elbow in the ribs, Aiden bowed his head briefly to the sovereign as they approached.

"Good morn," Covington said in greeting, his gaze slightly narrowed as he studied Aiden. "Exercising your muscles?"

"Aye," Kerrick answered when Aiden didn't. "We keep our men strong and skilled in case of attack. Might ye have a go of it, Lord Covington?" Kerrick nodded toward the slim sword the man had strapped to his side. "Or is your blade part of your costume?"

"Lord Covington is one of my best fencers," Charles answered with a smile, his brows raised. "I fear he would thwart you in seconds."

Covington cut the king a glance but smiled. "Flattery, I'm sure, Sire."

Charles laughed. "I'm the king. What use do I have of flattery? I speak the truth, Lord Covington." Charles threw out a beringed hand toward Aiden. "Show our Scottish cousins the skill of our English swordsmen."

Covington smiled, but it didn't reach his eyes. "I dare not say that I represent the skill of our country, but I have been known to beat an adversary or two."

"So modest," the king said loudly. "When you have beaten every man with a sword ever to be foolish enough to stand opposed to you."

"It is a different kind of battle," Covington said, sliding

his thinner sword from the scabbard at his side. "The English are trained to use the advantage of finesse and cleverness instead of brute force. The mind wins out over muscle every time." He smiled condescendingly at Aiden.

Aiden didn't disagree. He taught his men to use their minds in battle, but having the strength to cut a man in two certainly helped. It was the condescending way that Covington alluded that Scotsmen didn't use their minds, or had no minds to use, that made Aiden lift his sword.

"Join us, Covington. Show me how ye use your mind to slay me," Aiden said.

The woman, Jacqueline Beckett, looked worried. Her frown reminded him of another Beckett. "But Lord Covington has been riding in a coach for a fortnight. Surely he is not up to the rigors of swordplay," she said.

Covington's gaze slid to the row of warriors along the wall, all of whom looked a bit ragged after training. Did the dandy think Aiden was fairly spent since sweat darkened his short hair and shone on his neck? Stamina was something that all the Campbell warriors honed. Battles could drag on, and his men wouldn't lose their lives because they grew sloppy with exhaustion. At least not before the enemy did.

"I am fit as usual," Covington said and removed his long outer coat to hand to the lady, leaving him in a shirt, inner jacket, and his short pants over thick hose. "And you, Campbell, have been warned."

Aiden took one more swig of the ale in his flask and handed it to a cheered Kerrick. His men seemed instantly lifted as they came forward with the English guards to form a loose circle around the two of them. He'd fought English before, though mostly poorly trained infantrymen. He had learned to watch his opponents before they even began, and what he knew of Harry Covington, as he walked toward him, was that he led with his right foot, seemed to have a stiff left shoulder, and was cocky enough to think Aiden would be easily beat.

As they faced one another, Aiden noticed that some of the students had come out to stand at the top of the steps, Scarlet amongst them. But an audience didn't hinder Aiden. He'd learned to perform while judged unworthy from an early age. The fact he was considered the expected loser by the English around him honed his concentration to a knife's sharpness. Harry Covington was his prey, and it was only the two of them right now.

Covington took two steps inward, scraping his foot along the pebbly dirt, one hand behind him and his thinner sword before him. No doubt the weapon was sharp and would move quickly, its weight less than that of Aiden's. Aiden preferred the feel of his sword, the grasp familiar, an extension of his arm that he'd carried since he was a lad, a Campbell heirloom. A dark grin expanded his mouth. His father's sword would never fall to an Englishman.

*Clang.* Aiden blocked the man's strike and felt only a slight vibration from the weapon. Sharp and quick, but not very powerful. The men around the circle cheered as he and Covington moved around each other, deflecting and striking.

The Englishman was learning about Aiden just as he was learning about Covington. No doubt, Covington was clever and had studied the art well. But how often had the man needed to use his skill to defend his life? When one's life was on the line, the battle didn't follow rules.

Using his strength to keep the blade level, Aiden sliced his sword around, catching the button on Covington's waistcoat in an unanticipated strike. The man spun away, sweat starting to break out on his smooth face. "Nice," Covington said, his teeth clenched. Without giving Aiden time to rest, he ran forward, but one after another, Aiden blocked the man's strikes, back and forth.

They continued for several minutes, and although Aiden's arm was beginning to protest after fighting six other men, it continued to work as it should. Covington got in a slice that cut Aiden's shirt, bringing a line of red to the surface. The English cheered, and Covington smiled. "To the first blood?" he asked, indicating Aiden's arm.

"Nay," Aiden said and caught his sword with his left hand. "To the last drop of blood." He stepped toward Covington, who slashed defensively, but instead of blocking, Aiden ducked, rolling over his own head along the ground. As his legs came around, he used his booted feet to slam into the Englishman's shins, betting the man's surprise would keep him from slashing down before he was propelled backward.

Covington went flying, his balance completely shattered. He landed on his arse, his arms went out, his chest wide open. Aiden had continued his momentum and leaped to his feet before the Englishman could even take a breath. With both hands grasped around the hilt of his sword, Aiden braced his boots on either side of the sprawled man. With a ferocious yell, he raised his sword, thrusting it downward toward the man's chest.

A woman screamed as the wind gusted, driving a sudden swirl of snowflakes about them. Aiden stood, everything about him as hard as the granite-formed mountains of the Highlands around them. The point of his mighty claymore just touched Covington's waistcoat. The man's eyes bulged with surprise or fear or both, and Aiden held his gaze for a long moment.

"Lo there, Campbell," the king called, starting to come down.

Before he could reach him, Aiden lifted the tip of his sword away, stepped back, and lowered his arm for Covington to grasp. To all who watched, it looked like a goodwill gesture. Covington grasped his arm, allowing Aiden to lift him from the dirt.

"Fairly beat, though not adherent to any form of civil rules," Covington said. "But next time—"

Aiden drew the man in, speaking directly into his ear. He smelled of perfume. "If ye ever try to enter Scarlet's bedchamber again, I will skewer ye to the frozen ground." Without a glance, Aiden released the man with a slight shove and strode toward the wall, where Lawrence smiled and held out a fresh flask.

Leaning against the rough wall, Aiden wondered if not bowing to the king and queen after knocking the sovereign's champion on his arse would get him beheaded. The king frowned, and the woman, Jacqueline, fluttered around Covington, who stared at him, his eyes narrowed. At the top of the steps, Aiden saw Scarlet press a finger to her lips like he had done the night before when he asked her to think about her loyalty to Scotland. When she took her finger away, she smiled softly. She said something to her students, who clustered around her, and they all filed back into the keep.

"Phenomenal," Kerrick said under his breath, grasping Aiden's shoulder. "Worth ruining a shirt, I say." Aiden turned back to the bailey to see Covington look from the steps to Aiden. His aristocratic smile was back in place along with his rich coat, but his stare had hardened.

Aye, the man knew now. Aiden Campbell was definitely his enemy.

• • •

Green ropes of pine and holly hung in rolling swags across the walls of the great hall. Kirstin had enlisted several of the younger warriors to bring ladders and hooks to hang them. Holly and mistletoe adorned the crossed swords and Campbell clan shield above the hearth, and a long oak tree trunk lay against the wall to be slowly burned over the twelve nights of Christmas.

Many of the Campbells had been raised during the oppressive reign of Oliver Cromwell, who had outlawed the holiday completely. Even now, the solid Presbyterian government in Scotland did not acknowledge the holiday, despite their monarch's encouragement. So Scarlet found herself teaching her students about the basic Christmas customs, which they seemed to embrace quickly. Even Cat, who seemed to despise anything English.

Having finished laying pine boughs and ribbon along the mantel, Scarlet returned to the mosaic she'd begun on the stained wall. The blue piece that Aiden had stuck off to the side sat in the middle of a lovely, full rose. With all the insanity, she wondered if he'd noticed.

Lord, how her hands had turned numb and her legs weak as she watched him battle against Harry in the bailey. Harry was a well-known swordsman at court, earning him favors and accolades from men and women alike. Yet Aiden had bested him, not with brute strength, which he had in abundance, but with cleverness and agility.

She smiled and ran the pad of her fingertip over the blue piece. Aiden had thought she would remove it at first chance. She felt the tension in her face relax into a small smile as she built petals in deep red out from it. Even though one did not see blue inside roses, that didn't mean she couldn't create a unique rendition.

"What a creative art piece," Jacqueline Beckett said as she came up next to Scarlet. "Your student, Alana Campbell, said that these pieces had been her grandmother's and mother's china and pottery before the evil traitors shattered it. And here you are, making something lovely from the pieces."

The woman spoke without a hint of judgment, just open admiration. Scarlet slid a glance at her and then back to the new rose on which she worked. "The pieces were too beautiful to throw out, and we need to cover the burn marks on the walls. I hope to find someone to teach my students to create tapestries, so we can eventually replace the ones that burned."

"Oh?" Jacqueline said, excitement in her voice. "I've worked on several tapestries at my grandmother's house. She felt that one's attention and fingers must always be engaged to prevent Satan from leading one astray. Perhaps I could help your students get started during our stay."

Scarlet studied the beautiful young woman. She was trim and tall, with light-colored hair and blue eyes. Aiden said he didn't know her, yet the name said otherwise. "That would be...helpful. Thank you," Scarlet said. "Would you care to place some of the leaves and thorns?"

"I would like that very much," Jacqueline said, going to the table to retrieve some green and brown shards.

"Just a bit of the glue should hold it. I will fill in the cracks with plaster once I am finished with the entire design," Scarlet said, watching Jacqueline's slender fingers work. Had those fingers touched Aiden? She dropped her gaze. No, he would not outright lie to her.

"Lady Beckett," Scarlet said, raising her eyes. She waited until the woman looked at her. "Do you know Aiden Campbell?" The woman didn't say anything, but pink stained her cheeks. Scarlet stared into her blue eyes without blinking. "Although I haven't seen you speak, you two spend time looking at each other."

The woman swallowed, her finger coming up to twirl around some hair at her neckline. "I know *of* Aiden Campbell," she said slowly, as if choosing her words. "Though we have never met before now."

Relief uncoiled inside Scarlet so intensely that she found herself lowering onto a stool nearby. "Oh," she murmured.

"What then do you know *of* Aiden Campbell?"

Jacqueline's finger twirled her hair quicker, and her gaze scanned the room, where several of the Roses worked to finish the decorations before their class in the library. "My mother knew him."

"Is your mother still in London?" Scarlet asked, watching her.

"No, she died when I was young. I lived with my grandmother in Nottingham. I was raised by the same nurses that my mother had, so they would tell me about her growing up."

"How did she know him?"

Jacqueline picked up another piece and set it in a small blob of glue on the wall. "'Twas before I was born, and I've been asked not to speak of it."

Scarlet frowned. "By whom?"

Jacqueline exhaled a gust toward the mosaic. "By everyone, especially the queen and Lord Covington. Well, and my grandmother."

She turned a hastily stitched together smile toward Scarlet. "The queen misses you at court, Lady Worthington."

"Please, call me Scarlet. Even my students use my given name."

Her smile turned authentic. "And I am just Jacqueline, or Jacey, though I suppose not before the king or queen." She stuck another piece of green where a leaf might grow out of the vine. "Queen Catherine would like you to return with us to Whitehall."

Scarlet's whole body stilled. "I…" It took her a moment to find her breath. "I am committed to helping my sister run the school."

"I understand the draw of this beautiful land," Jacey said wistfully. "But it is so far from everything you know." She glanced at Scarlet. "Your heritage and customs. Like

Christmas," she said, indicating the hall. "I would feel so sad not to celebrate the birth of our savior."

"We are celebrating," Scarlet said. "Heritage and customs can be brought up here, where I'm learning about new customs like Beltane. Have you ever danced around a fire wearing a flower crown before?"

Jacqueline giggled. "No. My grandmother would call me a heathen and lock me in the church."

As much as Scarlet wanted to despise the young woman who kept drawing Aiden's glances, she rather liked her. "Well, if you decide to stay up here at the Highland Roses School, you will be able to celebrate Beltane without being made to repent."

Jacey's face lit up, and she clasped her hands. "I would like that."

"You are welcome," Scarlet said, standing again. "You could be our tapestry instructor, and I'm sure you have many other skills to pass along to ladies since you've spent time at court."

Her smile faded somewhat. "Lord Covington mentioned, though, that he may want me to return to court," she said. "If he wishes it, I must return." Her cheeks pinkened again. Was the woman fond of Harry? He was handsome, charming, and wealthy, the perfect scoundrel to lure in young damsels.

Scarlet curled her fingers around Jacqueline's arm. The young woman looked down at it and back up to Scarlet's gaze. "Lady Beckett, Jacey… Lord Covington is not what he seems to be." She lowered her voice. "You would do well to keep your heart far from him."

Jacqueline frowned as they stared at one another. "Thank you, Lady Worthington," she said, her voice soft but formal. "I appreciate your candor, but I have nothing to fear from such a fine man. I understand your unease, since he did not offer for your hand in marriage, but I am quite versed in modesty and patience. He runs a merry dance for certain. I will respond in kind."

Her gaze dropped back to Scarlet's hand, which she let drop, and Jacqueline walked away.

*Did not offer for your hand in marriage*? What exactly was that bastard telling people at court?

# Chapter Sixteen

"Where have ye been?" Kerrick asked Aiden as he caught him in the circular stairwell on his way down from the third floor. Aiden wasn't about to tell him that he'd been rummaging through Nathaniel Worthington's room.

"Has something happened?" Aiden asked, following Kerrick below.

Kerrick pulled him behind the stairs into the shadows. "William followed one of the English guards who rode out alone all the way to Castle Menzies. William pretended to visit someone in the village, and when he returned to the castle, the English soldier had left. Edgar Menzies's son seems to be taking the reins of the clan. He said the soldier was asking for Finlay, by name."

"Finlay? How the hell does he know Finlay Menzies?" Aiden murmured.

"Then, when William rode back, he saw the soldier discussing something with Harry Covington in the bailey, but when he walked nearby, pretending to collect something, they parted."

Aiden rubbed his fist against his bottom lip. "Covington knows Finlay Menzies." He focused on Kerrick. "And this soldier didn't ask Edgar's son for anything once he discovered he was in charge?"

Kerrick shook his head. "Seems Finlay was the only one the man wanted to speak with."

Aiden scratched his jaw. The Menzies chief, Finlay's father, had never seemed to fear English encroachment, and his son had continued to live serenely without even a wall around his castle for protection. As if neither of them worried that the English might try to take their castle or lands.

"I wonder if Finlay was friends with Captain Cross." Captain Cross, his head currently being delivered to England, was the English captain in charge of the company north of Killin. He was also a traitor, planning to assassinate the king at Finlarig. But he was dead, and Finlay was in exile from his clan.

"If he was working with Cross, and Harry Covington knows Finlay…" Kerrick left the rest hanging in the darkness of the alcove.

"Then Harry Covington might be a player in the plot to kill the king," Aiden whispered.

"Bloody hell," Kerrick said. "Speaking such without proof could get a man thrown into prison, Aiden. Even with proof." Panic made the man's voice higher pitched.

Aiden exhaled, frowning at Kerrick. "I'm not an imbecile."

Kerrick raked fingers through his hair. "Ballocks, having all these English dandies around is making my nerves itch." He scratched at his arm as if he had hives. "A man can't fart or belch without fearing he'll be called to task for insulting someone who could order his ballocks cut off."

Aiden looked upward and then to Kerrick. "I'll defend ye if the queen orders your ballocks cut off for farting before her."

Kerrick snorted. "This will be the most uptight holiday Finlarig has ever seen. And if ye bring up treason and assassination, it might be the bloodiest, too."

"Makes one think," Aiden said softly. "If we let the English kill off their own Catholic king, will we be celebrated or blamed?"

"Blamed," Kerrick answered without hesitation. "The Scots are always blamed." He sucked in a quick breath. "Maybe that's why Covington convinced the king and queen to come up to Finlarig."

Aiden nodded slowly, as possible plots started to become clear.

· · ·

"You think Harry wants the king dead?" Scarlet asked as she slid back on the pillow to look at Aiden in the darkness shrouding them. Her hair tumbled about them, the bedclothes lay skewed, and the fire had burned low, but neither of them felt cold after their passion.

"He sent someone to look for Finlay Menzies," Aiden answered, reaching forward to capture one of her curls between his finger and thumb as if testing its silkiness. He held it to his nose and inhaled. Scarlet twined her legs back with his under the blankets he'd pulled over them.

"Was Finlay linked to Cross and his plotters?" she asked.

Aiden shrugged, letting her curl slip away. "It would explain why the Menzies never worried about the English so close by when Cross was in charge." His palm stroked the skin down her side from her breast to her hip, where he grasped it gently in a possessive hold. She loved how he touched her so boldly. Even though they hid their attraction before others, once they shut her door, their fire burned all propriety and inhibitions to ash.

Scarlet exhaled, worry stopping her from pressing closer. "I think Lady Beckett's heart is at stake with Harry Covington."

Aiden pushed onto his elbow. "She's in love with him?"

Scarlet shook her head, watching Aiden closely. Neither Jacey or Aiden admitted knowing one another, but there was a connection. "She didn't go so far as to say that, but I fear she is being drawn in by his charm, and that would be dangerous for her."

She knew Aiden wanted to ask her about Harry, but his mouth remained tight as he studied her in the dim light of the waning fire. Scarlet laid her hand on his chest, stroking the muscles there under the light sprinkling of hair. She gazed into his eyes. "She says she hadn't met you before but knows *of* you."

"Ye were questioning her? About me?"

Lord. Scarlet felt like she walked a thin brick wall with Aiden. They both had secrets, secrets they wanted to know about the other. But the idea of giving voice to them, even when they could be exposed at any moment, made her want to curl in and hide away.

"I asked her if she knew you since the two of you seem to have some sort of connection, and she keeps looking at you." Scarlet lay back on her pillow to stare at the ceiling beams. "I was jealous, I suppose. She is beautiful."

She turned her head. "Was her mother just as beautiful?"

"I…" He started and stopped. "I'm not sure who she is yet, and that's the truth. The woman I knew didn't have a daughter like her." He leaned over her. "Let me figure this out. It has nothing to do with ye and me being together."

She wanted to argue. If he dreamt of an Englishwoman, who he may have loved enough for her to worm her way into his dreams, then she did have something to do with the two of them. And even though Jacqueline was too old to be Aiden's child, he may have had an affair with her mother years ago.

She gave him a small nod and smiled. "I will try," she said and lowered onto her pillow. "Now we must sleep for the Christmas ball will be tonight, and I expect you to dance with me."

"Even with the updated dance sheets that the queen brought with her, I haven't practiced," he said.

"You are a mystery, Aiden Campbell." She ran a finger along his jawline, smiling. "A Highland warrior who knows what a dance sheet is." She shook her head against the pillow.

"I've been told," Aiden said, "that to the English lady, the ballroom is a battleground. And a Highland warrior must be prepared for every battle."

Scarlet laughed, then narrowed her eyes. Who had given him such an accurate description? The secret Lady Beckett? "You are a very well-versed Highlander indeed." She reached up behind Aiden's neck to pull him down for one more kiss.

• • •

Aiden tied the cravat a third time around his neck as he stared into the mirror sitting in Nathaniel's room. He didn't feel guilty at all about rummaging through the Englishman's clothes. Scarlet's brother was down in London delivering heads to a monarch who was right now causing havoc amongst the Campbell clan as they tried to ready themselves for a bloody royal ball. And hell if Aiden was going to walk into it looking like a "homespun beggar."

Cravat tied in a suitable knot at his throat, Aiden studied himself in the mirror. He foking couldn't believe he was wearing English garb. He grunted at his image and stretched his shoulders, which felt a bit tight in Nathaniel's long coat. Otherwise, the men were of similar build and size. Even Nathaniel's tall leather boots fit Aiden's feet. The short pants were the slimmest Aiden could find in Nathaniel's trunk other than the rougher work trousers. These were of dark silk and cinched an inch above the top edge of the boots.

He tried on the one plumed hat Nathaniel had in his chest and discarded it. He'd go bareheaded rather than look like an ornamental bird. The rest of the costume was tolerable, and the rich fabric and cut made him look more like he might belong at court, perhaps as a warrior for hire, certainly not an aristocrat who spent his days reading poetry and beguiling ladies with false flattery.

Standing tall, he put his arms out and swayed, his feet finding the steps he'd seen on the dance sheet that Queen Catherine had shared with the students. During the first thirteen years of his life, his mother had shown him and Rebecca, though she was six years his junior, how to read dance steps and practice them. It wasn't something he ever thought to use again, but then Scarlet Worthington had come along.

*Bloody hell.* He stopped in mid step, letting his arms fall to his sides, fists clenched. He stared at his reflection. *Look what I've become.* He frowned, raising his hand to the cravat he'd just tied, ready to jerk it loose. But he stopped, glancing at his best kilt and sash on the bed. Homespun, even if he wasn't a beggar.

He wasn't ashamed of being a Scot nor living in a rural village. He loved the hills of wild heather, the soaring mountains and crystal-clear waterfalls. Sweet air fed the hum of life around him as he walked through the forests surrounding Killin. But tonight wasn't about any of that. It was showing Scarlet that he could be refined and still be a Highlander. That she could remain in Scotland and not fear that she'd only be surrounded by rough, fighting men in bloodstained and soil-smeared clothing. The English peacocks would be parading around tonight in their finery, and Aiden wanted to make certain Scarlet wasn't embarrassed by him.

Since when did he worry overmuch about what a lass thought of him? He rubbed his smooth chin where he'd shaved his beard away. Scarlet Worthington wasn't just some lass. Even though they still didn't trust each other with everything, he absolutely didn't want her to go back to England.

Aiden opened the door and, before he could change his mind, walked into the empty corridor to descend. Musicians had already begun a festive tune below, and the sound of conversation whispered up the steps. The whole town of Killin and surrounding Campbells had been invited. From the sound of it, most everyone was taking the opportunity to meet the king and queen.

He strode through the archway into the great hall. Half the village was already there, even Craig wearing his cleanest shirt and kilt. The ornery cur would surely curse him for his English clothes, but Aiden didn't care. Where was Scarlet? He glanced around the room but didn't see her.

"I thought ye were bloody jesting," Kerrick said as he strode over, a huge grin on his face as he looked Aiden up and down. "Your own da would flip in his grave to see ye so."

In actuality, Aiden's da would be the only one to understand his costume. He wasn't going to lose Scarlet to England without a fight. And since a fight with swords could cost the Campbell clan by labeling them traitors to the crown, he had to exchange his claymore for short trousers, hose, and a cravat.

"Hold your tongue," Aiden said, his voice low in warning, though it did little to stop the chuckle from escaping Kerrick's wide grin. He pierced the man with a sharp gaze. "And what do ye plan to do to keep Scarlet from returning with them to England?"

Kerrick's smile dropped. "Is she planning to leave?" His gaze scanned the room.

Aiden slid his hand to the sword strapped to his side, its familiar feel the only thing keeping him from going above to change. "She hasn't said, but I know the royals must want her to go back with them."

"What the bloody hell are ye wearing?" Craig asked as he clomped over.

"He's trying to keep Scarlet in Scotland," Kerrick answered before Aiden could open his mouth.

Aiden gave the man a hard elbow in the side, making Kerrick double over, clutching it. "Just showing these prigs that we are not some homespun country beggars," Aiden said.

"What Englishman did ye strip to get the clothes?" Craig asked, wiping a hand self-consciously over his hair that was actually combed for the first time that Aiden could remember.

"Nathaniel Worthington left these behind," Aiden said, his gaze going to the two chairs that had been set up for the king and queen. They'd been decorated with holly and velvet to look like small thrones, and the monarchs sat serenely, clothed in silk, wigs, and jewels. No doubt, Grey's da was bellowing at Heaven's gates as he watched the king hold court in the heart of Finlarig and Campbell territory.

More Campbells came in through the entryway, even Donald Campbell from Balloch Castle. Everyone wore their finest clothes, some bringing gifts for the royal couple. Aiden watched the king's mistress, Louise, walk with Jacqueline Beckett toward Harry Covington. The pompous ass stood by the hearth in a rich, yet less ridiculous costume than the king. Both of the Englishmen wore long wigs of dark curls.

Aiden's gaze slid to Jacqueline. Kerrick still hadn't discovered the woman's birthday, but the resemblance was so close that he knew she must be related to Rebecca and him in some way. He'd caught her looking at him but didn't know if she knew her lineage or not. If he could get her away from Covington, he'd ask her tonight.

Music played, and a line formed to present the monarchs with greetings and small gifts. As people exited the line, they moved over to the bounty that the king's cook, along with the help of Molly and some of the Highland Rose students, had prepared. Venison pies, roast goose, rabbit stew, braided breads, apple pudding, and of course tarts, since the Highland Roses School was known for them.

Craig began to cough into his fist. "Holy Mother Mary," Kerrick whispered as he stared in the same direction as the old blacksmith. Stepping out from the archway from the stairs, almost as one body, walked the students of the Highland Roses School. Only Molly and Izzy seemed to be missing from the group. The ladies wore flowing gowns that they'd been embellishing under Rebecca's superior guidance for the last few days, as fast as their fingers could move. But he hardly noticed the ribbons on their gowns for his gaze fastened on the one woman who led them all. Scarlet.

Her lovely dark auburn curls and creamy skin would catch anyone's attention, but it was what she wore that stopped his breath. The plaid design was familiar to all the Scots in the room for it was the green and blue lines of Campbell hunting plaid. A lace-edged smock came above the low neckline of the bodice. The plaid material draped down in a V to sit upon the purple petticoat, the top plaid skirt cinched up with a brooch on one side. Both layers flowed into wide skirts that shifted around her as she walked with the grace of royalty, her head held high as she displayed the Campbell colors.

"Seems someone else is using her costume to make a statement tonight," Kerrick said.

As if a silent command had been given, the stacked rows of Scarlet's students stepped out from the formation behind her. The ladies walked in graceful divergence as if their steps were part of a dance. Everyone in the room turned to watch, but Scarlet's gaze slid around the room until it landed on Aiden.

Connected, they stared at one another. Her gaze ran down

his costume, making her eyes widen. He grinned, stepping away from the wall to walk toward her, but before he could reach her, Covington came up. He took her arm, bending to say something to Scarlet that made her turn, though her smile became a mere mask. Aiden stopped in the middle of the floor, watching the bastard lead her to the monarchs sitting on their thrones. When Aiden glanced away, he realized that he stood in the middle of the floor like an abandoned suitor, and everyone stared his way. He inhaled long and turned toward the table. Hopefully someone had tapped the whisky.

Hamish stood by the table, chewing one of the tarts. He sucked in through his teeth. "Och, Aiden. I'd say Covington just sliced ye again." He shook his fat head, his smile spreading his sticky beard.

"Hold your tongue," Aiden said, but once again, his threats were answered by more smiling and a chuckle. *Mo chreach*. He wanted to meet the Englishman on a battlefield of mud and men, not silks and wigged prigs.

His hands curled into fists against his silk trousers. *Fok propriety*. He was walking over to her; proper manners be damned. He was just an ignorant Scot anyway, a brute from a savage land. But Scarlet had draped herself in his colors. His heart pounded behind the walls of his chest. Was she showing her decision? The one he'd asked her to make after thinking all around it?

Halfway across, Jacqueline Beckett met him. "Sir Aiden," she said, stepping up to him. "Might we take a turn about the room?"

Aiden glanced toward Scarlet as she spoke with Queen Catherine. Scarlet looked over to him, and her brows pinched slightly, but she continued to chat and finally turned her full attention to the queen. Jacqueline placed her hand on his arm, and Aiden raised it slightly as a gentleman would do. Years of training as a lad were being resurrected, yet this was no game with Rebecca before the sharp eyes of his mother before a simple hearth. This was a battle.

He led her toward the entryway. "You look quite handsome in English garb," she said.

He cleared his throat, knowing dozens of eyes were trained on him. "Ye look quite handsome as well, Lady Beckett."

"Thank you," she said demurely and nodded to Alana as they passed. Jacqueline looked up at Aiden. "There are many fine ladies this evening. I dare say that Lady Worthington has taught the Highland Rose School students to shine."

Aiden looked down at Jacqueline as they stopped near the dark entryway. The crowds had all entered, and no one stood near. "Aye, she has. The ladies in the Highlands can shine just as bright as the ladies down in London. We but have other endeavors to keep our hands busy on a daily basis, endeavors to keep us warm, fed, and safe here."

She made a small humming sound and nodded. "Yes, the set of tasks to keep one sheltered, fed, and protected here in the wild beauty of Scotland is vastly different from what I am required to do down in London at court."

The small catch in her voice made Aiden study her. Gone was the confident smile. It was replaced by a slightly haunted look, similar to the one Scarlet wore when speaking of her time at court. A protective feeling came over Aiden, and he leaned slightly toward Jacqueline's ear.

"Who are ye, Lady Beckett?" She turned big eyes up to him. "And why have ye come up here to Finlarig?" he asked.

He watched her upper teeth perch on her lower lip before it was quickly released, as if her training had almost abolished the habit of showing her worry.

"I have come here," she whispered, "to trade myself for Lady Scarlet."

# Chapter Seventeen

Scarlet barely heard the queen's question about local herbs. When she'd walked into the great hall, her stomach had flipped when she'd seen Aiden dressed like an Englishman. For a brief moment, she thought someone had forced him to switch out of his Highland dress, but nothing short of threatening to slaughter his clan would force Aiden Campbell to do anything he didn't want to do. Surely, he wouldn't dress for the king. Had he dressed in the short trousers and hose for her?

"I say," King Charles said, catching Scarlet's attention when Queen Catherine touched her hand. "You certainly look as if you fit into the Scottish life well enough." He eyed her gown, which the Roses had helped her alter from one of Rebecca's.

"Yes, your majesty, I have. I find it quite comfortable here." She bowed her head slightly, though she slid a glance to where Lady Jacqueline had taken Aiden's arm. Damn Harry for dragging her away from Aiden to talk to the queen.

"We miss you at court," Harry said, standing beside her,

though Scarlet refused to look at him.

Instead, she smiled at the queen. "How you must miss your homeland of Portugal, and yet you have found a new life in England."

"That is true," Catherine said. "I would not return now."

"And you've brought such rich and wonderful things to England," Scarlet continued. "Like drinking tea. What would I do without my morning tea leaves brewing?" She laughed softly as if she were at ease, though nothing done before these people was performed with ease. Especially after she'd seen what occurred behind closed doors.

Harry moved so that he was once again in Scarlet's peripheral view. "Queen Catherine would remain in England out of duty to her husband and king as well," he said.

Scarlet smiled at the queen and touched her hand to her heart, which thumped beneath the Campbell tartan of her bodice. "Since my heart has turned to the good people of Killin and the Highland Roses School, it is fortunate that I do not have such duty to perform. I will remain here until I die."

The king frowned, his gaze going to Harry and then back to Scarlet. "That is not what we wish at all. Without you at court, our poor Lord Covington practically mopes about the halls. None of the ladies have been able to lead him out of his melancholy, although they try. I, therefore, request that you return with us."

His words squeezed inside Scarlet's chest as if they were fingers clutching her heart, a bird caught in a monster's grasp. "Sire," she said, bowing her head. "I am flattered, but there has never been an understanding between Lord Covington and myself. My brother has not entered into any contract for my hand, and I am choosing to live north in Scotland as an independent woman."

The king waved his hand as if he could brush aside all that she just said, all her desires and freedom. "Lord Covington," he said, leaning to the side to see around Scarlet. "Make your heart known or lose your lady love forever."

He cleared his throat, and Scarlet felt her chin numb as her heartbeat soared in growing panic. Just then, the musicians started up a jaunty tune for a country dance. "Forgive me," Scarlet said loudly. "But I promised Sir Aiden Campbell the first country line dance." She curtsied low.

"Why... Yes, of course," the Queen said.

Scarlet could have kissed her for giving her permission to leave before the king could deny it. "We ladies are nothing if we do not keep our promises." The queen's gaze met Scarlet's, holding her for a moment, to make certain she picked up on the queen's warning. Scarlet nodded. She would make no promises that she could not keep, else find herself forced. Freedom was so fleeting as to be nonexistent at court.

Scarlet curtsied once more and turned, completely ignoring Harry as she walked away. She kept her stride measured and slow, even though she felt like a bird escaping a golden cage. Striding by herself across the floor where couples paired up in two long lines, Scarlet kept a direct route toward where Aiden stood in the shadows with the beautiful young Jacey. Aiden was staring down at the woman, his face a mix of confusion and shock.

Scarlet didn't care if she was intruding. "Pardon," she said briskly. "But I believe the first country line dance was promised to me. Aiden?"

His glance slid from Jacey to Scarlet, and his hesitation lit a fire inside Scarlet's middle. When she'd seen his costume, she'd thought he'd dressed to impress her, but perhaps he hoped to catch the eye of another. Yet, here Scarlet stood waiting, dressed from head to toe in Campbell colors, swearing to the king that she would stay in the Highlands.

Certainly, though, Aiden wouldn't just turn away from her after their intimate nights together. "Aiden?" she said, leaving all her questions in the inflection of that one word.

"Aye," he said, giving Jacey a nod and turning to Scarlet. "The dance."

Jacey looked pale, blinking her eyes as if she'd been stung by a slight. She forced her lips into a serene smile as Aiden left her to accompany Scarlet. His arm was firm, his fist clenched. Neither of them spoke, and he left her across from him in the line beside Kirstin, who danced opposite Kerrick.

Kirstin's cheeks were pink, and she smiled. "What a bloody wonderful ball," she whispered to Scarlet and then giggled, a finger to her lips. She was either having great success flirting with the men or she'd been drinking the whisky. Both should require a gentle reprimand from the school's matron, but at present, all Scarlet cared about was discovering what was going on between Aiden and Jacey while keeping herself from being tricked into promising to return to England.

Pairs of dancers stood across from one another, alternating man and woman along the two lines. Several of the English guards were participating, dancing opposite the ladies of the school. Of the Scots, only Aiden, Kerrick, and Lawrence were brave enough to step in.

The musicians started a strong tempo, and the ladies curtsied while the men bowed. Aiden looked natural, almost as if he belonged in a ballroom in his fine English garb. They came together, palms flattening against each other's. "Where did you find the clothes?" Scarlet asked, but he didn't have time to answer before stepping back. They turned toward the couple to their right, and Kerrick smiled at Scarlet while Aiden stared into the beaming face of Kirstin. "What fun," Scarlet heard her say.

"Something is wrong," Kerrick said as they stepped forward. His gaze passed between Scarlet and Aiden, but then they stepped back to face their first partners.

Scarlet met Aiden's palm again. It was warm and large,

and she couldn't help but remember the feel of it skimming the skin of her naked back. "I borrowed them from your brother," Aiden said, and she realized he was talking about the clothing.

Down the line, the couples met and retreated then turned to meet and back away from the dancers to their right. As Aiden came close again, he spoke low, his eyes shifting to take in the line of people. "I feel a noose tightening around us, but I cannot tell who is pulling it," he said and stepped back.

Palms together, Aiden and Scarlet turned. "'Tis how every ball I attended in England felt," she said. "I call it social imprisonment." They parted with the steps.

The top couple in line, at the far end, strode separately along the outside toward the bottom. As the end couple, Scarlet and Aiden became the second from the bottom, and they were to turn and greet their new neighbors. Scarlet's stomach tightened as Harry grinned at her from opposite Louise. One glance at Aiden and Scarlet was certain blood would be forthcoming.

Stepping forward, she met Aiden's gaze with a warning expression and a little shake of her head. Harry was goading Aiden here on the dance floor, trying to get him to lose control so that the king would intervene. The king would surely choose Harry's side, throwing Aiden out of the ball.

Louise passed close to Scarlet, her whisper coming at the right moment to pierce Scarlet's ear. "You are still desired at court." Louise met Aiden's palm, and they rotated, stepping back into place. Her words shot like poison through Scarlet's veins, yet somehow her feet continued to move.

Harry stepped forward to press his palm against Scarlet's. His words came low near her ear as they turned. "The king could do great things for your sister's school."

She turned away from him without meeting his gaze and

lifted her eyes to Aiden. They stepped together. "What the bloody hell are they saying to ye?" Aiden asked, his words loud so that Harry, Louise, as well as Kirstin and Kerrick surely heard him.

Just then, Alana and one of the English guards came down to the bottom, and she and Aiden were once again paired with Kerrick and Kirstin, at least for a few minutes. Kirstin, having picked up on the tension, wasn't quite as excited, but she was still much more pleasant than dealing with Louise.

As the king's mistress stepped into Aiden again, Scarlet heard her say, "What a strong figure you cut in your English costume. 'Tis a shame I can't bring you home with me. *Oui?*" she said in her mild French accent.

Scarlet's belly churned. The royals would gobble up everyone to bring home as playthings.

"Think of how many ladies would be begging to attend your sister's school if the king sanctioned it," Harry said before Scarlet retreated with the musician's set rhythm.

Anger added to the tightness in her stomach, making the food she'd eaten rise. As Louise passed her to turn, the woman opened her pouty lips. "Mademoiselle, think of the riches and luxuries you will have if you return to court."

So, Harry was trying to bribe her away from Scotland while Louise was trying to lure her toward England, the two working together. They moved down the row through another pairing with Kerrick before she was forced to meet Harry again. Through it all, Aiden's face hardened more and more, until she thought his teeth might break from clenching.

"King Charles would likely send funding to refurbish this ruin," Harry said to her and backed away.

Louise opened her mouth to say something as she passed. "The queen will—"

"Decide that she prefers me to you and send you back

to France, your Grace," Scarlet said, and stepped past. Her heart beat wildly as the threat left her mouth. It was likely no one had spoken to Louise de Kérouaille that way before. The woman's flushed, venom-filled face said as much.

Moving down the line, Kerrick stepped forward, once again partners. "Whatever ye said surely made the duchess sour."

"To match my stomach," Scarlet said, the hint of a real smile touching her lips as she decided that it would be good if Louise told Charles and Catherine that she despised Scarlet and didn't want her to return to court.

The music continued, laughter and the sound of rustling petticoats and tapping boots adding to the cadence in the hall. The holiday greenery and flowing wine and whisky worked together to make the party seem gay for everyone else in attendance.

Rebecca had partnered with Lawrence, and the two of them turned and glided into an odd gallop down the line on the outside, much to most everyone's mirth. Louise still looked annoyed, her eyes narrowing. She murmured something to Aiden that made him glance at Scarlet, one brow raised.

Scarlet met Harry once more, his palm pressing hard enough that their fingers intertwined before Scarlet could yank them back. He smiled at her, but the glint of annoyance in his eyes made a shiver run up her spine. "Drawing Louise's blood?" he asked. Had he heard the exchange, or could he read Louise's obvious disapproval?

Scarlet backed away, but she let a satisfied smile touch her lips to hide her rapid pulse. "Beware a rose's thorns," she said. "They are sharp and can cause pain or even death if underestimated."

She moved into line and then stepped forward to meet Aiden, but instead of meeting his palm with hers, his large hands gripped around her waist, lifting her up against him.

He turned her in the intimate La Volta step, setting her down so that he now stood next to Harry.

Keeping with the dance tempo, Aiden turned to Harry as Scarlet was forced to meet Louise, who stared with wide eyes at the change in partners. Aiden leaned into Harry, his hand on the hilt of his sword. "She isn't going back to England, ye *tolla-thon*, so stop hissing in her ear about it."

Harry raised an eyebrow, his feet keeping with the steps but his hands by his sides. "Are you so sure of that, Highlander? Have you known any Englishwoman who has found enough in Scotland to anchor her here?" Harry's face was tight with bitter humor and contempt. Was he talking about the mysterious Lady Beckett?

Aiden began to draw his sword. Without thought, Scarlet stepped forward to take Aiden's arm as if they were at the top of the dance and tugged him up the middle. His feet seemed to drag along, but eventually they made it through the startled dancers to the top where they continued to walk away from the two lines.

Aiden's fists were tight as he held his one arm out for her to take. "If I were but on a battlefield," he said, "I'd slice the man in two."

She pulled him before her near the archway to the stairs. "You *are* on a battlefield," she reminded him. "But it must be fought with slights, disguised threats, and sharp glances."

He huffed a deep, short growl. "I'd rather draw blood than frowns and sneers." He lowered his hands to her shoulders and exhaled before glancing out at the room then back at Scarlet. "Jacqueline Beckett spoke with me."

"I saw," Scarlet said, keeping her tone as light as she could. "What did the lovely lady have to say?"

He absently rubbed the hilt of his sheathed sword, his glance going out to the room. "She wants me to help her."

"Help her?" Scarlet said. "With what?"

He met her gaze. "She has her own battle going on."

"What is she fighting?"

The tension in his jaw was obvious as he spoke. "She fights against the same fate that sent ye up to Finlarig."

Scarlet stared at him, letting his words sink in. "The king wants her," she said softly.

He stared at her for a long moment. "*Mo chreach*," he murmured, grabbing the back of his neck. Aiden's mouth tightened, as treason and fury spread across his face. She had just confirmed that it wasn't Harry Covington alone who had sent Scarlet fleeing England. She watched Aiden turn narrowed eyes on King Charles. "Aye, the king wants her," he said. "She thinks if you return in her stead, he will leave her alone. Covington has told her as such."

"And she confided in you? Why you?" Scarlet asked without bothering to hide the tight note of jealousy in her words.

Aiden turned his full attention back to Scarlet. "Because… Jacqueline Beckett is my sister."

• • •

Aiden watched Scarlet's beautiful face. She looked so bonny and fresh in the Campbell tartan, though her tight curls and grace reminded him of the queen and courtiers. He'd said to Covington that she would never leave the Highlands, but the man's question, though asked to wound, was valid. Would an Englishwoman ever stay in the Highlands?

"Your sister?" Scarlet repeated. "Beckett?" She shook her head. "You said you've never met her."

"The name was my mother's, Alyce Beckett of Nottingham, a Viscountess who widowed young and met my father on a trip north on holiday. She was pregnant when she left us to return to England. Rebecca and I didn't know. I don't think our da knew, either, or he would have gone after her."

Scarlet stared at him. "Your mother...left you. She was English." Her face opened as if understanding had broken through her. "You hate Englishwomen not because one broke your heart—"

"She broke my father's heart," Aiden said. "And aye, she broke mine, too, a lad of thirteen years. Rebecca was only seven."

Scarlet pressed a hand against her chest. "She left her children," she whispered as if she spoke of great sin.

She met his gaze, and he saw pity there, something he couldn't tolerate. It curdled in his stomach, and he looked away, his gaze resting on the dancers starting a minuet. Foking Covington and the duchess walked back toward the king and queen.

He leaned against the shadowed wall. "Rebecca and I recovered, but we had to see our da suffer for years, quietly watching the south road, his hate for England growing each day, calling for her in his dreams and on his deathbed... It took nearly a decade before he discovered that she'd died within a year of returning to Nottingham. I wrote his letters for him, as my mother had taught me to read and write, but they went unanswered by any of her kin."

"Cruel," Scarlet whispered. Half her lovely face was caught in shadow while the candles from the other room lit her high cheekbone and the gentle slope of her nose.

"Ye are the only thing from England I've encountered that has not been cruel." He waited as if the statement were a question, and he realized how vulnerable he'd just rendered himself.

"And Jacey?" Scarlet asked lightly. "She has not been cruel. Or has she known about you up here all these years?"

He shook his head. "She claims to have only learned of

us from Covington when her grandmother grew ill and died before they came north, leaving her the estate in Nottingham. Apparently, the estate, without any other male heirs…is mine."

"Aiden," Scarlet said, her eyes wide. "A viscountess's son?"

"Not that I want anything to do with it, but I would claim the estate to give to my sister if the law requires."

Scarlet's hand rested on her mouth and chin. She let it drop. "So she could live independently, away from court."

He nodded, staring at Scarlet. "Is it far enough from court to protect her?" he whispered.

Scarlet exhaled, her gaze dropping. "I'm finding that Scotland may not be far enough."

He stepped closer, grasping her arms. "Aye, it is. Ye can stay, no matter what the royals have planned. No matter what they ask of ye, ye can say no."

She nodded, looking into his eyes. "But we need to save your sister."

The same questions rolled through Aiden. Scarlet still hadn't told him what had befallen her at Whitehall Court. And a warrior, fighting against an unknown foe, was at a disadvantage. But something in her eyes made him hold his tongue. Her nightmares were her own until she was ready to share.

"Aiden." Kerrick's voice made him drop his arms. Kerrick nodded to Scarlet and then looked at him. "Edgar Menzies and his son, Calum, just showed up. Calum's been named the new chief of the Menzies. They've come to greet the king and queen." No one moved, and Kerrick looked between them. "Thought ye'd want to know." He slowly backed out of the alcove.

"Go," Scarlet said. "We will untangle this mess later."

Aiden stepped to the opening but turned back to her.

"Ye look bonny, lass," he said, his accent thick. "Wearing our colors."

Her lush lips turned upward into a smile. "I wanted the king, and you, to know where I stood."

"And where do ye stand?" He needed to hear it again.

"I stand on the north side of the border," she said.

Aiden's chest loosened enough to allow a full inhale. Covington's talk of the school hadn't swayed her. He nodded and walked into the hall. His smile faded as he saw Covington next to the king, shaking Edgar and Calum's hands. Had the bastard really brought Jacqueline up here to trade for Scarlet like his sister said? Had he gone to the trouble to find something that he could use to persuade Aiden to convince Scarlet to return, not knowing that the temporary Campbell chief of Finlarig had... His heart pounded hard. Had fallen in love with her.

Love? His breathing was shallow, his brow low. Had he actually followed exactly in his father's footsteps? Love, the most powerful force to weaken a man.

Aiden stopped near the group where Edgar and Calum greeted the queen. "My son, Calum, has just been recognized as the new chief to the Menzies," Edgar said, as his son bowed low over the queen's hand.

"What happened to the old chief?" she asked.

"James Menzies died a year ago of disease," Edgar answered.

"What of his son?" Covington asked. "I believe he had a son."

Aiden's hands fisted at his sides, and he forced his focus on Harry Covington. "Finlay Menzies was a merry idiot," Aiden said, pulling everyone's attention. "He preferred to celebrate everything and anything rather than lead his clan."

"There is no crime in making merry," King Charles said with a dazzling smile that made Louise twitter like a bird atop bramble.

"When it is at the expense of his people, it is a crime," Aiden said slowly. Aiden bordered on traitorous innuendos. It was a much safer topic, in his mind, than his possible love for an Englishwoman.

As if looking to save his neighbor, Calum spoke up. "Finlay Menzies was a poor leader and ran away as soon as I opposed him. His cowardice proved his unfitness to be laird. My council and I will see the Menzies Clan as a strength again in the Highlands."

Covington raised the tankard he was holding. "To the new Chief Menzies, then. Congratulations are in order, and we happen to have a celebration going on. Please partake," he said, throwing his arm out wide as if he were the host instead of Clan Campbell.

Calum turned to Aiden. "Thank ye. And know that Clan Menzies is an ally of Clan Campbell of Breadalbane."

"Do not forget your allegiance to your sire, King Charles," Covington said.

Calum bowed to the king. "Of course. Menzies clan is loyal to he who governs the land."

The new Menzies chief seemed clever enough to know that he wasn't actually pledging to support Charles. However, Charles's condescending smile and nod quite clearly showed that he was not as clever.

Harry Covington's gaze rested on Calum as if assessing if he was treasonous or loyal. He finally smiled. "Shall I take you and your father over to the bounty that Titus, the king's personal chef, has laid out for the celebration." With a bow toward the monarchs, Covington led the Menzies away.

"It seems we have an Abbott of Unreason," Aiden said, watching the bastard saunter.

"Pardon?" Queen Catherine asked.

Aiden smiled, though it was wry. "The Lord of Misrule

for the Christmas festivities from decades ago. 'Twas called the Abbott of Unreason in Scotland. A fool to rule over the festivities."

The queen raised a gloved hand to her lips, hiding a smile. The king chuckled outright. "Perhaps we should make Lord Covington don a crown and order the dances."

Louise's dainty laugh won a grin from her king and lover. But was she lover enough to hold the roguish sovereign's attention? As Aiden watched the king follow his newly discovered sister across the dance floor, he doubted it. Did Louise wish for Jacqueline to stay here in Scotland, thinking the king would forget her with the distance? Had he forgotten Scarlet?

Aiden stared at the man, wishing to see inside his thoughts, when he felt a hand touch his. He looked down to see the quiet queen glancing up at him. "Would you take me to dance, Sir Campbell?"

The Queen of England wished to dance with him. Aiden's mother, if she could see him from the grave, would rejoice. Not that he had any wish to make her happy after she shattered his family by leaving them all.

He bowed. "I would be honored," he said, and she stood to walk with him toward the dancers, who made space immediately. A minuet was playing. The queen's participation seemed to refresh the musicians, and they picked up a more intricate song to the beats. Queen Catherine's feet moved in rapid grace. She smiled as she stepped out, turning to come forward to meet Aiden, who performed the same.

"You dance well, Sir Campbell," Catherine said. "A gift from your mother, perhaps?"

Aiden turned her in time. "She taught me as a lad," he said, not bothering to keep his smile. But his frown didn't seem to bother the queen.

She nodded. "Lady Beckett of Nottingham. Her own

mother, your grandmother, just passed away, leaving Lady Jacqueline Beckett alone, as I believe you know."

They stepped away from each other, the small steps taking them in mirrored circles. Aiden noticed Scarlet talking with Jacqueline, but he couldn't see their expressions. He came around to Queen Catherine once again. "Lord Covington would use her against you, you know this," she said.

"Why would he?" Aiden asked, the queen pulling his attention.

"He wants Lady Worthington. Once he realized where she was hiding, from her brother's letter, and then that an Aiden Campbell was in charge, he asked the king to investigate you. Lord Covington was quite enthusiastic when he discovered the young and beautiful Lady Beckett and asked her to accompany us. It is unfortunate for her that the king has found her youth enticing."

They moved apart, the queen's cool features showing no emotion to her discussion of her husband's roving appetite. She bowed her chin and turned, her tall tower of curls like an odd extension of her head.

Aiden kept a tight hold on his temper as he moved through the steps that his mother had taught him. It seemed sadly appropriate that her lessons would help him now in this battle where a sword would do naught but get him hung or shot.

He came back around to the queen. "Scarlet is a free woman. She has her brother's permission to remain in Scotland to help her sister with the school. She has no reason to return."

"Lord Covington thinks to trade one for the other," the queen said.

"They are not connected in any way."

"Oh, but they are," she said and turned, but instead of stepping back, she stepped forward as if chasing him, yet she made the move look like it was part of the minuet. "They are both beautiful and desired by the king, a man no one can refuse."

"I can refuse him," Aiden said, following the queen forward as she stepped back.

"A dead man cannot refuse him," she whispered, her warning coming like a hiss, the most emotion he'd heard in her voice.

"I would rather be dead than see Scarlet return to whatever hell chased her from England," Aiden said.

He turned the queen in a slow circle, their small steps keeping in time with the musician's beats. "Lady Worthington chased Lord Covington," Catherine said. "She was hurt when he refused to offer for her hand at the time because the king desired her, but Charles has said Lord Covington may now ask to wed her. He immediately began to persuade my husband to venture up here for Christmastide."

Aiden's blood rushed through him, making him want to charge instead of turn, bow, and continue the ridiculous little steps. "What does that matter if Scarlet refuses him?"

"Sir Campbell," the queen said, meeting his gaze. "How pray can you protect Lady Worthington from my husband? If she weds his favorite, Lord Covington can persuade the king to leave her be. If Lady Worthington returns with us to England, Charles will allow your sister to remain here as Lord Covington has already suggested to him. Both ladies will feel safe."

They turned and stepped, coming together one last time as the final notes of the minuet stretched out. "Pardon me, your majesty," Aiden said low, meeting her sturdy gaze. "The conception of safety is a personal opinion and must be built by that person. Lord Covington is a villain to Scarlet, not a hero, and not a possible husband." He leaned close to her ear. "And beware the schemer, your majesty, for he may endeavor to trick even you."

He bowed to her and offered his arm. She hesitated, then gently lay her gloved hand on his forearm to let him guide her back to her throne. Did she ever despair at not being able to traverse the room alone? All the webs of etiquette seemed to stuff the hall, making people walk in practiced, measured beats of expectation. It was all Aiden could do not to pull his sword and slice through it all.

"That was lovely," the king said, turning to them as the queen took a glass of chilled wine that Molly quietly offered.

"Your majesty is a very capable dancer," Aiden said.

"Capable?" the king said, laughing. "No flowery compliments to be had in the Highlands, where rugged men make their ladies swoon with words like capable and bonny."

"Pardon me," Aiden said low, turning to walk away before he said something even more offensive. He didn't wait for permission but left to stride across to where the Menzies ate, father and son talking together. Scarlet stood with Jacqueline near the alcove to the stairs, the pair still speaking, leaning into one another as if they shared secrets.

Secrets. They were everywhere. Scarlet knew his, but hers were still locked behind her bruised heart. He glanced at Covington as he heard him laugh several steps away with one of the British soldiers. That man had secrets; Aiden could practically smell them on him. His questions about Finlay. His decision to bring Jacqueline up to bribe Aiden, as the temporary Campbell chief, to let him drag Scarlet back to England. Was there more than lust or love behind his desire for her?

Battle energy flowed through Aiden, his hands fisting and releasing by his sides. "Ballocks, Campbell," Edgar Menzies said. "Ye look like ye want to rip into someone's throat."

"Maybe the Covington arse?" Calum said, his voice low as he took a drink of the ale that was flowing freely. The new chief was perceptive.

"I thought it was from him having to wear those tight trousers," Edgar said, looking over Aiden's costume, which just added to the heat inside him.

"Aye, why are ye wearing them?" Calum asked, crossing his arms over his chest. "Ye look very close to an English peacock in that silk."

Across the room, Aiden watched the queen and king stand. Queen Catherine beckoned to Louise where she stood with Jacqueline and Scarlet, and the three walked toward her.

Covington stepped up next to Aiden as if nothing but a simple festival were occurring. "The Scots surely know how to distill a smooth whisky," he said, pouring more into a small, broad-lipped cup. "Doesn't the word for whisky in your tongue, Campbell, mean water of life?"

Aiden cut a hard gaze to the man who talked to him as if they were friends. He'd frightened Scarlet, snubbed her in front of her peers, found Aiden's sister to entice the king, and was attempting to force Scarlet to return to the English court. Harry Covington was an enemy deadlier than anyone he'd met on a muddy, blood-soaked battlefield.

"If ye don't leave both my sister and Scarlet Worthington here in Scotland, the only thing on your tongue will be the blackness of death," he said.

Covington said nothing but took another sip, his gaze shifting to the middle of the hall where the king and queen stood, waiting for people to fall silent. Without any request at all, the room hushed, and the king smiled broadly, opening his arms wide.

"A joyous Christmastide to you all," Charles announced. "And gratitude to the people of Breadalbane for joining us here at Finlarig Castle for this merriment." Applause rose and then quieted as the king opened his mouth again.

Charles threw an arm out wide to Jacqueline. "May I

introduce a Christmas gift to the Campbells." He paused, a broad smile on his face. "We return Lady Jacqueline Beckett Campbell, Viscountess of Nottingham, to her Scottish family by blood, a full sister to your very own Aiden Campbell." Aiden's gaze flew across to Rebecca, who plopped down on the seat behind her. Alana took her hand, patting it, but her mouth was also slack.

"Lady Beckett will become an instructor at this wonderful Highland Roses School, replacing Lady Scarlet Worthington," Charles announced. Aiden's sight blurred with rage as he watched Scarlet's face remain impassive. *Nay.*

"She has left the comfort of her English home long enough and will journey back with us after Twelfth Night."

*Bloody hell!* Had she agreed to this? Aiden stared across at her but couldn't tell what expression played on her face. With all eyes on her, she gave a small curtsey to the king and queen, but she didn't look about. Had Covington and the queen and Louise finally convinced her that she was better off at court?

Covington raised his whisky cup. "Huzzah!" He took a sip as others joined him then set it down. His words came succinct and low. "See there, Campbell? Nothing in your bloody country is good enough to entice an English lady to stay for long. Not a man in a skirt or a lad who begged for but failed to keep a mother's love."

Aiden turned on his heel, his fist pulled back before conscious thought could slow him down. *Crack!* The pain in Aiden's knuckles as they smashed into Covington's aristocratic nose was the best thing he'd felt all evening. Before he lost all control and sliced the bastard through his gut, Aiden strode out into the brisk winter night.

# Chapter Eighteen

Scarlet paced in her dark bedroom. As she'd done for the last hour or so, she stopped to lean her ear against the door, but only silence filled the fourth floor. She tapped her fingers on the heavy wooden bar. Where was Aiden?

After he'd broken Harry's nose, leaving him bleeding and demanding the king arrest Aiden, she'd asked Kerrick to hunt him down while she put out the flames of retribution. Luckily, all her training from her manipulative mother and abusive father had given her the talents to keep Aiden's neck from the bloody block.

Harry had called for immediate execution since Aiden attacked the king's advisor, which, he argued, was the same as attacking the king himself. Scarlet quietly reminded Harry, before the king, that he did not have royal blood, and to think so made him a rival for the throne and therefore a traitor against King Charles. Then Cat told Harry to stop squealing like a stuck pig so she could set his nose correctly.

Scarlet had spent the next hour assuring the king and queen that Aiden Campbell was a loyal subject, and that he was likely jealous of Harry's courtly manner and easily angered by the man's slicing comments. "It's a cultural difference," she'd explained. "The Scots would rather battle with swords than words. Sir Campbell was at a disadvantage and only sought to battle the way he always has."

Scarlet filled her cheeks and blew out an exhale in a huff, rubbing at her head, which still ached from the lengthy game. For that's what battles at court were, games of favor and pride, but with deadly outcomes for the loser. How could she even contemplate returning to it? Was she actually considering the king's order? Her father would argue that there was no denying the king once an order left his lips in public. But Father lay silent in his grave, and Scarlet had devoured her taste of freedom here at Finlarig.

She leaned her forehead on the door. "Think, think," she whispered. There was a way out. She just had to find it without sacrificing Aiden's new sister. After all, she hadn't made any promises, so there was room to resist.

"Bastard." She cursed low, thinking of Harry. He was using Jacey just like he used other women to get what he wanted, whether it was a place beside the king or the woman he lusted after.

*Tap. Tap. Tap.*

Jumping back, Scarlet clutched her hands before her chest. Had her thoughts beckoned him? Would he say that the king demanded her presence? "Yes?" she asked softly.

"It's me, Kerrick."

Fear for herself twisted into worry for Aiden, and she leaned into the door, her lips moving an inch from the oak. "Did you find him?"

"Nay," Kerrick answered.

"Have you checked the dungeons?" she asked, her palms against the door.

"Aye. He's not there. I checked the town, too, and he's

not at Rebecca's. His horse is gone. He likely rode to his cabin for the night so as not to start a war with England. I'm fairly certain Grey wouldn't want him to start a war when he is trying to get the crown to lift the label of traitor from the Campbell clan."

Lord help her, Scarlet didn't want to become a Helen of Troy, dragging the Campbells into a war because of her. But she also couldn't imagine leaving Scotland to return to the hell she'd lived at court. "Thank you," she murmured. "And Kerrick…"

"Aye?"

"Walk by all the Roses' rooms and the one assigned to Jacqueline Beckett. Make sure they seem to be sleeping safely." She'd warned her students to bar their doors but worried that they could be tricked like she had been.

"I already did while hunting Aiden. All is quiet. Sleep now," Kerrick said. "Things will be better come morning."

Morning had never been Scarlet's friend. At court, mornings were full of ladies weeping or puking or worrying about things they'd done or endured the night before. The king was usually ornery before noon, and the queen was melancholy over whatever her spies told her of her husband's merrymaking.

"Sleep well, Kerrick," she said and heard him step quietly down the hall. She turned to lean against the door, watching the small flames in the hearth. She imagined Aiden doing the same in his cabin along Loch Tay. With a whispered curse, she pushed away from the door to wrap an arm around one of the bed's four posters. She ran her fingers down the beautifully carved ribbons of vines and flowers, all the way down to the heart that Aiden had said he'd added to the piece.

"This was for your mother," she whispered. Aiden's father, Rebecca, and young Aiden had given their hearts to the woman, and still she left them behind. Tears burned in

Scarlet's eyes. No wonder Aiden despised Englishwomen. The one he'd known, the one he'd loved as a son loves his mother, had turned away, abandoning him. She exhaled. Had Harry convinced him that Scarlet would do the same?

*If ye didn't have fear driving ye from England, Scarlet. Would ye choose to stay here rather than anywhere else in the world? Just think about it, think all around it, inside and outside of it, until ye are completely sure.*

His request came back to her, and she could see his earnest face before hers as they lay on the grand bed. He wouldn't let her answer then, placing a finger against her lips. His mother would have vowed to stay when she wed his father, and then years later, she'd left. Had Aiden not wanted to hear Scarlet's assurances because he thought they would one day be broken?

She dropped her face into her one hand as she leaned into the wood post. Breathing in slow, even breaths, she raised her face. "I need to see you," she whispered. As the plan solidified in her chest, making her heart pump hard, her shoulders relaxed. Gone was the lady who waited for someone to help her, keep her safe, a someone who may or may not ever arrive. Scarlet Worthington was taking her own safety, her own bloody happiness, into her hands. Determination overrode the trembling that suffused her.

Throwing legs into her warmest wool trousers under her skirt, Scarlet counted the knives to which she had access. She yanked on her heavy cloak and grabbed her gloves. Five knives sat in her pockets, easily accessed. If wolves were prowling tonight, she would be ready, or at least readier than the last time they'd chased her and Caora.

"Dear Savior, help me find him," she whispered, her eyes closed. "Amen." With strength, so as not to make a sound, she lifted the wooden bar, setting it on the floor, and opened the door. The corridor was empty. With luck and God's help, the great hall would be, too.

Scarlet exhaled in relief at the bottom of the stairs, and she flew on the toes of her boots across the empty great hall, keeping the heavy heels from cracking on the stone. A waning moon gave some light as she crossed the bailey toward the stables. *Damn.* She stopped. How would she get Caora out of the gate?

"Who goes there?" A deep voice echoed down from the guard tower.

"Shhhh," she said and ran over to see Hamish lowering himself to the ground.

"What are ye about, lass?" he asked, looking stern. He crossed his arms. "Running away again, are ye?"

The words resonated through Scarlet. Running away? She stood tall, firming her jaw, readying for the battle of negotiation that would get her out of the bailey. "No, Hamish, I'm not running away. For the first time in my life, I'm running toward something. Now open that bloody gate."

· · ·

Aiden slid the fine-grit stone along the edge of his sword, the sound of his strokes filling the cabin with a metallic keening. He sat by the hearth, cursing himself. *I should have stayed.* What happened after he left? Was Scarlet well? Had she barred herself inside her room? He'd ridden from Finlarig initially to prevent himself from changing the Christmastide celebration into a bloody battlefield of slaughter. Covington's words had sliced through the remaining, already frayed, threads of his discipline. "Fok."

The night, every word uttered by the Englishmen, the king, even the queen, had pressed him toward despair that, no matter what, Scarlet would leave. He'd known it from the start. What woman raised in finery would choose to live a homespun beggar's life?

Maybe at the start, if she were leaving something terrible behind, she thought she'd stay in Scotland. But if wrongs were righted, if she truly only had suffered a bruising of her heart and embarrassment when Covington didn't ask her to wed, and she had healed, wouldn't she return to what she'd always known? Even if she didn't go back to Covington, wouldn't she want to return to Lincolnshire? To her brother's estate where servants brought her rich foods?

"Foking, bloody hell," he said, standing, his sword in hand. He needed to go back. By now the town folk would be home in their beds. Even the court, which Scarlet said kept late hours, should be passed out in the fine whisky that had been flowing. He needed to make certain that Scarlet and his sister, Jacqueline, were not being harassed. No matter that he left to prevent more bloodshed and war, staying away was cowardice. If Covington cared for his own life, he better be snoring alone in his own bed.

Aiden doused the fire, threw on his cloak, and stepped out on his porch. A sliver of moon stood high in the clear black sky, with only a hint of wind. He'd put Eigh in the barn earlier and leaped off the porch to the dirt, heading that way. Most of the snow had melted during the sunny hours, leaving a darker landscape. One hand on his scabbard, he jogged across to the barn, pushing the door open. The smell of sweet hay filled his inhale, and Eigh's head came up over his stall. The horse snorted as if annoyed that Aiden had woken him.

"Ye can sleep back at Finlarig." He fed his horse an apple, patting his neck to wake him up. Aiden grabbed the bridle, shaking it straight. Eigh's ears twitched, and he raised his head, large eyes on the closed door. Aiden turned, dropping the bridle as he drew his claymore, his ears catching the deep thud of hooves. Had King Charles sent his soldiers after him? He almost smiled at the thought of meeting the challenge and waited.

One horse? Confused, he stood ready, and the softest of voices came through the door. "In you go, Caora. See, no wolves tonight." Scarlet? She pushed open the barn door, leading her horse inside.

"What the bloody hell are ye doing here in the middle of the night?" he asked, his voice booming.

Scarlet screamed, hand instantly grabbing hold of something he couldn't see in the dark. It whipped through the air. *Thwack*. And sunk, point first into the thick wooden brace next to the stall. "Blasted, bloody hell, Aiden!" She stormed forward. "I could have killed you."

"What are ye doing out by yourself in the middle of the night?" he asked again. His gaze went from her to her horse. "Unless everyone is drunk on whisky and you figured out how to wind the portcullis, Hamish is going to pay with his head for opening the damn gate for ye."

Scarlet stomped toward him, and for a second, he thought she might grab him, but she grabbed her knife instead, yanking it from the wood. "I am coming to find you," she yelled back.

"I don't need finding," he said and lowered his voice to normal. Why the hell were they yelling? *Blast*. Because she'd ridden out alone in the night. "There could have been wolves or worse, Englishmen about, maybe Finlay or Burdock. Both are still out there somewhere." He threw his arm toward the door where her horse stood, watching them.

"You left. Kerrick couldn't find you," she said, stepping in front of him. "You weren't at Rebecca's or in the dungeon."

"Of course I wasn't in the dungeon. Foking Englishmen wouldn't have taken me alive."

"Dammit, Aiden, I needed you," she yelled in his face.

Fury ignited the brittle kindling of worry stacked inside him. "Did that bastard touch ye?" Which bastard, he wasn't sure and didn't care. King or Covington, he'd slaughter them if they'd harmed her, and then he'd hate himself forever for leaving.

"What?" she asked, shaking her head, her hair in disarray from her hood, a glorious tumble of curls about her shoulders. "No."

"Then what did ye need me for?" he asked, matching her loud voice and frowning down at her.

She stepped up close to him, grabbing his shirt in both of her gloved fists. No words. Just raw emotions crossed her features. It was dark, but he saw worry and anger mixed with determination and longing. Standing on tiptoe, she yanked him down. Even in the shadow, her beauty caught his breath as she pressed her lips to his.

Fear for her, anger at himself, lust for vengeance—all of it welled inside him. A wave of feeling boiling up, and he wrapped his arms around her. Slanting his face, he deepened the kiss immediately, and Scarlet lifted her hands to his head, holding his mouth to hers.

Wild and fierce, their kiss consumed all of Aiden's thoughts. Inhaling through his nose, she smelled of warm, soft Scarlet. He groaned low in his throat and lifted her against him, pressing her closer as if there were nothing between them: no anger, no distrust or worry, and absolutely no clothing. He slid his hands down the gentle slope of her spine, over her curvy arse, lifting her against his aching member.

Scarlet's fingers scraped along his scalp as she plunged them through his hair, her lips clinging to him. "I… was so worried," she said, her words coming on little gasps.

He pulled back, still holding her close. "I am sorry, Scarlet, to go so far. I should have cooled down in town and returned right away."

"No," she shook her head, a dark laugh escaping her.

"Harry was calling for your head. 'Tis best that you were nowhere near."

"But ye rode out here a—"

She pressed a finger to his lips, stopping his words. "We've already had that argument. I think you should take me inside and make me warm." Her words ended in a seductive whisper. "Or would you rather I throw more knives at you? Because if you don't—"

He cut off her words by lifting under her legs. Scarlet's arms dropped around his neck as he carried her past her horse.

"Caora," she said.

"Will be safe and warm in here. I'll see to her later," he said, pushing them out into the crisp night air. He hugged her close in his arms, the weight of her relaxing his shoulders. Solid, warm, alive, and with him. He kissed her as they walked, his footing slow and secure on his own land. Och, the feel of her funneled down inside his chest, wrapping around as if she were binding him to her. How would he ever survive if she left?

. . .

Scarlet slid her backside up against Aiden where they lay on his large bed, the fire blazing in the hearth across the room. Their breaths had only just slowed, their passions spent for the moment. Her back grazed his chest, and Aiden brought his splayed hand to stroke down her belly, pressing her even closer into the shape of his body.

"Mmmm…" Scarlet hummed, a satisfied smile on her face.

He nuzzled her nape, kissing the skin of her bare shoulder. "I couldn't agree more," he whispered, his lips near her ear, giving her a tickling chill, which made her nipples harden again.

They breathed together in the silence of the night, the crackle of the fire the only sound. She tried to close her eyes but knew sleep wouldn't come with so much unsaid between them. Their passion had burned brighter than ever, but dawn would come soon, and mornings brought stark reality.

Scarlet inhaled. "Aiden…"

"Aye, lass?"

"You need to know, I'm not your mother." Her words were soft.

"I should bloody well hope not," he said.

She ran her fingernail gently along his arm, little circles in the fine hair there. "I won't leave you, no matter what the king says."

She felt the muscles of his arm tighten. His hand fisted where it rested before her, and she gently pried his fingers apart.

After a long moment, he shifted to lie on his back, and she rolled to face him. The fire cast gold and shadows over his face as he stared upward. "She thought she wouldn't leave the Highlands, either," he said. "I remember her happy with my father, him chasing her through the meadow flowers. 'Tis one of my first memories."

Scarlet waited, reaching to pull the quilt over them both. After a while, he opened his lips again, still staring upward. "I think…she may have lost a bairn after Rebecca was born. She cried, and nothing seemed to cheer her. It was a cold winter, the snows never ceasing." He shrugged slightly in the bed. "She talked all the time of England, her rich, warm estate in Nottingham. We'd heat bricks in the hearth to put in her bed."

The detail brought an ache behind Scarlet's eyes as she envisioned the two children trying to keep their mother happy. Was that why Aiden had brought a heating brick to her bed? She laid her hand on his chest, keeping it still.

"She would teach us to dance. Someone, maybe her mother, would send her letters from England. Sometimes the dance sheets for the upcoming court season would be enclosed. She'd teach us to read them. We began to call her Lady Beckett in hopes that she'd feel elegant here, but…" His words trailed off.

Scarlet saw the tension in his jaw and leaned forward. She kissed his chest, laying her cheek there to hear his heart beat beneath.

"Da even carved her that bed, trying to bring beauty to a world she had grown to despise, the work involved in everyday living here. No servants, no mother of her own, no real friends, as she kept her distance. She dressed us in ridiculous clothes that her mother sent from England, saying she didn't want us looking like homespun beggars. Rebecca was so young. She loved the dresses, but I hated the trousers and ended up pounding a number of lads for teasing me about them. And then one day…she kissed each of us…and…left in a coach that had come."

Scarlet inhaled, blinking back the tears. She swallowed, waiting until she could speak without any weeping emotion in her words. "She missed an amazing life with a loving husband, and two children who adored her." She propped herself on an elbow, looking down at him.

Aiden turned his head to meet her gaze. "Three. She was with child when she left. None of us knew. I doubt Da did, or he wouldn't have let her go. And then she died, and no one bloody told us for years." He shook his head as if remembering the day they'd learned of it. He must have been on the edge of manhood.

She touched his bristled cheek. "Aiden, I am not your mother. I have no one in England to entice me back with letters and lace. Even if I did, believe me when I say that nothing in England holds my heart like Finlarig and its people." She ran a fingertip over his full lower lip. "Like you."

"Alyce Beckett felt that way at first, too," he said.

"How could you know that?" she asked, shaking her head. "You weren't born when she arrived in Scotland. Perhaps she was never happy, even at first. And perhaps she would have returned after Jacqueline was born, but she died." She waited, but he just stared at the ceiling.

Scarlet planted her fists on his chest and leaned forward to stare into his dark eyes. "Stop comparing me to the only other Englishwoman you've known. We are all different people."

"But ye come from the same line of gentry. Hell, her first husband was a viscount, like your father. She sought to escape her first husband's memory, but once she got over his death, we couldn't keep her here. If…" He swallowed hard, turning toward her. "If Harry Covington asked ye to marry him now, said he loved ye and wanted to keep ye comfortable and happy all your life, would ye wish to return—?"

"Stop," she said, her voice loud. "You don't understand." She shook her head.

For a span of long, even breaths, he stared at her. "Maybe that's because ye haven't told me," he said, his voice low. He brushed his knuckles against her cheek. "Ye can trust me, Scarlet."

She flopped down on her back to stare up at the beams overhead. "Can I trust you not to ride back to Finlarig to slaughter a viscount and possibly a king?"

Aiden shifted until he leaned over her to kiss her forehead. He settled back in his spot beside her. "I will spill no blood tonight," he said, as if the statement represented an adequate promise.

"You already spilled blood tonight. Harry's nose gushed for an hour."

She glanced his way and saw a grin tip up the corner of Aiden's mouth, but he didn't say anything, just stared upward. Finally, he turned his head toward her. "I will not slice Covington or the king for what they've done in the past. At least, not mortally." She rolled her eyes. "Lass," Aiden said. "That's the best ye are bound to get."

She couldn't help but grin a little. His quip had helped loosen the tension she'd been holding in her shoulders. She breathed deeply and felt the gentle pressure of his hand lie across her arm, offering support but giving her room to think. Tentatively Scarlet touched upon the memories she'd locked up tightly, as if the fear and shame would go away if she refused to remember. But they hadn't. Fear and shame still laced her thoughts, like a poison trapped within her body. Could she lessen the taint if she spoke the words? Bled them out?

Aiden didn't say anything, just lay next to her, his warm palm along her arm. Scarlet closed her eyes and let the winter of a year ago trickle back into her mind.

# Chapter Nineteen

"I'm certain Harry will ask me to wed tonight," Scarlet said, smiling coyly at her sister's reflection in the mirror. Harry and Scarlet had walked the gardens the night before, talking of children and his country estate where he hoped they could live.

Evelyn paused, holding the peacock plume that she was attaching to the mountain of curls Molly had perched upon Scarlet's head. But then she smiled and jabbed the feather securely into her hair. "Are you sure he is the one?"

Scarlet turned to her, a look of shock raising her perfectly plucked brows. "Of course. He is the most influential man at court. He's handsome and witty. Father desired it before he died."

*Be an asset to your family, Scarlet. Evelyn has the astute mind, and you have your beauty and temperament. Do what you must to secure Lord Covington. He will see that the king thinks highly of the Worthington family.*

Scarlet pressed against the tightening in her stomach as she thought back on the last words her father spoke to her. Not of his love for her but of her duty. "I will be an asset to our family," she whispered.

Evelyn leaned in to her. "You already are, Scar, without wedding." Evelyn hugged her back gently so as not to muss her exquisite costume of pink and rose silk. "Marry for love and happiness. That is all I want for you."

Scarlet met her gaze in the mirror, her lips bending in her practiced pleasant smile. "Wouldn't that be lovely."

The evening progressed beautifully in the gilt ballroom at Whitehall Palace. King Charles and Queen Catherine hosted the ball to celebrate love, for it was St. Valentine's Day. Though, the royal couple rarely interacted, let alone looked to be in love. Charles spent his time dancing and laughing with several buxom women, including his two mistresses, Louise and Nell. Catherine retired early, and Scarlet couldn't help but feel pity for the resigned woman.

Harry spent much of his time staring at Scarlet, if he wasn't next to her. He looked the perfect gentleman in his wig and silk costume, and Scarlet watched many ladies frown with jealousy over his constant attention toward her.

"You, my sweet Scarlet, have caught the king's eye," Harry said in low tones as they stood sipping wine near the gold-threaded curtains.

A tendril of unease snaked through Scarlet, but then several ladies laughed, the king made a grand show of kissing Louise's cheek, and the musicians picked up a lively, festive tune for a contradance. Sounds of happiness dissolved Harry's comment as she placed her hand on his firm arm and they joined the two gathering rows of dancers.

The king did dance once with her, his wandering gaze stripping her pink gown away, but then he was dancing with

Louise and Nell, and Scarlet drank another glass of wine that Harry seemed prone to give her. By the end of the night, her steps were rather wobbly. Evelyn had retreated to get some sleep, and Nathaniel had returned to Hollings Estate when their mother sent a note saying she was ill.

*Meet me in the gallery at the strike of two. H.*

Harry's note lay folded in her pocket, a secret that made her stomach flutter. Or was that the wine. She giggled behind her glove as she looked in the mirror in her room, then she slowly stripped the glove off. A two a.m. rendezvous required less formality. She pulled the plume from her hair, letting her dark curls down over her shoulders. Scarlet dabbed a bit of perfume on her pulse and slipped out the door into the dark corridor of the palace. The faint whisper of her slippers and the silk of her dress followed her through the slumbering halls. She jumped slightly at the first strike of the clock and paused, leaning one hand on the wall while the other covered the bare skin over her pounding heart. The sound of giggling, followed by a deep male voice, came from behind the door closest to her.

Scarlet hiccoughed and continued on, listening to the end of the second strike resonate through the grand entryway where the clock stood. Her slippers seemed to move on their own accord, and she reached the gallery. It was dark except for one candle at the end, like a beacon, and she rushed toward it.

"Harry?" she whispered, and he stepped out from behind one of the curtains framing a dark window. His cravat was undone, as was his jacket. He'd taken off his wig, and his short hair lay flat with dampness. As she neared, she could smell the alcohol and tobacco on him with the underlying smell of sweat, likely from the long night of dancing with the ladies and talking politics with the men.

"I am here, my sweet pigeon," he said and pulled her into

his arms. Without any words, he kissed her, his wet mouth sliding along her lips as one hand held her back, the other pressed to her breast. She gasped against his mouth, but he didn't let go. The wine made her mind sluggish, but her stomach tightened, followed by a wave of nausea. Raising both hands, she pressed against his chest until he finally lifted his head.

Sucking in breath, Scarlet stared up into his face. In the light of the ballroom, his features had been exceedingly handsome, but in the shadows, alone, he looked altered, darker. As usual, she placed a smile on her lips. "Lord Covington, you take liberties," she said, admonishingly.

He ran a hand through his hair to his neck. "And you, Lady Worthington, should expect such roguish behavior when meeting a man alone at two in the morning." He smiled. "Is this not what you want, Scarlet. To be kissed and touched?"

Her cheeks warmed in the darkness. "A young woman desires the love that makes the kisses sweeter."

"Love? Well, certainly, Scar." He pulled her to him again, and she could feel his erection press against her. His fingers worked to ruck up her skirts. "Let me give you some love."

She kissed him, but when he touched the bare skin of her thigh she tried to step away. He backed her up until she felt the wall. Her heart raced. "What are you doing?" she breathed. His fingers worked up her bare legs, and she pawed at his hand. But he was stronger and continued until his fingers reached the heat between her legs, forcing them open.

She gasped as he pushed them inside. She tried to shove away, but he held her with his hard body against the wall, his lips sliding a wet trail up her neck to her ear. "Relax, Scar," he said. "You will like it."

"Stop," she said, but he continued, moving his fingers in her body. A hint of pleasure may have started, her body responding to the stimulus, but panic drenched her in cold fear. "I will be a maid on my wedding day," she said.

Harry withdrew his fingers and looked into her face. "Highly doubtful, but you've no need to fear my cock tonight," he said, his humor dark. "There is another cock that desires your virgin's blood."

Scarlet stared in horror at Harry. The flickers from his candle cut across his features, revealing a mix of lust and anger in the tightness of his jaw and eyes. "What?" she asked, the word barely a breath.

He leaned into her, his hot breath against her cheek. "I am doing you a favor actually. I'm not sure his majesty knows what to do with a virgin."

"Charles?" she asked.

"You were fashioned by God to be desired, Scarlet. Every man will want to bed you, even a king." He glanced around as if searching for a drink. "Tonight. But first I will get you used to being touched, show you how to hold a cock with your hand and, in time, with your mouth."

His crass words stunned her. He moved closer, grabbing again for her skirts, but she slapped at his hands, her heart pounding. "I thought...I thought you wanted to marry me." Tears burned behind her eyes, but she blinked them away. "We talked of children and your estate near Bath."

"Likely I will, eventually," he said, his gaze running down her, assessing her like she was a mare to be bought. "You are a beauty and of good breeding." He pressed against her. "But first I need Charles to trust me completely, and delivering you, wet and willing, to his cock will do just that."

The words shattered through Scarlet. "Deliver me?" she asked, her voice hard.

He rubbed his pelvis against her. "You will be obedient," he said and pressed his lips against her throat, inhaling the perfume she'd placed there. To think, she'd wanted to entice him. *Fool!*

"You would deliver me to another man?" she asked, pressing against his chest.

Harry lifted his head, annoyance on his face. "Not just a man. The king, you silly girl. But once he tires of you, I may offer for your hand. Although that depends on the reputation you earn in his care."

Fury welled up inside Scarlet, and she turned, stalking down the hallway. Before she could take more than a couple of steps, Harry's arms crushed around her from behind, halting her. "Unhand me," she yelled.

"Shhhhh," he hissed in her ear, practically lifting her from the ground as he half carried, half dragged her toward a door in the wall. One hand came up to clamp over her mouth. Her struggles were impotent against his strength. Fear made Scarlet weaker, her eyes wide over his hand. "Keep your mouth closed, else you find yourself gagging on something quite shocking, my sweet," he said, pressing his cock into her backside. Even with the layers of skirts, she could feel the hardness.

Slowly he removed his hand and turned the knob on the door, his other hand still around her. "Behold," he whispered as the door swung in, allowing them to see a candlelit room. It was a salon, one of many in the palace, with chairs, card tables, and a settee. Looking up from his position in a chair was King Charles, Louise sitting atop him, completely undone but for the tower of curls on her head. Her breasts jiggled before the king's face as she jogged up and down on his staff while the king's head lolled back on the chair. Another man stood watching them, his erect member out as he stroked it.

Scarlet struggled as Harry's hand slid up her bodice to yank the low-cut edge down, exposing her one breast. He cupped it hard and continued to rub himself against the back of her.

Charles, his eyes half closed in either pleasure or

drunkenness, pinched Louise's nipples hard until she squeaked. He smiled at the open door. "Come in. Come in," he said. "Join our small party." He groaned, reaching down as if to adjust himself. Louise glanced toward the door, a look of interest lighting her face as she saw Harry, but she didn't stop her rhythm. The other man moved to stand behind her, laying his hand down to stroke her moving backside.

Scarlet stood frozen, her body numb. Never before had she seen the act. Harry held her tight, and she felt her skirts slide up her legs as he once again dove his other hand under, seeking her out. She couldn't swallow or inhale properly, and sparks began to fire in her periphery. Lord help her. If she swooned, what would they do to her?

The king gestured with his hand, and his mistress stepped off him, only to turn around to lay her bare stomach over the back of the couch, presenting her parted cheeks. The king, his cock hanging low, gestured first to the other man, who moved forward eagerly to slide his length between Louise's lips.

Charles gestured toward Harry. "Come in, Lord Covington, and finish off sweet Louise. It seems the wine has taken my vigor. The lady you've brought and I can entertain ourselves while we watch the three of you." His words were slurred, and his lids lowered over his eyes as he sat naked in a high-backed chair, his long, dark wig askew.

The man in Louise's mouth groaned as he pumped, his eyes half closed as if pleasure overtook him. Harry leaned over Scarlet's bare shoulder, nipping the skin as he pinched her nipple. "Duty calls. Come, sit with the king." His lips came over to her ear. "If you please him, he will do great things for you and your family," he whispered.

*Be an asset to your family.* Her father's words beat with her pounding heart. Harry released her to grasp her hand, tugging her to follow him. Was this what she was meant for?

To be a king's mistress and perhaps the wife of a man who would use her for political gain? Her beauty was all she had, at least that's what her father always said. She righted her bodice and took two steps into the room. Harry smiled at her and gave her a nod. He let go of her hand and strode toward the waiting woman as he unbuttoned his trousers. Louise must have heard him for she arched her back, spreading her legs even more. Without warning, he slammed into her, making her moan though it was muffled. Harry grunted, and he leaned over her, grabbing her breasts as he beat fast and hard against her backside with each thrust.

Scarlet looked away, her gaze falling on the king. Charles stroked his limp cock as he watched Harry and the other man pound into his mistress. "Very nice," he said, his eyes closing, and his hand slid to the floor.

# Chapter Twenty

Aiden remained still where he lay in the bed next to Scarlet. Her whispered voice rose with her fear and fell when it held shame. His muscles had turned to granite as he fought against the fury making his blood rush. But he wanted, he needed to hear her every word. She might never speak them again.

"As if waking from a nightmare of shock, I realized that no one held me," she said, and he saw that she'd opened her eyes. Scarlet stared at the wood and plaster ceiling above them, the glow from the hearth lighting her beautiful face.

"So, I ran." The delicate arch of her brows rose. "Back to my room," she said, "where I tore off that awful gown." She shook her head on the pillow but kept her gaze on the ceiling. "I bolted the door and packed my things, holding my breath the whole time, listening for footsteps. But no one came. Knowing how the court slept late, I went to Evelyn's room just before dawn."

She inhaled, and he watched the rise and fall of her chest, the soft skin above the blanket as beautiful as a meadow draped in freshly fallen snow. He wouldn't touch her, not when she was so raw and he had such anger churning in him. Keeping his hand on her arm, he pulled upon his warrior's discipline not to react, letting her nightmare bleed out.

"Evie roused James and Molly, and we fled back to Hollings that dawn, where Nathaniel questioned me. Mother was too ill. Evie fended him off. The only thing I told him was that Lord Covington did not offer to marry me, and that I would never wed him if he asked. Mother died that night, and Nathaniel had too much to do with her arrangements and the estate to badger me."

He squeezed her arm gently, letting her breathe for long moments. She wet her lips. "Harry told people that he'd disappointed me when he didn't ask for my hand, and I fled in embarrassment. I could have remained in Hollings with that, a spinster, cared for by my brother. But a fortnight after I arrived home, Harry sent another note saying that the king desired me back at court." She swallowed, her other hand going to lie flat upon her chest. "He sent a jewel with it, like a payment perhaps. I…I sent it back, and when Evie said there was a chance we could come to Scotland, I grabbed at the escape." Her voice lowered, becoming small. "But he followed."

Her lips remained parted as she breathed. He waited to see if any more would come. He wanted to leap from the bed and ride back to Finlarig to slice his claymore through Covington and the king, but saying as much would only hurt her. And he'd rather die than see Scarlet hurt again.

Wind blew down the chimney, making the fire dance and flatten before rising again. Aiden cleared his throat softly. "I will take ye away, Scarlet. Ye will never need to see them again." He wasn't certain where they would go, but he would hide her here until he'd gathered supplies and made plans.

She rolled toward him, and the firelight showed the unshed tears in her eyes. One slid out sideways to trail over the bridge of her nose. He reached up to wipe it with the pad of his thumb, and she gave him a small smile. She shook her head. "No," she whispered.

His brows lowered. "No?"

"I am done running away," she said and pushed up onto her elbow to face him on the bed. "The things I've learned at the school, that you've taught me… Just knowing that I could defend myself gave me the strength to deal with Harry when he arrived." She glanced down at her hands. "I don't even think the king remembers, he was so drunk. He never even called me by name that night, and he hasn't mentioned it or looked at me more than anyone else. It makes me wonder if Harry was offering me to him without Charles asking about me." She met his gaze. "And now I worry he will do the same with Jacqueline." She shook her head again. "So, we can't leave."

The constant flow of fury through Aiden, and the effort to tamp it down to think rationally, made his jaw ache. He ground his teeth together and sat upright in the bed, rubbing his skull with both hands. "Then I will return with you and kill Covington."

Scarlet sat up so quickly, the covers flew back. "No," she said. "He is the king's most favored courtier right now. Charles trusts him and won't stand for violence against him. The king will retaliate, surely ordering your execution."

"The man raped ye," he said, struggling to keep the accusation from his voice. Scarlet shouldn't be the one to bear his anger.

"I was a maid when I first lay with you," she said.

"He violated your body and your soul, Scarlet." Aiden leaned in to stroke her cheek when she looked down at the covers again. "That is rape."

"I…I was foolish and went to meet him alone. Some would say I led him to believe I wanted him that way. That I was a wanton with him at the ball and would do anything to get him to marry me, that I—"

"Scarlet," he said, tipping her chin up to meet his gaze. "Did ye ask him to do those things?" He shook his head before she could answer. "Nay, he did those things to ye, not for ye. He stole your courage and your confidence, and attacked your body and soul. He is a villain who preys on those he knows are physically weaker. He deserves no mercy."

Tears welled up in Scarlet's eyes. "Then have mercy on me," she whispered.

He pulled her into him, holding her against his chest. "I don't underst—"

"How will I live if they kill you? If the king orders your execution or imprisonment? I… can't."

He kissed the top of her head. "Please," she said, her voice muffled. "I am the one who must face him. I am the one who must slay my nightmares." She pushed back, looking at him, her brows pinched. "Can you understand that?"

How many nightmares had he woken from where his mother turned her back on him? Too many. He exhaled, and some of his fury blew out with his breath. "I may not be able to understand what ye've felt, lass, but I do understand nightmares and how we long to slay them." He nodded and wiped his finger along her damp cheek. "I will help ye prepare to slay your demon, then."

Scarlet threw herself into his arms, and he fell backward onto the bed with her on top. She kissed him, and he caught her face in his hands, kissing her back. Wrapping his arms around her soft, warm body, he breathed fully. Aye, mercy. He needed it, too, for his heart felt full when he held Scarlet. She was becoming the one person in this life who could make the mess of the world seem right and just, the banisher of nightmares. She was softness when all else was stark and hard. Aye, he needed mercy, because he was falling in love with a beautiful, vibrant Englishwoman. Just like his father before him.

. . .

Scarlet set her foot in Aiden's hands, straightening her knee as he hoisted her onto Caora's back. It was nearly noon, and even though she'd made Aiden promise to stay hidden in Killin until Harry stopped demanding his execution, she was still worried. It was a victory that her fear was not for herself, but as she watched Aiden climb up on his white horse, she realized that fearing for someone else could be worse.

He pulled his horse, Eigh, close to Caora. "I do not like this," he said, perhaps for the hundredth time since she'd wrung a promise from him not to ride up to Finlarig with her.

She nodded. "So you have said." She looked into his clear blue eyes. "But you will be near, and I will send Kerrick or Hamish immediately to Rebecca's for you if needed."

"I will have Kerrick guard ye," he said, his frown fierce. "Though, it should be me."

She reached over to squeeze his hand. "How will you save me if you are dead or locked in Finlarig's dungeons?" Smiling, she sat back and produced one of the five blades she had hidden on her. "Your rose has her thorns sharpened." She inhaled, filling her lungs. "I am ready to face my demons."

He inhaled. "If Covington dares to touch ye, use surprise and then slice him well." Before they had left the cabin, Aiden had made Scarlet run through her training drills, using her body and then her blades to defend herself. Only when she was able to escape his hold and make him fall to the floor did he agree that she could return alone.

"I will," she said and followed his hand with her gaze as he lifted it to make certain her hair stick was also in place.

"Even if ye disarm yourself of daggers, keep your curls

up with the stick Craig made for ye." His gaze came back to meet hers. "And no matter what anyone says, do not open your bedchamber door to any man."

She nodded. "Let us go." Scarlet tapped Caora's side, and both horses carried their riders down toward the path that ran around Loch Tay. The day was bright, melting any remaining snow, although winter was just beginning. And for the first time since that horrible night at Whitehall, shame didn't weigh her down. She'd spoken the truth, the whole truth, and Aiden still judged her as honorable. What she had undergone was not her fault. It was the start of making herself believe it as well.

"A rider," Aiden said, pulling back on Eigh's reins.

Scarlet's heart rushed forward into a gallop while her horse paused next to Aiden. She squinted against the muted sun. "'Tis... Kerrick, I think."

"*Falbh*," Aiden said, and Eigh lunged forward toward the rider. Scarlet followed, the two of them tearing across the packed dirt.

"Ho, Aiden," Kerrick called out as they neared. "Ye must return to Finlarig."

"What's happened?" Scarlet asked, her eyes as wide as her heart was wild with concern.

"'Tis the queen," Kerrick said, his gaze going to Aiden. "And your new sister."

"Jacqueline?" Aiden asked.

"Aye, the two of them...have disappeared."

# Chapter Twenty-One

Aiden rode in front as the three of them tore around the bramble toward the lowered gate of Finlarig. They pulled up, halting their mounts as men shouted from the gate tower.

"Ye idiots, 'tis Aiden Campbell. And look, Lady Scarlet is with him." Hamish threw his arms out toward them. "Lower your bloody muskets before one of them goes off."

Two British soldiers, one on each side of Hamish, slowly lowered their muskets. Hamish ran a hand through his mussed hair, his eyes wide with annoyance as he met Aiden's gaze and nodded. "Been a beast of a morning," he yelled down.

"We've heard," Scarlet called up. "Let us in so we can help sort this out."

"No," one soldier yelled back. "The king says that the gate shall remain closed. If an attack is forthcoming, it must be in place."

Kerrick opened his arms wide. "There is no one about."

The British soldier squinted down at them. "So you would like for us to think."

"We will go through the door in the wall then," Scarlet said and threw her skirts over the side of Caora so she could dismount. "We will leave the horses out here."

As much as Aiden didn't like the idea of leaving Eigh outside the gates, it made sense, especially if he needed to ride Scarlet away from the castle quickly.

Leaving the three horses tethered, with long leads, in a woodsy area by a stream to the side of the castle, they met Hamish at the hidden door in the wall. Aiden let Scarlet walk in and caught Kerrick's shoulder, speaking low in his ear. "I want Covington alone." Kerrick nodded, and they filed inside, striding through the bailey, ignoring the frowns on the armed English soldiers.

"They were discovered missing two hours ago?" Scarlet asked, glancing up at the sun to see that it was as high as it would go on that winter's day.

"Aye," Hamish answered. "She wasn't disturbed as everyone was up late last eve, but when Molly went to bring her and Lady Jacey some tarts and fresh milk this morning, she found the king's room and the one next to it empty. The king said that he thought his wife had slept elsewhere, though I be thinking that *he* slept elsewhere and has no clue when she went missing."

"And Jacqueline was sleeping in the room next to it?" Aiden asked to confirm.

Hamish nodded. "She's been serving as Queen Catherine's lady-in-waiting. The Duchess Louise says Lady Jacqueline attended the queen last night before they went to bed around midnight."

"And the king?" Scarlet asked.

"Is as flustered as a plucked hen," Hamish said. They climbed the stairs, and he glanced at Aiden. "He thinks ye have something to do with the disappearance since ye left, too."

"Hours earlier," Scarlet said.

Hamish shrugged. "That Covington arse is heaping all sorts of blame on ye, Aiden." No doubt because of the man's broken nose and bruised pride. The man had no idea that Scarlet, the woman he'd manipulated and attacked, was the only one saving his bloody throat.

They pushed into the dark entryway where another English soldier stood. "Stand down," Scarlet said, as if she were a general. She stepped before Aiden to lead the way into the great hall where the king, Covington, Louise, and several of the students of the Roses School stood near the hearth.

"Aiden Campbell has nothing to do with the disappearance of the queen and Lady Jacqueline Beckett," Scarlet said, her words filling the room. "Has the entire castle been searched?"

"Arrest him," Covington yelled, stepping forward. Aiden nearly smiled at the sight of the man, his eyes blackened and his nose swollen with a small plaster over it.

"You will do nothing of the sort," Scarlet said, snapping around to stand between Aiden and the English soldier who had come forward.

"We've searched the castle," Alana said. "I know every room, and they are nowhere."

"I said," Covington started, but Scarlet interrupted, her hand pressing against Aiden's arm as he lay his palm on the hilt of his sword.

"Aiden Campbell is currently the chief of the Campbells. He was born and raised in this wilderness and knows all the hiding places. He is the strongest of men and the most cunning of warriors. If your majesty is to be protected from whoever has abducted your queen, you will need him to lead. Locking him in a dungeon would endanger your life further, your majesty."

Charles looked angry, though Aiden could spot the fear

in the shifting of his eyes. Scarlet was right, the man was frightened.

"Nonsense," Covington started, but Charles held up one hand.

"If you, Chief Campbell, have a way to ensure my safety, then you will remain in my charge," Charles said.

"The man was gone last night," Covington said, his voice low and respectful as he addressed the king. "He could have stolen them away and is now back to claim your life, sire."

"Aiden Campbell," Scarlet said, standing tall, "was at his cabin along Loch Tay all night in order to refrain from slitting your throat, Harry. He left hours before the ladies disappeared, and they were not taken to his cabin."

"How would you know that?" Covington said. "He could have left early and had his associates carry—"

"Because I was with Aiden Campbell all night long," Scarlet said. "It was just the two of us until Kerrick found us riding back this morning."

"You bastard," Covington said, his blackened eyes narrowing at Aiden. He turned to the king. "He has seduced Lady Worthington. The man is a scoundrel and should be locked up."

Would the king be angered that Scarlet was no longer a potential virgin mistress? Would he seek his revenge against the Campbells of Breadalbane? What would the repercussions be for killing the king and his associates here in the castle? For he wasn't about to let the man, or Covington, touch Scarlet.

"We are betrothed," Scarlet said, her voice strong. "Handfasted, as they would say here in the Highlands."

Alana squeaked, a smile on her face. Cici gasped loudly, her hands flying to her mouth at the same time Molly's did. Izzy grinned and ducked backward to scurry toward the alcove, perhaps to find her sister. Kerrick coughed into his fist.

"Is anyone else missing?" Aiden asked, keeping his face neutral. Scarlet must think their engagement might protect him, as if he needed protection. The only thing keeping him from running Covington through was Scarlet.

"Uh, aye," Molly said from behind Cici. "Titus, the cook. He was gone when I went to fetch the tarts this morn."

Hamish stepped forward. "He was seen pushing a handcart out the gate near dawn. The man on duty opened the gate, as he is your cook and said he was fetching more game from the butcher. There were tarps on the cart, bunched up. Two small lasses might have been hidden under it."

"How did you enter just now?" the king asked, his gaze sliding toward the entryway.

"Through the small doorway in the wall," Aiden said. "There are no other ways to enter Finlarig."

"Are you certain?" the king asked Aiden.

"Aye," Aiden said. "I can go through the door when we search for your queen and my sister. No need to raise the gate."

The king shook his head. "You aren't going anywhere," he said, his dark eyes trained on Aiden. "You will be my personal guard, as you are the best warrior here." Aiden's stomach tightened.

"I can protect you, your majesty," Covington said, and Aiden felt the hatred for the man well up through him, flowing through his limbs until his hands fisted at his sides.

Charles waved off Covington's comment. "We have no idea where to look for the queen, and I would have all of your warriors stationed here in case of a siege." The coward wasn't even going to let anyone look for his wife.

Aiden inhaled, forcing his thoughts away from the craven prig who was in charge of his country. "It would be safer for ye to wait for news in the school library on the second floor."

"Yes, yes," Charles said.

"I'm back out to guard the wall," Hamish said, giving an awkward bow before striding from the hall.

Scarlet glanced Aiden's way before looking back at the king. "I can show you above, where we can work out a plan for rescue," she said, indicating the steps.

"I said, there will be no rescue," the king said. "I will not fall into covenantor hands."

A man in fear of losing something dear to him would do anything to protect it. In this case, the cowardly bastard put his life above everyone else. The courtiers and students followed Charles and Scarlet to the steps, and Aiden followed Covington into the alcove, Kerrick at his side. Hatred churned like a hot spice in Aiden's middle, and only his promise to Scarlet was keeping him from burying his sword through the raping bastard's gut.

Kerrick glanced Aiden's way and snorted before taking a quicker step to catch Covington. "Two words, milord," Kerrick said.

Covington snorted. "Two words? How about asinine fool?" The man's gaze narrowed on Aiden.

Kerrick smiled wryly. "Nay." He nodded to Aiden. "The words I'd intended were *good* and *luck*," he said, drawing out the words. He jogged up the steps, leaving the two men alone.

"Step away," Covington yelled, but Aiden grabbed the front of his ruffled shirt, shoving him hard up against the back wall under the stone stairs. The bastard had held Scarlet against a wall, pressing into her, holding her against her will. Aiden's muscles contracted. It wouldn't take much to slide his hands up to Covington's neck. Scarlet had made him promise not to cut the man, but she'd said nothing about breaking him.

Covington's eyes shifted upward like he might cry out.

"Hold your tongue, else I cut it out," Aiden said, his voice rough in a deep hush. He could pull any number of daggers from his person to make good on the threat. He leaned into the man's face. If one could die from hateful thoughts and a piercing stare, Covington's heart would be shredded. "The only thing, Covington, that is stopping me from slicing ye end to end is Scarlet Worthington and a promise I made to her."

Covington opened his mouth and began to shake his head, but Aiden slammed his hand over the man's mouth and brought his face up to the man's ear. "If ye speak so much as one word to her or my sisters unless they've asked ye a direct question, I will slice off your tongue. If ye touch them against their wills, I will chop through your wrists until your twitching hands dangle from the bloody stumps."

The man swallowed under the pressure of his hand, struggling to step away, but Aiden's fury added to his strength, keeping him pinned. "And if your wee cock stiffens anywhere near my lady or sisters, I'll cut it off and feed it to the wolves that roam these hills. Neither Scarlet nor Jacqueline will be returning to England with ye."

Aiden removed his hand. "Are ye clear on this?"

Covington's lips pulled back, showing white teeth. "One word from me to the king, and you're a dead man, Campbell."

Aiden allowed a dark smile to turn up the corners of his mouth. "Ye've been spouting words to the king since last night, and he's just assigned me to protect his life, Covington. If ye have a care for your foolish head, I'd keep that tongue still if ye want to return to England with it attached."

Aiden opened his hand abruptly, releasing the English bastard. Covington reached up to pet down his shirt ruffles. "Step aside," Covington said. Aiden waited a full count of five before doing so. With one more cutting glance, the man hurried up the steps.

Warning given. Moving forward would be beyond his promise to Scarlet. Let the man try anything again, and he'd lose more than his straight nose.

. . .

"But your majesty," Scarlet said, her voice respectful despite the panic tightening her stomach. She watched Harry slide in through the library door, his face flushed. Aiden followed after him, but she couldn't gather anything from his closed expression. She looked toward the king. "They could be killed if we don't rescue them."

Charles waved off her comment, peering out the window into the bailey. "The covenantors want me off the throne, even though I am tolerant of all religions. But I am king and refuse to give in to their terror."

Scarlet walked over to him. "How do we know that this is the work of the Protestant radicals, sire? We have no information. They may want money."

"But there are radicals in the area," Charles said and turned, his gaze going to Aiden. "Perhaps we did not kill all the traitors."

"No one was expecting you here at Finlarig, your majesty," Scarlet said, looking between them. She couldn't let the king's suspicions turn against the Campbells. "Even your crests were covered on the carriages. You have only been here for two days, hardly time to make fresh plans for a strike against you."

"Aye," Aiden said, his one eyebrow raising. "Who could know ye were coming here for Christmastide to make plans for an abduction? We had no foreknowledge of your arrival. Only those traveling with you, or making plans for you to come here, knew."

The king's gaze cut to Harry. Harry cleared his throat. "I but wished to find a secure place for you and the queen to enjoy Christmastide, your majesty."

"Well, you did a damnably poor job at it, Covington," Charles said, his frown heavy.

"It could have been a last-minute plan concocted when word spread that you had arrived," Covington said in defense.

"No," Scarlet said. "Someone had enough forethought to hire and convince your cook to help with the abduction." Scarlet stole a glance at Harry. Was his motivation in coming to hide the king, convince her to return to England, or was there some darker motive?

"I can rally twenty Campbell warriors to search the surrounding area," Aiden said. "More by sending to Balloch Castle."

"No," Charles replied without hesitation. "Those twenty men shall remain here, for I am the real target."

"Your majesty," Covington said. "Think of the queen. We must send the Campbells to save her."

"And leave me unprotected?" the king asked.

"Ten then," Aiden said. "The rest will stay here—"

"No," the king said, turning to stare directly at Aiden. "The abduction is a lure."

"But your sire—" Covington began, his face hard and his eyes large.

"No!" the king yelled. "I require all the Campbells and English soldiers to be here, surrounding me. I am the king and therefore the crown of England, Scotland, and Ireland. I must be protected."

Covington yanked at his cuffs, his fingers clenching with ire. "Then," Covington said, stepping closer to Charles. "Have the Campbells on the outside of the wall, a first line of defense against any attack. With them before the wall, and the strong portcullis closed, no one will be able to enter."

Footsteps running up the steps made them all turn to the door as Hamish barged in, a parchment in his hand. "A ransom letter," he said. "Delivered by flying arrow from the woods. I sent Lawrence and William out to capture the messenger, but he fled on horseback before they could catch him."

The king strode over and snatched the letter from his hand. Scarlet drew close to peer over his shoulder, Louise on the other side, holding a handkerchief to her nose. They read silently.

*Return to London, Popish King. Either alone, as the coward you are. Or with your queen, having left two hundred pounds here in Scotland. Send the ransom into the woods north of the castle, else your queen and her woman will die.*

*Calum Menzies—Chief of the Menzies Clan of Breadalbane*

"Who is Calum Menzies?" Louise de Kérouaille asked, her whisper rough, as if she'd been crying.

"A traitor and a dead man, along with his clan," the king said, handing the letter to Scarlet, who read it out loud.

Aiden crossed his arms over his chest and frowned. "That isn't from Calum Menzies," he said.

"How so? He signed his name," Harry said, his words snapping.

"Calum Menzies isn't idiot enough to sign his own name and label his whole clan as traitors to the crown," Aiden said. "It is someone who wants to be rid of the Menzies' new chief."

Scarlet glanced at Cici where she stood beside Alana. Cici clasped her hands before her chin, her skin pale and her often busy lips still and closed.

"Finlay?" Scarlet said out loud, making Cici look toward her. Tears in her eyes caught the light from the windows, making her large eyes sparkle. Scarlet looked to Aiden. "Lieutenant Burdock would have signed a Campbell name."

"Who are these players?" Charles asked.

Aiden took the letter, scanning it. "Burdock is a rogue English lieutenant who worked against ye with Captain Cross and Philip Sotheby. He escaped capture and is believed to still be in the area," Aiden said. "And Finlay Menzies was recently ousted as chief of the Menzies, being replaced by Calum. He has also disappeared."

A small sob came from Cici, and she ran from the room, but the king didn't seem to notice.

"Send one man to the Menzies to see if this Calum Menzies knows anything of this letter," the king said.

Aiden nodded to Hamish, who hurried back out.

Scarlet cleared her throat. "We could still send someone out to meet the abductor. Perhaps a woman—"

"A woman will just be abducted," Harry said without looking at her. "To save the queen and her lady, we must send men, as many as can be spared."

The king looked to him. "And leave me without protection? No men, save the one, shall leave this area."

"The walls of Finlarig are strong," Harry said and bowed his head. "Your majesty."

"Did you even bring two hundred pounds?" Scarlet asked.

The king flipped his hand toward Harry. "My advisor insists that we travel with ample funds, hidden within the coaches." He turned to meet Scarlet's gaze. "But again," he said, his words clipped, "I have no intention of paying or sending men."

"But your queen," Scarlet said, her voice low but pleading.

"Has brought me no heirs and has confided in Louise that she is not with child but rather beyond her child-bearing youth," the king said.

Scarlet whipped her face around to Louise, who at least had the conscience to look down, her face flushing. How could she know that her comments to the king would possibly mean the death of her queen?

Scarlet looked to Aiden, who stood with his fists squeezed tightly against his braced legs. His sister, whom he'd just met, had been tangled into this deadly web. Without rescue, how long would she last? The queen had her royal status to protect her, but a young, beautiful woman might find a fate worse than death at the hands of criminals. Would Aiden go against a direct order from the king and leave to rescue her?

"Craig has armed the Campbell warriors," Kerrick said, his face grim. "I will go down to advise them. Three are already upon the roofline keeping watch."

"Aye," Aiden said, and Kerrick exited.

"I will see to Cici and Izzy," Alana whispered, her gaze on Scarlet before running out.

"Your majesty is safe in here," Scarlet said. "With Louise. I must see to my students."

The king waved his hand, dismissing her. As Scarlet walked past Aiden, she grasped his fingers, pulling him with her into the hallway. Once in the empty corridor, she grabbed both his arms.

"I am so sorry, Aiden, that Jacey has been caught up in this," she said, staring up into his closed features. "I know you want to go after her."

"I am," he said.

Scarlet shook her head, glancing at the library door where she could see Harry talking to the king and Louise through the crack. Panic made her words race. "No, you must do what Charles orders, or he will see you as a threat against him."

"What type of leader leaves his wife and an innocent woman to die at the hands of villains when his coin could save them?" he asked.

"I agree," she whispered. "I think he's acting on anger over Louise's revelation. She must have told him last night."

She exhaled long. "But I have another plan."

His gaze met hers. "Ye have a plan?"

"Yes," she said, glancing around. Her heart thumped hard, making her fidget. Fingers wrapping around his arms, she stared up into Aiden's pained face. "We will rescue the queen and your sister."

"We?" he asked.

"Yes, me, with my Highland Roses."

# Chapter Twenty-Two

"Nay," Aiden said, staring hard into Scarlet's face.

"I didn't ask for your permission," she said, the lovely shape of her eyes narrowing.

She dropped her hands from his arms, but his came up to clamp around hers. "Ye could be hurt, killed, Scarlet." Heaviness balled inside his stomach.

"I could be killed here, too. And whoever this is, whether it's Finlay or Burdock or some other conspirators, they won't be expecting trained ladies with knives hidden all over them. We can get in there because we are women, and then we will save Jacey and the queen without you violating a direct order from the king."

"Ye don't even know where they are being held," he said, one hand rising to grip his skull. The thought of Scarlet out in the woods with desperate men who wanted money and the king… It sent his blood racing. They wouldn't care who they killed. He shook his head. "Nay." Aiden caught her face in his hands. "I can't lose ye, Scarlet."

Her face softened, and she rose on tiptoe to brush a kiss

across his lips. "And I can't lose you," she said, setting back on her feet. "If someone doesn't go to save Jacey, I know that you will, and the king will be furious. Harry will make certain of it. But he's made no orders against the women in the castle going. He wants men to protect him."

"Scarlet," Aiden said, but she placed a finger over his lips. He fought to keep from grabbing her, throwing her over his shoulder to lock her away somewhere in the castle.

"You said yourself this morning," she said. "When I finally escaped your hold that I could protect myself, and I did. I am ready."

"Ready to live without being afraid," he said, his words coming past her finger, and she lowered it. "Not to go to war."

She nodded. "I'm not afraid." She smiled, breathing deeply. "For once in my life, I feel I have a real purpose." She glanced to the side and then back at him as if trying to find the right words. "Saving someone. This feeling of truly helping. I want to go."

The heaviness inside Aiden extended out to his arms, making them ache to pull his sword. All he wanted to do was protect the beautiful, brave woman before him. She stared at him, her gaze asking him to understand. "I will be good at this," she whispered. "You've trained me, and they won't expect me."

"The others?" he asked, his mind trying to latch on to a worthy reason for her not to go, but he couldn't find an argument other than he would die if something happened to her.

"I won't order any of the Roses to go, but if they want to help, I will lead them and we will save Jacey and Queen Catherine," Scarlet said. "You stay here and make sure the king knows that you are protecting him." She squeezed his hand. "You can save the whole Campbell clan from English persecution if you win King Charles over with your defense."

"Bloody foking hell," he cursed low.

"Yes," she said, a determined grin on her face. "War is hell, out there." She lay her palm flat over his heart. "But more so inside here. Usually, as women, we must sit home and watch our loves ride into danger. This time we can do something to help."

He pulled her into his arms. "How do ye survive this?" he asked, kissing the top of her fragrant hair.

"Embroidery, weaving," she murmured against his chest. "Soapmaking." She pulled back, giving him a teasing smile, though he noticed that her breathing had grown rapid. "Find something to keep your hands and mind busy."

He dropped his hold and exhaled long. She smiled, knowing that he would let her go. "First…" he said, catching her chin with his fingers. "Ye said we were betrothed." His heart beat faster.

"I did," she whispered. "A ruse to explain my…"

He kissed her, a warm press, slow and deep, his fingers stroking her curls. He pulled away, resting his forehead on hers. "Ye are going to war," he said. "Perhaps ye should ask me to wed before ye go? It might give me something to keep my mind busy while ye battle."

Scarlet's gaze moved between his eyes as if trying to ferret out if he was being serious. She opened her lips and closed them, wetting the bottom one. "I…I love you, Aiden Campbell," she said. "Think about that while I'm gone." She turned, hurrying into the tower of stairs.

Aiden's chest hurt, and he inhaled past the ache. "I love ye, too," he whispered, the admission making him more afraid than he'd ever been in his life.

• • •

"We should wear our training trousers," Alana said, rushing

to a wooden chest. Izzy hopped from foot to foot, her silence not hampering her excitement. Cici stood still, her eyes slightly swollen from tears. Cat sat on the edge of Alana's large bed, propping herself up on her hands.

"You do not need to come with me," Scarlet said to the small group gathered in Alana's room. "It is dangerous."

Cat pushed off the bed and crossed her arms. "We are dangerous."

"Roses with thorns," Alana said, grabbing her hair stick out of her bun, making her waves fall down.

"These men could have muskets," Scarlet said. "They could…do more than shoot us."

"Not if ye kick them in the ballocks like ye did to Finlay," Cici said and wiped her nose on her handkerchief. She shook her head. "He's never been a good brother—cruel, actually. Sending me away so he could have his late-night romps through the castle. But he's still my brother."

Scarlet hugged her. "You should stay here, Cici, in case he is involved. I wouldn't do that to you."

She sniffed. "But if he is threatening to kill the queen and another lady…" She backed up. "He'll be damned for it. Maybe I can reason with him."

Scarlet squeezed her hand and looked at the waiting faces. "There are five of us, then."

"Kirstin, Martha, Rebecca, and Fiona will want to come," Alana said. "I know they will."

Cat nodded. "And we'll all be armed with blades."

"How will we get out of the gate?" Alana asked. "You've said that the king ordered the door and gate to be barred. No one is to leave through them."

"Aiden knows that we are leaving," Cici said. "He will sneak us out."

Scarlet shook her head. *Aiden.* Her heart squeezed just thinking of him worrying over her. "He can't help us in any way, or the king may say he's going against his orders. If he were seen, it could make the king think he's against him. It could hurt all the Campbells of Breadalbane." She looked to Alana. "There must be another way out of the castle and the wall. A tunnel, perhaps, that you've seen."

She shook her head. "There is the back door into the gardens by the kitchen, but nothing that leads through the wall. Grey had it reinforced after Lieutenant Burdock's setting us on fire. We must go through the door by the gate tower."

*Good lord.* "That won't do," Scarlet whispered, her mind racing. "There are armed English soldiers out there with smoking muskets." *Blast.* Would her plans dissolve like that?

"Maybe…" Cat said, her word trailing off as she moved her jaw to the side, her lips puckering in thought. She looked to Scarlet. "Have ye noticed all the animals in the bailey lately?"

Of course. Scarlet had been tripping over chickens, a pair of peahens, and a peacock. Also, a donkey had appeared in the sheep barn with Snowball and his mother. "Yes."

"The donkey belongs to Alana's grandmother," Cat said. "And I saw peahens and that cock near her cottage."

"Elizabeth Campbell?"

"Gram?" Alana said at the same time as Scarlet.

Cat nodded. "I think she's returned to Finlarig and is hidden somewhere inside. I would look in on her when I was at my cottage in the woods. These are her animals, and I know she wouldn't leave them behind alone. Somehow, she's been sneaking them inside."

Scarlet thought about the strange noises she'd heard, like the braying and the art book dropping, and the candle glow she thought she'd seen once in the library. Could the elderly woman be living in the castle? "And no one has seen her enter or leave?" Scarlet asked slowly.

Cat shook her head. "I think she's come through some secret way."

Scarlet nodded, hope flaring inside her chest. "Everyone dress in their dark training trousers and black shirts. Find your blades, too. Then return here, and we will search for that secret passage."

. . .

Molly hurried with Scarlet down the third-floor hall to Alana's room. "You think she's coming and going somehow through the library?" Molly asked.

"I've seen candlelight and heard unexplained noises," Scarlet answered as they passed a paned window. Beyond it, the sun was starting to go down. She was already dressed in her dark trousers and shirt, her hair tied back with two sharp iron spikes, *sgian dubhs* and a *mattucashlass* strapped under her shirt and inside her tall boots.

"'Twould explain the shite I had to clean up there," Molly said. "Lady Alana swore it wasn't one of her dogs, and your lamb was out with its mother." The woman raised her skirts to keep up with Scarlet. "In the mornings, I go by to set up for your class. Chairs are moved. Books are misshelved. Crumbs are about, and I found an empty bladder of wine one morning."

"She must be living behind the walls," Scarlet said. "We will have to get the king out to search it."

Molly grabbed Scarlet's hand as they reached Alana's door. "Be careful, milady."

The thin woman had a tremendously tight grip, threatening the flow of blood to Scarlet's arm. Scarlet patted her hand. "Cat, Izzy, and Alana know the forests around Finlarig. They will follow me to the queen and her lady once the villains find me with my pretend bag of coin that Cat's putting together."

Molly nodded and glanced side to side, leaning in as if there were ears listening. "I mean around the old woman. She's wily, and I've heard she carries blades and poison."

"Alana's grandmother?" Scarlet asked, finally wiggling her hand out of the maid's grip.

"Fiona says her mother said the grand lady was on the edge of lunacy and thirsts for English blood," Molly said.

Scarlet's brows pinched together, and Molly nodded again. "'Tis the harmless looking ones that can bite the hardest," she said, as if she had firsthand experience with things biting her.

"I will be on guard, Molly," Scarlet assured her, adding it to her list of details that could disrupt her plan.

With a quick knock, she and Molly pushed into Alana's room, where the four Roses waited, their bodies in black clothing, buns up with steel spikes sticking out of them. Alana's dog, Robert, trotted over to sniff them.

Alana paced, tapping her lip. "Before it was a library, it was the chief's room—always had been, ever since it was built two hundred years ago by Black Duncan. Likely my grandmother learned about a passageway while it was her room."

She turned toward Scarlet, and all of them stood, waiting. Scarlet nodded to them, her heart pumping fast. "Step one. We need to get the king out of the library."

Molly raised her hand, fingers wiggling. "I can help with that, milady."

"Very good," Scarlet said, glancing at the window where night was falling. "Because time is running out."

• • •

"I wish to be served here in the library," the king said. Aiden watched Molly tremble as she curtsied so low that it looked like she might fall onto her face. He'd been forced to stand guard with Covington and Louise as the king hid away.

Still in her pose, Molly spoke, her words aimed toward the floor. "The cauldron is too heavy for me to carry, and I wouldn't burden anyone trying to protect the king and castle. If you take a turn with the lady down to eat, you can check on the securities set up by Chief Campbell's men."

The woman was trying to get the king out of the library. She stood up but kept her eyes cast downward. "And the spirits, they haunt this room," she said with a little nod. "They taint the stew and toughen the meat when I serve it in here."

"Spirits?" Louise clasped her hands and looked upward like ghosts might be floating amongst the ceiling beams.

The king's brows drew together. "Nonsense," he said from his seat by the fire.

"Yes, your majesty," Molly said, but then made the sign of the cross over her chest in slow, exaggerated movements. Louise moved forward to perch on the edge of her chair.

*Wooooo.* The sound came from down the hallway, echoing. Louise jumped. Aiden looked out into the corridor. "It is empty," he said.

Louise touched the king's arm. "Let us take a walk about. My legs are turning to stone sitting in here all day. And I prefer my stew meat tender."

Covington walked past Aiden without acknowledging him. "I will tour the defenses outside," he said.

"The stew, your majesty?" Molly whispered. She raised onto her toes and then back down. "I'm afraid the rough soldiers will eat it all."

"Into the wilds of Scotland for Christmastide," Charles said, his voice filled with annoyance. "It will be a pleasant diversion," he said with a scowl toward the door where Covington had just exited. "On how many counts could Lord

Covington be utterly wrong?"

Aiden walked out behind the king and his mistress toward the stairs. Glancing back, he watched a shadow move silently along the corridor toward the library. Gentle curves that could make a man weep with want, clothed in soft black wool—he'd know Scarlet's grace anywhere. What was she doing creeping around the corridors?

"Campbell?" the king called from below.

Bloody hell, he'd been rendered into a blasted nursemaid. Turning back to the stairwell, he descended, the thud of his heavy boots echoing. *Good God, keep the lass safe.* His head filled with his silent prayer.

· · ·

"I don't see any odd cracks in the walls," Alana said, tapping her leg to make her wolfhound sit next to her.

"Perhaps behind the hearth," Scarlet whispered as she ran her hands across the stone, her fingertips diving into any little crevice she could feel.

"If he barks, he's likely to give us away," Cat said behind Scarlet as she continued to search. "And he's huge, up to your waist now. He likely won't fit into any passage we find."

"He won't make a sound," Alana said with confidence. "He was a rascal as a wee pup, but he's following my rules now," she said. "And he is powerful enough to drag a man to the ground."

"To lick him to death," Cat said.

"Whether biting or licking, the villain won't be getting up with Robert on him," Alana defended.

Scarlet dropped her hand, wiping the stone dust on her trousers as she surveyed the room. Cici exhaled. "We've checked every part of this room." There was a definite whine in her voice. "My hands are becoming chafed from petting the stone walls."

Scarlet turned in a tight circle, hands planted on her hips. What had been unchanged in the room since the castle was built? The hearth. The bookcases. Not the ones that Evelyn had ordered from England, but the two deep bookcases that flanked the stone hearth. She stood to one side and studied the oak, its large knots swirling down the side. She moved around to see the books. Something looked slightly strange, as if the one side of the bookcase was thicker than needed. She ran a hand over the oak knots, feeling the holes in the middle. Down low was another hole that seemed deeper in shadow. She pressed her fingertip into it and felt…cold.

"I've found something," she said, pushing farther into the knot. She curled her finger, catching the wood, and pulled back. The panel moved outward with her hand, exposing a closet no bigger than a man.

"I had no idea that was in here," Alana whispered next to her, peering over her shoulder. Robert's large head pushed against Scarlet's knee as if he wanted to look, too.

"It must lead out of here," Cat said. "If Gram Campbell was bringing her animals in this way."

Scarlet looked down the dark, narrow stairs beyond the closet built into the side of the bookshelf. "Where is she now?"

Alana stepped past her, holding a candle high to light the steep descent. She cursed in Gaelic and looked at Scarlet over her shoulder. "Up and down these steps? She could be broken at the bottom." She leaned her hand against the stone wall and started to descend. "Gram," she called down the tunnel. "Come, Robert." The dog plunged down the steps to follow Alana.

Scarlet motioned to the others. "Cat, close the door behind us." Izzy passed Scarlet a candle, one for each of them, and they slowly descended the uneven slabs of stone through the narrow passage. Thank God, they were all wearing the slim trousers, as boned hoops would have made the descent nearly impossible. The candlelight only reached a couple of steps ahead, and there were no handholds except for the uneven stones in the walls. "Careful," Scarlet warned. If one of them fell above, she could knock all of them to their deaths. Her heart pounded, and she concentrated on breathing the damp, musty air.

"Gram?" Alana called from ahead.

"Alana?" came a distant voice.

"Thank God, you're alive," she called back.

"Don't fall," Scarlet called after her, but found herself hurrying along, as well. How the hell did the old woman get a mule up these steps? And chickens. And a peacock?

"Bloody hell, what a beast," came the elderly woman's voice from below. "Goodness, child, what are ye wearing?" Elizabeth Campbell's tone was filled with both surprise and disapproval.

Stepping down toward the glow of lamps, Scarlet entered a stone cell at the bottom. Cat, Cici, and Izzy followed closely on her heels. The room was half the size of one of the bedrooms above. A small bed took up one wall. "Have you been living here?" Scarlet asked.

The woman looked more ragged than the last time Scarlet had seen her at Evelyn and Grey's wedding, though she wore the same frown. Even though no one spoke of it, it was obvious that she resented the Worthingtons for taking over the castle, which had been her home.

"They are trousers for easier movement when battling," Alana said and took her grandmother's hands. "Gram, the queen and a Campbell woman have been abducted. We need to sneak out of the castle to rescue them."

"The queen? Of what?" she asked, her brows furrowing.

"Of England, Scotland, and Ireland," Scarlet said. "King

Charles is right now residing in Finlarig, and his queen was stolen, along with Aiden Campbell's sister."

"Rebecca?" Elizabeth said, her hand going to her throat.

"No," Scarlet said. "Her name is Jacqueline, and she was born down in England, raised there."

The elderly woman glanced off for a moment, shaking her head. "I knew that woman was with child when she left. Terrible, sad woman, their mother."

"Gram," Alana said. "What are ye doing in here?"

Elizabeth glanced at Cat. "When my neighbor in the forest left, and that man who used to bother her kept coming around, I figured that I needed to find a safer place to live, since my family abandoned me there."

"Gram, we didn't abandon ye. Grey asked ye, and so did Evelyn, to come back to Finlarig."

Elizabeth looked around, seeming to ignore her. "This was the safest place I could think of, but the animals stunk up the room. Figured they could be cared for above." She patted her leg to get Robert to come over. He sniffed her hands, his long tongue unrolling to lick them.

"Lady Elizabeth," Scarlet said. "You are always welcome at Finlarig. It is still your home. We can move you above soon, but right now we need your help to escape the walls, so we can meet the villains to save the queen and Aiden's new sister. Does that door lead beyond the walls?" she asked, indicating a latched door.

The woman studied her, her frown still in place, but she gave a brief nod. "Aye. It comes out in the family gravesite, the crypt room." Scarlet had seen the family graves when she'd toured the grounds with Grey and Evelyn. It sat off to the west, surrounded by trees, a squat stone mausoleum in the middle.

Elizabeth squinted her eyes and glanced up the stairs. "So, the bloody King of England is sitting up in my castle?

Someone should slit his throat."

"Gram," Alana said as Cat snorted. "Don't ye go near him."

"Lady Campbell," Scarlet said, catching Elizabeth's gaze. "Think of the favors your clan will receive if we bring the queen safely back and ensure the king's safety. Even if you despise him, he is the most powerful man in the land. If he thinks highly of the Campbells of Breadalbane, he could protect your entire family." She nodded to emphasize the truth in her words.

"Bloody hell," the woman murmured and huffed. She lifted the wooden bar from across the door and pushed it open. "Come along then. Let the Merry Monarch and his woman be beholden to us." She waved for them to follow her out of the tiny room into another cold room of smooth stone. Robert wagged his thick tail, making them all dodge it as he led the way.

Cici shuddered dramatically. "We're inside a bloody tomb."

Elizabeth laughed softly. "Black Duncan's bones are off to the side. Leave them be or he'll haunt ye."

"Robert," Alana called, pulling him around the neck to keep him close.

Cici squeaked softly and pressed into the back of Scarlet as they filed through the small door, bending low to step out into the darkness of the forest. Scarlet breathed in fully of the chilled night air. Through the trees, she could see the lit torches along the roofline of the castle. The moon was only a sliver, and with the snows melted, their black shirts and trousers blended into the night. All of them, except for Alana's grandmother, wore their hair in tight buns, stuck with one or two sharp hair spikes.

She motioned for them to blow out their candles and follow her behind a dense copse of trees. Only the one lamp that Elizabeth had brought with her remained lit. They stepped close together into a ring.

"First," Scarlet said. "Someone needs to run to Kirstin and then to Rebecca, Fiona, and Martha to see if they will join us."

Izzy raised her hand. "Good," Scarlet said, nodding. "You are swift. Bring whoever will come back with you here as fast as you can." The girl sprinted off through the woods while Alana held Robert so he wouldn't follow.

"I know where they are likely holding them," Elizabeth said, making the remaining four turn to her. She smiled, her face cut with shadows, reminding Scarlet of a wood carving of an old witch.

"How would ye know that, Gram?" Alana asked.

"That English soldier, the one who took Izzy before…"

"Burdock?" Cat asked.

"Aye. I was seeing him around and inside your cottage for the last month. At first, I thought he was looking for ye, but he came back and put iron bars on the windows and boarded up the back door ye had. Thought maybe he was moving in himself, hiding as he was. I was going to tell Grey, but then he said he was leaving for England."

"And ye didn't tell him then?" Alana asked, her lips pinched in dismay.

Elizabeth shrugged, and with her hair sticking out oddly, she gave the impression of someone who didn't have a firm grasp of her mind. "The man had left for a couple of weeks, so I didn't think of it, but he came again after Grey left, so I decided to move here."

Alana ran her hands over her face, much like her brother did when he was upset. "Lord, Gram, if Cat had gone back, Burdock could have caught her there."

"Oh, I knew Cat had turned traitor and moved in with the English in the castle," Elizabeth said, looking at Cat.

"But I can't blame ye, with your sister here."

Cat rolled her eyes heavenward but didn't say anything.

"So," Scarlet said. "The villains might be led by Marcus Burdock. And he could have them at Cat's old cottage." She glanced out into the night. "I plan to meet the villains at midnight, like they instructed in their letter, with a bag of coin."

Cici looked around. "Which is where exactly?"

Cat pulled the pack she'd been carrying off her back. "Bag of rocks with a few coins on top, just like ye asked for," she said, swinging it off her shoulder to set before Scarlet.

"Well done," Scarlet said, lifting the weighted bag. "By showing the scoundrels a few gold coins, the bag will hopefully win me a trip to the queen and Jacey. For it's doubtful that they will bring the ladies close to Finlarig." Scarlet let the slight breeze cool her warm cheeks. Her pulse was beating so fast that she would soon start to sweat, even out in the winter temperatures.

"Ye want them to take ye, then?" Alana asked, her eyes wide. "Burdock and perhaps Finlay Menzies?"

Scarlet swallowed. "I suppose yes, with all of you following me, possibly to Cat's cottage." She nodded. "Yes, that's the plan, for them to take me."

"Ye are brave," Alana murmured, and Scarlet glanced around at the other grim faces. Even Cat's expression was pinched with concern.

"We must all find our courage to do what is right in this world," Scarlet said. Facing Finlay would be unpleasant, but she'd fought and won against him before. Thankfully, the demon who stalked her dreams remained inside the walls of Finlarig.

# Chapter Twenty-Three

Aiden watched Harry Covington walk the inside perimeter of the bailey wall. He stopped at each English soldier to have a word with him. There were five of them now, as one had been sent north to the English encampment headed by the newly promoted Captain Morris. Each of the four held a smoking musket, ready to fire.

Covington stopped by two of the soldiers who stood together. The three bent their heads inward as if speaking low. Covington glanced up toward where Aiden stood next to King Charles at the bottom of the stairs, his mistress at his side, but then he looked away, walking on to another soldier. Hands clenching and unclenching at his sides, Covington seemed gripped by nervousness.

"'Tis getting dark," Louise said. "We should go back inside." Charles pulled her affectionately into him and murmured something in her ear that Aiden couldn't hear. She smiled and kissed his cheek. The woman had already given him a son, and if Queen Catherine was killed, Scarlet had told him that Charles would likely wed Louise. Was that part of why the man wouldn't let warriors leave to rescue the queen?

Aiden's fist tightened around the hilt of his sword. The politics of this predicament only added to the tangle. And he was certainly not a politician. He'd rather force everyone to give up their secrets and plots at sword point. But he wouldn't jeopardize the Campbell clan of Breadalbane by acting on his own wants.

Shite. How did Grey do this all the time as chief? Shouldn't he be back by now? It was Christmas in a couple of days, and Aiden had had enough of playing chief. Aiden wanted his freedom back to carry Scarlet to his cabin where he would make love to her and convince her to remain with him forever.

*I love you, Aiden Campbell. Think of that while I'm gone.* Blast, he'd thought of little else. Except now, his instincts kept bristling the hairs on the back of his neck as he watched Covington whispering to yet another English soldier inside the walls. He'd convinced Charles to keep most of the Campbell warriors outside, leaving the four English soldiers, Hamish, Kerrick, and Aiden inside. Only the English soldiers had muskets. The others stood armed with swords, shields, and bows, spaced evenly outside the castle wall.

Covington moved across the bailey with clipped strides of his polished leather boots. "Your majesty," he said with a little bow of his head. "I don't know why the English camp north of here hasn't sent any men. Perhaps our soldier was waylaid by the traitors." He stood tall. "I request permission to ride there myself to bring more reinforcements to guard you."

The king played with the end of his thin mustache. "You are a brave man, Covington." He nodded. "You may go, but make haste as night falls." He glanced at Aiden. "I would send Campbell here with you, but you might be in even more danger." He chuckled slightly, tucking Louise's hand into the crook of his arm.

Covington didn't even look at Aiden, but turned on his heel, striding toward the door hidden in the wall where Kerrick had re-entered. The portcullis remained down. Aiden's jaw hardened, as he knew that the bastard would likely use his horse, still tied outside. Maybe Eigh would throw the man, saving Aiden the trouble of breaking his neck.

As Covington stopped before the small door, he had another word with the English soldier standing there. The soldier nodded, opening the door in the wall and closing it after Covington went through. Glancing around, the soldier stood before the door as if guarding it. Aiden watched him carefully but then looked toward the king as the soldier's gaze perused the entire bailey. Aiden crossed his arms and braced his legs in a casual, waiting stance that belied the quickening of his pulse. For the soldier who'd let Covington out had failed to secure the door, leaving open an easy entrance into Finlarig.

Letting his gaze slide along the top of the keep wall where Kerrick patrolled, Aiden side-stepped closer to the king. "Your majesty, I was wondering..." He turned to face the lacy, jewel-bedecked man, who looked out at the inadequate defenses he'd brought with him.

"Yes?" Charles intoned.

Arms crossed over his chest to keep his hand from his sword, Aiden spoke slow. "How well do ye really know Lord Covington?"

. . .

Scarlet smiled at the group of eight trouser-clad ladies, her Highland Roses, every one of them anxious to help. Elizabeth Campbell stood with them, though with her angry pout, she still looked reluctant.

"Cat," Scarlet said, turning to the one Rose who looked comfortable in her fighting gear, a bow over her shoulder and blades strapped around her thighs. "Once I leave to meet the abductors, you will be in charge." Cat nodded, straightening even taller. "You all will follow me to wherever they are holding the queen and Jacey," Scarlet said.

Elizabeth crossed her arms. "At Cat's cottage."

Scarlet nodded to her. "Very likely." She looked to the others. "In which defensive skills do you each feel the most confident?"

"I've been able to throw my *mattucashlass* the farthest and straightest," Alana said, producing one from her tall boot. "And I have Robert." She patted the dog as he sat at her side, his nose to the air. "He will listen to my commands. Won't ye, boy?"

"I'm better at throwing than Alana," Kirstin said. "But we're both good." She patted her tall boots where she must have blades hidden.

Fiona cleared her throat. "I can throw rocks." Scarlet's brows rose, and Fiona twirled one of her loose curls with a finger. "My ma says it isn't right for ladies to throw blades outside our cottage, so I've been practicing with rocks." She smiled. "I can hit a cow in the forehead ten yards away."

"Fiona," Alana whispered harshly.

"Only once," she answered. "I truly didn't think I could throw that far. Old Besse was fine. 'Twas a small rock."

"Very well," Scarlet drawled out.

Cat pointed to the bag that she'd fashioned to look like the ransom. "Take a couple of large ones out of there." Fiona bent to it, tugging the ropes open.

The night sat still around them with hardly a breeze. Winter seemed to hold its breath, listening to their plans. Scarlet breathed in the cold like it was quenching water. Her hands were chilled, but she felt a little trickle of sweat slide down between her breasts.

"I brought blades," Martha said. "The two most balanced, which I throw the best."

Cici cleared her throat. "I can scream."

"We all can scream," Fiona said as she clattered the rocks in the bag.

"If Finlay is involved…" Cici said and exhaled long. "Well, he hates my scream. It makes him fall down, covering his ears. I think he sent me away partly because of it. He says I scream like a banshee." She tipped her head. "It's powerful."

Scarlet clasped her hands before her so that she wouldn't lay her palms to her cheeks. She wet her dry lips and pressed them into a smile. "It could be a very effective diversion while some of you sneak into the cottage to free the prisoners." Scarlet turned to Cat, who nodded, even though she looked more like she'd rather roll her eyes.

Izzy raised her hand, flapping it in the air over her head. "And Izzy will be our ears," Cat said. Izzy dropped her hand and nodded. "She's silent, small, and can sneak around to listen to what anyone is saying," Cat said. "I know all her signals, so she can use her hands to tell me what people are saying across the way." Izzy nodded again.

Scarlet's stomach tightened. "I wish you would stay back, Izzy." She held up her palm as Izzy's face fell into a frown. "I'm just worried you'll get hurt." The girl splayed her hands out to them all. "Yes, I worry that any of you could get hurt. In actuality," Scarlet started and sighed. "I worry that I've led you all wrong by asking you to help."

Cat drew closer. "Just because we are lasses doesn't mean we can't contribute to the security of our clan. We have grown stronger and have skills."

"We are ladies saving other ladies," Kirstin said. "We'd want someone to save us if we were taken by those beasts."

"We are the Highland Roses," Alana said with a smile, her hand resting on Scarlet's arm. "And our thorns are sharp." She hit the final *p* in the word with force.

Izzy made claws with her fingers as if they had thorny tips, and Scarlet noticed that the girl had indeed trimmed her nails to points. Good Lord, what would Evelyn think of her students now?

Elizabeth chuckled, shaking her head. She scratched the back of one ear. "This school has filled ye full of bloodlust."

"Gram," Alana said. "We've learned that we can do more than sit and pray."

Elizabeth shook her head. "These are strange times." She looked to Scarlet. "If I was young, I'd run with ye. But I suppose I'll stay behind and pray." She snorted.

Alana gave her a hug. "Ye've helped us get out of the castle, Gram."

Scarlet took the bag of rocks and coins, sliding it over her shoulder. "Wait," Elizabeth said. "Ye need to cover those trousers, else they know something is afoot." She slid back into the mausoleum, quickly returning with a soiled skirt. "I had this just inside," she said. "I was going to wash it."

"Thank you," Scarlet said and climbed into the skirt, tying it closed on the side. Anyone paying attention would surely see that she wasn't dressed like a lady, even with the skirt, but it would help.

She looked to Cat and nodded. "Don't lose us. They could be on horseback."

Izzy jumped up and down and pointed into the woods. "She brought back the two horses tied outside the wall when she got the others," Cat translated.

"Two?" Scarlet asked. "Weren't there three?" Kerrick's horse, Caora, and Aiden's mighty Eigh.

Izzy shook her head, frowning, and held up two fingers. Scarlet nodded. "Thank you for your quick thinking," she said to Izzy, who grinned widely.

Scarlet took a deep breath. "To save our fellow women, then," she said to her team. "The Roses have great courage. Thank you, ladies."

"We will follow right behind ye but stay hidden in the woods," Cat said.

Scarlet nodded once and turned to stride off through the woods toward the main road near the path to Finlarig. She didn't want to be seen by the warriors outside the castle, but she wanted to be seen by the men looking for the ransom. Her borrowed skirt smelled like a dirty barn and caught on the twiggy wood of the winter bushes. She contemplated stepping out of it, but Elizabeth was right. To be taken as a simple lass, she must be in a skirt.

With only a sliver of moon, the road was dark, helping to keep her concealed from Finlarig. She crept carefully to the road since Aiden may have ordered the men to scout the surrounding area. But the king's order to stay at the wall to protect him must have kept the Campbell warriors in place, for the road was barren of men and movement. Around the corner from the castle path, Scarlet stepped out, her boots crunching on the pebbles. She shifted the bag of coins and rocks to her other shoulder, her heart pounding in her ears as she strained to listen.

Somewhere behind her, the Roses would be creeping close while staying hidden. What if no one came? Should they continue on to Cat's cottage? It was late, but was it midnight yet? Should she stand out in the open, waiting? *God give me courage*. What would stop the fiends from shooting her and taking the bag without bringing back the queen and Aiden's sister? Nothing.

The more she mulled over their possible treachery, the more Scarlet longed to return to the cover of the trees. She could find the Roses, and they could go together to Cat's cottage. There would be no other reason for Burdock to be reinforcing Cat's windows and blocking the back door other than to hold a captive.

*I'll wait 'til the count of one-hundred.* Then she would find the Roses. Scarlet shifted nervously and began to count in her head. *Thirty-five, thirty-six, thirty-seven—*

*Crack.* A branch broke, and she spun in the dark toward a tiny lamp up ahead, her heart pounding. She held her breath as five men emerged from the shadows. Five. How could she fight five of them if rape and murder were on their minds? *The Roses.* They were a bit back in the woods. She inhaled, holding her ground.

Scarlet fished around in the bag and produced a gold coin before her. "I've brought the coin. Where are the queen and her lady?"

"Well now," the man in front said, a smile cracking his scruffy face. "The coward sent a woman? How kind of him." The others chuckled behind him, the sound of their deep voices stirring the panic in her middle.

"Where are the queen and her lady?" she repeated.

The leader stepped closer, peering at her in the glow of the lamp. "I don't think we've been properly introduced, milady, though you look quite a bit like your sister."

"You have me at a disadvantage, sir," Scarlet said.

One of the other men chuckled. "That we do."

The leader plucked the coin from her fingers. He tossed it in the air and caught it. "Burdock," the man said. "I am Marcus Burdock, and you, Lady Scarlet Worthington, will need to come back with us to claim the queen."

"And Jacqueline Beckett, the lady with the queen," Scarlet said. Or had something horrible befallen Aiden's sister?

Burdock nodded, watching her closely. "If the coin is in there then you can have them both. If not..." He glanced at the other men. "We will add a third to our royal party."

Scarlet's breath caught inside her until she forced an even exchange and nodded. The Roses would liberate them before they had time to realize the coins barely equaled twenty pounds. "Onward then," she said, and one of the men yanked the bag from her hands. He smelled of sweat and wood smoke and spirits. Another man, wearing a kilt instead of the dirt-stained English uniform, grabbed Scarlet's arm, and she recognized him as the man she'd witnessed thrusting into the woman in the great hall of Castle Menzies.

He smiled down at her. "Come along now, lass." Scarlet made her feet move and turned to stare straight ahead into the darkness. They walked for long minutes before stopping, two of the men dodging off into the woods to bring back four horses.

*Blast.* They were continuing on horseback. Had the Roses left the two horses behind when the men were on foot?

"Up ye go," said the Menzies scoundrel, and lifted her. Scarlet almost kicked the horse, stealing it away, but stilled her legs, waiting for the man to climb behind her. Her mission was to find the queen and Jacey, not escape. *Deep breaths. In and out.*

Nausea slid through her stomach as the man's arms came around her, and he pulled her backside into the V of his thighs. Panic fought inside Scarlet, but she squashed it back. *I'll pierce his eye with my hair spike if he touches me.* The solid plan calmed her nerves, and he leaned forward, prompting the horse into a gallop through the night.

Scarlet had never visited Cat's cottage in the woods, so she had no idea if they were headed there or another place entirely. If the Roses couldn't keep up, and the villains' hideaway was somewhere else, it would be completely up to Scarlet to save the three of them. How many men were waiting at the end of the ride? Good Lord! She was acting on the flimsiest of plans.

She breathed in the night wind that rushed by her face, tugging at the knot of hair she'd fastened with two hair spikes. *I am strong and armed. I am powerful. I am brave.* She repeated the words over and over, although she didn't feel very strong just then. But the men hadn't even thought to check to see if she was armed.

Up ahead, Burdock veered off the road to the left, the horses plunging into the forest along a slim path. They slowed in the darkness, avoiding broad branches that could pluck a man from his horse, though they still scratched Scarlet's arms. She ducked her head low over the horse's neck, inadvertently pushing back into the man seated behind her. He leaned forward over her back.

"Keep wiggling that fine arse of yours, and I'll pull off the trail for a bit of fun before we make it to camp."

"Touch me and die," she yelled, letting him know that she wouldn't take his threats silently. She sat upright, her one hand before her face to fend off the branches.

"Leave her be, Jack," Burdock called.

Jack leaned into her ear, inhaling long. "If ye don't have the proper coin in that bag you brought, I'll be the first in line to teach ye a lesson about lying. And I know your tricks, lass, after watching how ye kneed poor Finlay."

A bile-filled bubble of panic pressed up her throat. Perhaps puking on the man would cool his ardor. She'd add that to her list of weapons, along with two deadly hair spikes, two *sgian dubhs*, one *mattucashlass*, and pissing.

"I've more tricks than that, you soon-to-be-damned beast." She twisted in her seat to glance his way. "And I have no weakness about spilling your blood," she said through her clenched teeth. "Then God can teach *you* a lesson," she said. Scarlet didn't know how God-fearing Jack might be, but he didn't whisper any further crude threats during the ride.

Firelight pierced the night up ahead, and smoke drifted into the trees. Single-file, they rode into a clearing where a squat cottage sat before a small outbuilding for animals. A low murmur of deep voices filled the night as about thirty men waited on foot and horseback. Good Lord. It was an army.

The men began to trot out. Burdock nodded to them as they passed. "We'll be joining you soon," he said, continuing on to the far side to dismount near the fire. Jack pulled her down off the horse. Were the queen and Jacey inside the cottage?

Two men stood near the cottage door, talking, one in a kilt and the other in… a tailored court costume. Scarlet's breath stuttered to a halt, her jaw freezing open as Harry Covington turned to gaze at her.

A frown grew across his face. "Scarlet?" His gaze cut to Burdock. "What the hell are you doing bringing her here?"

Burdock jumped down from his mount. "She met us with the ransom," he said, dropping the bag on the ground by his horse.

"But King Charles said no one was to rescue the queen," Harry said, stalking toward her.

*Inhale, exhale. Slow breaths.* Scarlet repeated the words in her mind, willing the pinpricks of light to vanish from her sight. She squeezed her hands, hoping the feeling in them would return, and swallowed, squaring her shoulders. "He said no *man* could rescue her. He did not specify for women."

"Shite, Scar," Harry said, grabbing her upper arm to give her a little shake. She swallowed to hide the grimace at the hard pinch. "You shouldn't be here." He ran a hand up his forehead to his short hair. "Damnation."

"You shouldn't be here, either, Harry," she said softly, her gaze sliding to Burdock as he spoke with the man who remained.

"So, the whole army has gone to Finlarig, since Charles isn't sending an army to get his queen back," Burdock called to Harry.

"Yes," Harry said, while staring at Scarlet. He lowered his voice. "I came to tell them that the plan had changed when Charles refused to send the Campbells to save his queen, the unfeeling bastard. If she had been with child, he'd have sent at least half the Highlanders after her, leaving the castle with limited protection."

Scarlet closed her eyes for a moment then blinked them open. "You planned the queen's abduction to pull away the defense around the king." Her heart thumped hard. Harry Covington was the traitor. The man closest to the king. She shook her head. "Why didn't you kill him?" she whispered, her teeth bared.

Harry released her arm and tugged on his gold-stitched cuffs, pulling the lace edges free from his jacket sleeves. "And risk being labeled a traitor before taking over a new Parliament? My reputation must remain free of that taint to rule after that Popish liar is off the throne."

*Good Lord.* Her heart beat against her breastbone. Harry's ambition stretched far. He leaned closer to her until she could smell his dinner on his breath. "You could be my queen," he whispered.

His queen? When he would drag her unwillingly to give her virginity to a king he despised? When he would jump upon the king's mistress without a thought about her watching? When he could act like the king's best ally while plotting to depose him?

"You will never be king," she said out loud, pulling Burdock's gaze from where he spoke with the four other men who'd brought her there. Harry grabbed her arm, dragging her toward the cottage. Apparently, he hadn't shared his grand ambitions with the riffraff.

"Lord Protector, perhaps," Harry whispered close to her ear. He looked over toward the men. "I haven't orchestrated all of this for the past year, ingratiating myself with that incompetent blue blood only to have it fall apart because he doesn't care for his queen enough to send men to rescue her."

Scarlet's mind slid back over the last year, as Harry became a court favorite at the time Philip Sotheby and Captain Cross had been plotting. She stared hard at the man she'd once thought of as the most handsome in London. "You were plotting with Philip and the English captain to lure King Charles up to Campbell land to assassinate him and blame the Scots."

Harry's frown turned into a grin. "And I thought your sister, Evelyn, was the smart one." He shook his head. "Philip was supposed to take her to heel, yet now his head has been delivered to Whitehall." He chuckled. "Actually, she did me a favor, as the man was vicious and had wild aspirations."

"Like you," Scarlet said. "Aspirations that will lead you to the Tower."

Harry sucked in through his teeth, shaking his head. "A smart girl wouldn't keep giving me reasons to see that she never leaves these woods."

Anger nudged past the fear that twisted in her stomach. "Is that your proposal, then? To your queen? A death threat?" She crossed her arms over her chest and schooled her expression into one of disappointed annoyance, which her father had used nearly every time she approached him. "You are a colossal waste of a gentleman," she said with as much disdain she could muster.

*Crack.*

Pain, burning and sudden, burst across her cheek, and Scarlet flew backward, her backside slamming into the ground. Pinpricks of light sparked before her eyes, and she curled her fingers into the damp ground where her splayed hands had caught her. Fire prickled the cheek Harry had slapped with brute force. He stood over her, his one hand fisted at his side as he shook the sting from the one he'd used on her. The features she'd once thought handsome were contorted in rage, his teeth stacked in a grimace. He took a step away, only to pivot back to her, offering her his hand.

She stared at the appendage without moving.

"Take it, Scar."

She met his gaze. "Or what? You'll kill me?" She narrowed her eyes and spit out the blood she tasted on her tongue. "But you've already decided that, haven't you?"

He didn't say anything, and she shook her head, turning away from him to lift herself from the wet leaves and dirt. By the time she stood, he'd stepped back.

"I really have no idea what to do with you now," he said, fixing his damned shirt cuffs again.

"And have you decided what to do with me, Lord Covington," a woman's voice came from the cottage door. Queen Catherine stood there, her hair down about her shoulders, her costume a mere robe over her sleeping smock. Scarlet could see Jacey standing behind her, the young woman's eyes wide as full moons.

"God's teeth," Harry swore, striding toward her. "Who the hell untied them?" As he stepped up to the vulnerable, yet proud, figure of the queen, a large man, his skin dark as night, came out of the cottage to block her. Titus.

Arms crossed, standing nearly a head taller than Harry, Titus was a mountain of dark granite. "I did."

Harry stopped before the Moor. "You imbecile. Now that they've seen me..." He threw a hand out to indicate the women standing behind him. "You've just sealed their deaths."

A soft cry came from Jacey.

"No," Titus said. "You said nothing bad would happen

to her majesty and her lady. Yet bad has already happened." His dark eyes caught the reflection of the torch Burdock held as he came closer, his men with him. Titus ignored them, his gaze moving to Scarlet. "And to the woman you said would be your wife."

"You bloody black devil," Harry said. "You've just lost your position and..." He leaned in toward Titus. "You've just lost your sister."

Titus had a sister? One who he was willing to commit treason to protect?

The man, Jack Menzies, raised a musket at Titus, obviously waiting for a word from Harry or Burdock. The other three men with Burdock stood ready and silent.

Scarlet glanced at the perimeter of the clearing, but she saw no one. Had the Roses been left behind? Was this even Cat's cottage? Was she truly all alone?

"The word, Covington," Burdock said.

Harry threw his hand up with a casual wave of his fingers. "Kill him."

Before Scarlet could even contemplate the best form of attack or defense, she whipped the dagger from the pocket built into her shirt, aimed toward Jack, and with a precise shifting of her weight, released the blade through the air. The musket blast shattered the stillness, followed by Jack's scream. He dropped the smoking gun to the dirt, his hands going to the blade stuck into the center of his throat.

Scarlet's gaze whipped back to Titus, and her stomach lurched as the large man doubled forward, falling onto the ground. Jacey screamed behind him, rushing out past the queen. Blood soaked outward, staining the shirt Titus wore, the red a horribly macabre contrast to the white linen. Scarlet's hands flew to him, yanking at the shirt, but she was suddenly grabbed from behind, her feet lifted from the ground.

"You little bitch," Burdock yelled in her ear as he twirled

her around, throwing her toward the corner of the cottage. Scarlet landed on her aching backside, her head jarred. She watched the other men run to Jack, trying to help him, but her aim had been true.

"You can stand before God to be judged now, Jack," she said, and then realized Harry stared at her next to the ladies bent over Titus.

He wore a surprised grin. "My, Scar, you've become a bloodthirsty barbarian up here in the wilds."

She slid a hand against the curls stuck to her forehead and pushed up, yanking her borrowed skirt off her legs. Standing straight, wearing only her black fighting attire, she unsheathed a *mattucashlass* from her tall boot. "No, Harry, I've become a Highland Rose."

He laughed. "Is that supposed to strike fear in me?" He shook his head and waved to Burdock, who'd reloaded Jack's musket. "I hate to say this, my dear. I'd thought to marry you, but now I see you are not lady enough to be my match. You can join your Highlander in death today." He waved his hand at Burdock.

Scarlet held her breath, staring at the muzzle of the gun. She was going to die.

*Aiden.* Sorrow and remorse for the pain her death would cause him billowed up inside her. Would he ever forgive her for leaving Finlarig to find the queen and his sister? For leaving him alone like his mother had done?

The night breeze blew, and her heart pounded, forcing Scarlet to inhale. With the cocked musket pointing directly at her chest, there was no escape. Even if she yanked out another dagger, the weapon would fire before she could move. She drew in her last breath.

A scream, like that of a maniacal banshee, shattered the night.

# Chapter Twenty-Four

"He's my most trusted advisor," King Charles said to Aiden. They stood inside the keep with Louise and Kerrick, whom he'd called down from the castle wall.

Aiden glanced at his second in command. Kerrick's gaze was steely. "Ye watched him, too?" Aiden asked Kerrick, and he nodded but held his tongue. Aiden turned to Charles. "My instincts are telling me that the man is up to something, and now he's ridden off to give information to whomever his contact is."

"Contact?" Charles said. "Harry knows no one in this wild place. He's a refined Englishman, a constant at the court."

Louise placed her hand on Charles's arm. "Who has been currying favor with some of the more parliamentary-loving members in London," she said softly. Charles turned, searching her gaze, and she nodded. "Your majesty, he has done everything to find your favor, yet spends his time talking with those who would love to see England run by a parliament without a king."

"He's never given me any indication that he wants me off the throne," Charles said, his gaze going to the floor as if he was turning inward to examine his interactions with the man.

"I know nothing of your court," Aiden said. "But I do know war. And Covington spoke with several of your guards in whispers, at length with the two nearest the door through the wall. After Covington departed, they did not re-lock the door."

"What?" the king said. "It's a direct route into the castle for those who know where it sits."

Aiden nodded. "And Covington suggested leaving the rest of my men outside the castle walls when he heard ye wouldn't send half of them away to find your queen."

Charles's nostrils flared wide as he inhaled. "Arrest those two guards and lock the door."

"They have us at a disadvantage," Kerrick said. "Seeing as how ye've given your men muskets, and we have swords."

Louise laid her palm flat over her bare chest. "*Mon Dieu*," she said softly. "Perhaps I should sit with Lady Worthington and her pupils above." She tugged on the king's arm. "And you, Charles."

Fury sat in the set of Charles's jaw as he realized he might have been tricked. He was a king, but he was also a man, his pride craving vengeance. "You go, my dearest," Charles said. "I would have a word with these soldiers near the door in the wall."

Aiden didn't know if Scarlet and her students were still in the castle. They hadn't left by either of the means he knew about, so hopefully they were above, still strategizing. It was past midnight, the time when the ransom was supposed to be delivered. So any attack on the castle would come soon. He should probably point that out to Charles.

Instead, Aiden and Kerrick followed the striding monarch out the front doors and down the steps into the torchlit bailey.

Charles traipsed directly toward the door in the wall where two of his English soldiers stood, their muskets lit. His long, ruffled coat flapped as he walked, the slight breeze teasing the stiff curls of his ridiculously long wig.

"Step aside," Charles ordered, and the wide-eyed soldiers stepped to either side of the unbarred door. "Why was this not locked after Lord Covington left?" he asked, staring directly at the taller of the two.

"Your majesty," the soldier said, not meeting his gaze directly. "We were told to guard it but not to set the locks."

"For what reason?" Charles asked. He twisted his hand as if using a key, an order for the other soldier to lock the door. The man made a long show of looking for the large iron key, though he could easily have just lifted the bar that sat beside the door to brace it from the inside. "Speak up," the king ordered.

The two soldiers looked at one another, the shorter man sliding his hand to a dagger strapped to his side. Prickles of warning raised the fine hairs on the back of Aiden's neck. There was desperation in the shorter soldier's eyes, along with a solidifying determination. The two together meant that the soldier had decided to give his life to his cause. His anxious gaze narrowed on the king, his target.

The soldier drew the dagger, whipping it from its sheath at the same time Aiden grabbed the king's arm, yanking him back behind him. The king yelled in angry surprise, which turned to a shocked gasp as the blade flew through the air. Its point stuck into the ground where the king had been standing.

Kerrick came up behind the king with Aiden in front, blocking him on both sides. Not that Aiden was a supporter of anything so blatantly English as the bloody king himself, but the man was unarmed, untrained, and on Campbell lands. Aiden wouldn't have the clan blamed for Charles's assassination.

Everything happened like lightning then—fractured, powerful, and shooting off in all directions. Aiden pulled his claymore, standing before the king, and thrust forward, catching the end of the lit musket as it fired, deflecting the shot to the side.

The king cursed behind him, and Aiden saw Kerrick grab the man around his middle and drag him, high-heel shoes kicking, across the bailey toward the safety of the keep. But before he could take three steps, the Campbell war cry rose up with mounting voices outside the wall. "*Ionnsaigh!* Campbells *ionnsaigh!*"

With a forward thrust and slash, Aiden sliced off the arm of the shorter soldier, tipping the musket he was leveling to the ground, still clutched by his bloody hand. He screamed, falling, and Aiden leaped over him, his boot kicking off the man's back as he slammed the hilt of his sword down on the tall soldier's hand, forcing him to drop his musket. Aiden grabbed the man by the throat, shoving him against the stone wall, his two knuckles pressed into the man's windpipe.

"What the foking hell is going on?" Aiden asked, his question a command, yelled in the man's face.

Beside them, the stone-covered door swung inward, and men rushed inside, a line of kilted and trouser-clad men, brandishing swords. Aiden dropped the soldier to throw his weight against the door, but he caught the glint of a sword coming toward him. He twisted in time, the blade slicing through his shirt and skin across his back. The sting told him it was superficial. He spun around to come face to face with Finlay Menzies.

The man's eyes widened, his frown growing as he bared his teeth. "Thought I might find ye here, Campbell," he said.

Despite the battle surging behind Aiden, with Hamish raising the portcullis to allow the Campbell warriors inside, Aiden felt his first smile of the night. "Finlay Menzies," Aiden said his name, relishing it, the coil of cold anger tightening in his gut like the fist he held around his hilt. "Ye made the biggest mistake of your life when ye lied to Scarlet to get her out of her room."

Finlay spit on the ground. "Her leaving in the middle of the night raised a bloody lot of questions that got me exiled from my own home, my rightful place as chief. When I finish with ye, I'll be taking a long moment to thank the bitch myself."

With that, Finlay lunged, his sword clanging against Aiden's. The young man was stronger than he looked but had little experience in battle. He attacked with unchecked emotion, charging over and over while Aiden slid each of his attacks to the side with minimal effort, letting the fool tire himself out. Out of the corner of his eye, he saw Kerrick fighting off a man in a tattered English uniform, perhaps a deserter with Burdock. He didn't see the king. Hopefully Charles had barricaded himself inside the keep with the women.

Frustrated, sweat dripping down his clenched face, Finlay swung with both of his arms, using his momentum to try to cut through Aiden's middle. But the sword was slower than Aiden, who pivoted out of the way and sank his blade into Finlay's stomach. The man screamed, falling to the dirt. "For Scarlet and any other lass ye attacked," Aiden said and spun away to help Kerrick beat back two men in Menzies plaid.

Aiden met their swords, driving them back until they tired enough to hesitate. Another swing met the enemy's neck, slicing through and dropping him to the ground. Aiden spun in time to watch a group of three running toward the steps of the keep with a handheld battering ram. It slammed into the wooden double doors, making them bow but not break. When they retreated to take another run at it, Aiden ran toward them. But two more English soldiers, one of whom had accompanied the king, attacked him.

"I'm protecting your damn king, ye idiots," Aiden yelled.

"We want no king," the one in his bright red uniform called.

"I don't bloody hell, either," Aiden said. "But I'll be dead before I let ye murder him on Campbell land. Stop or my blade will send ye to hell."

The dirtier of the two laughed, lunging forward, and then the soldier in the crisp uniform attacked, too. Aiden dodged the first and met the sword of the other, deflecting it, the clangs becoming part of the cursing and sounds of sliding steel around him. His body moved with a steady rhythm, turning and swinging, taking in the smallest hints of what his opponents would try next. Without conscious thought, he responded to the shifting in their weights as if able to read their minds. It was how Campbells trained, and he prayed the younger warriors were using their instincts as well.

With a twist in the opposite direction, Aiden caught one soldier with a slash across the middle, so as not to lose his sword, since he had a second attacker. The slashed soldier grabbed his stomach, dropping his sword. The dirtier of the two ran at him, but Aiden was ready and buried his sword in his chest. Yanking the weapon free of the man's shattered ribs, he spun around, arms held ready to meet the next opponent.

Hamish shot arrows from the gate tower where Lawrence wrestled a Menzies off the ladder. William took on one of the English outcasts, meeting the man blow for blow until William fell back. Aiden leaped forward, running across to slam into the man's back before he could lower his sword into William's chest. The man fell forward, face in the dirt, while Aiden jumped on his back, yanking his face around by the hair. "Are ye working for Burdock?" Aiden yelled in his ear.

"Get the bloody hell off me," the man yelled, his English

accent obvious.

"Or do ye battle under a different Devil's orders?" He flipped the man over, shoving his *mattucashlass* against his swallowing throat, hard enough to cause blood to seep from a shallow cut. Aiden leaned in. "Where the fok is Harry Covington?"

The man spit, baring his teeth. "He's likely rutting on top of your woman."

Aiden stared at the man's red face, his brutal words sinking in as his mind raced. Covington was outside the castle walls, while Scarlet was still safely inside. Wasn't she? He glanced toward the stone fortress, and his stomach roiled with fear. *Bloody hell!*

• • •

The scream tore through the night, and Scarlet ducked down, her legs, without the hindrance of skirts, leaping to take her behind the cottage. The musket went off, making her jump, but no fire bit into her body. Burdock had missed. Hallelujah for Cici's banshee scream.

Scarlet ran around the other side of the solid cottage, peeking out to see two arrows fly across the space in rapid succession, striking Burdock in the chest. Cat leaped out of the night, carrying her bow, her face tense with concentration as she slid her dagger from her boot to leap upon her once-tormentor. Knees pinning Burdock's arms, she didn't see another English soldier run toward her.

"Cat," Scarlet yelled, but before Cat could even turn, a large rock smacked the runner in the center of his forehead, throwing him off his feet. A knife followed, hitting him in the hand, and he yelled as he hit the ground. Another knife flew from Kirstin where she stood on the edge of the bushes; it hit the man's shoulder.

One of the soldiers grabbed the fallen gun, working to reload it, but Fiona threw several rocks, hitting him in the eye, nose, and head. Blood gushed from his nose, and he bent over, cursing. Alana ran into the clearing, Robert leaping ahead of her to tackle one of the men, his teeth coming down on the man's arm to shake him in his jaws.

A high-pitched scream came from the far side, different from Cici's scream. Scarlet turned to see Izzy with her hands cupped to her mouth. Izzy? Screaming? The realization stunned Scarlet until Izzy began to frantically point behind the cottage. Scarlet gasped softly and pivoted, getting halfway around as Harry slammed his body against her, pinning her to the cottage wall.

His large, open hands pressed against her shoulders. "You little bitch. Trying to ruin all the hard work I've accomplished. Ingratiating myself with the merry ass, sitting by with a blasted smile on my face while he leads our country to ruin."

He leaned into her face. "First, your sister kills Philip Sotheby and her Highlander kills Cross, our link into Scotland. And now that I've mended the mess and convinced Charles to come up here, you're trying to ruin my plans again. I even found the girl, Jacqueline, to bring up here to convince you to come back to England so I could protect you from all this. And what appreciation do I get?"

The more he talked, the darker his face became, until fury made his words snap out with spittle. Mouth contorted with rage, he spoke through his teeth. "And now I foking have to kill you, all of you! Think I won't because you are ladies? Ha! I'll do more than kill you, Scar," he boasted. "I'll peel you naked first."

Beyond the cottage, Scarlet heard a woman scream and another yell. Had the tide turned against the Roses? Good Lord! She'd drawn them into this. *Please save them,*

*God.* Blood rushing in her ears, Scarlet fought to keep her breathing even. *Think. Don't panic. Think.*

Harry pressed his mouth against her ear. "Hear that? Your stupid Roses are already dying." He pulled back, a maniacal leer on his face. "And you owe me a good fok before you stop breathing. I kept away from you to give you to the bloody king, to further win his trust. But none of that matters now. Your dying memory can be of me between your legs and leaving you to be found that way."

Harry used his thick body to trap her against the wall, his hard cod jamming into her stomach. His hands dove down to shove at her trousers.

"No!" she screamed in his face. "Get off me! Stop." Twisting, she fought, scratching and pushing, but he pressed his weight into her chest, pinning her shoulders, which made her hands useless.

*Ye have powerful legs, lass. Use them.* Aiden's voice filled her mind, his encouragement and faith urging her to escape. It washed through her, giving her strength and helping her breathe and think. Without the hindrance of heavy skirts, her legs were free to fight.

"Bloody hell, you are armed," Harry said, throwing away the two daggers that were strapped to her hips. His fingers yanked the ties at the top of her trousers.

"If you touch me, you will die, Harry Covington," she said, her words seething.

Free of fear, her tone made him pause as if surprised. Harry's eyebrow rose in wry contemplation. "We shall see then, Scarlet dear. One of us will die, then, as I'm definitely touching you." His fingers curled into the top of her trousers.

"No," she screamed as loudly as she could. At the same time, she lifted her boot, slamming the heel down on his foot. He grunted, backing up slightly. "No," she screamed again as her knee shot upward, straight into his erection.

Harry yelled, lurching forward, his hands grasping her arms in a bruising lock as he fell forward.

"No!" Scarlet reached up, yanking her hair sticks out of the bun at the back of her head. Curls tumbling down, she grasped the iron spikes in solid fists, driving them forward into Harry's chest.

He screamed, eyes going wide. His hands clawed against her as he fell, taking her with him to the ground. Scarlet fought against his weight, pounding his chest, hitting the ends of the sticks protruding like thick needles. She hit his recently broken nose with her fist, and he gasped. Blood poured from it again as crimson soaked through the white ruffled shirt covering his chest.

Fury and disgust whirled through Scarlet like a ferocious storm. She lifted her legs to use her feet to push against his heaviness until he rolled away from her to stare at the dark sky above. With a gurgled breath, he stilled. Taking large gulps of air into her burning lungs, Scarlet turned to the side and vomited.

"Scarlet," Alana yelled, running around the side of the cottage. Robert leaped over to Scarlet, his wet tongue hanging out. He jammed his nose into her face, sniffing. "Oh God! You're covered in blood! Cat!" Alana called.

Cat ran around the corner, falling to her knees before Scarlet. "Where are ye cut?" she asked, her voice firm.

Scarlet shook her head, wiping her mouth as the dog continued to sniff her all over as if checking for injuries. "'Tis his blood, not mine." She looked up, meeting Cat's gaze. "Highland Roses fight to survive." She blinked but knew she'd lost the fight to keep her tears inside. They washed out of her eyes, and she bit back a sob with the back of her hand across her mouth.

"Thank God," Kirstin said as she ran up in time to hear Scarlet.

Cat nodded to Scarlet and reached down to help her stand. "Killing is nasty business." She spit toward Harry's unmoving form. "Sometimes there's no other choice."

"The others?" Scarlet asked, hurrying around to the front of the cottage. Her stomach tightened again at the scene. Jacey wrapped linen around an unconscious Titus in the doorway of the cottage, the queen, unbound and dirty, handing her rolls of material to use. Jack lay where she'd struck him with her flying dagger. Burdock lay with two arrows sticking out of him. The other men lay dead or unconscious. Robert ran from man to man, growling and sniffing, as if to make certain they wouldn't rise again.

Scarlet spun to Alana, which made her wobble with dizziness, and she wrapped her arms around herself. "Fiona?"

"Her leg is badly slashed," Rebecca said, pointing where Cici was hovering over someone lying behind low bushes.

"She will heal," Cat said. "I stopped the bleeding."

Izzy leaped out of the cottage, dropping more wrappings to hurtle into Scarlet's arms, hugging her. Scarlet hugged her back, kissing her head. "You helped save me." She pulled back to look into Izzy's mud-spattered face. "You spoke."

"She spoke?" Cat asked, bending before her sister. Izzy's mouth stretched into a wide grin.

"She screamed to get my attention," Scarlet said. "So I had a second to realize Harry was about to grab me."

Cat met her sister's smile with her own and nodded. "Maybe words will come again," she said and pulled Izzy against her into a hug.

"Fiona's going to need stitches," Cici said, walking up to them, shaking her head. Her shirt was ripped, and she held it closed over her bosom with one hand. Rebecca and Alana hurried past her to see Fiona.

"We need to get her to safety," Martha whispered. But where was that?

Silence descended, broken only by whispers as they checked each other's wounds, and the sky above them began to lighten to a dark gray.

Scarlet turned as Queen Catherine walked toward them. The Roses, in ripped and stained shirts and trousers, gave small curtseys, and Scarlet bowed her head. "Your majesty. I'm sorry you have had to witness such bloodiness."

"Especially from ladies," Martha said, and Cici nodded vigorously.

Even undone and in her robe, the queen walked with dignity, slim shoulders back and chin high with courage. She reached forward, grasping Scarlet's bloodstained hands, and squeezed. She glanced toward the Roses. "We do what we must do to fight for what is right and just. I am proud of and thankful for all of you." She spoke from her heart, bowing her head to them all with slow grace. Scarlet could see why she remained the Merry Monarch's wife despite his scandalous ways. She, too, did what she must to guide him toward the right.

"We are very welcome to be of service," Scarlet said. "Your majesty."

She sighed. "We will see if I am still queen or if Lord Covington was ultimately successful as his small army met the warriors of Finlarig."

"I will stay with Titus," Jacey said, glancing up. "He kept them from us, protecting us until they shot him." She looked back down at him. "They promised freedom for his younger sister if he got us out of the castle, but he didn't know that Harry Covington's plan included killing us."

The queen caught Scarlet's sleeve, tugging gently for her to meet her gaze. She spoke low. "Charles wasn't willing to send anyone to save us, was he?" Sadness mixed with muted anger in her gaze.

Scarlet let regret show on her face. The queen met her

look for a long pause and then turned toward the horses that Kirstin and Izzy had rounded up—Caora and Eigh, and the horses Harry and his small group of villains had used.

"We don't know what we will face when we return to Finlarig," Scarlet called out. The sky above continued to brighten as dawn broke over the forest. "Anyone who would care to stay here may."

Cat stood up from Titus's side, nodding to Jacey. "Just keep him still and resting until we return. Try to give him water if he wakes." She strode toward a horse. Scarlet went to Caora, pressing her forehead to the horse's nose for a moment before helping the queen up onto the filly's strong back. Scarlet watched the others mounting the horses then climbed up from a log to ride in front of the queen.

"You are all going?" Scarlet asked. "They could still be fighting, or worse. Harry's army may have won." She swallowed past the ache in her throat and wiped again at her eyes. Aiden could be injured or dead. The thought made her want to rush back to Finlarig no matter what was happening.

"Of course we are going," Cat said, a bit of annoyance in her voice. "We are Highland Roses, and, as these bastards found out, our thorns are deadly."

Around the clearing, every student nodded. Although she was grim, filthy, and exhausted, hope unfurled inside Scarlet. "*Falbh!*" she called to Caora in Gaelic, and they plunged through the woods toward Finlarig.

# Chapter Twenty-Five

Aiden tore through the splintered front door to find the king and Louise dodging behind the table, away from a man brandishing a bloody sword, while Kerrick fought another. Aiden leaped an overturned chair to tackle the man who wore a Menzies kilt, easily dispatching him.

Louise screamed, and Charles helped her to another chair where she slumped against the back, her eyes fluttering with a near swoon. Kerrick grunted as he pulled his sword from the other man's middle, then nodded to Aiden and ran back out into the bailey.

Aiden glanced at the king, but his gaze went to the stairs above. "Ye are unharmed?"

"*Mon Dieu*," Louise said, looking at him. "Because of you, *Monsieur* Campbell."

The words slid off Aiden. "Where are Scarlet and her students?"

Louise shook her head, while Charles spoke. "Louise went above. Searched every floor, but couldn't find them. They have been seized like Catherine."

More likely, they found a way out of the castle without anyone seeing. Which would mean the English soldier's last words out in the bailey could possibly be true. *Rutting on top of your woman.* The words cut like the sharpest of knives. How could he have let Scarlet go? Even if at the time he didn't know the man of her nightmares was also a traitor. Regret surged through Aiden—regret and desperation.

"Barricade yourselves in your bedchamber on the top floor," he yelled at the king as he ran back outside.

Dawn was brightening the courtyard, revealing the bloodied corpses and unconscious soldiers. William ran up to Aiden, blood smeared along his forehead, his shirt cut. "We have them caught," he said, and Aiden realized that Hamish had lowered the portcullis while two Campbells guarded the door in the wall. Once the tide had turned in favor of the Campbells, the bastards couldn't escape. Those few who remained standing were being tied up with rope. The dead were being dragged toward the gatehouse.

"Kerrick," Aiden called, and his friend ran over. "The ladies, Scarlet and her Roses," he said, pulling in a breath. "I think Covington has them."

"Open the gate," came a demand from outside the wall, and Aiden ran with Kerrick toward the portcullis, which was rising without hesitation.

Two carriages stood on the outside with two men on horseback. One was Scarlet's brother, Nathaniel, and the other was Grey Campbell, the chief of Finlarig. "What the bloody hell is going on here?" Grey yelled, his gray horse leaping into the bailey. More curses came as he dismounted, pulling his sword free as he viewed the bloody and body-littered battleground. "Aiden?"

The carriage door opened, and Evelyn barreled out. "Good God in Heaven," she called, racing forward. A hand went to her mouth as she dodged around a dead English soldier. "Scarlet!"

"We were attacked by an army run by Harry Covington and Finlay Menzies," Aiden said, grabbing the reins of Grey's horse. "I think they were part of the plot involving Captain Cross and Philip Sotheby."

"Harry Covington?" Evelyn said. "Scarlet?"

"Is not here," Aiden said, throwing his hand out to the steps of Finlarig, where it was obvious that Charles couldn't follow orders. He stood looking out. "But the bloody king is."

Aiden mounted Grey's horse while they stood stunned, looking back and forth between the king and Aiden. He had no time to waste. Each second ticked by with the pounding of his heart. Scarlet could be under attack or even... No, he couldn't think it, wouldn't think it. Scarlet, with all her warmth and softness, her quick wit and courage, couldn't be dead. "Kerrick," Aiden yelled. "Explain it to them. I'm going to get Scarlet and the rest of the Roses."

"The Roses? Harry has my students?" Evelyn said, her words sounding numb, though coming loud in the heaviness of the bailey. Campbells were checking bodies and dragging the dead while Hamish jumped down from the gate tower to run over.

"Aiden," Hamish yelled, jabbing his finger in large motions toward the raised gate. Hooves clopped against the packed ground as horses rode into the bailey, Scarlet on Caora at the lead.

Violent relief exploded inside Aiden, and for a moment he felt weak, leaning forward on his hands where he sat Grey's horse. She rode directly to him, and he straightened. "My God, Scarlet," he said, realizing that he could hardly catch a breath. Her dark clothing hid much, but he could tell it was smeared with blood. Her hair was unbound, her curls free and wild about her. Dirt smudged her cheek where a bruise stood out against her lovely pale skin. But she was alive, and she was the most beautiful sight he'd ever seen.

As she drew close to him, she smiled. "You were right."

He took in every detail of her glorious, alive face. "Of course," he answered, breathless, and she laughed. "How exactly…" He swallowed hard against the tightness of his throat. "How exactly was I right this time?"

She cocked her head to one side. "I was ready. My demon didn't stand a chance."

Aiden huffed out an exhale and reached forward, pulling her off Caora's back, hardly noticing the woman seated on the horse behind her. Scarlet smiled broadly as he wrapped his arms around her atop Grey's horse, his mouth descending to kiss her soundly. He inhaled and pulled back to capture her face in his hands. "Ye're alive. Thank God, ye are alive." He kissed her forehead, her nose, and then brushed across her lips. "I love ye, Scarlet Worthington."

"And I love you," she replied, making his heart fill so much, he could imagine it bursting.

Someone cleared their throat, and Aiden glanced down to find Grey and Evelyn staring up at them. Evelyn's lips fell wide open like a fish left beside a riverbank. She blinked, looking between the two. Her mouth closed and opened twice before she finally found her voice.

She cleared her throat. "So," she said, her arched brows rising. Her arms rose slowly out from her sides, only to flop back against her skirt as if in surrender. "So, you've…gotten trousers for all the students while I was gone."

"Trousers and daggers," Alana said, lowering her dog from the back of Aiden's horse. Robert loped off toward the bodies in the bailey.

Cat jumped down from her horse and helped Fiona dismount. Martha ran over to help Fiona, her leg bandaged and bloody, hobble toward the keep. William ran over to pick Fiona up, carrying her to the steps.

"We have thorns now," Cat said to Evelyn, a wry smile on her lips. Aiden caught the slight turn of her freckled face as she met Nathaniel's gaze where he stood below Scarlet. Nathaniel kept his frown, and Cat gave a soft snort before continuing toward the keep.

"Thorns?" Evelyn called, her gaze catching on Cici with more questions in her eyes.

"Aye," Cat called behind her. "We are Roses with deadly thorns." She raised her bow with one hand and a *mattucashlass* with the other.

Evelyn turned to Scarlet. "Thorns? The Roses have thorns now?"

"It seems we do," Scarlet said, smiling down at her. "I'll explain everything, Evie."

The queen clicked her tongue and guided Caora over to where the king stood surveying the field. He hurried down the steps to help her dismount and pulled her into a hug. Maybe there was some tenderness between them.

"Aye, I think some explanations are in…" Grey's words ebbed off as he stared at the gate where his grandmother, clothed in her blue cloak, walked sedately inside, her gaze straight ahead. "Gram?" Grey called, more shock than question in his voice.

"She's been living in a secret tunnel under Finlarig," Alana said.

"Bloody hell, what?" Grey asked, jogging to follow his grandmother, but she reached the king and queen before him. "Are ye armed, Gram?"

"I'm always armed," she called over her shoulder. "But not to worry."

"Oh lord," Scarlet said.

"What?" Evelyn asked, turning to watch.

"She has no love for them," Scarlet said, but the old woman came level with the queen and gave a small curtsey.

Elizabeth Campbell's words came clear and strong across the hushed bailey. "Welcome to my home. I am Elizabeth Campbell." She indicated the splintered door as if it were whole and there weren't bodies of traitors littering the courtyard below. "I believe the Highland Roses School serves tea. Let us find some inside, as we all seem to be in need of fortification."

· · ·

"I just…" Evelyn said, shaking her head. "I can't believe all this happened in a few short weeks." She narrowed her eyes at Scarlet. "How long was I gone, again?"

Scarlet chuckled as she finished tying the stays around Evelyn's widening waist. "Long enough for me to know that you're definitely with Grey's child."

Evelyn turned, a huge smile on her face. "I told him once we reached London. He was so worried that he yelled at everyone and brought two midwives to inspect me."

Scarlet laughed. "Due in early summer, then?"

"Yes."

Scarlet clasped her hands. "What a wonderful Christmas gift, finding out that I will be an auntie."

They walked out the door of Scarlet's room arm in arm. Grey and Evelyn had taken one of the small bedrooms while the king and queen still used their bedchamber, but Scarlet had brought Evelyn's clothes into her own room.

"I wasn't sure if we'd make it home in time," Evelyn said. "Especially with Grey insisting that I couldn't be jostled. I thought Nathaniel might punch him, but we picked up speed once Grey decided it was safer for me and the baby for him to cradle me before him on his horse, which is how I rode most of the days."

They walked down the turning stairs, Scarlet going in

front to help protect Evelyn in case she tripped. It had been two days since the battle against the assassins, and it was a Christmas blessing that most had come out of the turmoil alive and well. Even Titus was beginning to heal after Cat and Jacqueline had pulled the iron bullet from his chest and sutured the hole closed. Aiden's new sister was an accomplished healer, too, and seemed to have a fondness for the mysterious Moor who had protected her and the queen.

"I think you were gone almost four weeks," Scarlet said. "Enough time for me to bring three new students in, along with Aiden's new sister as an instructor."

"And a herd of lovely white sheep for Nathaniel," Evelyn said. "Not to mention saving the queen and king of England, Scotland, and Ireland." They stepped down to the bottom. "Ousting a traitorous neighboring clan chief, convincing Cat and Elizabeth Campbell to live at Finlarig, thwarting that treasonous bastard Harry Covington, and..." Evelyn took a full breath, tugging Scarlet to look at her. "And getting Aiden Campbell to fall in love with you."

Fluttering in Scarlet's stomach caught at her breath as she smiled. Yes, she was nervous, more so than when she'd informed Aiden that she was going to save the queen. For her newest plan didn't involve the safety of her body; it involved the safety of her heart.

Evelyn's eyes narrowed as she gazed at her while they stood outside the great hall, the sounds of gaiety and music drifting from inside. "That smile is a worried smile, Scar. What has you nervous now? Burdock is dead, Harry is dead, Finlay is dead. There isn't another villain about whom we should be concerned, is there?"

Scarlet felt a real smile grow. "There are always villains, Evie. You know that." Scarlet held up a hand when Evelyn opened her mouth, her eyes round. "None of whom are here right now."

She tucked her arm into Evelyn's as they walked into the decorated great hall. Despite her early grumbles, Aiden's grandmother had orchestrated the Christmas decorating like a woman reborn to command a household. They hadn't celebrated Christmas at Finlarig since the 1500s, but it was the king and queen's holiday. Since they were visiting, Elizabeth Campbell had Kerrick set the Yule log in the fire, and all the Highland Roses had gathered winter holly and mistletoe to hang in long garlands. The mantel was draped with candles, holly, and gaily wrapped gifts, which Alana kept calling Hogmanay gifts that couldn't be opened until the New Year's Eve.

With the end of the great threat, King Charles was in a jolly mood, drinking merrily with the Campbells and calling them the most loyal of men. Louise and the queen spoke pleasantly, and Jacqueline popped in and out to visit with them when she wasn't tending Titus, whom the queen had defended to Charles for his heroism.

"Then, what has you worried?" Evelyn asked, obviously not willing to let it go.

Scarlet patted her hand. "Still the older sister, always watching out for my happiness." She leaned in to kiss Evelyn's cheek. "You'll just have to see," she whispered in her ear and guided them toward the hearth where Grey and Aiden talked with the king and Calum Menzies, the new Menzies chief.

Scarlet's heart raced seeing Aiden. Clad in his crisp white shirt and dress kilt, his hair long enough now to curl around his ears, he was the handsomest man she'd ever seen. And if all went well tonight, he'd be hers forever. Forever without him worrying that she'd leave him like his mother had.

"You must come to London again," Charles said to Grey as they walked up. "I will throw a ball in honor of your brave clan."

"Perhaps after my lad or lass is born," Grey said. Charles didn't seem to notice the reticence in his tone and laughed, nodding.

"Yes, bring them along, and with your best warrior here," Charles said, patting Aiden on his shoulder. But Aiden was only staring at Scarlet.

"Not likely," he murmured and stepped forward to pull Scarlet close, his lips brushing against hers. Despite the busyness of the last two days, with answering questions, burying the dead, and figuring out the players in the deadly scheme, Aiden had come to Scarlet each night. Their fire, erupting upon contact, had consumed them. They'd held each other all night long, as if making certain that they were both truly alive and together.

He bent toward her ear. "Lass, ye look as lovely as the most perfect rose." She wore a deep red gown edged with green.

She smiled up at him. "You are writing poetry again."

"Poetry?" the king said. "Lady Worthington used to be ringed by interested suitors spouting poetry to her at court." He laughed.

Scarlet watched a shadow pass over Aiden's gaze, but he smiled despite it. She'd do anything to banish that shadow forever. "Come," she said, tugging him to follow after the king as he made his way to where Queen Catherine sat. The queen nodded to Scarlet, her gaze shifting briefly to Aiden, then she stood.

"Lady Scarlet Worthington," she intoned. Despite being a small and humble lady, her accented voice rang with true majesty.

Scarlet curtsied and rose. "Your majesty." Aiden bowed his head briefly.

The queen looked out on the crowded hall where all the villagers from Killin and from around Castle Menzies had gathered. All the Roses were there, once again in dresses. Even Fiona, with her leg stitched and wrapped, sat nearby, smiling as her mother fussed about her, bragging to everyone about her daughter saving the queen. Izzy stood next to Cat, who wrapped her arms around her little sister. Cici waited, smiling with some of her old friends from Castle Menzies, the ones who hadn't supported her terrible brother. And Elizabeth Campbell came up to link arms with Evelyn as she stood by Grey.

Queen Catherine held the pause for a count of five and then spoke out as if she addressed the London court. "I personally give thanks to you and your Highland Roses for coming to the aid of myself and Lady Jacqueline."

"Yes," the king added, nodding as if he'd decreed it.

Catherine looked back to Scarlet. "And in honor of your bravery, I order you…" She paused again. "Never to return to England."

A hushed murmur filtered from the crowd. Scarlet felt Aiden's arm tighten under her hand. "Never?" the king asked.

"Never," Catherine repeated. "You may visit your brother if you wish, but you are to remain, until the end of your life, living here in Scotland, amongst these good people. You will help your sister, Lady Evelyn Worthington Campbell, to run her royally backed school for ladies."

"Royally backed?" Charles asked low, but Catherine patted his arm and continued.

"Your Roses have shown great courage and skill in thwarting the enemies of justice and right. We order you to continue in your good works here in Scotland." She shook her head, glancing at Aiden. "And nowhere else." She turned back to Scarlet. "Do you accept, Lady Worthington?"

Scarlet slid her hand off Aiden, her heart beating wildly in her chest. "I accept under one condition."

"Speak it," Catherine said.

Scarlet turned to Aiden. "I will stay here in Scotland until the end of time itself, as long as…Aiden Campbell agrees to wed me."

The whole room held its breath. Not a single person even shifted or coughed as Scarlet gazed into Aiden's frowning face. Oh Lord. He couldn't turn her down, not when she'd put her heart out for everyone to see. Scarlet swallowed, wetting her dry lips. "Aiden Campbell," she said, her breaths coming too quickly. "I love you. Will you marry me and keep me here in Scotland until the end of days?"

Aiden's face relaxed bit by bit, like ice thawing on a spring day, until a grin played on his perfect lips. "Scarlet Worthington."

"Yes?" she whispered.

"I pledge to keep ye with me in Scotland until the end of days," he said, and she released the breath she'd been holding with a small huff of laughter. "Even if I have to tie ye to me." He pulled her closer. "I love ye, Scarlet. Aye. I will wed ye, lass." His warm lips pressed against hers, and Scarlet wrapped her own arms around him, molding her body to his as the room erupted around them in cheers.

"Lord help us," Elizabeth Campbell said beside them. "First, she has the ladies wearing trousers, second, we have to celebrate Christmas, and then, she asks a man to marry her. All our ways are being shattered. What's next?"

Someone hushed her, and Aiden released Scarlet from the kiss. He gazed into her eyes. "Even the most shattered mess can be made into something stronger and more beautiful if we pick up the pieces."

"I said that to her," Evelyn whispered with a smile, and Grey pulled her closer.

Scarlet laughed as she stared up into Aiden's blue eyes. "My warrior poet," she said, pulling him closer for a kiss. Forged from ashes of nightmares, their binding love was the most beautiful creation under heaven, made from the shards of their pasts.

# Epilogue

"Where are ye?" Aiden called from below.

"I'm up here in the second bedroom," Scarlet replied and listened to the heavy footfalls of her husband as he rushed up the steps in their cabin on Loch Tay.

"What are ye doing in…?" His words stopped as he stood in the doorway of the small room down the hall from their bedchamber. "In here?" he finished as he stared at the wall where Scarlet had been laboring all day, while he worked with Grey at the castle on the cradle for Evelyn's baby, due in a few weeks.

"I think it is time to start fixing up this room," she said, stepping off the stool. She backed up to look at her mosaic. "I used some of the leftover pieces from Finlarig, and Rebecca gave me some of your mother's plates that you broke after she—"

"Is that…?" he asked, cutting her off.

She smiled broadly. "Two roses," she said, pointing. "One red. One blue."

"With a third…wee rose under them," he said slowly, and she heard him step up behind her. "A purple rose—a mix of the two?"

"Why, yes," she said and looked up into his question-filled eyes. She tilted her head. "Perhaps you should ask Grey to help *you* to build a baby's cradle."

"You are with child?" he asked, his words breathless.

She nodded, a smile forming so broad that she felt tears squeeze from her eyes. "Due around Christmastime," she said. "Or Hogma—"

Scarlet half squealed, half gasped as Aiden caught her up to him, spinning her around as she laughed. He set her gently on the floor and cupped her cheeks, pressing a kiss to her lips. Scarlet's heart soared, her happiness mixed with Aiden's, so high that she felt like she could float.

"She will be lovely like her mother," he said, pulling her into his chest.

"Or he will be brawny and clever like his father," she said.

"Could be, but I have a feeling it's a wee lass," Aiden said, running a broad hand softly along her slightly rounded abdomen. He kissed her forehead, staring down into her eyes. "A beautiful lass, strong and clever. The perfect Highland Rose."

• • •

*When Queen Catherine sends a letter to Finlarig Castle, requesting a Highland Rose to help King Charles, which student is brave, lethal, and talented enough to journey to London to save a king? Find out the answer in* The Wicked Viscount, *book #3 of The Campbells series!*

# Acknowledgments

*The Savage Highlander* certainly caused me pain! After writing the first three chapters, my computer had a "critical fail" even though it was only thirteen months old (one month past the warranty) and showed no signs of illness. I want to acknowledge my fabulous husband, Braden, who worked for a week to try to recover those lost words and twelve months of marketing material, which I hadn't backed up properly. During that time, he drove my poor, dead laptop around to the Geek Squad, helped me up when I sobbed all over their showroom floor, drove us to a "computer whisperer" who worked on it for days only to pronounce it truly dead, and then helped me buy and load a new computer as fast as he could. Through it all, he was kind and supportive, and never once said "why didn't you save it to the chicken" (my flash drive is a chicken).

We now have a paid company who backs up EVERYTHING on my computer every night. However, as I neared the end of the book, I thought I lost the last 6,000 words! But Braden managed to find it and is looking into what happened. So, a huge thank you goes to my Highland Hero. Without you, this book might never have been finished!

Also...

At the end of each of my books, I ask that you, my awesome readers, please remind yourselves of the whispered symptoms of ovarian cancer. I am now a seven-year survivor, one of the lucky ones. Please don't rely on luck. If you experience any of these symptoms consistently for three weeks or more, go see your GYN.

· Bloating

· Eating less and feeling full faster

· Abdominal pain

· Trouble with your bladder

Other symptoms may include: indigestion, back pain, pain with intercourse, constipation, fatigue, and menstrual irregularities.

# About the Author

Heather McCollum is an award-winning historical romance writer. She is a member of Romance Writers of America and the Ruby Slippered Sisterhood of 2009 Golden Heart finalists. She has over eighteen romance novels published and is a 2015 Readers' Crown Winner and Amazon Best Seller.

The ancient magic and lush beauty of Great Britain entrances Ms. McCollum's heart and imagination every time she visits. The country's history and landscape have been a backdrop for her writing ever since her first journey across the pond.

When she is not creating vibrant characters and magical adventures on the page, she is roaring her own battle cry in the war against ovarian cancer. Ms. McCollum slew the cancer beast and resides with her very own Highland hero, a rescued golden retriever, and three kids in the wilds of suburbia on the mid-Atlantic coast. For more information about Ms. McCollum, please visit www.HeatherMcCollum. com.

URL and Social Media links:

Facebook: facebook.com/HeatherMcCollumAuthor
Twitter: https://twitter.com/HMcCollumAuthor
Pinterest: https://www.pinterest.com/hmccollumauthor/
Instagram: instagram.com/heathermccollumauthor/

*Don't miss The Campbells series...*

THE SCOTTISH ROGUE

THE WICKED VISCOUNT


*Also by Heather McCollum...*

HIGHLAND HEART

CAPTURED HEART

TANGLED HEARTS

UNTAMED HEARTS

CRIMSON HEART

THE BEAST OF AROS CASTLE

THE ROGUE OF ISLAY ISLE

THE WOLF OF KISIMUL CASTLE

THE DEVIL OF DUNAKIN CASTLE

*Discover more Amara titles...*

## TEMPTING THE HIGHLAND SPY
### a *Highland Hearts* novel by Tara Kingston

It had been one glorious night, and Harrison MacMasters, Highland spy, never thought to see jewel thief Grace Winters again. Now he's forced to protect her as they join together to catch a killer, even though he can't trust her with anything, especially his heart. Grace will do anything to keep her family from the poorhouse, including a pretend marriage to the one man who tempts her to make it real.

## FORGETTING THE SCOT
### a *Highlanders of Balforss* novel by Jennifer Trethewey

Virginia Whitebridge is trapped in a loveless, abusive marriage. Her husband took her inheritance and tried to kill her. After a close escape, Virginia feels protected thanks to the Scottish Highlands and the Highlander Magnus Sinclair. But she must go back to England to reclaim what's hers. It's just Magnus's luck that he's fallen for a woman he can't have. To keep her safe, he must follow her to the one place he loathes—England. Where he is too large, too uncivilized, too everything. Despite omens that death awaits him there, Magnus vows to help Virginia go to London and restore her fortune. Get in. Get out. Or die trying.

## A Lord for the Lass
### a *Tartans and Titans* novel by Amalie Howard and Angie Morgan

Lady Makenna Maclaren Brodie is on the run from her clan for the death of her husband and laird. Even though she is innocent, she and her maid run to the only safe place she knows...and right into the arms of the handsome French lord she'd met a year ago. An unapologetic rake, Lord Julien Leclerc is focused on one thing—expanding his empire and increasing his fortune. However, when the widowed Makenna arrives on his doorstep in the Highlands, all bets are off.

## The Devilish Duke
### a novel by Maddison Michaels

Devlin Markham, the "Devil Duke" of Huntington, needs a woman. And not just any woman. If he can't woo eccentric bluestocking Lady Sophie Wolcott within the month, he can kiss his fortune goodbye. But he finds love a wasted emotion and marriage an inconvenience. And Sophie seems unmoved by his charm… When Sophie learns her orphanage is in danger, she'll do anything to save it. Even marry a ruthless rake. Even one targeted by a killer.

Printed in Great Britain
by Amazon